1999

055431447

VILLAGE SQUARE

The Eyes
Of The World

Other novels by Anne Melville

The Lorimer Line
The Lorimer Legacy
Lorimers at War
Lorimers in Love
The Last of the Lorimers
Lorimer Loyalties

The House of Hardie
Grace Hardie
The Hardie Inheritance

The Dangerfield Diaries

The Trantivy Trust

A Clean Break

The Russian Tiara

Standing Alone

The Longest Silence

Short story collection

Snapshots

The Eyes Of The World

Anne Melville

PIATKUS

Copyright © 1998 by Anne Melville

First published in Great Britain in 1998 by
Judy Piatkus (Publishers) Ltd of
5 Windmill Street, London W1

This edition published 1998

**The moral right of the author
has been asserted**

*A catalogue record for this book
is available from the British Library*

ISBN 0-7499-0445-3

Set in 10/12pt Times by
Action Typesetting Ltd,
Northgate Street, Gloucester

Printed and bound in Great Britain by
Bookcraft Ltd, Midsomer Norton, Avon

BOOK ONE

Terts

Part One: Schooldays
Part Two: Girls
Part Three: War
Part Four: Eye-Openers
Part Five: Inheritance
Part Six: The Dying of the Light

BOOK TWO

Jolene

Part One: Sunset in Colorado
Part Two: Going Home
Part Three: Memories
Part Four: Bombshells
Part Five: Kinderley
Part Six: The Going Down of the Sun

BOOK ONE

Terts

Part One

Schooldays

1

Mortimer James Bradley, aged twelve and three-quarters, sat in silence at the breakfast table, awaiting the regular morning ordeal. What would he have to talk about today?

Breakfast in the Bradley household was the only meal which parents and children took together, and all members of the younger generation were under an obligation to contribute to the conversation: it was part of their education. Although during his working day Henry Bradley was an autocrat, at home he could be described as a benevolent despot. He encouraged his four children, within reason, to be heard as well as seen. It was his business to make sure that, when the time came, the firm which bore the family name should be handed on to his heirs in a healthy condition. But of equal importance, he considered, was his responsibility for making sure that the members of the next generation would be fit to receive their birthright.

On this particular June morning in 1902 Richard and Bingham were away at school. Mort and his younger sister, however, would each be expected to make some comment on whatever topic their father chose to discuss. They did not have to wait long.

'So that's all over at last, then. Let's hope they've learned their lesson.' Mr Bradley, opening *The Times*, gave a satisfied nod as he announced that the Boer War had come to an end.

'I'm glad they're not going to kill each other any more,' said seven-year-old Libby. The remark was appropriate to her age and was received with approval. Mr Bradley turned his head to await his son's contribution.

'It's too late for all the dead children, though,' said Mort.

The temperature of the room dropped to freezing point. Leonard the footman froze in the act of replacing the silver lid on a dish of kidneys, reflecting that Master Mort was going to get himself into real trouble one of these days. Mrs Bradley froze with her teacup to her lips, not knowing exactly what her third son was talking about but suspecting that his tone of voice was intended to be provocative. Libby, who adored the brother closest to her in age, froze with apprehension of the beating which was likely to come his way.

'What are you talking about, pray?' asked Mr Bradley.

'All the children who've died in the camps. And their mothers.' Mort wriggled uneasily. He had not, as a matter of fact, intended to provoke an argument. He was quoting something he had read, with which he assumed everyone would agree. Twenty thousand of the women and children who had been removed from their homes and herded into guarded camps had died of illness. Or so somebody said.

Mr Bradley, lowering his newspaper, managed to hold on to his temper as he explained the position to a boy who was perhaps too young to understand the realities of war.

'When you are dealing with an enemy who wears no uniform, who pretends to be a peaceful farmer until your back is turned and then shoots you, and who finds shelter and food and horses in every scattered homestead and farmhouse, there's only one way to deal with him. You have to empty the land, so that you know anyone still at large is your enemy. The children and their mothers were removed for their own sakes. Otherwise they might have been killed in the fighting.'

'Yes, sir.' Unfortunately, though, Mort did not know when to stop. 'But then, if you take the children from their homes and put them all together, there ought to be doctors there, and medicines, because children are always getting ill.' Mort himself had recently recovered from scarlet fever. The doctor had insisted that he must be nursed in isolation for eight weeks. It didn't sound as though there had been anyone to look after the children in the camps in that sort of way.

'What nonsense is this?' Mr Bradley's well-nourished face purpled with rage at the thought that one of his sons was unpatriotic: a Boer-lover.

'I read it in the newspaper. There's a lady called Miss Hobhouse who's found out all about it and she thinks we ought to stop it.'

'You don't have to believe everything you read in the newspaper, for heaven's sake!'

'Oh,' said Mort, confounded. 'I thought if it was there, it would be true.'

'It ought to be. But not all the people who write that sort of thing can be trusted. Politics comes into it. You need to know something about the writer before you can decide whether to trust him. The only way to be sure about anything is to see it with your own eyes.'

'But nobody can see everything that happens in the world.' Mort was not trying to be difficult. He was genuinely confused.

'That may have been true in the past. But now there are photographs. Looking at a photograph is as good as seeing for yourself. The camera doesn't lie. What are you doing, reading the newspaper, anyway?' Mr Bradley looked suspiciously at his copy of *The Times*, as though to make sure that no one else had been at it before it was brought to him, newly ironed.

'I only read it after you've finished with it. I'm always a day behind.'

'You shouldn't be wasting your time with that sort of thing. Gossip and scandal. If you have free time when your lessons are done, you should read history, not politics.'

'Yes, sir. But Mr Townsend says that today's politics are tomorrow's history, so I thought I *was* reading history, in a way. And Mr Townsend says that an educated gentleman should be able to read *The Times* from cover to cover and understand every word of it, so I've been practising to see how far I can get.'

'Mr Townsend should concentrate on your Latin and Greek.' Mr Bradley considered for a moment. He did not, as Libby had feared, intend to beat wrong-headed opinions out of his third son. It was not the boy's fault if his tutor was filling his head full of nonsense. 'How old are you now, Mort?'

'Twelve and three-quarters, sir.'

'Yes. Quite. It's time, I think, for you to join Richard and Bingham at school. Next September, then.'

2

'You're not to call me Richard at school,' said Richard. 'Only when we're home again for the hols.'

'You don't call me Bing either,' said Bing. 'Richard's Bradley major, Bradley ma, and I'm Bradley mi. You'll be Bradley tertius. Terts for short, probably.'

Mort considered this point with interest. He had always disliked his Christian name, Mortimer. It wasn't a proper Christian name at all, but his mother's maiden name. More to the point, it was the name of Lord Mortimer, his maternal grandfather.

Lord Mortimer, who owned a grand house and several thousand acres in Oxfordshire, had no sons of his own. He had two daughters, the elder of whom had also produced only daughters. The younger one was Mrs Bradley. When Lord Mortimer died, the title would be inherited by some distant cousin who lived in Canada. But his estate was not entailed. It could be bequeathed to whomsoever he wished. Mort strongly suspected that he had been given his grandfather's name in the hope that this in due course might bring him more of the considerable Mortimer fortune than a mere third grandson could otherwise expect. That was another reason for disliking it. It was a second-hand name and it was a sucking-up name.

In practice his parents always called him Mort; but he had begun to dislike that as well as soon as he started to learn French and realised that it meant 'dead'. Starting at Croxton might give him the chance to escape from the hated name. Neither masters nor boys would ever address him by his Christian name, or even know what it was. He realised from what his brothers had told him that the mark of popularity or friendship was to be called by a nickname. It should be easy enough to let it be known that although Bradley tertius was his official label, his friends could call him Terts.

I am Terts, he thought to himself silently, giving an obedient nod to acknowledge his brothers' continuing instructions. There was so much to remember. Croxton had its own special vocabulary and he would be tested on his knowledge of it on the first evening of term. A new boy, for example, was called a servitor and must be prepared to run errands for the prefects for the whole of his first year. In addition to that, he would be a slave to one particular boy, his slavemaster, who would be entitled to beat him whenever he made a mistake. Terts, who was not Mort any longer, was not worried about being able to manage his lessons – which were not actually called lessons, but tasks – and he was not worried about getting on with other boys of his own age. But he didn't much look forward to being somebody's slave.

Only one day was left before the beginning of the school term and, as they watched the housekeeper pack his trunk, his elder brothers were full of last-minute hints. They meant well, because otherwise he might have found out the hard way that he was not to put his hands in his pockets until he was in the Eleven, or to walk across Greatney's Grass until he was in the Sixth, or to whistle ever. But the sheer number of possible traps was making him nervous.

'You'll be slaving for Pettifer,' said Bing reassuringly. 'The list went up at the end of last term. He's quite a decent chap. He'll probably give you a beating quite early on, just to show what happens if you slack, but after that you should be all right as long as you keep his study clean and look willing all the time.'

Terts didn't like the idea of an early beating, even if it was only intended as a warning. And although his brothers had already described to him the duties that he would have to carry out in his first year, he still found it odd that his father should pay for him to clean muddy boots and make tea and act as a kind of housemaid when at home he never had to do anything of the sort at all. There were servants for that sort of thing. But he would do his best to keep out of trouble.

That had been Richard's first piece of advice: that the best thing for a servitor was not to be noticed. For the whole of his first year he should keep the rules and hand in his tasks and impots on time and turn up punctually for the games which would be compulsory for him, but he should do nothing to make him stand out from the rest. In his second year it would be different.

By then he should have discovered something he could be good at, and it would be quite in order to start making a name for himself.

Bing, for example, had a natural talent for sports and games, and an aggressive nature which caused trouble when it showed itself in a shortness of temper but was an asset in Corps exercises and on the rugger field. He had been picked for Junior Colts in his fourth term and would undoubtedly end his school career as Captain of the Fifteen. Terts, who was more slightly built than his brother – and who took no great pleasure in the prospect of being hurled to the ground and having his face rubbed into the mud – was never likely to rival Bing in that sphere. He would have to find his own path to distinction.

The trunk was full. All three boys sat on the lid while Mrs Warren pulled down the metal clasps and then left the heavy load to be carried downstairs later. While the two elder boys hurried off to enjoy their last day of freedom, Terts continued to sit on the trunk, swinging his legs so that his heels drummed against its solid side.

One stage of his life was coming to an end. It was not just that in twenty-four hours' time he would have become a schoolboy. Something more important than that would be happening. Until now he had been a child at home, doing what he was told. He would still have to do what he was told at school, of course, but there would be choices to be made, and the choices would determine the direction of his adult life. It was a weird feeling, not knowing yet what the choices would be.

One choice, though, he had made already. From now on he would no longer be Mortimer or Mort. He was Terts.

3

'Service!'

Automatically Terts came to a halt and looked around to see who was calling. Pettifer, for whom he slaved, was safely out of the way on the cricket field. But any of the school prefects was entitled to shout for a boy to run an errand. After the call was heard, the first servitor he saw had to do the job. Terts was still a servitor, and would remain so until the end of his third term at Croxton. If he were noticed deliberately trying to get out of sight, he would be given an immediate stroke of the whippy cane which every prefect carried as his badge of office.

By the beginning of the summer term Terts had become adept at pinpointing the direction from which the call had come and making an unobtrusive escape; although it was sometimes wiser to keep still than to be caught running away.

On this occasion the call was echoing between Big School, which housed most of the classrooms, and the chapel. The chapel was a free-standing building, designed in imitation of a Greek temple and raised above ground level so that there were eight rows of stone steps all round. Taking care to move quietly, Terts climbed the steps and walked along the outer side of the chapel, keeping as close to the wall as he could. The important thing was not to run, so that if he was seen he could pretend to have been on his way to obey the summons.

'Service!' This time it was not so much a shout as a bellow. And as he reached the end of the chapel building he was confronted by the bellower.

'Oh, it's you, Terts. Come and give us a hand, will you?' said his brother.

Terts was both indignant and surprised by the confrontation. Bing was not a prefect. He had no right to call for service. And why was he dressed in rugger kit on the first day of the cricket term? Curiosity prompted the younger boy to see what was going on, but he dawdled ostentatiously to make it clear that it was only because he chose to that he was moving in that direction.

What he saw increased his puzzlement. It was not just Bing who was dressed for rugger but the whole of Dempsey's junior team, which had won the Colts Cock House Cup at the end of the previous term. Or, at least, they had won it on the field, but had unfortunately chosen to celebrate their victory that evening by breaking bounds and going into town, to the Red Lion. Here, as they sipped their beer, they had been spotted by one of the masters. In a sullen ceremony the next day they had been forced to hand over the coveted trophy to School House, their defeated rivals. Bing had spent the whole of Easter holiday grumbling about it – although not within his father's hearing.

Now the team had reassembled. Fourteen boys, with hair neatly slicked down and rugger kit clean and pressed, were sitting in three rows on the chapel steps. There was a gap in the middle of the group for their captain.

'Colts Cock House Fifteen always has an official photograph,' explained Bing, as Terts wondered what was going on. 'But they cut us out last term, because of all the fuss. We did win, though, so I don't see why we shouldn't have one. I tried to get Brabham's to send someone up, but they said they couldn't without an official order.'

Mr Brabham owned a photographic studio in the town. In the first term of each school year he despatched an assistant to take the nine house photographs, and in each of the other terms he came in person to immortalise the School First Eleven or First Fifteen and any other teams whose achievements deserved to be recorded for posterity. Each photograph was set behind a gold-edged mount and the names of the boys thus distinguished were written in neat letters below.

'Anyway,' Bing continued, 'Maddison's got a camera of his own. We just need someone to take the photograph, so that we can all be in it.'

'I never have,' said Terts, made anxious by the responsibility. Bing's team included all the house hefties, who would not lightly overlook any failure on his part.

'It's all set up,' his brother assured him. Two of the chairs used in chapel by the masters had been carried out to form a small platform. 'Whatever you do, don't touch the camera. Just look through that sort of window there: the viewfinder.'

Terts bent down, taking care that not even an eyelash should disturb the camera. He found himself looking at a neatly packed group of tiny figures: no longer bullies, but lilliputians. But there was no time to reflect on the suddenness of their diminution, because instructions were coming hard and fast.

'Take hold of this sort of wire thing,' Bing commanded. 'Don't pull it straight in case it jerks the camera. Put your thumb on this plunger at the end and two fingers under this metal ring. What you're going to do is press the plunger down till the knob touches the ring and then wait and then press it down again. We shall have to keep quite still between the two presses, and so must the camera.'

Still nervous, Terts put his hand into the right position and flexed his thumb to make sure it was ready to move.

'How long do I wait?'

'Count to thirty. First of all you let me get into my place. Then you say, "Are you ready? One, two, three". After three you press for the first time. Then you count to thirty. Then you press the second time. Then you tell us we can move again.'

He moved off and climbed into his place in the centre of the group. Like the others, he sat with his knees apart. Between his strong, thick thighs he set the Colts Cock House Cup. The sight of that almost startled Terts into a comment. It must have been stolen from School House. But he knew better than to ask questions. He began to set the operation into motion.

'Are you ready? One, two – Franklin, all the others have got their arms folded except you. Does it matter, you looking different?'

Franklin folded his arms. Terts felt a moment of sheer delight. It wasn't very often that a servitor could tell somebody two years older than himself what to do. His eyes, close to the viewfinder, searched hopefully for some other failure of conformity that he could criticise and correct, but without success.

'Are you ready? One, two, three.' His thumb pressed smoothly down and he heard a faint click. His eyes stayed close to the viewfinder, staring at the team.

They would all want a copy of this photograph. Their mothers would frame it. It would hang in a study or billiards room. While its owner grew older and older, it would remain unchanged. Franklin, as the years passed, would have sideburns and a white walrus moustache. He would drink too much and limp with gout. But in the photograph he would always be a boy, frozen in time in the pose dictated by Bradley tertius. Would he feel pleasure in looking at the group and remembering a day of triumph; or would he spend his later years regretting that he was a boy no longer?

With a sharp intake of breath Terts realised guiltily that he was forgetting to count. Probably the time was past already, but he counted another quick thirty just in case. A smile spread over his face as he realised that the team, frozen into immobility, were doubtless well aware that they should have been released by now: but anyone who opened his mouth to protest would spoil the photograph. Once again he was in control.

'Twenty-nine, thirty,' said Terts, and pressed for the second time.

As he had expected, there was a burst of indignation.

'That was too long,' Bing told him. 'I was counting myself.'

'Sorry. You didn't say how fast I was supposed to go.'

'Doesn't matter,' said Maddison, the owner of the camera. 'As long as we didn't move, the longer the better.' He smiled in a friendly way at Terts, who was emboldened to ask questions about how the camera worked. The Bradleys had once, soon after Libby's birth, sat for a family group, but the camera on that occasion was a large one which was set on a tripod and fed with heavy glass plates. He had never seen anything as compact as this before.

Maddison, who would not normally have bothered with a boy two years his junior, seemed pleased to explain about lenses and refraction and light and exposures. 'Of course, a camera like this only takes quite small pictures,' he said. 'But they can be made bigger. I don't know how you do that yet, but it can be done. I've only had this since Christmas, and I didn't bring it to school last term in case somebody pinched it or chucked it about. Thanks, anyway.' He folded up the camera carefully and hurried off. The rest of the team had disappeared already, anxious to sneak back into the house and change before they were noticed. Bing, in addition, would presumably have to restore the cup to its proper home.

Terts sat down on the chapel steps, still warm where the group had been posing, and thought about the unexpected interlude. He savoured his moment of power over the bigger boys, and he sympathised with his brother's wish to record the victory which Dempsey's had certainly won on the field. But another thought niggled at his mind. The team had not actually been entitled to hold the cup. The name engraved on it for 1903 would be that of School House. The photograph was a lie, in a way. An understandable lie, a white lie, but a lie all the same and he, Terts, was responsible for it.

He remembered the conversation which he had had with his father a year earlier. It was about the concentration camps in South Africa and how people might write untruths about them. Words couldn't be trusted. Only seeing was believing, Mr Bradley had said, but there was an implication – he couldn't remember after such a long time whether it had been put into words – that since not everybody could physically see everything, photographs were the next best thing. The camera couldn't lie.

But yes, it could lie, and it just had. When that gouty and white-haired Franklin at the age of seventy showed the photograph of Dempsey's Colts to his grandson, he would be suggesting, although not in words, that the name engraved on the cup was Dempsey's. What the camera was truthfully saying was that Bing and his team had acted out a sort of fib, but that was far too complicated for anyone ever to work out.

The only answer, thought Terts to himself as he stood up and prepared to go on his way, was for a photograph to be taken without the subject knowing anything about it. Not posing for the camera. In fact, perhaps deliberately trying to hide from it. If only he had Maddison's camera in his hand now and could take a picture of Bing trying to sneak the cup back into School House! That would be really true.

But he hadn't got a camera and so he couldn't take the photograph. As he went on his way again Terts screwed his right hand into a loose fist and looked through it as though it were a telescope or a viewfinder. He paused to focus on a blackbird which was tugging a worm out of the ground. 'Click!' he said at the very moment when the last of the worm emerged and the bird's head jerked backwards. It was a true picture: or would have been if he had been properly equipped. That actual blackbird had caught that actual worm. This was good sport. With his fist still to his eye Terts left the shelter of the chapel wall.

'Service!'

This time it was a genuine prefect who was calling. Once again Terts kept quite still so that he could not be caned for running away. Round the corner of the chapel crept another servitor: Mabey, a boy in his own form. He was making exaggerated movements and biting his bottom lip with concentration in his efforts not to be heard escaping.

'Click!' said Terts.

Mabey spun round, startled and angry. With reason, as it turned out, for the prefect had heard the word spoken and arrived within a second to claim his service. Terts volunteered to do it; that seemed only fair since he had given both of them away. But Mabey had been seen trying to escape. Already the prefect's cane was lashing at his trousers. Terts's hand was still raised to his eye. He had more sense than to say Click out loud this time but he registered the scene as though he were still looking through Maddison's viewfinder. Life, he realised for the first time, was a series of pictures.

4

The Bradleys had no country estate of their own, and needed none. Mrs Bradley's father, Lord Mortimer, lived alone – except for the servants, of course – in Kinderley Court, his country seat. He sent his son-in-law regular invitations to the shooting, and encouraged his daughter to bring her children for a long country holiday each summer. In addition, it was understood that the whole family would spend Christmas with him each year.

The first day of each holiday tended to be nerve-racking for the boys. Their grandfather treated them as though they were the sons he had never had: but with one difference. Had he fathered boys of his own, the eldest would automatically have become his heir, but amongst his grandsons he had the power to choose. Terts was not yet of an age to worry about inheritances, but both Richard and Bing were aware of the possibilities. It was to be assumed that Lord Mortimer would keep the estate in the family, but no one knew how his mind would work. Would he choose Richard as his heir, because he was the eldest grandson, or would he deliberately not choose Richard because of the inheritance from the Bradley side of the family that would come his way one day? And if not Richard, then who would it be?

It was not a matter to which Terts ever gave any thought. His grandfather was not an old man; well, not very old. And to give Henry and Edith Bradley their due, they never suggested in so many words that the boys should attempt to ingratiate themselves with their grandfather in any specific way – perhaps because they felt certain enough that one or other of their boys would be the fortunate heir. All the same, the departure for each visit was always marked by a strong emphasis on the need for good behaviour. Even without understanding precisely what they thought was at stake, Terts found it hard to behave naturally when he first arrived.

But the constraint didn't last for long. Once the first greetings had been exchanged it was understood that the children would need to stretch their legs after the journey. There were dogs and horses to be greeted and favourite parts of the estate to be explored. It was full of pictures. Terts no longer said 'Click' out loud when his fist framed an interesting subject, but he thought it in his mind. Click to a robin perching on the handle of a spade in the walled garden. Click to the dead crows strung on a line by the gamekeeper's cottage. Click to the gamekeeper himself, keeping the boys at a safe distance as he pushed a stick into a poacher's trap to make it snap shut.

Terts knew better than to ask his parents directly whether he could have a camera for his Christmas present: that was not the done thing at all. The best he could do was to mention his new interest in taking photographs on every possible occasion. He had made loud comments on the subject throughout the summer holidays and then again in the days before the family packed up for the Christmas visit. Not until Christmas Day itself would he learn whether they had taken the hint.

Christmas Day came, and his father gave him a gun.

'No point in getting you measured at Purdey's until your hands and arms have finished growing,' Mr Bradley said. 'But this will do you for a few years, and now that you're fourteen you should be sensible enough to handle it.'

Without thinking, Terts promptly proved him wrong by putting the gun to his shoulder and taking aim at a blackbird outside on the terrace. 'Click,' he thought to himself as he lowered his head to get the bird in his sights. Then, as he turned to express his thanks, he was abashed by the expression on his father's face.

'Sorry, father. But it's never been loaded, has it?'

'That's not something you should ever take for granted.' But Mr Bradley was in a good Christmas Day mood. 'It's the hunt tomorrow. But the day after, we'll go out together and see whether we can bag a few rabbits for the pot, eh?'

'That would be good fun. Thank you very much.' It would not have been polite to let his father notice any disappointment. Nor would it be wise, in the presence of his grandfather, even to hint that he preferred watching live rabbits to eating dead ones. Lord Mortimer took it for granted that pheasants and foxes and trout and rabbits existed just to be killed.

The disappointment did not last long. 'Open my present next,' said Bing. He was holding out a box wrapped in green paper. Inside the wrapping was a camera.

'I didn't have the rhino to get anything as good as Maddison's,' Bing said, watching his younger brother's face to make sure that the gift was appreciated. 'Five bob was the most I could manage. But the chap said that these Brownies did a pretty decent job anyway. Just right for a beginner, he said.'

'Gosh, thanks, Bing. It's jolly generous of you.' The boys were given very little pocket money and were usually reduced to home-made presents between themselves.

Bing came closer, and dropped his voice to a whisper.

'It's a sort of thank you. For keeping your mouth shut.' The photograph of Dempsey's Colts, which Terts had taken, had been proudly displayed by Bing to his parents at the beginning of the summer holiday, and his younger brother had refrained from making any comment. Bing raised his voice to a normal level again. 'Unlike your gun, this is loaded. I got the chap to put a film cartridge in, in case you didn't know how. It will take six pictures.'

Terts repeated his thanks and put the camera to his eye, just as he had earlier put the gun. As in the case of the gun, he made no attempt to squeeze the trigger. The precious six shots must not be wasted, and he would need to read the instruction book in order to learn whether pictures could be taken indoors at all. But it gave him pleasure simply to look through the viewfinder, framing a small part of the rich Christmas canvas.

There was the Christmas tree, with its candles burning and the rapidly diminishing pile of presents round its foot. And there was Libby's small impatient hand, stretching quietly out to reach a parcel which had her name on it. Terts waited until he had both the hand and the parcel in his sights. 'Click!' he thought silently to himself. That would have made a picture.

There was his mother, who was going to have another baby quite soon. She had told the children that just before they left for Kinderley, although of course they had all noticed already how fat she was growing. She was sitting down now, looking tired and happy at the same time as she watched her family opening their presents. Terts pointed the camera directly at her and caught the smile which lit up her face and filled her eyes with love and pleasure as Libby clasped her new doll to her chest. Click. Once again the movement was only in his mind, not in his finger; but oh, this was going to be good sport.

The hunt, he decided. He would take pictures of the Boxing Day hunt. The meet would be at Kinderley Court, so there would be half an hour in which the riders would be assembling and not moving too fast. He could photograph his family, and the hounds. Yes, the meet would make a fine start.

Now that he was fourteen, Terts himself would have been allowed to ride to hounds if he had wanted to, as long as he promised to be careful. Richard and Bing were already members of the hunt. Libby was far too young, of course. One of the grooms would take her out on a leading rein, following the hounds – but slowly – to start with and then cutting across to some point from which she might hope to see the end of the chase. But Terts was in between. He was allowed to choose, and he chose to do what he had always done and to watch. He knew the countryside almost as well as his grandfather. He was a fast runner and could calculate how to take short cuts and keep the hunt in view. It was a marvellous sight, seen from some hilltop above: the red streak of speed which was the fox, followed by the eager hounds and then by the line of smartly-dressed riders, urging on their mounts. As a picture Terts always found it thrilling. The problem was that he was really on the side of the fox.

Six pictures. As the hunt assembled on the morning of Boxing Day Terts moved around as unobtrusively as he could, choosing what he would record. It seemed only right that his first snapshot should be of Bing, the giver of the camera, sitting straight-backed on his grey. It was a posed picture, because the young photographer needed time to step backwards and sideways until the whole of the horse was fitted inside the viewfinder, and so the subject had to be asked to keep still.

The picture of his mother was posed as well. As soon as Mrs Bradley realised that the camera was pointing in her direction she complained that it was unfair to record her in her present bulky state when in two months' time she would once again be as slim as before. So Terts was invited to come up close and take just her face. She turned it from side to side, smiling all the time, until he said 'Now!' and pulled the little metal lever: the trigger which opened the shutter.

It was probably sensible to start with two such co-operative subjects, but that wasn't really what Terts wanted to do. Of all the pictures which he saw in his mind, the best were of people who were getting on with their ordinary lives without realising that anyone was watching them. But now that he was holding a real camera in his hands, he didn't quite see how to remain unobtrusive.

He was not the only photographer at the meet that morning. A young man, after a word with Lord Mortimer, was setting up a tripod on the steps of Kinderley Court. Terts went up to join him.

'Is this the best place?'

'It is for me.' The young man glanced down to see what Terts was carrying. 'Not for your Brownie, though. You need to be closer than this. I should concentrate on individuals or small groups, if I were you.'

'Are you taking yours for a newspaper?'

'Hope so. Local paper.' He bent down to put his eye to the camera while his hand adjusted the focus. 'They've never printed photographs before,' he said as he straightened himself. 'Only drawings. But they've got a new machine and they said they'd give me a chance to show what I can do. If they like it, I might get a regular job. It's all the rage nowadays, photographs in newspapers. My name's Albert Dennison.'

'How do you do, Mr Dennison? I'm Terts. Lord Mortimer's my grandfather. I want to take a photograph of him, but not just looking straight at me and smiling.'

'Should be easy enough. The thing is, to know what's going to happen next. If you were to get yourself near your grandfather's horse – but outside kicking distance, mind – you'd know that the stirrup cup will be coming round in a few moments. The tray will be held up. Your grandfather will lean down to take his glass. He'll turn his head to the side, but he'll be looking at the glass, not at you. So all you need is to be pointing your camera not at where he is now but where he'll be when he leans down. Snap, and you've got him. In short, you don't go to the picture, the picture comes to you. You've just got to be sure that you get there first, that's all.'

'Yes, I see. Gosh, thanks, Mr Dennison.' Delighted by the lesson, Terts hurried off. He caught Lord Mortimer in exactly the position which Mr Dennison had suggested. He caught Richard leaning forward to pat his mount on the head. And he took Libby standing behind a group of hounds. Perhaps the movement of the hounds would spoil the picture, but the only way to find that out was by trying.

The last shot in the cartridge was reserved for his father, but Mr Bradley's chestnut, Major, was in a restless mood, continually shaking his head and turning round on the spot. But anyway, Terts had had a better idea. He had decided to try an action shot. It might not work – but then, all these first attempts were really experiments.

And now the hunt was off, streaming down the long drive. Terts waited until the distant call of the huntsman's horn gave him a clue to the direction of the chase; then he began to run.

His first vantage point gave him a view of the fox itself, with the hounds in full cry behind. He waited until the first riders came into sight. There were four or five riders ahead of his father. Mr Bradley would not like that. Terts did some quick calculations in his head and began to run again.

Panting with effort, he came to a halt ten minutes later beside a high thorn hedge. Unless the fox outwitted him by doubling back, this was the direction in which the hunt would come. At the bottom of the field there was a fence which could be jumped and a gate which could be opened, but these were slightly away from what was likely to be the direct line. Mr Bradley, anxious to get into the lead and knowing that his horse, Major, was powerful enough to jump the hedge, would hold to a straight line. At least, so Terts guessed, and it wouldn't matter in the least if he had guessed wrong. Half hidden, pressed close to the hedge, he waited for his picture to come to him.

And here it came, just as he had envisaged it: the hounds jumping through the fence, the main group of riders following their line, and Major, alone, keeping to the higher ground. The galloping hooves made the ground shake with their weight and energy as he approached the hedge. Terts was close enough to see the excitement in his father's eyes as the horse collected himself, ready for the jump.

Terts took half a step forward. His camera was pointing upwards, ready to snap the horse and rider as they soared at full stretch over the obstacle. But even that slight movement was enough to catch Major's eye. At the very last moment he checked his stride, putting his head down and rearing his hind legs into the air. As Terts's finger moved to take the shot, it was only Mr Bradley who soared over the hedge.

5

The crash as his father hit the ground was followed by a terrifying silence. Terts held his breath, desperately listening for some sound to tell him that his father was picking himself up, swearing in fury, brushing himself down. But there was nothing to be heard except the galloping of the other hunters as they sped away from the safe fence lower down the hill and Major's unhappy neighing as his forelegs reared into the air, conveying his knowledge that something was badly wrong.

Perhaps it was only for a few seconds that Terts was frozen into immobility, but they were long seconds. Then, panting with fear and distress, he tried to look through the hedge. It was too thick. He ran further up the hill, searching for some gap through which he could squeeze.

Another horseman was approaching. It was Bing, whose own mount was not strong enough to keep up with the leaders of the hunt and who must have glanced up the hill as he approached the fence and seen that Major was riderless. Terts, by now fifty yards away and caught by thorns as he tried to force his way through the hedge, knew that he ought to explain what had happened, but once again found himself unable to move. If his father was badly injured or dead, it was because Major had been alarmed by a movement which was unforgivable, which nobody would in fact ever forgive.

Puzzled and alarmed, Bing hitched Major's reins round a sapling and then tried, as Terts had tried, to peer through. Failing to see anything clearly, he remounted and rode down the hill and through the gate which by now had been opened to let some of the ladies through. Tears ran down Terts's cheeks as he waited and watched. A few minutes passed. Then Bing reappeared, riding at full gallop towards Kinderley Court.

Terts began to run. He was a fast runner and did not pause even when his heart and lungs became so pinched with pain that he could hardly breathe. Inevitably, though, Bing reached the house before him. By the time Terts came within sight of Kinderley, two footmen were already running down the steps of the courtyard, carrying a stretcher, while a groom and his lad ran to harness the carriage horses before taking them to the nearest point which could be reached by road.

Mrs Bradley appeared on the top step. Her face was white, and she leaned against one of the pillars as though without its support she would fall. Her hands were pressed across her stomach, and as Terts watched she suddenly doubled up in pain, uttering a sharp cry which he could hear even at a distance. He moved closer, although taking care not to be seen. Mrs Bradley's French maid came hurrying to her side, her face as anxious as that of her mistress. Calling for one of the other servants to give additional support, she began to lead Mrs Bradley inside, but paused to call down to Bing.

'Dr Wilkinson, he is out with the hunt. Tell him please, your mother needs him. Quick-quick.'

Bing, who had been about to lead the way for the footmen at walking pace, made off at a canter instead, leaving Terts more miserable even than before as the last vestige of hope faded. If the doctor was to go to his mother, who was merely ill, it could only be because there was nothing to be done for his father.

Quietly he made his way into the house and up to his room, expecting at every turn to be confronted by accusing glances. But the household was in such a state of upheaval that no one paid any attention to a scratched and dishevelled fourteen-year-old boy.

His heart was pounding with more than the exertion of the run. In a daylight nightmare he seemed to see once again the terrifying picture of his father flying through the air – only now it was not his father but himself: projected upwards and knowing that in a few seconds he would crash to the ground. He stuffed the fingers of his left hand into his mouth to stifle a scream of terror, and bit frantically at his finger nails. In his right hand he was still holding the camera. As his breathing and heartbeat at last began to steady themselves, he set it down on a table and sat on the edge of his bed, staring at it.

Only a few hours earlier his father had reminded him of the rules to be observed when carrying a loaded gun: all the precautions which must be taken, all the foolishness which must be avoided. No one had warned him that a camera could be a lethal weapon as well. He should have realised for himself, when he thought of what his two Christmas presents had in common: the cartridge, the trigger, the viewfinder which served the same purpose as the sights of a gun. He had intended to shoot a picture but instead had killed his father as surely as though he had shot him with a bullet.

The gun, still in its case, was lying on the table with the rest of his Christmas presents. A long time passed as Terts stared at it, feeling himself drawn towards it. He deserved to be punished. He deserved to die, as his father had died. And then he would never need to confess what he had done. A moment of pain would be a lesser punishment than a lifetime of guilt, cast out from the family. Because when his mother discovered that he was to blame she would never want to speak to him again; would never love him again.

But it was the greater punishment, not the lesser, that he ought to accept. And if he were to die in what would look like a stupid accident, no one would know why. His mother, already so upset, would have to endure the shock of a second bereavement. Was it really fair to inflict such pain on her? Besides, he had not yet been given any cartridges for the gun. He would have to steal them from his grandfather's gun room, and that was always kept locked.

He heard the gong for luncheon while he was still staring at the gun, but even the thought of food made him feel sick. No one came to see where he was. Although the servants were continuing the normal daily routine, perhaps none of the family had any appetite. Or perhaps they were all sitting round the table and discussing what should be done with a boy who had behaved so irresponsibly.

But no: none of them could possibly know what he had done. There were no witnesses to his stupidity. Except the camera. Turning his eyes away from the gun at last, Terts gazed at the Brownie instead as though it were an explosive only waiting for the fuse to be lit. He had taken a photograph of Bing that morning and Bing, the donor of the camera, would sooner or later demand to see how the picture had come out. The others would want to look as well. Richard, who was clever, would not take long to work out the significance of the fatal sixth exposure. What was to be done?

There was someone at the door of his room. Grainger, the butler, was a large and aloof man, who would normally have delegated the bearing of a message for one of the children to some inferior servant. But today his voice was compassionate.

'His lordship would like to speak to you in the library, Master Mortimer.'

Terts stood up, automatically obedient to the summons. But the butler's unusually gentle voice offered a suggestion.

'I'm sure his lordship will be willing to wait for a moment or two while you, er, wash your hands.'

Terts looked down. His hands were filthy and streaked with blood where the hedge had scratched them. He could feel, too, that his hair was tousled. He nodded, picked up his hairbrush and made his way to the bathroom.

Five minutes later he appeared in the library. Bing and Richard were sitting on the window seat in gloomy silence, while Lord Mortimer and Dr Wilkinson, standing in front of the fire, talked in lowered voices.

'Ah, Mortimer.' Terts's grandfather never used the abbreviation of his name and was not even aware of the nickname by which he was nowadays known. 'I see you've heard the news already.'

Terts realised that he had forgotten to wash his tear-stained and dirty face. He nodded miserably. Lord Mortimer, who was not as a rule a demonstrative man, came across to his grandson and put an arm round his shoulders.

'It's a bad business. Very bad. But hunting's a dangerous sport, Mortimer. Each of us knows when we set out in the morning that we may not all come back in one piece. Your father died suddenly, without suffering, while he was doing something he enjoyed. We must mourn his loss, but not the manner of his going. If you see what I mean. It's your mother we have to think about now.'

'How is she, sir?'

It was Dr Wilkinson who answered. 'The baby she was expecting has arrived early. A little boy. Very small. He'll be needing a lot of care.'

'And Mother?'

'Your mother's very upset, naturally. And very tired. She'll need to rest. I've arranged for a nurse for her and a wet nurse for the baby.'

What was a wet nurse? Terts frowned in puzzlement, but was given no opportunity to enquire.

'It will take her a long time to recover from the shock,' said Lord Mortimer. 'You three boys – and little Libby, of course – are the ones who can help her most. I'm sure I can rely on you all to support her. She needs to be sure that nothing else has changed. That she still has a loving family around her. If you see what I mean.'

There was a muffled 'Yes, sir' from the three young Bradleys. Terts felt the hand which was resting on his shoulder give an affectionate pat.

'You're upset, my boy. I can see that. Naturally. Go back to your room and rest if you want to. We'll let you know when your mother's well enough to see you.'

Dragging his feet, Terts went upstairs. It was clear to him now that he could never confess.

6

By noon on the day after their father's death, Terts and his two brothers were on their way to acquire mourning clothes. Aunt Florence, who had been spending Christmas with her father-in-law in Cheltenham, had hurried to be with her sister as soon as she heard the news, and volunteered to make the necessary arrangements for the children. Outfitting the boys was comparatively simple, even in a provincial city; but Libby would have to have a dress made for her. Terts, who had lain awake for half the night trying to decide what to do, leapt at the chance of a brief freedom in Oxford.

'While she's being measured, may I go and visit a friend, Aunt Florence?'

In normal circumstances his aunt would have recognised the unlikelihood of the fourteen-year-old having any acquaintance in Oxford and would in any case have wished to keep all her nephews in sight. But she was distressed by the tragedy which had struck her sister's family and flustered by the need to shop in an unfamiliar place. She not only allowed him to go, but told him to take the carriage in order to be sure that he would be back within half an hour without becoming lost.

As soon as he had heard that morning that he was to be taken into Oxford, Terts had copied the address of the local newspaper from his grandfather's copy. Now, clutching his camera, he hurried into its busy office and asked to see Mr Albert Dennison.

'He doesn't work here. Sorry, lad.'

'Oh. I thought he said –'

'Bit of the wishful if he did. He'd like to, all right. Came in yesterday with the last picture taken of that gent who died in the Kinderley hunt. We bought that.'

'Where could I find him? I want to talk to him.'

Although Terts himself was not aware of it, his voice had changed from the anxious and slightly breathless tone of his original enquiry to the confident demand of a public schoolboy of good family. The sub-editor whom he had approached must have recognised the difference – or perhaps, thought Terts (noting that he was no longer addressed as a 'lad'), had caught a glimpse of Lord Mortimer's carriage waiting outside.

'Miss Wootton, give the young gentleman Bert's address, will you?'

Five minutes later, after Membury the coachman had made two enquiries as to the whereabouts of the Jericho district, the carriage drew up in a street so narrow that nothing would be able to pass it. There was no bell to pull beside the door of the small terraced cottage, so Terts knocked on the door and then, when no one answered, hammered more loudly.

'All right, all right.' Bert, when at last he appeared in shirtsleeves, looked none too pleased to be disturbed. 'I was in the darkroom. What can I do for you?'

'I'm Terts Bradley. We met yesterday at Kinderley Court.'

'Oh yes. I was sorry to hear about your father. Unfortunate.'

'Could I talk to you, please?'

With some reluctance Bert opened the door. Terts found himself standing in a small sitting room made to seem even smaller by the presence of a bed.

'Only one bedroom and I have to use that for my work,' Bert explained apologetically.

'Yes, of course. That's what I wanted to talk about. I wondered if you'd mind telling me what I need to do to print my photographs?'

'You don't have to do that yourself, Master Bradley. A Brownie, wasn't it? All you have to do is to send the cartridge off to Kodak and in three or four weeks they'll send you back the prints. A bit of cash is all you need, not know-how.'

'But I want to do it myself.'

'Well, I'm sorry. I can't just say to you "Do this and that" and expect you to make a good hand of it. You need equipment. Special paper and special chemicals and special containers to put them in. And a darkroom. And a way of knowing what you're doing in the dark. It's not worth setting yourself up just for the odd snapshot.'

'Yes, but ...' Terts tried to think of some way in which he could avoid an explanation. 'Well, Mr Dennison, you've got the equipment here, haven't you. Could you give me a sort of lesson? Help me to make the prints using your stuff. I'd pay for your time, naturally. I've got a sovereign. One of my Christmas presents.'

'What's the urgency, that you can't wait for Kodak to do it for you?'

'The pictures are private. I don't want anyone to see them.'

'Oh! Been taking dirty pictures, have you? Little ladies with no clothes on?'

'Of course not.' Terts's voice, which he thought had finished breaking, shot uncontrollably upwards into a shrill treble. He was tempted to walk out indignantly; but he needed this man's help.

'If you want me to help you, then I'll be bound to see what you've taken. Can't be done without that.'

'But I could ask you, couldn't I, to ... to ...' Terts searched for the proper grown-up phrase. 'To keep it confidential.'

Bert stared at him for some time without speaking. Then he said, 'Sit down, Master Bradley, won't you?'

Terts looked around and sat on the only chair which was not covered with articles of clothing. Bert remained standing.

'If I were a bounder,' he said at last, 'I'd take your money and develop your photographs and let you go away thinking that your secrets were safe with that honourable gentleman Mr Albert Dennison. But I'm only half a bounder. So I'll tell you the truth.'

There was another pause. It seemed that telling the truth went against the grain.

'I told you yesterday, I want to get regular employment. My knees under the table. Best way for me to get on the payroll is to turn up in the editor's office with what's called a scoop. Something that nobody knows except me and one other person, and that other person wanting to keep it quiet. Something that the editor will want to print in his paper if he can find out what it is, and his way to find out won't be to give me money, but a job.'

'That's a sort of blackmail.'

Bert shook his head vigorously. 'Blackmail would be if I went to that one other person and asked for money to keep quiet about what I knew. Going to the editor in the way I said is just naming a price. Ordinary business transaction. Now then, you've got some kind of secret hidden inside this camera of yours, is that right?'

Terts didn't answer. He had been a fool to come and a fool to suppose that Albert Dennison would be stupid enough and kind-hearted enough to come to his aid without asking questions.

Bert was still thinking aloud. 'Not likely to be anything with yourself as the subject. Your first day with a camera, you wouldn't be on to that sort of thing. But one of your brothers, perhaps? A grandson of Lord Mortimer, doing something he shouldn't?'

He paused again, and again Terts kept his expression under control, determined not to let the photographer learn whether any of his guesses came near the mark.

'Well, I don't know what it is that you don't want a stranger in the Kodak laboratory to see. No idea. I'm not going to bang you on the head and steal your camera so that I can find out. But if you hand over the camera and ask me to spread your secret out in front of my eyes as well as yours, you're expecting too much if you think I won't remember what I've seen. And use it if it's worth using. I'm being straight with you because you're a young lad and you haven't had time yet to learn how the world works. It's your lesson for today. Never trust a journalist – or someone who wants to be a journalist – not to tell the truth.'

'Don't you mean the other way round?' Terts by now was confused as well as disappointed.

Bert shook his head vigorously. 'I mean what I said. I don't suppose a young gentleman like you reckons much to a chap like me. A bit of speculative work but no regular job. Not much money. Not much of a home and lucky to have what there is. But I know what I want to do with my life: tell the world about the crimes which are hidden from it. There needs to be someone like me to be the eyes of the world, so that people will know. Maybe it'll only be once or twice in my life that I see something important. But I have to be looking out all the time. I'm looking out now. If there's a crime in your camera, you'd do well to leave.'

Clutching the Brownie even more tightly, Terts stood up and began to back towards the door. Yesterday he had thought that Albert Dennison was a pleasant young man, but now he found the intensity of his voice frightening. He had claimed that he wasn't going to knock his visitor over the head, but all the same ... Perhaps it was just as well that Membury was still sitting with the whip in his hand just outside the door.

The door was opened for him politely. Bert smiled as he said goodbye and became once again the pleasant young man.

'Your secret may not be as bad as you think, not really,' he said. 'But do remember, won't you, that you have to be very careful to take your cartridge out in the dark. Because if the light gets in, you lose your pictures and there's nothing to be done about them.'

'Yes, of course. Thank you. I'm sorry to have wasted your time.'

It was a relief to be safely back in the carriage and back into the ordinary sort of life in which aunts scolded their nephews for being late and causing anxiety. The problem had not, of course, gone away; but Bert, for all his apparent unhelpfulness, had provided the solution.

Alone in his bedroom at Kinderley Court, Terts prepared the envelope in which to send his negatives off to be developed and printed. Then, in the cold grey light of a December morning, he opened the back of the camera.

The problem was solved, but his feeling of guilt could not be so quickly removed. All he could do in the end was to try to learn more lessons from the incident than the one which Bert had specifically spelled out.

The first photograph he had ever taken, of the rugger team with the cup to which it was not entitled, was a lie, and he was ashamed of taking it. The most recent photograph, of his father flying head-first over the hedge, was a true record of what had happened, but he was ashamed of this one too, because he was responsible for the consequences.

From now on, he pledged himself, it was going to be different. He would take ordinary photographs, like the one of his grandfather stooping for the stirrup cup, which were simply pleasant records of an occasion. And perhaps when he was older he would be able to do what Bert wanted to do and take other photographs which would reveal secrets: which would tell the world about crimes that people were trying to conceal from it.

The eyes of the world. Bert had used that phrase, and Terts liked it. One day perhaps he too might be the eyes of the world. But in the meantime there was one firm resolve to be made. To make public the shameful secrets of other people was one thing. But never again would he take a photograph of which he himself might be ashamed. Never.

7

Eight days after his father's death, Terts was once again summoned to his grandfather's library. Lord Mortimer was standing in front of the log fire with his legs apart, toasting his back. Bing was standing as well, as stiffly as though he were a soldier awaiting orders. Libby, looking pale in her black dress, sat quietly on a footstool, while Miss Raynor, her governess, had found a place on the window seat.

'All here, then.' Lord Mortimer drew breath as though to make a speech. Tentatively, Terts interrupted him.

'Richard isn't ...'

'Right then, let's start with Richard. Your brother's gone up to London. To Bradley's. To be interviewed by the partners. His uncles. He'll be offered a job. Not much doubt about that. Nothing wrong with nepotism, as long he's up to the work.'

'Is he going to leave Croxton then, sir?' It was Bing who asked that question.

'Have to, won't he? Should think he'd be glad enough to go. Boys can't wait to get away from school, can they?'

Neither Bing nor Terts was prepared to answer that question. Their brother had hoped to go to university before joining the family firm. But perhaps there was no money for that sort of thing any longer.

'Are we very poor now that Father has died?' asked Terts.

His grandfather gave a kind of snort which was difficult to interpret as either yes or no. 'I shan't let you starve,' he promised them. 'No one expects you two to go out and work for your living yet. But look at it this way. Richard is the head of your family now. It's time he began to make his way in the world. To be a support to your mother. They'll expect him, your uncles will, to start at the bottom, and the sooner he gets going, the sooner he'll reach the top.'

The two boys were silent, unsure whether they should be sorry for their elder brother or envious of him. Lord Mortimer used the silence to embark on the statement from which he had been diverted.

'Now then, about the three of you here,' he said. 'Things are bound to change. Can't expect life to go on as it was before your father died. There's no point in keeping up a house in London. Richard can live with one of your uncles to start with. By the time he's ready for a bit more independence, he may be earning enough to find lodgings on his own. But the rest of you will make your home here with me. Good country air. Outdoor life. Much healthier than making your way through those filthy London streets.'

'Are Bing and me going to leave Croxton as well?' asked Terts.

'No, no. Go on as you were. Come here for the holidays, that's all. Well, you did that often enough anyway. Libby and the baby and your mother will be here all the time. Your mother won't want the responsibility of running a London household on her own. This will suit everyone best. I've talked it over with your Bradley uncles. You stay with me, each of you boys, till you're seventeen or so, and then they'll set you up for work.'

'It's very good of you to offer us a home, sir,' said Bing.

'Glad of the chance. Though sorry for the cause of it, naturally. Rattling around on my own here. Glad to have a bit of life in the place. And your mother ...'

Until then Libby had listened to the conversation without joining in. Now she rose to her feet, her eyes wide with anxiety.

'Is Mother going to die as well as Father?' she asked.

'Gracious, no.' Lord Mortimer bent over to pick her up and then lowered himself into a leather armchair and jogged her on his knee. Libby was his pet. 'No, she'll be back with you all before too long, I hope. But she's been ill and she's been upset. It may be a little while before she's strong and happy again. You'll have Miss Raynor to give you your lessons still. And there'll be a nursemaid starting on Monday to look after the two of you and the baby and his nurse.'

'When's the baby going to be christened?' asked Bing.

'Done already. On the day he was born. In case he didn't last the night. Poor little scrap.'

'So what's his name?' asked Libby.

'Aden. Don't ask me why. Your mother should have called him Henry. She wasn't in any fit state to think about it. Well, it's done now. Aden. Now then. Go off and find Mrs Yetton. Talk about rooms. Miss Raynor will come with you. You'll need a schoolroom, Libby. And now that you're all going to live here, you may want to change from the rooms you've been using for holidays. I want you to feel at home. Comfortable.'

As Libby slipped off her grandfather's lap, Terts stepped towards him and held out his hand.

'You're being very kind to us, Grandfather. Thank you very much.'

Startled by the formality, Lord Mortimer shook hands. 'Off you go, then.'

There were twenty-three rooms on the main bedroom floor of Kinderley Court. The housekeeper made it clear that not all of them were on offer. The best were naturally reserved for Lord Mortimer and his weekend guests, and for Mrs Bradley. Aden and his nurse would need three rooms between them, and another three must be set aside for Libby and Miss Raynor. Even so, there was enough choice to make the process of dashing from one room to another enjoyable.

It was agreed that Richard would probably like to have a place of his own for future visits, so Bing was happy to stay alone in the room which the two elder boys had shared in the past. Terts, however, chose somewhere new: a corner room with windows on two sides, so that he could look out in different directions. Next to it was a small box room with no windows at all, and he had his eye on this as well. Although he didn't know exactly what Bert had meant by a darkroom, this room was as dark as it was possible to be. One day, when he had learned how to develop his own photographs, he would put in a claim for this room as well.

At first he was excited by the move, but as he sat on the edge of his new bed, waiting for a maid to bring his clothes from the old room, he began to feel miserable again. His father was dead, his mother was ill, it sounded as though the new baby was by no means certain to live and Richard had been abruptly snatched from the family. Nothing would ever be the same again. And it was all his fault. How could he ever hope to escape from the guilt of that one thoughtless movement?

Bing, arriving to inspect his brother's new quarters, could not be expected to understand about the guilt, but was unexpectedly sensitive to his anxiety.

'It'll be all right,' he said. 'We're lucky to have Grandfather.'

Terts nodded his agreement. Lord Mortimer held and expressed strong views about politicians who failed to value the landowners who provided the country with food and gave employment to labourers and servants; and on the subject of foreigners, Roman Catholics, Jews and farmers who shot foxes he quickly became apoplectic. But within the family he was affectionate and generous. His wife had died soon after the second of his daughters married and left home and he was undoubtedly sincere in saying that it would give him pleasure to have members of two younger generations living with him.

'Yes,' agreed Terts. 'Lucky.' He gave a sigh. 'Well, I wonder how Richard's getting on.'

Richard arrived back at Kinderley the next day, accompanied by the trunks, already packed, which his brothers would need for the school term which was about to start. As soon as he had emerged from a brief visit to his mother's bedroom, his two brothers clamoured to hear his news.

'Tell us all about it,' commanded Bing. 'Right from the beginning.'

'Well, I had to report to the Partner's Room at eleven o'clock. And it was very odd. There were the three of them, sitting behind a long table, and I didn't really know what to call them when they spoke to me. I mean, they've always been just uncles up till now. I kept wondering, was it still all right to say Uncle Alfred or should I call him Mr Bradley?'

'What did you decide?'

'I just said "sir" all the time. But it still feels strange, not knowing quite how to think of them in future.'

'So what did they say?'

'They started off by telling me that I wouldn't be going back to Croxton. That was a bit of a shock, because Father had always promised that I could go on to Oxford if I wanted to. I did mention that. I supposed perhaps there wouldn't be enough money for that now, but Uncle Howard said no, it wasn't that. Just that working at Bradley's would give me knowledge and opportunities that would prove a far better recipe for success in the world than the ability to write Latin and Greek verses.' It was easy to tell from Richard's voice that he was quoting what he had been told without necessarily believing it. 'He made it sound as though Bradley's was a kind of university itself.'

'What does Bradley's do?' asked Terts. It was a question he had never dared to put to his father, because by the time he became curious about it he recognised that he ought to have made enquiries years earlier.

'They buy things from all over the British Empire and sell them here. And quite often they start by lending money for a workshop to be built so that the things can be made, or they buy land for farmers who can't afford to get started. It all provides income for people in poor countries. According to Uncle Adolphus, we help to keep the British flag flying all over the world.'

'You said "we",' Terts pointed out. 'So you're going to work there, are you?'

'Not much choice, is there? But I think it will be interesting. And they were all very nice, the uncles. I wasn't to think that I was being taken out of Croxton because I'd done anything wrong. They'd written to the school already. They read out bits of a letter from the Head Man. I'd have you know that I'm intelligent and hard-working and a good example to the younger boys!'

The two younger boys present on this occasion made noises appropriate to this display of swank. 'So when do you start?' asked Bing.

'Same day that you go up to term. It will be a dull job to begin with. In the mail room. Uncle Howard said they'd want me to have a spell in every department, starting at the bottom. But there were hints that if I did well I might finish up in the Partners' Room in the end.'

'So I should think!' exclaimed Bing, demonstrating that he shared his uncles' view of family entitlement to quick promotion.

'And the rest of you are going to live here, Mother tells me.'

Bing and Terts nodded. For a moment all three boys were silent, considering the ways in which their lives had been changed.

'You won't be Terts at Croxton any longer, Terts,' Richard pointed out. 'Bing will be Bradley, and you'll be Bradley mi.'

This was one change which had not occurred to Terts, but it took him no time at all to dismiss it.

'Only to the gowns,' he said, using the Croxton word for masters. 'As far as everyone else is concerned, I'm Terts for life.'

8

Someone was blubbing. Not with the noisy sobs of a small child who hoped to attract attention and be comforted. This was the sibilant gasping of a boy who knew that to cry was shameful but could not quite conceal his distress. Terts changed direction and silently made his way towards the sound.

He was carrying his camera. The school year which had just started in September 1904 would be Bing's last at Croxton and his younger brother had decided to prepare a leaving present to give him next June. It would consist of a set of photographs of school life, taken at intervals throughout the year. Terts proposed to stick them neatly on to a large sheet of paper and then take it down to Brabham's to be framed. It should provide a good memento.

At the moment when he heard the sobbing he was on his way to the rugger field to take the first shot. Bing was Captain of Rugger this year, so this was the most appropriate place to begin. But there was plenty of time: the game had only just started. He turned a corner, and then another, and found himself in the Old Pump Yard.

Once upon a time, when Croxton was first founded and consisted only of the present School House, a pump in the centre of a courtyard was the only means of washing themselves provided for the boys. By now it was merely a part of the school's history, but it still worked. A thirteen-year-old boy was using it. He had stripped to the waist and was pumping with one hand whilst leaning forward underneath the flow so that the water splashed over his shoulders. His back was bruised and bleeding. Terts could count six distinct red weals where he had been struck from one direction, but the battered flesh suggested that further strokes had descended at right angles to the first.

Automatically, Terts raised his camera to his eye and recorded the scene, wincing as he did so almost as though he could personally feel the pain of the water stinging into wounds on his own back. Only then did he move round to the other side of the pump so that he could be seen.

Gulping in an attempt at self-control, the boy released the pump handle and straightened himself. Terts recognised him as being a member of his own house, Dempsey's. His name was Rose, which was unfortunate for him, since in combination with his frail figure and slightly girlish complexion it encouraged his contemporaries to call him Rosie. But boys of his own age, though they might tease and even bully, would have no right to give him a beating. Only a prefect could do that.

This beating must have been particularly severe. Terts wondered what he had done to deserve it. Rose was a new boy, a servitor, who had only arrived at Croxton at the beginning of this term. Although he might inadvertently have offended against one of the many unwritten etiquettes of dress or trespass, it was difficult to think that he would have been deliberately wicked in any way which would justify such a punishment.

'Turn round,' said Terts.

The boy obeyed. Although Terts was only just fifteen, Rose in his present fragile state probably felt that any older boy had better be obeyed. Terts wound on the film and took another photograph, as close as he could, of the bleeding back.

'What did you do?' he asked.

'I don't know.' The boy bit his lip in an effort to stop the tears flowing again. 'How can I know what I'm not to do again when I don't know what I did?'

'Who gave you the beating?'

The question had the effect of stiffening the thirteen year old's resolve. He stopped crying and wiped the back of his wet hand across his face. 'I can't tell you,' he said.

'Why not?'

'He said if I squealed he'd give me a beating that would make this one feel like the stroke of a baby's finger.'

'It's not right,' said Terts. 'No one ought to hit you like this, especially so early in your first term.' Even as he spoke, he remembered how Bing and Richard had warned him, before he started at Croxton, that he would probably be given an early beating as a lesson to stay on the right track. 'Who's your slavemaster?'

'Jenks. But it wasn't him.'

'Jenks, hey?' Terts knew Jenks, who was a friend of Bing's. Jenks could be sarcastic and unkind and it was easy to believe that he could be cruel.

'It wasn't him, I say!'

'Then tell me who.' Any of the prefects would have the right to strike a servitor who was too slow in answering a call for service, but as a rule they were content with a single whip across the shoulders with the narrow cane they carried. A formal house punishment, by contrast, would be administered on the buttocks with a heavier cane but with not more than six strokes – and it was unlikely that a new boy would have given sufficient offence to deserve this. It must be Jenks. In the privacy of his study, a slavemaster could do anything he chose. But this was too much. It wasn't right. Terts found himself burning with as much indignation as though he had suffered the punishment himself.

What could he do about it? There was no point in complaining to the Head of House who, like Bing, was a friend of Jenks. The housemaster, if approached, would say – as he always said – that discipline was a matter for the boys themselves. The Head Man would not want to be bothered with what he would see as a house matter, especially since Rose would almost certainly continue in his refusal to name his tormentor, for fear of worse punishment to come. Terts sighed helplessly.

'You'd better go and see Matron,' was the best he could suggest. 'She'll put something on it for you.'

Rose opened his mouth to argue, but Terts guessed what he was going to say.

'She won't squeal,' he promised. 'Only if you're infectious.' Matron had made her position clear a long time ago. If the boys injured each other in unauthorised fights, she wanted to be allowed to disinfect and bandage them immediately, and knew that they would only report to her if they could be sure that no questions would be asked.

Terts watched as the younger boy picked up his shirt and covered up his battered back. Then he resumed his walk towards the rugger field. He had already learned that his Brownie was no good for moving subjects, but he managed twice to catch the scrum in a more or less static state, and in a third shot took Bing poised in concentration as he prepared to convert a try.

He found it difficult, though, to put the memory of the sobbing servitor out of his mind. There must be something that could be done to stop this sort of savagery. Terts himself had not had too bad a time in his first year because his two elder brothers would have made clear their disapproval of any punishment which was not deserved. But boys were sent to school to be educated, not to be whipped like animals. If their parents knew what went on, they would surely not send their sons to a school like Croxton any more. But no one would ever tell them, because the life of any boy who squealed would be hell for the rest of his school career.

A solution presented itself only a few weeks later, when he happened to run into Rose again on the same day that his photographs arrived back, developed and printed, from the Kodak laboratory. The thirteen year old looked ill and unhappy. His eyes were ringed with black and his shoulders were hunched together as he walked nervously down a corridor. When Terts stood in his path to stop him, he jumped as though he had been hit again.

'How are you getting on?' Terts asked him. 'Everything better now?'

'No. I hate this beastly school. I wrote to my parents and tried to get them to take me away.'

'What did they say?'

'I think the mater might have agreed. She sounded upset when she wrote. But the pater just said that I was going to have to spend the rest of my life mixing with people who'd been to Croxton and other schools like it, and if I ran away from the first difficulty I'd never have any friends or any respect from people. But I haven't got any friends anyway and I don't care about being respected. I just want to get away from here, and they won't let me.'

'Hard cheese,' said Terts; but he spoke in an abstracted way. He had thought of a solution. If Rose were to leave Croxton, he would be safe from retribution; and to leave was what he wanted to do. So it could do no harm if . . .

Terts was not senior enough to enjoy a share of a study, but now that he was no longer a servitor he had a small cubicle which he could make private with a curtain. That evening he took from the new set of prints the close-up photograph of Rose's bleeding back. On a page torn out of a school notebook he wrote on capital letters with his left hand: 'THIS IS YOUR SON IN HIS SECOND WEEK AT CROXTON. DID YOU SEND HIM HERE FOR THIS?' He put the photograph and the message into an envelope and sealed it. It would not take long to discover the address of Rose's mother. All the boys' outgoing letters had to be placed on a tray outside the housemaster's study, so that he could approve their destinations.

Three days later Dempsey's housemaster called a meeting of the whole house in the dining hall. This was unusual; but what was unheard of was that it was the Head Man – never before known to interfere in house matters – who strode on to the dais. He was followed by a couple who must be Rose's parents. Mrs Rose, formidably large in tweeds and fox fur, looked intently at the assembled boys as they rose to their feet, as though hoping in some way to recognise the sender of the anonymous letter. Her husband, darker in complexion and unobtrusive in presence, had an ugly face but one which seemed to Terts unusually intelligent. His eyes also were searching the room, but in a different way from his wife's. He was taking everything in: making an assessment. Terts, immediately attracted to him, was prepared to bet that he would say nothing at all, but was nevertheless convinced that he was the one in control of the situation.

As for young Rose, looking too small and young to be at school at all, he cowered in the background as the headmaster delivered a lecture on the responsibilities which attended the right to impose discipline. Then he demanded to know who had inflicted a beating so frenzied that the scars had not yet healed.

A murmuring, quickly silenced, went round the hall, but no confession was made. In a second lecture it was made indirectly clear that if Mr Rose received no satisfaction he intended to air the matter in the public press. The reputation of the school would be damaged. Was there someone in the hall who was prepared to carry the burden of that guilt for the rest of his life?

Terts hardly noticed how long the second silence continued, for he had been surprised by an interesting thought. That was what he could have done!

If he had sent the photograph to a newspaper, it might not have been necessary to mention Rose's name at all. But then, he would have been the one responsible for damaging the school, and he was too loyal to wish for that.

The headmaster was tired of waiting. 'Will Rose's slavemaster please stand up?'

Every head turned to the back of the hall as Jenks slowly rose to his feet.

'It wasn't me, sir.'

'Then who was it? You owed this boy a duty of protection in return for his service. You must know who attacked him.'

'I'm afraid I can't say, sir.'

'Then I can only believe that you did in fact inflict this punishment yourself and that you aren't man enough to own up to it.'

'No, it wasn't him.' Rose was suddenly galvanised into life. 'I've said all the time that it wasn't Jenks. He was nice to me, after he saw I was hurt. It wasn't Jenks.'

'I suggest that the only way for you to repay his kindness is to stop wasting everyone's time and give the name of the real offender. Otherwise, I shall continue to believe –'

Terts noticed that Mrs Rose was bending down to whisper something to her son. Perhaps she was telling him that he would be leaving Croxton with her that day and need never return, for after a moment's hesitation he whispered something back.

Mrs Rose straightened herself and tugged at her fox fur to straighten it. 'The boy's name is Bradley,' she announced in a voice that carried to the back of the hall.

There was a hiss of amazement, but Terts did not join in the whispering which followed. He was overwhelmed by the horror of what he had done. It was one thing to bring down Jenks, who was always making nasty remarks; but to expose his own brother to the headmaster's caning which would undoubtedly follow was unforgivable and would never be forgiven. Although perhaps Bing need never know who had betrayed him ... It was, after all, Rose who had pointed the finger.

'Stand up, Bradley.'

Terts was the only boy who did not turn his head. He had no wish to see his brother at this moment of disgrace.

'Were you responsible for beating Rose?'

'Yes, sir.'

'You will come to my study in half an hour. The rest of you may dismiss.'

He turned to lead the way out, but Mrs Rose had something to say before she left. Mothers normally stayed in the background on school occasions, but this one seemed to be made of sterner stuff.

'Just one thing,' she announced in the same ringing tones as before. 'I'd like to thank whoever it was who sent me the photograph of my son's injuries. He hadn't mentioned them himself. We should never have known. It was a courageous thing to do. Thank you.'

What a stupid, senseless, floss-brained woman! Terts could hardly believe his ears. What sort of thanks was that, to let everyone know who was responsible for the punishment of one of the most popular boys in the house? And Bing himself would be the first to guess. If she had only kept quiet, Rose's identification would by itself have been enough. No one would have looked any further for a squealer. But now ... Mrs Rose had called the unknown boy courageous, but this would be the day when Terts would really need his courage.

In the week after his father died, he had made himself two promises. One was that he would use his camera, whenever he could, to expose shameful actions which ought to be known: and he had done that. The other was that he would never again be ashamed of any photographs he took. That was going to be harder.

The interview which he knew must come took place an hour later, when he was summoned to Bing's study.

'Was it you?'

'Yes. Bing, I'm terribly sorry. I never –'

'Don't call me Bing, Bradley minor.'

'I'm sorry, Bradley. I thought it was Jenks. I would never have done it if I'd known it was you.'

'So it would have been all right if you'd got Jenks expelled, would it?'

'Expelled!'

'I am not to return to Croxton next term. Rose's father, it appears, owns a newspaper and two magazines. He thought it might be interesting to run a series of articles on life in our great public schools. Slimy little toad! Just because he never went to one himself. Wouldn't have him, I shouldn't think. Blackmail, I call it. And the Head Man hadn't got the guts to stand up to him.' Bing's voice was shaking with anger.

'Bing – Bradley ma, I mean – I really am most awfully sorry.'

'You realise what it means? I shan't be able to get into Sandhurst now. My whole career destroyed before it even starts.' Bing was not academically clever, and it had already been agreed with the uncles that he would be more suited to the army than to Bradley's. 'My life ruined ... and all because some stupid little squirt has to stir up trouble in what's none of his business!'

There was nothing more that Terts could say. Overwhelmed by the enormity of what he had done, he waited in silence for the beating which must surely follow. But perhaps the Rose episode had taught Bing a lesson about the dangers of losing his temper. He stared coldly at his brother.

'It's too late to start whining about being sorry. You should have thought before you did it. I shall never speak to you again. Not for the rest of my life. You're not my brother any longer. Do you understand? I shouldn't think anyone at all with an ounce of decency in him will ever speak to such a filthy little sneak. Except Rose, I suppose. You can go and sob on his slimy shoulders. Now get out.'

Outside the study door, Terts leaned against the corridor wall, trembling with sympathy for his brother, and guilt and apprehension on his own account. Bing couldn't possibly mean what he had said about not speaking again ever, could he? Yes, he could. And he was one of the most popular boys in the school. If he let it be known who was responsible for his disgrace, there might well be a period of complete ostracism.

But the photograph was honest. It recorded something that had happened and that ought not to have happened. And if revealing it was the only way to help an unhappy boy escape from what he saw as a prison, then revealing it was the right thing to do. It was unfortunate that in helping a stranger he had betrayed a brother, but it was not wrong.

All the same, Bing must be wishing by now that he had never given a camera to his younger brother. It was quite on the cards that he would seek it out and smash it up. Straightening his shoulders, Terts hurried off to his cubicle to find the camera and conceal it. It was a disquieting thought that the taking of photographs meant more to him than the friendship of a brother, but it was true.

9

At first there was nothing untoward about the start of the holidays. Lord Mortimer's coachman met Bing and Terts off the train as usual and probably did not particularly notice that there was no conversation in the carriage as he drove it to Kinderley Court. Libby, who loved Terts dearly, rushed out to greet him with a hug and a stream of chatter about the dogs and horses and how well she was doing in her lessons and how they were all invited to visit Aunt Florence and how –

'How's Mother?' Terts asked her. At the time when he left Kinderley for Croxton in September, their mother had still not recovered from the birth of her baby and the death of her husband. Even though nine months had passed, she was spending most of her time in bed. Her letters to school, though, had been cheerful enough, so he hoped that by now she had recovered.

The question dampened Libby's liveliness. 'She's still in bed. I go up at five o'clock every day for a game, but she doesn't play for very long. The baby's getting bigger, though. He's not going to die after all.'

'Good. Can I go up to see her straightaway, d'you think?'

Libby didn't know, but Grainger, the butler, provided an answer by intercepting Terts and Bing as soon as they entered the house.

'Lord Mortimer would like to see you both in the library.'

Terts's heart sank. There could not be much doubt about the subject of the forthcoming interview, and if he was expected to attend as well as Bing, it must be because his part in his brother's disgrace was known.

As usual, Lord Mortimer was standing in front of the fire. After greeting the two boys, he seemed uncertain how to go on; and what he had to say, when at last he came round to it, was not at all what Terts had expected.

'I'm afraid I have to prepare you both for some bad news,' he said. 'Your Mother –'

He paused, swallowing a lump in his throat, while Terts stared at him in horror.

'Is she dead, Grandfather?'

'No. No. But I'm afraid she's not well. Not well at all. The doctor has warned me, so now I have to warn you. We may not have her for very much longer.'

There was a long silence. The two boys stared in disbelief at their grandfather, who in turn stared down at his shoes.

'You'll stay here, of course, after ... This will be your home. No change in that. I'll do what I can to take your father's place. But it's a bad business for you, losing them both within a year, perhaps. Bad for little Aden, as well. I'm sorry.' There was another silence.

'May we see her?' asked Terts at last.

'Yes, of course. Go up to tell her you're back. One at a time. And not more than five minutes each. She gets tired. You'll be cheerful, of course. There's no call for you to tell her, Bingham, about this Croxton business. Well, wait a minute. While you're here, we might as well get this over. Can't pretend nothing's happened, can we? I had a letter from your headmaster this morning.'

Terts turned to leave the room. It would not improve Bing's temper if his younger brother were allowed to witness the dressing-down which was bound to come.

'No need for you to go, Mortimer. Now then, Bingham. This business didn't sound quite straightforward. Weaselly sort of letter, I thought. And more punishment than crime, on the face of it. Let's have your side of the story. What did you do?'

'I beat a boy.'

'A boy called Nathan Rose. Did you beat him because he was a Jew?'

Bing, who until this moment had been stony-faced, looked surprised.

'I didn't know he was one. I didn't think Croxton had any Jewish boys. Why should they want to come to a Christian foundation?'

'So that they can pretend that they're as good as anyone else, that's why.' Lord Mortimer's views on this subject had always been intemperate. 'Grandfather turns up from some bazaar or ghetto, hardly able to read and write, and sets up as a money-lender. Next generation goes into banking, does well.

35

Clever with money, a lot of them. Third generation has to be turned into an English gentleman, so they pack him off to somewhere like Croxton and hope that no one after that will ever know where he came from. Well, if it wasn't that, what was the beating for, then?'

'I put the lists up for the first week rugger. All the servitors get a game, so that I can see whether any of them are likely to be any good. Rose crossed his name off. Put a line through it, just like that!' Bing's voice rose in indignation. No doubt he had never known such impertinence before.

'So?'

'So I sent for him. When I ticked him off, he was cheeky. Said he hadn't realised that playing games was a punishment which he wasn't allowed to dodge. He was quite happy to play fives, but he didn't fancy rugger, thank you very much. So I gave him a caning, to teach him a lesson. Six strokes on the buttocks.'

'Nothing against that, since you're a prefect, I imagine.'

'No, sir. But he went on being cheeky. After he'd pulled his trousers up, he had the gall to thank me for getting him off rugger officially, since he was sure that Matron would sign a note saying that he wasn't fit to play now. He started limping, pretending he couldn't walk. I was still holding the cane. I – well, I lost my temper. I did hit out at him. I wanted to make him blub.'

'Hm.' Lord Mortimer considered for a moment. 'It can't be the first time that this sort of thing's happened at Croxton. Anyone ever been expelled for it before?'

'I don't think so, sir. A prefect was stripped of his badge about three years ago. That's the worst I can remember.'

'So what was different this time?'

'His father owning a newspaper, I should think, and threatening what he'd do if no one was punished for hitting his baby boy.'

'And how did your headmaster find out who was to be punished? Who sneaked on you?'

Terts held his breath. This was the moment when Bing would take his revenge. Deliberately prolonging the agony, Bing took his time about answering. He continued to look straight ahead at his grandfather, as though unaware that his younger brother was in the room.

'The boy himself,' said Bing.

'Just what we might expect!' Lord Mortimer was still indulging his contempt for the Jews. Terts, almost sighing with relief as he began to breathe normally again, could tell that his grandfather was considering the position carefully before pronouncing a verdict.

'Well, now then, listen to me, Bingham,' he said at last. 'I'm not going to condone your loss of temper. You've had time to think about that and be sorry, I imagine.'

'Yes, sir. I shan't let it happen again.'

'Quite. Quite. Well then, I don't see why Mr Julius Rose, father of Master Nathan Rose, should be allowed to get away with wrecking the whole career of an Englishman who wants to serve his country. I take it you'd have told him you were sorry if you'd been given a chance?'

Bing made no answer to this supposition, but his grandfather, thinking aloud, pressed on without waiting for a comment.

'So we'll have to see how we can manage to get you into Sandhurst after all. I'll have a word with one of the Croxton governors, get him to lean on the headmaster for a decent report. He may be feeling a bit ashamed of himself by now, for letting an outsider tell him how to run his school. Your part is to pass the entrance examination. I'll find you a crammer. You might have needed one anyway. Best thing will probably be for you to board with him. It'll mean hard work. Are you prepared for that?'

'Yes, sir. Thank you very much. Very much indeed. I won't let you down.'

Lord Mortimer brushed away the thanks. 'You'll make a fine soldier, I'm sure of it. Damned if I'll let a greasy Israelite trip you up before you've even started. But remember: hold on to your temper in future. Now then, you'll be anxious to see your mother. Mortimer, you go up first. Give Bingham a chance to get it steady in his head, what he's going to do.'

In the drama of the past few moments, Terts had almost forgotten about the sad news with which the conversation had begun. Now his spirits were once again subdued as he led the way out of the library. With one foot on the bottom stair he turned back to address his brother.

'Thanks, Bing.' He could say Bing, and not Bradley, now that they were at home again.

Bing, crossing the hall, continued to look straight ahead, not indicating in any way that he had heard the remark. Even though he had not betrayed his brother's part in his downfall, he was clearly not yet ready to abandon his vow of silence.

It was a miserable start to the holiday. Terts's heart was heavy as he dragged himself up the wide, curving staircase. Only a year ago he had been a member of a happy family, excited by their regular Christmas visit. And now his father was dead, his mother was dying, Bing was never going to speak to him again and Richard was not really part of the family any longer. He was fond of Libby, but she was too young to share in many of his pursuits, and he hardly knew the baby at all. The only consolation he could think of was that he still had his camera for company.

Part Two

Girls

1

'I'm to come out!'

Libby would be celebrating her eighteenth birthday in January 1913 and now, a month before that momentous occasion, she flung herself in excitement at Terts when he arrived for his Christmas visit. 'Aunt Florence is going to present me at Court and Emily can be a chaperone now that she's married and Grandfather is taking a house in Mayfair for three months and I can take Nutmeg with me and put him at livery and ride in Rotten Row every morning and then I'm to have a ball at Kinderley. You'll be my escort, won't you, Terts?'

'Steady on!' Terts laughed affectionately as his sister bounced up and down at the top of the steps leading up to the courtyard around which Kinderley Court was built. She had run out to greet him as soon as she heard the carriage and, although she might be so close in age now to the status of a young lady, her loosely tied long hair, plain dress and unrestrained exuberance still spoke of the schoolroom. 'If you go on standing in the snow without a coat you'll be dead of pneumonia before anyone has a chance to present you anywhere.' He refused to discuss the matter anymore until they were both seated in front of the schoolroom fire. 'Now then. What does an escort have to do?'

'You must know all that sort of thing, living in London.'

'But I don't mix in the exalted world of debutantes. And I rather suspect that most of that world turns up its nose at young men who work for their living.' Like his brother Richard, Terts had gone straight from school to Bradley's.

'Well, the main thing is that you'll take me to balls and make sure that I always have someone to dance with and never have to sit out by myself. So if somebody asks for a dance and I don't like him I can look at my programme and say I'm engaged for that number, and then dance with you, but if your name is in the programme and somebody more exciting comes along I can drop you and say I'd be delighted.' Her eyes sparkled with mischief at the prospect. 'And you make private arrangements with the other brothers, that they should dance with me and you'll dance with their sisters.'

'But suppose I don't like their sisters!'

'Doesn't matter what you like! Anyway, you're bound to get on with one or two of them. I'm offering you a marvellous opportunity to meet the cream of society. It's time you got married. You're twenty-two.'

'Thank you for telling me. But it's not time at all. The uncles offer me magnificent prospects but not much in the way of day-to-day income. And they expect me to keep office hours. If I'm still dancing at three or four every morning I may not be at my brightest when I reach my desk at eight.'

'They won't mind. I'm sure they'll give you time off if you ask. It would be useful for business if one of their nephews was to make a really good connection. An heiress. Or at the very least, a girl from an old family. I don't know about Uncle Adolphus himself, but Aunt Louise would love to be able to boast that her nephew is married to the Lady Anne or the Honourable Diana.'

'I think you may find that your fellow debutantes, the Lady Annes, are more interested in the eldest sons of dukes than in a third grandson of a baron. Is that why you're doing this, Libby – to find yourself a grand husband?'

'He doesn't have to be grand.' But the question sobered his sister down and she was silent for a moment. 'I don't meet anyone here,' she said at last. 'I mean, I act as hostess for Grandfather when he has people to shoot, but they're always his own age; never mine. It's been different for you. Going to school and going to work, you've been able to make friends. But I haven't got any friends at all except Emily and Lucy.' Emily and Lucy were their cousins, Aunt Florence's daughters. 'And Nutmeg,' she added. Nutmeg was her horse.

Once again she was silent, thinking about it. 'It's lonely,' she confessed at last. 'Grandfather's so kind and I love Miss Raynor dearly. She's been like a mother. But all the things she teaches me are intended to be useful not in this part of my life but in all the rest of it. It's as though these first eighteen years are just time to be lived through before real life begins. And I've had enough of waiting. I want to enjoy myself. To be with people.'

'There must be other girls of your age in the county.'

'Yes. And this is where I shall meet them, in the London Season. This is when I can really start making friends of my own. Women friends, I'm talking about, but yes, their brothers as well.'

'So you have three exciting months in London and then you go off to live in some other house just like Kinderley, to be lonely again.'

'No, it will be quite different if I marry. I should have my husband for company and –' She flushed slightly. 'And children. And friends to visit and to entertain. And although I can only be a debutante once, I can do the Season every year if I choose. That's if I find the right sort of husband, of course. And I don't expect Aunt Florence will allow any other sort to come near me.'

'And is that all you want, Libby? To spend eighteen years being prepared to make a good marriage and then the rest of your life bringing up daughters to make good marriages in their turn?'

'What else is there?' With one of the abrupt movements which she would have to learn to control before her presentation, Libby stood up and walked across to the window. 'I suppose I could say that what I'd like most of all would be to stay seventeen for ever and to live here with Nutmeg. But that's not going to happen, is it? I shall grow older. And Grandfather's seventy-seven. When he dies, am I to be taken over as part of the furniture by whoever inherits Kinderley? I have to find some kind of future for myself, and what else am I fit for? Would you suggest that I should become one of your lady typewriters?' Bradley's had within the past year taken the revolutionary step of employing young women for the first time.

'No, of course not. You're quite right. Some lucky chap is going to pick a pearl with you. When you think that most girls of your age have been under their mother's thumbs all their lives, while you ...! As well as being able to play the piano and paint and sew and spout French and German with the best of them, Mrs Yetton has taught you how to run a household, Grandfather has taught you how to be a hostess and you've been mothering Aden ever since he was born. You deserve to net not simply an eldest son but a duke in person.'

'You shouldn't tease me, Terts.'

'Well, I'm not teasing, really. I want you to have the very best. Not just a rich man. A kind man. It's such a big thing for a girl, isn't it, finding the right husband?'

'Just as important for a man to find the right wife.'

'True. But in my case, there's no sense of racing against the clock. I can enjoy my freedom for a little longer yet.'

'Yes.' Libby was all smiles again. 'Until one day I introduce you to my new very best friend and you fall head over heels in love with her. Now then, are you coming to say hello to Nutmeg?'

'Only if you wrap yourself up first. Grandfather's doing the accounts, I suppose?' As he grew older Lord Mortimer had taken to retiring to his library for two hours after luncheon each day. It was generally understood that 'doing the accounts' was his euphemism for taking a nap and that he was not to be disturbed.

'Yes. Wait here, then.'

'How's Aden?' asked Terts when his sister reappeared wearing stouter boots and with a warm shawl round her shoulders.

'He's odd,' said Libby frankly. 'He doesn't like riding or walking. He reads all the time. He learns Latin and Greek with the vicar but he has all his other lessons with Miss Raynor and me and he's really clever. It's been very hard on me, because I'm supposed to keep ahead of him, but I'm having enough trouble just keeping up. I'm becoming a very well-educated young lady. Aden ought really to go off to prep school, to have more company. But Grandfather's afraid he might be bullied, being so small for his age. He says schoolboys don't like swots. Come on, then. Here's some sugar for you.'

'For Nutmeg, you mean.'

'Of course.'

They walked companionably towards the stableyard. Although Terts could ride well enough he had never shared either Bing's fearlessness on horseback or Libby's devotion to each of her ponies in turn and now to the horse which would be sharing the Season with her. His own enthusiasm was for machines. With part of his inheritance from his mother's marriage settlement, which had been handed over to him on his twenty-first birthday, he had bought himself a two-stroke Calthorpe motor bicycle – and on every visit to Kinderley he tried to persuade his grandfather to acquire a motor car. But without success. Kinderley was hopelessly mired in a horse-drawn age.

Arriving at the stable, Libby held out her hand. Terts pulled out his folding camera and took a snapshot just as the horse stretched its long head towards her and delicately took the sugar lumps from her flat palm.

Libby was used to this sort of behaviour, but registered a protest on Nutmeg's behalf.

'Why do you always put me in your photographs and never take Nutmeg on his own?' she asked. 'In fact, why do you only photograph people and never flowers or houses or anything else?'

'I do take houses sometimes. I enjoy thinking about the sort of life that's been lived inside them for hundreds of years. Usually I don't take them more than once, though, because they stay the same. What I enjoy about photographing people is trying to get inside their heads just at the moment when I do it. Trying to guess what they're thinking.'

'I expect they're usually wondering whether they're looking beautiful or whether their hat is crooked.'

'That's when they're posed, yes. But what's more fun is to take them without them knowing. As well as the Kodak, I've got a new camera now, with a set of different lenses. I can take people from further away, when they don't know that I'm even looking at them. And then afterwards I look at the print and I think, "How did that man get that scarf?" or "Why is that woman so unhappy?" and in a funny sort of way I feel myself into their lives.'

'You can't get it right, though, can you, if you aren't even acquainted with them?'

'I suppose not. I don't really know. All that I'm sure of is that I can't get it right with horses.'

'Yes, you can. Take another one now.' She moved to stand behind the horse's head, stroking it and rubbing her chin against it. 'You know what I'm feeling: that I can't wait to get to London. And you know what Nutmeg's feeling as well. When is that stupid man going to give me the rest of my sugar lumps?'

'You're right.' He took the photograph and offered the sugar. 'I shall mount this as one of a pair. Libby with her hair down, with Nutmeg. And then, in four months' time, Miss Elizabeth Bradley with her hair up, with ostrich feathers. Come on, let's go on. Grandfather will be awake for his tea by now.'

Terts's own arrival had completed the Christmas party. Bing was serving with his regiment in India and Richard had recently married one of his Bradley cousins and was spending the holiday in London. There would be a Bradley cousin for Terts as well in a year or two, if he wanted one. But she was still only sixteen. There was plenty of time to think about that.

He began to think about it, in fact, later that day, when he went upstairs to change for dinner. Well, not about his cousin, but about girls in general.

Had he been too hard on Libby, seeming to criticise her for having no ambition outside marriage? Was his own case any better? Whatever he might say now, no doubt he would indeed marry within the next few years and then he would have to slog away in an office for the rest of his life in order to support his family and see his sons in turn find work and wives. Was that all there was to existence: days of boring work simply in order to make sure that life went on in a new generation?

He was dealing with the accounts of an investment in India at the moment, as he worked his way through each department of the family firm in turn. Bradley's had lent the money to finance the building of three factories in Agra and the establishment of a trading company which imported and sold their products. Lord Mortimer, whose anti-Semitism led him to anathematise all Jews as money-lenders, might have been surprised to find that two of his grandsons were in much the same business.

It was one of Terts's current responsibilities to record every quarter the payment of the contracted interest on the loans and to check that the correct percentage of the profits was also paid over. In a small way, he consoled himself, he was helping to give employment to dozens of Indians who might otherwise have starved. But although he tried hard to humanise his task by imagining the fathers of families as they worked away and accepted their wages and took them home to feed their children, he couldn't do it. It was not just the physical setting which made it too difficult, but the culture of a society which was unfamiliar to him, and likely to remain so. He would never go to India. He would never see any of these people whose work was indirectly helping to pay his salary. He was expected to be interested only in figures, numbers, and he found them deadly dull.

'You'll fall head over heels in love,' Libby had promised him; and perhaps one day he would. But what was the value of that experience except as the bait which for a year or two might reconcile him to life inside the trap of work and marriage? There was a sense in which he wanted to meet girls, but a much stronger sense in which he was afraid of what they could do to him.

So much agonising, with so little real danger! In Society's terms, his mother had married beneath her. Libby might triumph over the stigma of having been born to a landless and untitled father by virtue of her youth and beauty and happy nature, but that would not apply to Terts himself.

He studied his appearance in the glass as he tied his bow tie. Recognising that as her brother he was indeed the most suitable escort for Libby, would there be anything in his looks to let her down? He was tall and thin – and because he was allowed to use his grandfather's accounts to order his suits in Savile Row, his shoes at Lobb's and his shirts as Harborow's, he could guarantee to be well-dressed on every occasion. Nobody would describe him as handsome, but there was nothing actually wrong with his face – except perhaps for a slight lop-sidedness about the mouth. One corner seemed to turn up and the other down. But nothing to make him stand out in a crowd.

In short, he was unobtrusive: unnoticeable. It was a useful characteristic for someone who liked to take photographs unobserved. And equally useful, no doubt, for the brother of a debutante. He would be there when he was needed and invisible at all other times.

Terts's affection for his sister was very strong. Just as she had mothered Aden since their mother's death, so he had appointed himself Libby's protector when she was left fatherless. Yes, if she needed his social support, she should have it. But it would be entirely for her sake; not for his own.

2

'Are you decent?'

Terts waited for Libby's reassurance before opening the door. This was the great day, the day of her presentation at court, and there was a female panic in progress. It was something to do with a pair of shoes which ought to have been worn for the fitting but had not, so that a last-minute alteration to the hemline of her dress had become necessary.

As he stepped into the room, he was greeted by a comic sight. His sister, decked out in all her finery, stood straight-backed and with her head held high. Her hair was up and ornamented with ostrich feathers. She wore no personal jewellery, but her court dress was embroidered with hundreds of tiny pearls. Its train had been carefully spread out on the floor behind her and the whole effect would have been a stately one were it not for the figure of the dressmaker who was down on the ground, crawling round with pins in her mouth as she adjusted the errant quarter-inch of length.

She looked up, startled, as Terts came in and hooted with laughter. He had come to take a formal photograph of Libby in her presentation dress before they left, so that she would not need to join the queue of girls who would go straight from the palace to Mayall's, the official photographers. But the dressmaker's expression, and her ungainly position on the floor, tempted him first of all to pull out his folding camera for a quick shot of work in progress.

'You look a little unusual yourself,' Libby pointed out, thinking that he was laughing only at her. It was true. As the brother of a debutante Terts was invited to Buckingham Palace to watch her make her curtsy, but since he was not entitled to wear any uniform he had been forced to dress in black velvet court dress.

The dressmaker signalled that she had finished and Terts helped her to her feet. 'Don't move,' he said to Libby, while he carried in his tripod.

By now – counting the Brownie with which his addiction to photography had begun – he owned four different cameras and delighted in experimenting to find which was most successful in different circumstances: outdoors or indoors, with natural or artificial light, for a stationary or moving subject and – the biggest difference of all – for a posed picture or one which nobody knew was being taken. He had come a long way since that humiliating moment when he had appealed to a newspaper photographer for help in developing and printing his film.

At the age of fifteen, deciding that modern languages would be more useful to him than Latin and Greek, and that he was more interested in science than any other subject, he had managed to transfer from the Classical to the Modern side at Croxton. In the course of a lesson on the refraction of light he had discovered that one of his teachers shared his enthusiasm for photography, owned all the necessary equipment, and was willing to help his pupil experiment. By the time he left school, he was well educated in at least one subject.

Today's picture was to be posed, so after he had put the smaller camera away, he had all the paraphernalia of glass plates and a black cloth to prepare. Libby first of all waited patiently and then stood without moving for the necessary time.

'Now for the curtsy,' he commanded. Naturally he would not be allowed to take any photographs at the presentation itself.

Libby sank to the ground, her head demurely bowed, trying not to wobble as Terts counted out the seconds. Then the session was brought to an end by Aunt Florence, who came to see whether they were ready to leave. Lucy, still too young to be presented, looked wide-eyed at the cousin who had so abruptly become grown-up, while Emily, who at twenty-one was a mature married woman, nodded her approval.

As a social occasion, the presentation could only be described as tedious. So long was the procession of carriages that it took more than an hour even to reach Buckingham Palace. Then there was a long wait before all the debutantes were assembled and the king and queen arrived to a roll of drums. At last the ceremony could begin, but more than two hours passed before the last of the eighteen year olds made her deep curtsy, to be rewarded with a nod of the royal head.

During the first part of the wait Terts was content to study the crowded room. Although all the girls wore white, the scene was made colourful by the sashes and orders boasted by members of the diplomatic corps, by the gold braid of court chamberlains, by the sparkling tiaras of the older women who would be making the presentations and by the bright uniforms of most of the watching brothers and fathers; and when the king himself arrived, he was attended by young pages in scarlet livery and by a dozen Indian orderlies whose feathered turbans rivalled the ostrich plumes of the debutantes.

Only when the band began to play and the presentation began did Terts turn his attention to the young women for whom this ceremony was staged. A ceremony, he thought at first, that was almost sordid in its significance. Like slaves paraded for sale they were on display; available not for labour but for matrimony, to the highest bidder.

As time passed, though, his mood changed. Their mothers might be plotting marriages, but it was easy to see that for the girls themselves there was a different significance. Before the big moment came they were nervous and shy, but as they dipped low, heads bent, their mood was one of solemnity. This was the female equivalent, perhaps, of the oaths which their fathers and brothers swore on joining the army or navy. They were pledging their loyalty to the king, the empire, the whole fabric of society. The frivolity of dances and flirtations would come later; for the moment there was an almost religious seriousness to their earnest young faces.

And Libby was right to think that some of these girls would become her friends. Even tonight, when few of them knew each other, they had gathered in little groups as they waited for the royal family to arrive. New relationships were being explored. Perhaps, Terts told himself sternly, it was a kind of jealousy which made him dislike the thought of his sister being courted by young men; but certainly he must support her need to find friendship amongst the girls of her own generation.

He looked more critically at the debutantes as each in turn stepped forward. If they were the cream of British society, it was not the smoothest of creams. Unlike the older women who presented them, they wore their court dresses awkwardly and were clearly unaccustomed to the tight corsetry in which they were caged and nervous about the security of their elaborately dressed hair. Many of them were on the plump side and their unpowdered complexions were not always perfect. They looked exactly what they were: girls only one step away from the schoolroom. It would be interesting, thought Terts, to make a photographic record of Libby's first Season: to catch, if he could, the gradual change from child to sophisticated woman. Yes, he would do that. His only previous attempt to record a whole season had ended in the disaster of Bing's expulsion from Croxton, but nothing like that could happen in this case.

And now it was Libby's turn to make her curtsy. It was hard to refrain from applauding as she rose again with a smile on her lips. She was Out.

A few days after the presentation Terts arrived home to find his sister waiting for him with a new bundle of invitations. Right from the first moment of planning her debut she had impressed him by the efficiency with which she was organising her new life in society. It was their grandfather's housekeeper, no doubt, who had taught her the importance of diaries and lists. Certainly it was useful to Terts himself that he should be told so clearly in advance when his company would be needed; for unlike most of the young men who acted as escorts for their sisters and cousins, he was still expected to report for work whenever he could.

The Bradley uncles had, as a matter of fact, proved surprisingly sympathetic to their nephew's social needs. Although, following the shock of his father's sudden death, Richard had moved without complaint from school to office work – and, more recently, to marriage – the uncles seemed to recognise that a young man was entitled to a fling at some point in his life. Perhaps, also, as Libby had suggested, they could see the possible advantages to be gained if either their niece or their nephew, or both, should make good marriages.

So at a formal meeting between the partners and the youngest family member on the staff, it had been agreed that Terts had worked hard and efficiently since leaving Croxton and that some relaxation might be permitted during the limited period of the Season. It was just as well, for Libby was an indefatigable dancer and often went to more than one dance in an evening. It was regularly three or four in the morning before Terts was able to fall exhausted into bed, so he was grateful that he need not always report for work at eight.

On this particular day he had done a good afternoon's work. His bachelor apartment had been sublet for the Season. Since he would have to escort Libby home every night, it made sense that he too should live in the house that Lord Mortimer had rented. He was in good time today to dress for the opera. The Imperial Russian Opera Company was appearing at the Theatre Royal in Drury Lane and, whether Libby enjoyed opera or not, it was necessary that she should be able to talk about it. First of all, though, she needed to give her brother some new dates for his diary, and before even that could be done he asked her about the success of the tea party which Aunt Florence had held for her that afternoon.

Terts could not help finding the subtle gradations of entertainment amusing, although the females of the family seemed sometimes to regard them as matters of life and death. The tea parties which took place early in the Season were organised by the mothers – or in Libby's case, of course, her aunt – amongst their own friends, so that all their daughters could meet each other. In addition, Aunt Florence had also arranged a series of dinner parties, from which the young people, with their chaperones, would move on to one or more of the dances which took place almost every night. The London house they had taken was not suitable for an elaborate dance; nor was the garden large enough for a spacious marquee. But the news that a ball would be held at Kinderley at the end of the Season had been fed into the network of gossip early, so that all those who hoped to be asked to it would be sure to invite Libby to their own social events.

Compared with balls and dances, a tea party was a dull affair, but this one proved to have had an unexpected consequence.

'I showed off the pictures you took of me,' Libby told him. 'Everyone thought they must have been done by a professional, and wanted to know who it was. When I said it was my brother, I could almost see them all making a note that you must be invited to their very best things – with me, of course – in the hope that perhaps you'd offer to photograph them as well.'

'That would be a nice change, to be invited in my own right!' exclaimed Terts. He was well aware that in the eyes of most hostesses he was a shadowy figure. They did their best to ensure that there should always be a sufficiency of young men at their dances in order that none of the girls should be left as wallflowers, but there was a clear differentiation in their minds between men who were catches in the marriage market and those who were only asked to make up the number of partners. Terts knew his place. To be invited for his own sake for once would be amusing.

For Libby it would be not so much amusing as important.

'So we shall be asked to Lady Kenward's dinner for the Marchioness of Glencross's ball,' she said. 'Aunt Florence is dizzy with anticipation.'

'And are we acquainted with the Marchioness of Glencross? That's to say, does she know that we propose to honour her with our presence?'

'Not yet. She just asks Lady Kenward to take a party on to the ball.'

Terts raised his eyebrows to indicate that this was hardly a complete explanation. Patiently, as to a social ignoramus, Libby explained the position.

'The Marchioness of Glencross has a sister, Lady Cox. The two sisters are bringing their daughters out together, so this ball, in Glencross House, is a joint one for the two of them. Lady Cox is married to Sir Robert Cox, Bart, who owns acres and acres of Scotland. Sir William Kenward owns a rather smaller grouse moor which marches with the Cox land, and the Coxes and the Kenwards are great friends. Meanwhile, down in the south, the Kenwards have a house in Gloucestershire and Lady Kenward and Aunt Florence are great friends. As a result, Lady Kenward's daughter was the first of this year's debutantes I ever met and we've rather clung to each other ever since. So you see, it's all quite simple. The Kenwards put us on their list and the Kenwards are already on the Coxes' list and the Glencrosses are happy to see any friends of the Coxes.'

'As you say, crystal clear. And I pay for our invitation, do I, by telling plain Miss Kenward that she's a beauty and I long to take her photograph.'

'Yes, you do. And she *is* plain, so you'll need to work at it. You'll have to dance with her as well, of course.'

'And presumably the marchioness also has a daughter who has to be danced with?' Terts had had time by now to learn the etiquette of these occasions. 'Is she also plain?'

'I don't know. But you'll do it, won't you, Terts? Offer to photograph Cynthia Kenward, I mean. This will be a big thing for Aunt Florence.'

'Yes, of course.' Terts understood what she was saying. Their aunt, as the daughter of a baron and the wife of a baronet, was perfectly respectable, but did not belong in the highest echelon of society. She was not a snob and was perfectly content to do her best for her niece at her own level; but access to one of the most sought-after invitations of the Season would be more than just a triumph in itself. When Libby was seen at one ball of this kind she would automatically qualify to receive other invitations of a similar kind. The Season was dominated by an almost invisible web of social approval. Members of the older generation were securely in place, but it was accepted that there would always be room for new young people to make their mark, if they were the right sort. If Terts's small talent could help his sister to take a step upward, he would do what he could.

When the evening came, he found himself placed at dinner next to Miss Kenward, almost certainly at her request. She was a pleasant, unsophisticated girl, not yet at ease with her formal hair style, which she continually touched to make sure that it had not collapsed. Terts did his duty, paying the necessary compliments and making the hoped-for request that she would pose for him. Her glow of pleasure made her look almost pretty. It would be interesting, he thought, if he could manage to capture that, creating a permanent record of a beauty which had never in fact existed – for Libby had been right to warn him that her new friend was plain. It would please the girl, and the achievement would in a different way please him as well. It was in no grudging manner that he promised to arrange a time.

For the moment, though, there was the ball to be enjoyed. Half a dozen taxis took the dinner guests to the mansion in Park Lane. While Libby disappeared to a cloakroom to check that her hair was tidy and her dress in good order, Terts looked up towards the reception area. The marquess and marchioness stood at the top of a curving, flower-decked staircase. Next to the marchioness stood a black-haired young woman who was overloaded with diamonds and whose stiffly cut dress added years to her age, which was presumably eighteen. Lamb dressed as mutton, Terts thought to himself sympathetically. But she was a good-looking girl, and no doubt it would not be too long before she managed to escape from her mother's taste and establish her own.

A long procession of couples moved up the stairs towards them, each in turn pausing for their names to be announced, before stepping forward to be welcomed. Then they took a few steps forward for a second reception. Once again a husband and wife and daughter were waiting to welcome them. But there was a difference. This daughter – Miss Cox, presumably – was, like her cousin, wearing the uniform of a debutante. White shoes, long white gloves, low-cut white dress. But this was a different kind of dress. Although the tightly-fitting sash, of the same material, showed off its wearer's tiny waist, the clever cut of the skirt gave a simultaneous impression of slimness and fluidity. It was a skirt made for dancing – and the unobtrusive tapping of a toe in time to the music which was already playing suggested that its owner could hardly wait to get on to the dance floor.

Terts, however, was not interested in clothes. As Libby returned to say that she was ready, she found him gazing in a kind of awe at the most beautiful girl he had ever seen.

3

Her name was Venetia.

'Isn't it too, too pretentious?' she said to Terts later in the Season, after they had become friends. 'But Bart and Lady –' which was how she always referred to her parents '– spent their honeymoon in Venice and I was born nine months later, so I suppose it was some kind of sentimental gesture. The idiotic thing was that, having inflicted the name on me, they never used it themselves. I was always Netty in the nursery. Until I was about seven, when apparently I announced that Netty was a name for housemaids and I wished to be Venetia from then on. And having once given that order, I never had the courage to change yet again. So Venetia it is.'

'It's a wonderful name.' Terts didn't care what she was called as long as he was inside the magic circle which was allowed to call her by her Christian name. From that first glimpse at the Glencross ball he had been besotted by her beauty.

Her hair was golden and although she had put it up, she allowed a few waving strands to hang down beside each ear, softening the effect. Her complexion was fair. She tutted at herself for the frequency with which she blushed, but Terts found the faint colouring of her cheeks irresistible. Like every other girl of her age, she was forbidden to wear any cosmetics, but her mouth was naturally rosy. Her eyes were blue, the unclouded blue of a summer sky, and seemed always to be smiling. Her arms were slim, her back was straight, her neck was long and her body was so slender that when Terts danced with her it was as though he held a feather in his arms. She was perfect.

On that first evening he had no opportunity to partner her, in spite of his pleadings. Her programme was full, she said, smiling in a friendly way even though she had never met him before. Girls – as Libby had taught him – were not always truthful about the initials they scribbled in the tiny dance cards which hung from their wrists, but in this case he could see for himself that she was dancing every number, and it was reasonable that at her coming-out ball she should give preference to her own guests rather than her friend's. So Terts had to content himself with devoting more attention to Miss Kenward than was strictly necessary. Libby had explained to him about 'sets', and this was a set to which he wished to belong.

It was with Miss Cox in mind that, a few days later, he devoted all his skill to turning her friend Cynthia into a beauty. His first shots were of the formal kind she would expect to see, and he followed them with a pair of dreamy seated poses. When he came to print these two he would deliberately make them hazy, to give her face a soft and luminous quality.

After those were out of the way he began to talk as he worked, making her smile, making her laugh in a way which no professional photographer would ever do. 'Peter Piper picked a peck of pickled pepper,' he said. 'Repeat it. Go on, repeat it, over and over again. Faster, faster.' And, abandoning the tripod, he waited until she was almost helpless with giggles before moving round her with the hand-held Rolleiflex which was his latest pride; making her giggle even more at his antics. His Aunt Florence and Lady Kenward, who were quietly chatting in a corner, looked up in momentary anxiety lest they should be neglecting their duties as chaperones, but were glad to see that no impropriety was taking place; only youthful mirth.

His motive for trying so hard to produce a flattering result was both uncomplicated and successful. So delighted was Lady Kenward by the prints with which he presented her, and the unexpected blossoming of her daughter revealed by them, that she showed the portfolio to all her friends. Soon she was passing on new requests, which he dodged with a fine display of modesty. This was only a hobby, he explained: something he was glad to do just for Libby's closest friends. But if it was a question of Lady Kenward's goddaughter, Miss Cox, well then, of course ...

There were no tricks of light or mood needed to make Venetia look beautiful. He was not exaggerating when he told her, laughing, that he would be able to make his fortune by selling her likeness on a picture postcard.

'But you won't, will you?' For a moment she was alarmed, and then burst out laughing. 'Oh, I see. You're a tease. I might try that trick on Lady. She'd probably buy your whole batch up to keep it off the street. You'd make your fortune.'

'But alas, I am a gentleman. I shall have to die poor. Are you going to Lady Elphinstone's masked ball tonight? Yes, of course you must be. May I have the supper dance? If you say no, I shall give you such dark shadows under your eyes that your mother will send you straight back to the country to rest.'

'Can you do that? Surely the camera always pictures what it sees?'

'And so it may do; but once the man behind the camera disappears into his dark-room all sorts of wickedness may go on. That's why I like to do all the processing of my pictures myself, instead of sending the films away.'

'Then may I come into the dark-room with you? To stop your wickedness in its tracks.'

'I hardly think your mother would approve of that. There would be no room for a chaperone.'

'Does it work the other way?' asked Venetia. 'Can you make someone beautiful who isn't? At least, I know you can, but how do you do it?'

'How do you know that I can?' He was taking the informal photographs now and was happy that she was willing to relax and chat.

'Because I've seen those pictures of Cynthia. Cynthia's my best friend. She has the nicest nature of anyone I know. But I'd never thought of her before as being even pretty. She always used to say herself that she looked rather like a horse. But you managed to make her look really quite lovely, and since then I find myself looking at her and thinking that, yes, she is good-looking. I can't tell whether she's grown to look like her photograph, so to speak, or whether the difference is my eyes and I'm seeing what you saw. Whatever it is, you've done her a marvellously good turn. She was terrified of coming out, because she thought everyone would either laugh at her or ignore her, but now she's really enjoying herself and I'm so happy for her.'

'Is that why you're allowing me to take you?'

Venetia shook her head. 'It was Lady who fixed that up. But I'm glad about it, as a matter of fact. Because when I'm old and ugly it will be nice to open an album and think, "Well, I had my moment".'

'You'll never be ugly, however old you grow. Some kinds of beauty last for ever.'

'I don't believe that. While I was waiting to be presented I was looking at the group of duchesses – did you see them? The ones who have the entrée. Bart is always talking about how lovely they were when he was a young man, and look at them now! Stout and over-dressed and frumpy, and I'm sure that at least one of them dyes her hair. Everybody goes on and on about how elegant and distinguished they are, but it isn't true, it's just that they're duchesses.'

'I hope you'll never be a duchess,' said Terts sincerely. He had finished his task by now, but was reluctant to let her go. 'One more posed shot, if you will. Sitting over there.' He pulled up a second chair and sat down to face her, a few feet away. 'I want you to lean slightly forward with one hand on your knee and the other gesturing towards me, so.' He moved his own hand and waited for her to copy him. 'Now look straight forward and think the words "I love you", but stop on the "I", with your lips apart.' He mimed that as well, to show the expression he wanted.

Venetia raised her eyebrows in mischievous amusement. 'But Mr Bradley, I hardly know you!'

'You're talking to the camera, not to me. One day there'll be someone to whom you'll want to give a photograph like this. Just pretend he's sitting here now. Think, "I love you".'

The maid who was acting as chaperone looked on in surprise as Venetia did as she was asked. Terts himself could hardly breathe, so overwhelmed was he by real and not pretended love. Luckily, his subject was unaware that the Rolleiflex camera had no need of the long exposure times which had been called for at the beginning of the afternoon, for several seconds passed before he remembered to trigger the opening of the shutter.

'Thank you very much,' he said at last. 'But you haven't answered my question about the supper dance tonight. The labourer, you know, is worthy of his hire.'

'I can't promise anything until I have my programme.'

But she would keep it for him; he felt sure of that. They were at ease with each other in an immediate and marvellous manner. So often it proved that the prettiest girls were the dullest, with nothing to say and no sense of humour. But Venetia was not like that. She was bright and sparkling and – oh, there were no words to describe her.

Later, in the tiny, windowless box room which he had had cleared for his use, he watched the latent images emerge in the developing tray. At one moment, as he gently rippled the fluid, there was nothing to be seen but blank sheets of white paper and then suddenly, gradually, the pictures began to take shape. Like a ghost materialising. Like an idea of beauty becoming real. It was hard to be patient. He was tempted to pull the sheets too soon into the air and to press them to his lips. He could feel his heart aching as he waited.

When it came to the last one, he stared at it as though mesmerised. It was unlikely in the extreme that he would prove to be the man to whom Venetia offered this picture, with its promise of love; but he would keep a copy for himself and pretend. Libby had promised that he would fall in love with one of her friends, and she was right. He was head over heels in love with Venetia Cox.

4

Perhaps it was because the Season was so short that everything seemed to happen at breakneck speed. Within a week of the Glencross ball Terts and Libby had encountered Venetia on eight separate social occasions: within three weeks they were secure members of her circle.

It was known as Venetia's set in spite of the fact that the most socially prominent of the group was her cousin, Lady Sylvia, who was not merely the daughter but the only child of a marquess. An heiress. A catch. Eligible young men were already circling and swooping, but she hardly seemed to be interested. Her mother would deal with all that. She was a placid, dull girl who was content to swim in the wake of her more vivacious cousin.

It was Venetia who, after attending nine fancy dress balls within three weeks, commanded all her circle to arrive at the tenth dressed as though it were four o'clock in the afternoon; disguised as 'ordinary people'. It was Venetia who started a craze for gate-crashing. Hostesses, she argued, ought to be pleased that such delightful young guests should choose to attend their entertainments in preference to those to which they had been invited.

It was Venetia, too, who demanded that Terts should put his talents as a photographer to an unusual use.

'We are going to turn ourselves into the Landmarks of London,' she announced. 'I shall write down twenty places and everyone must draw one out of a hat and tell Terts so that he can be there to take a photograph and anyone who doesn't do it won't be invited to my uncle's Cowes party.'

'What do you mean by "do it"?' asked Hugh, a cousin of Cynthia Kenward who had been pressed into escort duty in much the same way as Terts himself. 'If I pull out Cleopatra's Needle, do you expect me to climb it?'

'Of course not. Just to stand next door. But you won't get that anyway. Too dull.'

'I think I'd prefer to be dull,' said Cynthia, knowing how her friend's imagination was likely to work. But she put her hand into Hugh's hat without protest and, to her relief, pulled out Chelsea Hospital.

'You must be dressed as a display of flowers,' said Terts, entering into the spirit of Venetia's project. 'So that you look like part of the Chelsea Flower Show. When shall we arrange it?' He turned in mock severity to Venetia. 'It's all very well, each of you having to go to one place, but I shall have to turn up at all twenty. I must insist that the organiser attends on every occasion.'

'Well, naturally.' Venetia was quick to agree. 'In fact, we shall all go everywhere. No fun otherwise.'

'Buckingham Palace!' There was a wail from Lady Sylvia as she unfolded the slip she had picked. 'If anyone sees me posing for a picture there, I'll be banished from the Court for life.'

'I'm the one at risk,' Terts pointed out. 'You only need to be standing, not knowing what's going on. I'm the one who might get caught holding a camera. Although, I think ...' Yes, it would be easy enough. She was not a girl who would be prepared to make herself look ridiculous. He would take her, prettily dressed, at a garden party. On the far side of the lake where nobody would notice, but with the palace in the background. He smiled happily at Venetia: a partner in her enterprise.

Some members of the set chose their own poses. David and Diana, for example, the inseparable twins who were so shy that they hardly spoke to anyone but each other, insisted on sharing a site, and dressed up as Beefeaters to stand in front of the Tower of London. It was one of the advantages of the Season's plethora of fancy dress balls that nobody's mother was likely to query the need to hire yet another costume.

Most of the best ideas, though, were Terts's own. When Lady Jane, who was almost as pretty as Venetia, picked out the Royal Academy slip, Terts ordered her to wear her most dramatic hat so that he could photograph her head and shoulders within a large golden frame. The Honourable Beatrice, who was plump and awkward and all too often inappropriately dressed, agreed that all but her face should be wrapped up like a mummy on the steps of the British Museum. Muriel, a good sport, stood in front of the Royal Opera House in Madame Butterfly's Japanese costume, miming the gestures and open mouth of a prima donna in full song without regard to the stares of passers-by; while her brother Rupert, not to be outdone, held up the traffic beneath Admiralty Arch while he was photographed in admiral's uniform.

It was a relief to Libby, who was less extrovert than some of the others, when her landmark proved to be Rotten Row.

'You've already got a picture of me riding,' she reminded her brother. 'Part of your record of the Season.'

'Too ordinary. We must think of something more original. Suppose you and someone else were to pair up as a pantomime horse! Or you could stand on Nutmeg's back, like a circus rider.'

As he had expected, these suggestions were firmly rejected. He left her for the moment and turned his attention to Cynthia's cousin. Hugh's landmark was Tower Bridge, and Terts had an idea for this as well. He led the group to an assembly point in the centre of the bridge.

'I want you standing on the balustrade, exactly in the middle with your legs wide apart, so that if the bridge were to open this minute you'd be split in half.' He knew, of course, that it would certainly not open without warning.

Hugh looked slightly doubtful, but prepared to climb up. It was Libby who protested violently, holding him back.

'No! No, you mustn't! Terts, that's far too dangerous. There's nothing to hold on to at all. He might fall!'

There was an unusual degree of anxiety in his sister's voice which startled Terts. He looked at her closely. She was still holding on to Hugh's sleeve and now, as she let it go, her face was suffused with a blush. It was the first indication she had given him that he was not the only member of the family to have fallen in love this summer.

'You're quite right,' he agreed. 'Well then, follow me.'

Except for Muriel, who danced later into the night than anyone else and so was later to rise in the morning, all Venetia's set were in attendance, together with Lady Sylvia's maid who was acting as chaperone for the whole party and who followed at a distance with a permanently bemused expression on her face. Terts led them first to Tower Pier and then on to London Bridge. He took a dozen photographs, some of Tower Bridge from a distance and others of Hugh standing with his arms wide apart above his head. Later, in his temporary dark-room, he would experiment to see whether he could somehow make it seem that Hugh was hanging from the bridge. It would be an interesting exercise.

Later that day, when they were for a few moments alone together, Terts put some direct questions to Libby.

'What does Hugh do? I've never asked him.'

There was a sense in which it was a foolish question. Some of this year's escorts were officers whose regiments did not apparently require very much of their time or attention. But most of them lived on their country estates for the greater part of the year, entertaining and being entertained, and hunting, shooting and fishing during the seasons which so conveniently filled the parts of the year when London was dead. They did not, in the sense which most people would understand, 'do' anything at all.

'He acts as his father's land agent. His elder brother, the one who'll inherit, is in the Navy. And he – Hugh, I mean – has got a special interest in dairy cattle. He breeds them to show. And wins prizes when they produce more milk than anyone else's.'

'Do you like him? Like him 'specially, I mean?'

For a second time that day Libby was unable to control her blush.

'Yes, I do. We enjoy the same sort of things. Living in the country rather than London. Riding. And reading. Most of the others never seem to read at all, except magazines, but with him I can talk about all the books I've read with Miss Raynor and he has interesting things to say about them. But the real thing is that he's so good-natured. Like Cynthia. It must run in the family. You like Cynthia, don't you?'

'I like her, yes, but –'

'But not as much as Venetia! Yes, I realise that. You're lucky, being a man. You can take the initiative. It's difficult for me to know ...'

Terts was not so sure that he was lucky. Although he and Venetia had become partners in her latest project, he knew that he was only one amongst many admirers: and probably the one with the least to offer. Hugh Kenward, doing the Season only as a favour to his cousin and probably looking forward to the moment when he could return to the country, was not part of the matrimonial merry-go-round. It was easy to tell from his behaviour that no one was pressing him to make a 'good' marriage – but he must be aware that he would never again have the opportunity to choose from amongst so many marriageable young women. Libby would make him a suitable wife in a better sense than the social one, and there must be a fair chance that her feelings were reciprocated. Terts had already noticed that his services as emergency dancing partner were required less and less often these days.

In the meantime, there were still three or four more of the landmarks to be photographed, including Venetia's own.

'The River Thames,' she told him. 'And I must tell you straightaway that I can't swim, so if you plan to have me bobbing about in the water, think again.'

'Would you like to be a figurehead?' he asked her. 'On the prow of a boat. I noticed just the thing – a sailing ship – when we were on Tower Bridge yesterday.'

'No, I don't think so. It sounds madly uncomfortable. I'd rather look pretty beneath a parasol.'

'Right.' Venetia was the only one he was not prepared to bully. The group assembled next morning in a fleet of small boats. Distancing himself slightly from his subject, Terts devoted a whole film to Venetia looking elegant, Venetia looking ravishing, Venetia pretending to be asleep, and lastly, from a little further away, Venetia with the dome of St Paul's Cathedral rising above her head.

'Finished,' he said at last. Venetia put down her parasol, sat up straighter and prepared to stand up.

'More over, David,' she commanded. 'I want to try rowing.'

The boat wobbled violently. From all around came a shout of 'Sit down!' Only Terts did not join in. Like the others, he saw that she was in danger of falling into the water; but, almost to his own shame, he found himself wanting this to happen. From childhood he had swum in the Kinderley lake. If she fell, he could rescue her. He would see her wet clothes clinging to the line of her breasts. He would hold her body close to his own. He would save her life and she would be grateful to him for ever. Overwhelmed by his desire for her, he waited for his chance to prove a hero.

Venetia staggered slightly and then fell backwards on to the cushions, grimacing at the bump. David, meanwhile, was using the oars to steady the boat. The incident was over. It was a more subdued party than usual which made its way back to the pier from which the little fleet had been hired. Terts had to make an effort to appear his usual cheerful self.

'What does your mother actually think you're doing at this moment?' he asked Venetia half an hour later as he helped her ashore.

'Having breakfast out. I've told her it's the latest fad. Girls-only breakfasts. The joke is that it only took about two days after I first mentioned it for the word about the "latest fad" to spread, and now I keep getting invitations to hen breakfasts from people who want to be in the swim.'

'And do you go?'

'Certainly not. I tell them all that I never eat breakfast. And I don't let any of the rest of us accept either.' She gestured towards her friends as they shook down their dresses after the crumpling effect of the small boats. 'It's one of the rules.' Laying down ridiculous rules to distinguish between her set and the rest of the world was yet another of Venetia's enterprises and the others took pleasure in following her lead.

Terts's pleasure was more complicated. He was in the apparently enviable situation of being surrounded by pretty girls: valued as a dancing partner and to some extent courted because of his skill as a photographer. The oddity of being a man who worked for a salary had the curious effect of making him neither dangerous nor desirable. Even the most nervous of debutantes felt in no danger of an unwanted proposal from him while, conversely, even the most dutiful of daughters felt under no obligation to entice him into a conservatory in the hope of compromising him. He was just Libby's brother, who could be relied on to take pity on anyone who too often found herself a wallflower.

All this gave him the freedom to be popular without the imprisonment of being openly attached to just one member of the circle. This was hard, when a recognised attachment was what he most desired. Did Venetia not realise that beneath his frivolous pretence of devotion lay a genuine desire for her love?

5

Afraid of frightening Venetia away, Terts postponed any serious discussion until the night of Libby's ball.

Not since Aunt Florence herself came out more than thirty years earlier had there been a ball at Kinderley Court and the preparations were worthy of an army getting ready for battle. Some of the staff who had been hired for the London house were kept on to come to the country. Leaving Lord Mortimer's own cook to prepare the hot dishes on ranges with which she was familiar, the supercilious temporary chef and his *patisseur* made themselves responsible for everything that was to be served cold, while Aunt Florence, who would act as her father's hostess, brought extra maids and footmen from her own home to cope with all the house guests.

Nine of the nearest county families would bring parties to the ball, but Terts and Libby made sure that the Coxes and the Kenwards would be amongst those staying at Kinderley itself. This was a night on which every male guest would ask Libby to dance, so Terts had no duties to perform in that direction. He wasted no time in booking Venetia not only for the supper dance but for the quadrille which was due to follow it.

'They've enough to make up the figures without us,' he said when the time for that formal dance came. 'Shall we walk by the lake?'

Automatically Venetia looked round to see where her mother was, in time to see her disappearing into a card room. Shrugging her shoulders, she agreed with a smile. At country balls like this the strict rules of London behaviour were relaxed. Other couples were already strolling on the terraces and towards the rose garden. She took Terts's proffered arm and with her other hand lifted her skirt a little as they walked down the gentle grassy slope.

'If we go round to the other side, there's a fine view of Kinderley across the water,' Terts suggested; and although this made their walk much longer she did not demur.

They reached the viewpoint which he had chosen earlier in the day and turned to face the way they had come. Terts felt his heart swelling until he could hardly breathe. This was a night he would remember for the rest of his life. The sound of the orchestra floated towards them over the water; and through the ballroom windows they could see the dancers as they advanced and retreated in elaborate patterns. Outside, on the candle-lit terrace, other couples sipped drinks and chatted. At this distance, all the women were elegant and all the men were handsome in their formal clothes. And Kinderley Court itself, with almost all its windows lit, was beautiful as Terts had never seen it before. Only one thing was needed now to make the evening perfect.

Beside him, Venetia gave an admiring sigh.

'It's lovely,' she said. 'So old, and so exactly right for its setting. You must love living here.'

'Yes, I do. But – what I love is you, Venetia. I love you most frightfully. I want to marry you. Will you? Tell me you will.'

She turned her head to look at him. There was just enough moonlight to pick out the paleness of her dress and the whiteness of her shoulders, but not quite enough to let him interpret the expression in her eyes.

'We've had a lot of fun together,' she said. 'But getting married is different.'

'Of course it is. That's why ... That's what I want. To have you with me all the time.'

'Can you afford me?' she asked, and laughed as Terts reacted with astonishment to the unexpected query. 'That's not my question. It's what Bart will ask. He'll tell you that I'm an expensive object to maintain, and that I have no skills whatsoever to help me support myself. I'm a little ashamed of that, actually, but I'm supposed to be proud of it. I'm expected to think that the more I spend on clothes and maids and dinner parties, the more my husband can feel proud to have me. There was something Lady said to me right at the start of the Season. "You'll get a lot of proposals," she said. "Your father and I will protect you from the duds. But of the rest, bear this in mind," she said. "When all fortunes are equal you can be guided by your feelings. But when all feelings are equal, you would do well to be guided by the fortunes."'

'And have you had a lot of proposals?'

She shrugged her shoulders, not prepared to boast.

'Perhaps I should really ask, are all your feelings equal?'

'No, of course not.'

What did that mean? Was she encouraging him? 'I can look after you,' he said, desperate not to let himself be talked out of her. He knew it wasn't true; not at the moment, anyway. But he had a small income from his mother's settlement and his grandfather would perhaps be prepared to make him an allowance and if he worked really hard it would surely not be too long before he could join his uncles in the Partners' room at Bradley's and take a share of the profits instead of making do on a salary. Sir Robert was a wealthy man and would want to be generous in making a settlement on his daughter, to tide them over any early sticky patches. If they loved each other, it would be all right.

'Oh, please,' he said. 'I can't live without you. Tell me that you love me.'

'I love you,' she told him. They were the sweetest words he had ever heard in his life. 'But ...'

He refused to let her continue, closing her lips with a kiss which he would have liked never to end.

'So will you marry me? May I go to your father? Can we be engaged?'

With a shake of the head she toppled him from delight to despair.

'I don't want that. Not to be engaged, I mean, not yet. All this ...' She waved a white-gloved hand towards the candle-lit terrace, the dancers in the ballroom. 'All this is something that will never come again. 'Being young and happy and –'

'And beautiful.' Terts filled in the word she was too modest to pronounce.

'I wasn't going to say that. Young and free. I may still be under Bart's thumb in a sense, but just for a while I have choices. About the whole course of my life. As soon as I've made the choice, I shan't have them any longer. This sort of freedom can only be for a very little while. Lady has already started wondering aloud whether I'm going to be the only debutante of my Season to end the year unengaged. But Bart sees it the other way round. He thinks I'm too young to tie myself down. And I feel that too. I realise it's a frivolous thing to say, but I'm afraid I'm a frivolous person. I want to enjoy myself while I can. Libby must feel the same. Ask her.'

Terts shook his head, knowing that Libby's feelings were quite opposite. For her too this was a time of choice, but she was eager to be offered the choice and to make it and settle down. Remembering that not long before he had thought she was making a mistake, it was illogical of him to regret Venetia's attitude. The only consolation was that as long as she remained determined to preserve her freedom, he could continue to hope.

'Is there anyone else?' he asked.

'Not that sort of anyone else, no. But what there is –' She gestured once again towards the ballroom windows, through which it was possible to see that the quadrille had come to an end; and the note of seriousness was banished from her voice. 'Somewhere over there is a young man to whom I have promised the next dance. I ought not to have come so far.'

She turned to lead the way back, but Terts held on to her hand.

'Say it again.'

'Say what?'

'That you love me.'

'I love you. Madly. But you mustn't kiss me again like you did before.'

She was too late. Already Terts was holding her close. Her small, firm breasts pressed against his chest, while with one hand he stroked the cool skin of her back. How could he bear to let her go? How could he somehow manage to keep her for himself?'

The rest of the evening passed in an emotional whirl. He was the luckiest of men because Venetia loved him. He was the unluckiest of men because she would not engage herself to marry him. His feelings were not greatly soothed when, at five o'clock in the morning, he stood with the rest of his family to watch the last carriage depart. The house guests by then were already in their rooms, with a general instruction that they were not to be woken in the morning. Libby, beside him, squeezed his hand.

'I have some news,' she said.

He guessed at once from the sparkle of her eyes what it must be. Had he not been so absorbed in his own affairs he would have realised much earlier what had happened.

'You don't need to tell me. You're about to become Mrs Hugh Kenward.'

She nodded her head happily. 'It's not official yet, because his parents haven't met me. I'm to go down to Cornwall to stay for a month. But he's asked me and I've said yes so it's all settled really. Apparently he asked Grandfather's permission this morning. I mean, yesterday morning. Grandfather doesn't really know him, of course, so he just asked Hugh what his income is and who he hunts with and whether he has a decent home to offer me. After that, it was apparently up to me.'

'I'm very happy for you, Libby.' He kissed her, although not in the same way that he had kissed Venetia four hours earlier. His congratulations were heartfelt, but when at last he reached his bed it was with the feeling that he had mismanaged his own situation. He should formally have requested Sir Robert for Venetia's hand before anything else. But then, he had not been sure, not quite sure, of Venetia's feelings until he asked her. And Sir Robert would not have accepted his financial situation without making more detailed enquiries and was in any case, it seemed, in no hurry to see Venetia married.

At one moment, as he tossed and turned, the situation seemed hopeless. Then, at the next, he fired himself with a determination to succeed, to grow rich and important. He would work all hours of the clock, impressing his uncles with his diligence. Before the winter was over he would plead for – no, demand – some assurances about his future prospects. Once he became a partner he would be wealthy and important; he might even be able to earn a knighthood so that Venetia would be a Lady like her mother.

It was only as he was on the brink of falling asleep at last that he remembered how he had first greeted Libby's news about her coming-out. He had been glad, hadn't he, that there could be no pressure on him to marry? He had recognised that falling in love was a trap which would condemn him to a life of boring business in the interests of making money and had felt sure that he would not for a very long time be prepared to surrender his freedom in such a way.

In other words, what he had felt six months earlier was what Venetia felt now. He ought to be sympathetic and even relieved. But his last waking thoughts defied that logic. How long would he have to wait before he could rejoice in being a prisoner?

6

The wait was not as bad as Terts had feared. Lady Cox's letter of thanks for the Kinderley ball was accompanied by an invitation for him to join a shooting party at the beginning of the grouse season. Venetia must have arranged it. She must be taking his proposal seriously. She must be hoping that her parents would accept him as a suitor. His spirits rose again.

Terts was a good shot. He had been allowed a stand at his grandfather's shooting parties ever since his sixteenth birthday, and even before that had been encouraged to shoot for the pot. As he packed his guns in preparation for the visit he was pleased that it would offer him the opportunity to show off one of his talents.

So good was his bag on the first day, in fact, that it prompted him to request an interview with his host.

'You've got a good eye!' said Sir Robert approvingly, looking up from the game book while his other guests, in the next room, settled down to cards. 'Mostly pheasant at Kinderley, I suppose. But it's not the shooting you want to talk to me about, eh?'

'No, sir. It's Venetia. I am very fond of her.'

'So she tells me. But what I tell her is, hold your horses. She's a pretty girl, and she'll still be pretty in a year or two's time. I'm in no hurry to get rid of her, and she can't unbuckle the reins herself until she's twenty-one.'

'Two years is a long time to wait, sir.'

'Time to find out whether you're serious about each other. Time to see – both of you – whether anyone else is going to catch your eye. I haven't much use for the goings-on in London. Or in the country, come to that. Wives asking for rooms well away from their husbands, so that someone else can slink along the corridors in the middle of the night.'

'I can promise you –'

'I don't want your promises,' said Sir Robert. 'I'm not offering you anything, so I don't ask anything of you. I'm not saying no, d'you understand, but I'm not saying yes. What I *am* saying is that there's to be no hanky-panky. Venetia may be high-spirited, but she'll be a virgin on her wedding day or I'll want to know the reason why!'

'Well, of course –' Terts was prepared to be indignant, but Sir Robert waved his protest away.

'Not saying anything against you, my boy. If Venetia wants you to keep her company next Season, that's her choice. But you're not to think it means anything. If you were formally going to ask me for her hand today, I'd be writing to your grandfather tomorrow to ask how much he's prepared to settle on you. But you're not asking, because I won't let you, and so I'm not asking either.'

'I'm sorry about that. But thank you at least for not turning me away.'

'You must come and shoot again. A pleasure.'

Terts accepted that the interview was over, but it seemed that Sir Robert, in spite of what he had just said, could not resist asking one question.

'Kinderley's not entailed, then?'

'No.'

It was a truthful answer. Only after he had closed the door and returned to join the other guests did Terts realise how misleading the monosyllable might have been. Had Venetia said something to make her father believe that Terts would inherit his grandfather's estate one day? Had Terts himself – or Libby, perhaps – said anything to make Venetia believe it? Ought he to correct the impression? Yes, he ought – but he knew that he would not.

If Sir Robert had been prepared to consider allowing a formal engagement, then he would have had the right to investigate a future son-in-law's expectations. But he had deliberately turned his back on that path and it would be no one's fault but his own if he were to wander down a byway. By the time the inevitable enquiry came, his daughter's attachment might prove too strong to be broken.

Terts promised himself that he would make the truth about Kinderley clear to Venetia: but the truth was only that he didn't know what the truth was.

Once before, when they were all much younger, the young Bradleys had wondered amongst themselves which of them would be chosen as their Lord Mortimer's heir; but Terts had made a resolution that he would never try to find out and would never even allow himself to think what he would do if the choice fell on him. He had seen too many people made lazy or disappointed by hopes which were not fulfilled, and too many old men made bitter by the realisation that their deaths were eagerly awaited. Terts loved the grandfather who had taken the place of his father, and he was not prepared to let the relationship be influenced in any way by guesses or hopes.

In the meantime, his situation, although not perfect, was the best he could have expected. It would all depend on Venetia. If she let her feelings become known, they would be invited to the same house parties and would be regarded as a couple when the next London Season began. As long as Venetia continued to love him, everything would be all right. Between the demands of working days and the delights of country house weekends, the winter would soon pass.

And pass it did, until the turning pages of the calendar diverted Society from its country pursuits and saw the start of another Season. Afterwards, like everyone else of his privileged kind, Terts looked back on the summer of 1914 as a sunlit haze of happiness. It was not only the pleasures of the time which filled his heart with delight as he enjoyed them, but the certainty that they would continue unchanged year after year.

In every succeeding London Season, he could be sure, there would be dances and dinners and tea parties. Political hostesses would compete to tempt the intellectual élite to their tables while others captured the lions of high society. The king and queen would make their gracious progress at the start of Royal Ascot, old men in pink socks would watch young men rowing at Henley and yachtsmen would prepare for Cowes Week. Fortnum and Mason would pack up hampers for Derby Day, milliners would decorate hats for the Chelsea Flower Show and dressmakers and embroiderers would try to soothe fingers made sore by non-stop sewing. Above all, girls in pale, pretty dresses would dance and flirt and accept grand alliances and perhaps even fall in love. It was, of course, love which for both Libby and Terts transformed that summer into a season of delight.

Libby was by now officially engaged, her wedding planned for the end of June. She was to be married from Kinderley Court, with her grandfather giving her away. The first part of the honeymoon would be spent at Hugh's home in Cornwall. Later they would travel to Italy, before returning to supervise the building of a new house on the Trelowen estate. Work had already begun on this, and although from time to time Libby declared herself fraught with anxiety in respect of all the decisions to be made about the decoration and furnishing of her new home, in fact she was completely carefree. So radiant was her happiness that Terts did not have the heart to tease her for her lack of worldly wisdom in accepting the first offer of marriage she had received instead of collecting proposals in order to select the most advantageous.

Terts was as deeply in love as his sister, although unlike Libby he lacked the assurance of a formal engagement. Venetia's father remained adamant in his refusal to let her marry before she was twenty-one, and considered that three months was quite long enough for an engagement to last before a wedding day. Was he secretly hoping that his daughter would come to her senses during the long waiting period and find a suitor with a more brilliant station in life to offer her?

Venetia was not disposed to quarrel with her father's decision, but often repeated what she had said on the night of the Kinderley ball. She loved Terts madly, of course she did, and there was nobody else who had any place in her heart. But this three-year period between her debut and her twenty-first birthday was the only time of comparative freedom she was ever likely to enjoy in her life and she was not prepared to relinquish it so soon. If he truly loved her, he would understand.

He did indeed truly love her, but that did not prevent him from sometimes feeling frightened. She was so beautiful, so vivacious, so desirable, so popular. Well, that was an argument in his favour. She was all these things and yet she was in love with him. Yes, it was a marvellous summer, the summer of 1914.

Libby was married on June 29. Once again Kinderley was filled with flowers and laughter. All the young people in the house party were high-spirited as, after the bride and groom had left for their honeymoon, they prepared to amuse themselves for a day or two longer on the croquet or tennis lawns, or boating on the lake. Only Lord Mortimer, retreating to his library with the newspaper for which he had had no time earlier in the day, felt a chill cloud come over the day as he read the news of an assassination in Sarajevo.

He said nothing at the time to spoil the party. But later, when the guests were preparing to leave, Sir Robert Cox invited both Terts and his grandfather to come to Scotland for the Glorious Twelfth. Terts accepted with alacrity and was surprised by Lord Mortimer's hesitation.

'What's worrying you, Grandfather?'

'I don't like the look of things. By August the twelfth a rather larger shooting party may have begun.'

Terts and Venetia combined to tease him out of his gloom. If he was talking about war, that was impossible. How could events in Serbia have anything to do with England? Nothing could spoil this wonderful year. Or so they thought.

7

Arriving at Kinderley for the August Bank Holiday weekend in 1914, Terts was surprised to be greeted by his sister.

'What are you doing here, Mrs Kenward? You're supposed to be on your honeymoon.'

'Hugh thinks that war will begin in a day or two.'

'I'm sure he's right.' By now Terts had had time to realise that Lord Mortimer's understanding of the network of treaties which divided parts of Europe and drew others into alliances had been more accurate than his own.

'So he's volunteered. He expects to go off to France almost at once. He doesn't want me to be on my own; and anyway, our house isn't ready. I could have stayed with his parents, of course, but I don't really know them very well yet, so we agreed that I should come back to Kinderley. It'll only be for a few months, Hugh says.'

'He's probably right about that as well. Everybody thinks it'll be over by Christmas.'

'I suppose so. But in those few months ... It frightens me, Terts. After all, we can't win a battle, can we, without people getting killed?'

It was hardly surprising that she should be upset. He gave her a reassuring hug.

'Anyone who manages to snatch the beautiful Miss Bradley away from all her other admirers must have Lady Luck sitting on his shoulder. You mustn't worry. Where's Grandfather?'

'Out in the garden. It's an odd thing. He seems to have become ten years younger. I mean, he's an old man really, but suddenly – well, for example, he spent all this morning in the walled garden with Parsons, discussing how we could grow fewer flowers and lots and lots more vegetables. We've always grown practically everything we need for the house, but now I think he's going to feed the village as well. Or at least to send baskets down to all the women whose sons or husbands have joined up. Anyway, he's looking forward to seeing you. He'll tell you all about it.'

'Come on, then.' Terts led the way into the garden, because he had news of his own, to be announced to both of them at once. 'Hugh's not the only member of the family to volunteer,' he told them. 'I've signed up for the Royal Flying Corps.'

'Good for you, my boy!' Lord Mortimer beamed his approval, but Libby looked aghast.

'To fly aeroplanes? Up in the sky!' Libby, who had never seen an aeroplane, clearly felt that for her brother even to take his feet off the ground would be dangerous enough, without the additional hazard of Germans firing at him.

'It'll be like driving my motor bike, but faster. I've always liked machines better than horses. You know that. It will be exciting.'

Libby was still looking at him doubtfully. 'You've always said that you can't imagine how Bing can bear to kill people. So how can you –?'

'I'm afraid this is one reason why I've chosen the RFC. A rather shameful reason.'

He paused, wondering how to express himself without sounding soft. Over the past few days, once he had recognised that war was inevitable, he had agonised over the part he should play in it. There was no compulsion on anyone to join the British Expeditionary Force. Although he wanted to do his bit, he could not envisage himself ever having the resolve to stick a bayonet into the guts of a fellow human being and watch him die. To stay in the air, above the battle, seemed to provide an ideal solution.

'Once I've learned to fly, I think there'll be choices,' he told her. 'I was discussing it with a staff-captain when I went to the War Office. They need reconnaissance pilots and observers and wireless telegraphists and photographers and people to interpret the photographs as well as the fighter pilots who try to shoot down other pilots. I told him that I had a special interest in photography. He wrote that down.'

'You're not going off straightaway, are you?'

Terts shook his head. 'No, not today. They'll send me a telegram. I suppose they only have a limited number of training planes.'

'All right with your uncles, is it?' asked Lord Mortimer – his tone suggesting that if it was not all right he would have a word or two to say on the subject.

'I imagine they recognise that they're bound to lose most of their young men for a bit. And Richard doesn't intend to volunteer. Family responsibilities, you know.' There was no need for anyone to ask about Bing. After Sandhurst he had joined the Indian Army. Although his letters since then had mainly described polo or tent-pegging or pig-sticking or escorting important visitors on tiger shoots, he would undoubtedly be eager to put his military training to more belligerent use.

That was enough talk about the war. Terts changed the subject to that of the vegetable garden and found his grandfather eager to discuss it.

'So, no more pineapples or melons after this year,' Lord Mortimer warned when he had finished detailing his plans for a wider degree of self-sufficiency. 'Not right to use fuel to heat the greenhouses for luxuries; and we shall lose men from the outside staff; bound to.'

'But the vine!' pleaded Terts. 'It's more than a hundred years old. You can't leave it to freeze.'

'Well, perhaps just the vine. And a few peaches in with it. But that's all. Are you going riding, you two?'

'Yes!' Libby sprang to her feet and Terts smilingly followed suit. Just for a moment the old man held him back with a hand grasping his own.

'You're doing the right thing, my boy. Proud of you.'

They smiled at each other: in the ten years since Henry Bradley's death the two of them had become like father and son. Then Terts went off to change into his riding clothes.

'How can you bear to go?' asked Libby an hour later. They had brought Nutmeg and Barney to a halt side by side on the highest ridge of the estate and were gazing down at the distant house, so peacefully sheltered, with the glistening lake on one side and the three great avenues of trees fanning out through the park on the other. 'It's so beautiful. So peaceful. I'm sure – at least I suppose – you're right to volunteer. But how can you bear to leave all this?'

'Perhaps because it isn't really this that I'm leaving, but a couple of rooms in London.'

'But it may be yours one day.'

He looked at his sister curiously. 'Why do you say that?'

'Well, I don't know, of course; he doesn't talk about it. But I think Grandfather would like you to have it. He has this sort of feeling that Richard and Bing are Bradleys. He's been a father to the rest of us, but not really to them.'

'There are three of us left; not just me.'

'Aden's too young and I'm a girl. And anyway, I shall be living in Cornwall soon. But mainly I just think he likes you best. And it would give him a special pleasure to get you away from Bradley's. I'm sure, if he did leave the estate to you it would be on condition that you settled down to live here. You'd like that, wouldn't you?'

Terts took a moment to consider the question. It was certainly the case that he would like to get away from Bradley's. The boring repetitiveness of office life had been one of the factors which inspired his eagerness to volunteer. Working for a family firm held a great many advantages as far as future prospects were concerned, but also the one great disadvantage that it was almost impossible to move to any other job without giving offence. The call of his country had provided an excuse that was not to be missed.

Would he grow bored with Kinderley if he were to find himself spending the rest of his life here? It was hard to say. Probably not, because with the estate would come a private income from the tenanted farms. He would have the freedom to spend part of each year travelling: to see the world. In the past he had deliberately refused to let himself wonder about his grandfather's intentions, because it would have made him feel that he was looking forward to the death of a man he loved. But now that Libby had put the idea into his mind . . .

'Did you ever talk about this to Venetia?' he asked her abruptly. 'Was it the sort of thing she asked you: what my prospects were?'

Libby looked slightly disconcerted by the question. 'Well, I expect the subject came up once or twice. I mean, obviously she was interested.'

'But you didn't say anything definite?'

'Oh, no. How could I, when I don't know?'

Was she telling the truth? It would have been natural enough for her to exaggerate the prospects of her favourite brother. He hoped that she had not misled Venetia to a degree which would lead to disappointment.

'I think it will be Bing,' Terts said. He had had time to think about it by now. 'He would do the hunting and shooting much better than I'd ever want to. None of his interests are on the Bradley side, but I can quite see him as a country gentleman. Yes, I'm sure. Grandfather will leave Kinderley to Bing.'

Libby, realising that it was pointless to argue about something so speculative, continued to pursue her earlier train of thought.

'What about Venetia now, Terts? Have you told her yet that you've volunteered? What's she going to think?'

'I hope she'll feel proud of me. She wouldn't want to feel I was a coward, skulking at home while everyone else goes off to war. You're pleased about Hugh going, aren't you?'

'I suppose so. I mean, yes, of course. Except that I don't really see why we have to have a war at all.'

'To protect Belgium.'

'Yes, but working backwards from that, all these treaties! And just because of one assassination.' She gave a sigh, defeated by the complications of international politics. Then she flicked Nutmeg's reins and dug in her heels. 'Come on, boy!' They finished their ride without any further conversation.

Terts did not have to wait long for his summons from the War Office, which ordered him to report on August 16. That date would allow him to spend the Glorious Twelfth with Venetia's family in Scotland, as had been arranged earlier.

He took the first opportunity after his arrival on the eleventh to express his regrets to Sir Robert that his stay would be such a short one and explain it with the news that he had volunteered. As he expected, this was met with approval.

'So I wondered, sir, whether you might reconsider ... I mean, I quite understood why you wanted Venetia not to marry before she was twenty-one, but in the circumstances ...'

'The circumstances make the waiting all the more important. A young woman getting married needs an establishment of her own and a husband on hand to help her run it. Not goodbye and back in six months' time, however worthy the reason. She'll be safe here with her mother and me and by the time she comes of age you'll both have had time to be sure that you're right for each other.'

'I'm sure now, sir. I'll never be more sure.'

'I'm sorry, but she can't marry without my consent and I'm not prepared to change my mind about making her wait.'

'It used to be the custom in the old days,' said Terts, choosing his words carefully, 'that a young man going into battle was allowed to wear his lady's favour. To tell the world what he was really fighting for. I don't care so very much about Belgium. I shall be fighting for my country and a way of life that I don't want to see changed; but most of all for the woman I love.'

There was a long silence. It seemed that perhaps Sir Robert's defences were weakening.

'This is against my principles,' he said at last. 'As a general rule, I don't believe that a long engagement has much to be said for it. But I do see that the war makes a difference. You're right to do your bit. Shouldn't have any respect for you if you stayed at home. And I suppose you want your attachment to Venetia to be publicly recognised while you're away. Well, you may speak to her if you wish. If she's prepared to commit herself to an engagement, I won't object. But you may find that she doesn't want to clip her own wings. And whatever happens, before there's any question of an engagement turning into a marriage, I shall need to know that you're in a position to support her.'

'Yes, of course. Thank you, sir. Thank you very much indeed.'

He hurried off to find Venetia. 'A walk!' he demanded. 'After all those hours in the train, I need fresh air.'

She agreed happily, delaying only long enough to change into boots sturdy enough to protect her feet from the scratchy heather. It was one of the unexpectedly marvellous things about her, that someone who was so obviously in her metier in the social events of London life should be equally at home in the country.

At Kinderley they had walked together round an ornamental lake. Here, they strode across the moor towards a much larger loch. But Terts's question was the same on each bank.

'I've got things in the right order at last,' he said. 'Your father says that I may ask you to marry me. So I'm asking. Will you marry me, my darling girl?'

'You mean, get engaged?'

'Yes. I want the whole world to know that you're mine. I want you to wear my ring on your finger. I want ... I want you so much. Say that you will. So that I can think of you all the time I'm away at the war, and know that you're thinking of me.'

'Of course I will. Darling Terts.'

Probably anyone in the castle who happened to be looking out of a window could see them, but they fell into each other's arms without caring. Venetia gave a deep sigh of happiness.

'Shall you be able to get the ring before you leave?'

'I have it already.' He had been determined before he left London that he was going to make Sir Robert surrender. Taking the box out of his pocket, he slid the ring on to her finger. The diamond, which had cost more than he could really afford, sparkled in the sunlight as he raised her hand to his lips.

The engagement was announced that same evening and generously toasted in champagne. It should have been enough to content Terts, but served only to increase his desire.

'Why should we need to wait?' he asked her next day. The ladies of the party had come on to the moor for lunch, and had stayed to watch the afternoon shoot. As they walked back to the castle Terts and his fiancée were able to fall a little behind. 'Why shouldn't we go the whole way and get married?'

'My father –'

'He's given his approval. We don't need his formal permission, not here in Scotland. We could go off to Gretna Green. Tomorrow morning, without telling anyone. Say you'll marry me now, tomorrow. Please, Venetia.'

'Oh, Terts, darling!' She gave the high, amused laugh which so much delighted him at dances and parties, but which now promised disappointment even before she spoke. 'We can't do that, not even in Scotland. If you're thinking of all those eloping couples holding hands over the blacksmith's forge, you're years out of date. We'd each have to be resident for three weeks first, and you haven't got time for that. Besides, the family would be furious. I should be cut off without a penny.'

'What does that matter?'

'It does to me, when I only need to wait a bit to get a decent settlement. That's the sort of thing that'll make all the difference later on. And it isn't as if we'd be able to settle down together as a married couple. I mean, you're not going to be here, are you?'

'You're being too practical. Have you no romance in your soul?'

'I suppose not. But I do love you. You mustn't think that I don't want to marry you, because of course I do. Madly. But in the right way. With a proper wedding and all our friends there and my parents pleased and smiling.'

'Well then, if you won't run away, will you let me come to your room tonight? Because it's so frustrating! I can't bear it any longer. I need to show you how much I love you. Darling!'

'My room's next to my mother's. It's impossible.'

'Well, you could come to mine, then. Everybody does it. You know that well enough.'

'Not before they're married. It wouldn't be right. You know that, really. You wouldn't want to marry me if I were that sort of girl.'

'But it's different. We're engaged. And I love you so much.'

'I love you too. But I want you to respect me as well. Don't let's talk about it any more, darling. As soon as I'm twenty-one ...'

'It's too long to wait.'

'I'm sorry.' She was silent for a moment, and then smiled as brightly as though they had been discussing a triviality. 'You'll do your training in England, won't you? You're bound to get some weekends off. And leaves. I'll come down. We'll have a good time together. And in two years ...'

Terts was tempted to point out that he was about to go to war and that in two years' time he might not still be alive. But possibly it was a thought of that kind which had made her father so adamant about the need to wait. For his own part, naturally, he had every intention of staying alive. But it looked as though this particular battle was lost.

He gave a sigh of surrender. But it was impossible to be unhappy for long. He was engaged to be married to the only girl he would ever love. And the war would be over by Christmas.

Part Three
War

1

The day on which Terts first reported for duty was one that for the rest of his life he never forgot. Every detail stayed in his memory; but there were three moments which imprinted themselves on his eyes with particular clarity. As a newly arrived cadet he knew better than to produce a camera on that first day; but although, later on, he attempted to recreate these early glimpses of military life for his album just as he had originally seen them, whenever he looked at those photographs in later life it was really the first impressions he was remembering.

The very first impression of all was the extreme fragility of the aeroplanes which he would soon, if all went well, be flying. They seemed hardly more substantial than the models that all the younger boys at Croxton had constructed out of balsa wood and Japanese silk and glue in the aviation craze which followed Bleriot's successful crossing of the Channel. Seen from a distance, these full-size machines appeared mainly to be made of canvas and certainly were held together – and presumably controlled – by an elaborate criss-crossing of thin piano wire. The idea of entrusting himself to such an apparently makeshift contraption would have seemed ludicrous had it not been for the fact that half a dozen of the aircraft were at that very moment circling above their heads.

There was little time to think about this, because what was to provide the second of the day's indelible memories arrived with unexpected swiftness. Just as on the first day at school, the new cadets were shown to their quarters in order to deposit their kit, and then were immediately ordered to assemble in front of the O.C.

He welcomed them briefly, introduced their instructors and gave a brief outline of their training. Then, in an unexpected display of sympathy for their feelings – a softness which was not to be repeated during the six weeks that followed – he announced a treat.

'The first time you get into one of these for training,' he said, indicating the aeroplanes on the ground, 'you'll have your head full of instructions and you'll be so busy trying to do the right thing that you'll hardly have time to realise you're in the air at all. So I've authorised your instructors to give each of you a quick flip now. Two circuits, that's all, six of you up at a time. Alphabetical order. Sergeant Lucas! Take over!'

'Sir!'

After that, there was no time to think about the solidity of the machines. The early position of Bradley in the alphabet ensured Terts one of the first flights. He was issued with a helmet, goggles and gloves, and pointed towards a biplane. Ordered not to touch any of the controls, he strapped himself in and gripped the sides of the open cockpit with a mixture of excitement and apprehension. This had nothing to do with any fear of danger: he was only concerned that the experience might not come up to his expectations.

All his senses were on high alert. Although at the time he was hardly aware of details as two mechanics tugged away the chocks that were wedged under the wheels and the Longhorn began to trundle bumpily forward, afterwards he was able to relive the experience second by second. They were rushing along the ground. They were surely going to hit the hedge. But no; the bumping had stopped and the hedge was below them. They were climbing, soaring, flying.

For a few seconds he was unable to breathe, as though to be surrounded by air made it unnecessary to take any into his lungs. His body was filled with a kind of ecstasy. Even with a girl he had never experienced such bliss before. Briefly he closed his eyes – but that was a waste of these few precious moments. Two circuits would not take long.

Leaning over the side of the cockpit he looked down at the neat landscape, divided by hedges into small squares of green or brown. Black and white cows stood in some of the green squares, as small and wooden as if they had come from a Noah's Ark, while, tiny as a clockwork toy, a plough was being pulled by two horses in one of the brown patches. Terts was reminded of the very first occasion on which he had looked through the viewfinder of a camera and had seen the muscular rugger players of Bing's house team suddenly diminished into insignificance. No wonder God was always imagined as being up in the heavens, looking down on puny mankind.

Now they were into the second circuit, sweeping a little more widely. A railway line could be identified by the train which appeared on it, its engine puffing black smoke. A small stream flowed into some larger river. No doubt the junction could be located easily enough on a map; but not yet by someone who had only just arrived in this unfamiliar part of the world.

There were other shapes to be observed as well: the shadows of clouds which had begun within the past few seconds to move more swiftly than before as a breeze sprang up. Their rounded or wispy edges softened the straight-lined rectangles of farmland, and while the ground immediately between them and the late autumn sun was darkened to a purplish grey, the unshadowed grass looked all the brighter by contrast. This would be heaven for a painter – but perhaps a frustrating heaven, for the shapes and colours refused to pose but changed with every second.

They headed back towards the airfield. The wind, catching the Longhorn at a different angle, tossed it about like a ship in a storm, but Terts hardly noticed. He was looking down at the group of cadets who were awaiting their own turn to fly. Still small, but growing in size with every moment that passed, they were watching the circling aeroplanes, wondering how it felt to be up there. Terts for his part knew exactly how they were feeling. He could put himself inside their excitement as though he were not himself but one of them.

The aeroplane was about to land. How fast it was going! The ground, only a foot or two below them, rushed past on either side. There was the very slightest of bumps followed by an immediate braking which pressed his body so tightly against the harness that for a second time he found it difficult to breathe. Then the machine turned and rattled back to the spot where the others were waiting.

Terts thanked the pilot and climbed out. Another of the cadets was already crossing towards them, ready for his turn.

'What was it like?' he asked as they crossed.

'Marvellous!' It was the expected response; but to himself he tried to be more specific. What was it, exactly, that had been marvellous?

The answer took him back once more to that day when Dempsey's Colts had posed for their photograph. He remembered how, afterwards, he had run through the school grounds looking through the telescope of his fist. Click! Click! One small scene after another, as though it were a photograph, cut off from the larger world around it.

Looking down from the aeroplane had in one sense been quite opposite. The view was not diminished but enlarged, framed only by the horizon. But it brought with it the same feeling of something seen for the first time: seen from outside and with a new clarity. Once he was allowed to take his camera up in the air, Terts promised himself, both these pleasures would come together. How glad he was that he had chosen to enlist in the Royal Flying Corps.

He watched with interest as 'his' Longhorn took off again. Now he was the tiny figure on the airstrip – yet at the same time he was in the cockpit again, re-experiencing the exhilaration of take-off, looking down at the shadows of clouds.

By now the wind had increased in strength and two or three of the second batch of cadets showed signs of having felt airsick; they staggered slightly as they found themselves on terra firma again. Not, however, the young man from Terts's plane. He vaulted athletically out of the cockpit and came running towards Terts, clearly longing to share his excitement. Terts, for his part, moved spontaneously forward to greet him.

'Was I right? Marvellous?'

'Absolutely ripping!'

They grinned at each other with no need of any more elaborate vocabulary. This was the third of the three moments which Terts would remember for the rest of his life: the beginning of his friendship with Arthur.

He was not Arthur to start with, of course. 'My name's Lennox,' he said.

'Bradley.' They shook hands and walked together to discover what was due to happen next. It was a matter-of-fact beginning; but important all the same. No doubt each of the new cadets recognised the need to make friends in this new life amongst strangers. The only difference in Terts's case was the speed with which he and Arthur took it for granted that they would become companions: willing to support each other and able to rely on each other.

They came from different social backgrounds. Arthur was a grammar school boy and at first a little overawed to learn that his friend had been educated at Croxton. Like Terts, he was an orphan, but instead of being brought up in a grand house with siblings and servants he had shared a small bungalow with the elderly aunt who adopted him when he was ten. He was six years younger than Terts, having volunteered straight from school; and, in contrast to the sophisticated delights of the Season, his social life seemed to have been confined to the activities of the local Presbyterian church. In that strait-laced society, it appeared that even to kiss a girl represented practically a proposal of marriage, so it came as no surprise to Terts to learn in due course that his new friend was still a virgin.

That state was not likely to continue for too long, for Arthur, fresh-complexioned and fair-haired, was outstandingly handsome and his schoolboy enthusiasm must surely make him immediately attractive to women. He and Terts were both tall and athletic, but while Terts's body was thin and rangy, Arthur's was muscular, filling his uniform in a more substantial manner. They promised each other a weekend on the town together once their training was complete.

The details of their past lives emerged only gradually, of course, in brief exchanges of confidences. Their immediate concern was to fulfil all the RFC's requirements and earn their tickets. Together they discussed the inevitable successes and shames: the first solo flight, the first crash landing. Terts took a photograph of Arthur leaning against his machine after that first solo flight. He gave a print to his friend, to send to his aunt, and made another for himself.

The main concern of all the cadets during this period was to notch up a sufficient number of flying hours; but there was another side to their training as well – a necessary reminder that they had volunteered to do more than just learn to fly.

There were mechanical sessions in the hangars. Although there would always be mechanics to carry out any necessary overnight repairs, it was the responsibility of the pilot to be able to check his machine's airworthiness, and there were likely to be occasions on which he would have to land a damaged aeroplane, possibly behind the enemy lines, and rig up some kind of emergency repair. Terts and Arthur had both owned and tinkered with motor bicycles before joining up and were quick to get the hang of this.

There were also classroom sessions. The cadets were taught not only how to read maps but how to read the ground in order to navigate. They were instructed on the various purposes of reconnaissance and how to interpret small details like the changed position of a trench or any unusual amount of activity on a road or railway line. They needed to recognise and report every new position of the enemy's guns, and must know how to tell their own artillery to adjust their range of fire. For that they had to study wireless telegraphy and memorise a code of instructions using gestures or flares.

As an important part of all this observation they were taught, with the help of slides projected by a lantern, how to interpret aerial photographs. What they were hardly taught at all, to Terts's disgust, was how best to take the photographs. The pilot was responsible for keeping a steady line above whatever was to be observed and recorded, and it seemed to Terts that it would only be a matter of luck if the regular exposure of plates by the observer disclosed anything useful. But it was not for a cadet to be critical.

The last of all the classroom sessions was taken by the O.C. himself. By this time each of the cadets had earned his pilot's certificate on the training Longhorn, but they were still probationers and now were about to be posted to other aerodromes in order to acquire experience on a variety of machines.

'Just one last thing,' said Captain Sheffield as he came to the end of his remarks. 'When you get out there, at the front, never forget that more pilots are killed by a lack of concentration than by the Hun. From the moment when you take charge of your plane, every thought and sense you possess must be devoted to the task in hand. You may be angry because you've had a quarrel or sad because your grandmother has died or worried because – well, because of anything. But all those thoughts have to be put out of your mind completely. You have a task to perform and you must think of nothing else until it's done. Remember that it may not only be your own life at stake. Good luck, then, men.'

Before reporting to their new posting – which in the case of both Terts and Arthur was Gosport – there were a few hours of freedom to enjoy. Terts took Arthur along with him to the Waterloo station canteen where a voluntary service provided food and cups of tea to soldiers who were just leaving for the front or were returning from it wounded. Venetia was just as slim and lovely in her unfamiliar uniform as she had been in her ball dresses. Terts embraced and kissed her without regard for the interested audience.

'You're the most beautiful woman in the world and I adore you,' he whispered into her ear before pulling himself away and speaking more formally. 'May I present my friend Lieutenant Arthur Lennox? Arthur, Miss Venetia Cox. We're hoping, Venetia, that you have a friend who might like to make up a foursome for the evening.'

'That won't be too difficult.' Venetia smiled at Arthur as she shook hands. In the course of the past three months he had grown a blond moustache which had immediately changed him from a handsome schoolboy to a handsome young man. Yes, any girl would be happy to spend an evening with him.

'And I think you'll find,' Terts told his friend after they had made arrangements for the evening and left the canteen, 'that if Venetia chooses one of her debutante cronies to bring along, you needn't worry that a kiss or two will be regarded as a proposal of marriage.' The stern rules of that Presbyterian upbringing had caused a good deal of laughter between the two of them – although in fact it was no more than a year or two ago that any of Libby's friends would have been considered compromised had Terts taken her out of the sight of her chaperone for more than a few minutes. How times had changed! Venetia was still under twenty-one, but nowadays she would laugh at the idea of being chaperoned.

The evening was a success. The knowledge that there would not be another such occasion for many months added an extra edge to their pleasure in the bright lights, good food and company – and in Arthur's case, too much to drink, for he had never tasted champagne before. Terts himself was not entirely sober as he kissed Venetia a passionate goodbye.

'We ought to be married,' he said. 'I want to be married to you.'

'There's plenty of time. All the rest of our lives. Take care of yourself, darling. I love you.'

'I love you.' He repeated the words to himself as the taxi drove the two men on to catch the last train. But there was an uneasiness in his mind, all the same. He was returning to a world entirely of men – but Venetia would remain in a world which still held enough men to make him anxious.

She had told him in the course of the evening that she intended to enrol in the VAD and train to be a nurse. Now that it was clear that the war would not after all be over by Christmas, pouring out cups of tea was too trivial a contribution. Terts admired her for the decision, but was disturbed by it on his own account. Wounded men were liable to fall in love with even the plainest of nurses, and Venetia was so beautiful. All her patients were bound to adore her. How could he hope that she would be true to him? He ought to have married her. But he couldn't marry her, not without her father's consent, until she was twenty-one. Would she still be waiting for him when he had his next leave?

Only time could answer that question – and now, when he had reported in at Gosport, time began to pass at a faster pace. While he had been training, others had been fighting. There were casualties already and the new recruits were urgently needed at the front. In his new posting he was hurried from one type of aeroplane to another: from biplane to monoplane, from front to rear cockpit, from front- to rear-mounted engine, from a machine with a tail plane to one with only a balanced elevator. There were nerve-racking moments, but they ended in triumph when the moment came for Terts and almost all his companions to be awarded their Wings.

An official group photograph was taken on passing-out day. It reminded Terts of the House photograph at Croxton. He took his place in the group as proudly as any of them, but afterwards he moved amongst them with his own camera, recording individually the young men whom he might never see again. They were to be divided between four different postings now, in France or Belgium, but someone in authority had taken note of friendships between the pilots, recognising no doubt how important it was that they should have confidence in each other on the battlefield. So when Terts and Arthur raced to read the lists which had been posted in the Mess, they discovered with relief and pleasure that they were to be together.

It was a solemn moment, nevertheless. They had taken pleasure in learning to fly for its own sake. Now they were reminded that it had all been only a preparation for the real work of helping their army on the ground to kill while doing their best not to be killed themselves. But the solemnity did not last long. They both felt themselves to be immortal, and it was time for them to do their bit.

And so at ten o'clock next morning it was without any feeling of doom that Terts pulled on his leather coat, sheepskin boots and flying helmet, polished his goggles, checked the route on his map and strapped himself into his cockpit. At a signal from his Flight-Commander he started his engine, warmed it up for a few minutes and gave it one last roar before allowing it to tick over as he waited to take his place in the line which taxied down to the far end of the aerodrome. Then, turning into the wind, he opened the throttle and took his aeroplane smoothly up into the air. Off to the war.

2

The battle of the Somme began at dawn on July 1, 1916. The letter from Venetia was received by Terts on the last day of June. It was hard to remember, afterwards, which was the more devastating.

For seven days before the offensive the British and French artillery kept up a non-stop barrage against the German lines, and on each of those seven days the pilots and observers of A Wing were sent out to photograph the effects of the bombardment. The Morane Parasol which Terts usually flew for such reconnaissance was under repair; he was allocated a BE 2c instead.

'Why is it always me who gets lumbered with this monster?' he grumbled to his sergeant-gunner as they walked together across the tarmac.

'Because you're the best of the pilot-photographers, sir.'

Terts gave a mock groan. Probably that was true, but it was a compliment he could have done without. When flying the Parasol, which was a monoplane, he needed only to keep steady in position while his observer, behind him, took the photographs; but in the BE 2c, a biplane, the observer sat forward, with part of the plane beneath him and wires all round to obscure his view. The camera, therefore, was mounted outside the fuselage next to the pilot. It was the pilot who – while still flying the aeroplane with his left hand – had to lean over the side and look through a ball and cross-wire sight. Then, when he was immediately above the spot which he wanted to photograph, he pulled a ring on the end of a cord to make an exposure. That part was easy enough, but he next had to stretch his arm out into the wind and push the camera handle back and forward again to change the plates before pulling the string for the next exposure.

Throughout all this procedure, which might need to be repeated twenty-four times, he was a sitting duck for Archie, the anti-aircraft fire from the ground, and for the German Fokkers which at any moment might swoop down out of the sun to attack him. Sergeant Day was armed with a Lewis gun; but, unlike the Fokkers which could shoot through their propellers, the BE 2c seemed to have been specially constructed to make it most likely that the gunner would damage his own plane.

The stress of each day's operation was very great and made worse by the knowledge that it would be repeated the next day, and the next. Worse still was Terts's rapid realisation that the barrage was having very little effect – except, presumably, that of alerting the Hun to the fact that an offensive was about to begin. The Germans had dug themselves well into defensive positions and were simply sitting the bombardment out. Although Terts was not required to study the photographs he had taken, he regularly asked to do so, as being the only way of finding out whether he was operating efficiently; and he could see how little change there was from day to day.

The last day of this preparatory week, June 30, dawned wet and cloudy. Looking out at the driving rain, Terts could not resist a sigh of relief. There could be no flying today. While some of the others settled down to a game of cards after breakfast, he returned to sit on the edge of his bed and write a letter to Venetia.

These letters were never easy to write. It was tacitly accepted by all the pilots that their families and loved ones should never be allowed to learn just how dangerous their work was. Since almost the whole of Terts's day was devoted to inspecting and testing and flying and reporting on his aeroplane, that left little else to describe. Often the best he could do – apart from expressions of love – was to tell anecdotes about the other members of his Wing, though it was unlikely that Venetia would feel great interest in men she had never met.

There was a new factor today, though. All along the lines, knowing that the offensive was about to begin, men would be writing letters home: the sort of letters which would probably be torn up in relief if the writers were still alive at the end of the day, but which otherwise would be included in the bleak package of personal effects to be delivered to some mourning wife or mother. Thousands of letters which would all contain the same phrases: 'Thank you.' 'I love you.'

Naturally Terts could not refer directly to this in his own letter. Although the censors were undoubtedly holding up all outgoing letters for the time being to make sure that no references to the forthcoming battle slipped through, it was against both regulations and common sense to allow any clues to creep into what he wrote. But the thought of all those men, many of them barely literate, struggling to express their feelings in words, gave Terts a theme for this letter of his own.

My dearest, darling Venetia,
I've just been counting my blessings. Thinking of all the men in the trenches, and the mud and lice and discomfort they have to endure, and comparing their lives with my own pampered existence. A comfortable bed. (Well, I might not have thought so three years ago, but judged against a bunk in a dug-out, it rates as worthy of the Ritz.) Dry uniform. Decent food. The day-to-day company of men I can trust with my life. And above all, the knowledge that I love and am loved by the most marvellous, most beautiful girl in the

He was interrupted by Arthur. 'Photographic patrol at two o'clock.'
Terts put down the letter and stood up to look out of the window. The rain seemed to have stopped, but so low was the cloud that there was little chance of getting any decent shots – not, at least, without flying within rifle range of the enemy.
'Cracker must be mad.'
'He's had his arm twisted. 15th Corps are in a panic. Some of yesterday's stuff didn't show what they wanted. They seem to think the whole offensive will be doomed if they don't know whether or not they've knocked out a particular bit of Hun artillery. There's just one silver lining, though. Your Parasol is back in action. You won't have to struggle with The Monster any longer. Briefing at one o'clock. Dick Spalding will be with you.' Lt Spalding

was a young officer who had only recently come out from England. Although he had completed his pilot training and notched up the fifteen hours' flying time which was nowadays considered sufficient, it was always considered a wise precaution to let new arrivals enjoy their first experience of flying in a war zone in the observer's seat of a more experienced pilot.

'Right.' Terts registered his disapproval of the patrol with an ostentatious sigh. Then he folded the unfinished letter and put it away. The Parasol had been in the hands of the mechanics for four days. It would be necessary to check it over with extreme thoroughness before taking off. He started the process at once.

It was not a pleasant afternoon. The low cloud forced Terts to keep below two thousand feet and the bombardment was more intense than any that he had yet heard or witnessed. How could the Corps commander expect clear photographs when the whole of the enemy line was covered with the white smoke of exploding shells? And had he forgotten to tell the gunners that there would be friendly aircraft in the air? They were supposed to pause when one of their own planes was passing, but today it seemed that they were gripped by a kind of powder lust. Shells passed above and below the Parasol, their wind eddies flinging it up and down. Terts thanked his lucky stars that at least today he could leave his observer to take the photographs while he himself concentrated on keeping the aeroplane steady.

It seemed a long time before a double tap on his shoulder told him that the job was finished and they could head for home. The one thing to be said for flying in this weather was that the Huns had not expected such lunacy and their Fokkers were still on the ground. But if Terts thought that the danger was over, he was wrong.

The guns were still firing and by now the continuous noise was intolerable, Terts's head ached as though every shell were pounding itself into his forehead. And suddenly, as they approached their own lines, it seemed that this was not only a matter of imagination. The aeroplane was so low beneath the clouds that he could see the muzzles of a row of howitzers, and they were pointing straight at him. The missiles themselves were invisible, but as the shells whizzed past on either side, he found himself overwhelmed by a kind of panic which he had never felt before.

They were trying to shoot him down. His own side! What did the crazy buggers think they were playing at? There was no point in swerving or diving, as he might have done had the enemy been on the attack, for he was as likely to fly into a shell as to avoid one. Almost blinded with fury, there was a moment in which he was tempted to dive over his own artillery and open up with his Lewis gun.

His fears proved to be well justified. There was a bang which first of all knocked the aeroplane sideways and then caused it to vibrate uncontrollably. The Parasol was not easy to fly under the best of conditions. Although the engine was more reliable than any other, the fact that there was no fixed tail plane, but only a balanced elevator, meant that the pilot could never relax control. As he fought now to steady the machine, it went into a dive, pointing straight at the offending artillery post. It would serve them right if he crashed into the bunch of cretins – but since he and his observer would certainly be killed, he did not allow that thought to linger for more than a split second. It was perhaps in order to remove just such temptations that the powers-that-be had decided not to issue pilots with parachutes.

At least now the gunners knew he was there! As he screamed down towards them he was close enough to see their anxious faces looking up before they ran for cover. He hoped they were terrified. Serve them right. But although his mind might be dominated by hatred, his hands were automatically powered by many hours of flying experience. After what seemed a lifetime of desperate struggle he was able to pull out of the dive and then correct the upward swoop.

'What's the damage?' he shouted back when at last they were flying level again, but still vibrating in a manner which spelt trouble. The shell which hit them had fortunately not exploded, but it would have been heavy enough to break any wires it hit.

It was one of the responsibilities of the observer to report on the condition of the plane, but on this occasion there was no answer. Terts twisted round so that he could look back, and saw the young lieutenant sitting bolt upright, his hands gripping the sides of the cockpit and his face frozen in terror. No one could blame him for that. It was always worse for the observer in an emergency, because there was nothing he could do about it. The pilot at least had the distraction of trying to save himself.

At last they were through, behind the lines. By now the continuing vibration had convinced Terts that the damage was probably to the engine at the rear. Since it had brought them this far, there was no reason why the landing should be particularly hazardous. Nevertheless, he circled the aerodrome three times. This would alert the ground crew to the fact that there might be an emergency but also, more importantly, it gave him time to settle his nerves.

After he had brought the aeroplane to a halt he sat without moving for a moment while the chocks were set in place. He was aware of his observer scrambling out of the cockpit behind him and, a few seconds later, heard the sound of him vomiting. By the time Terts himself climbed wearily down, the young man was standing with his forehead pressed against the body of the Parasol, breathing heavily as he tried to bring himself under control.

'A touch of sea-sickness?' It was not done for anyone even to suspect fear in others. 'Not surprised. The equivalent of a Force Ten gale in the Bay of Biscay, I'd say. Sorry I couldn't keep her any steadier for you, that last bit.'

'They were shooting at us!' Lieutenant Spalding's moment of panic was brought under control by indignation. 'They were aiming straight at us!'

'Not really.' As the older and more experienced officer Terts knew that his duty was to reassure, although his own stomach was still churning as violently as his observer's. 'They don't know what they're shooting at. It's all geometry to them. Angles. They know they can't see their target, so they don't bother to look. I sometimes wonder if they even realise that they're killing people at the other end of their beautiful trajectories. If it's any help, this may be the worst you ever have to face. With any other sort of attack, you can always run away. It's trickier when the guns are between you and home. Give me the plates. I'll hand them in. You go and get your boots off.'

'Thank you, sir.' But the young man took only a few steps towards his quarters before turning back. 'You handled her jolly well, sir. Thank you.'

'My neck on the line as much as yours.' Terts managed a smile, but his mind was still seething. What he would most like to do now was to get drunk: hopelessly, obliviously drunk. But the offensive was due to start next day, and he would have to be in the air before dawn. This was no time to risk a hangover.

After handing in the plates, he met Arthur in a corridor, clutching half a dozen letters.

'Blighty bag's in. Some for you.'

They would be from Venetia. It was three weeks since her last letter had arrived, but Terts had not worried about the delay. It was well known that the squadron mail officer had a tendency to hold up incoming correspondence in the days leading up to a big push in order to make sure that every man received at least one letter from home on the night before. It was apparently assumed that this would be good for morale, and perhaps it was. Arthur, however, had news which cancelled out this moment of cheer. 'Scott and Douglas haven't made it back. Shot down.'

'By whom?' asked Terts bitterly, but he did not wait for an answer. He intended to put in a report which would redden a few faces: but not until the coming battle was over.

It was a disappointment to find that only one of his letters was from Venetia; but no doubt she had written it, as often in the past, rather like a diary, with news added day by day. He carried his post back to his quarters, but did not open any of it immediately. Taking off his boots, he stretched himself out on the bed and breathed deeply as he tried to bring the trembling of his body under control. It was a bad sign that the stress was getting to him like this. For the past eighteen months he had seemed to lead a charmed life, and for that to continue it was necessary that he should believe himself to be, if not immortal, at least confident of survival until this mess was over. Today, in the artillery fire, his confidence had been dented. It was something which he had observed in other people. This was a time of danger.

The return from any mission required a period of winding down as the tension of mind and body gradually relaxed; but on this occasion the period was longer than usual. At last he gave a single deep sigh, expelling from his body the last memory of the day's patrol, and began to tear open the first envelope. He would leave Venetia's letter until last, so that her words would linger to cheer up the rest of the day.

Libby first, then. Usually her letters were light-hearted, describing the various mishaps which resulted from the gradual disappearance of domestic and garden staff and her own efforts to take over unfamiliar duties. But this time she was in sombre mood as she poured out her anxieties about Hugh in view of the terrible casualty lists which appeared in the newspapers day after day. And that was not the worst of it.

We have news of Bing at last, and I'm afraid it's bad news; very bad. I don't know how much you on the Western Front hear about what's going on in the rest of the world and I can't remember when I last passed on anything we knew here, but it can't be recently because it's at least six months since we last heard from him.

Still lying almost prone, Terts lowered the letter on to his chest, almost afraid to go on reading. Was she going to tell him that their brother was dead?

Bing's life in the Indian Army immediately after leaving Sandhurst had sounded idyllic. There were exercises and manoeuvres to be practised, but no fighting. His days were devoted to various sports and his evenings to the entertainment of the young women who came out from England to join their fathers and enjoy the social life. In his first year there he had referred to them as the Fishing Fleet, because it was well understood that the aim of each one was to catch herself a husband from the 'right' regiment; but it was not long before Bing had been netted as one of the fish.

Young officers were not allowed to marry without the consent of their superiors, who normally specified a minimum age or rank. But the rules had been slackened with the outbreak of war, and just before the cavalry brigade received its orders to embark for Mesopotamia, Bing had married a Miss Violet Cunningham, who none of his family had yet met. Within a fortnight he had been forced to leave her; but he had put the fortnight to good use, and his son was born in July 1915.

The brigade, in the meantime, had successfully captured Basra, thus safeguarding the oil supplies which would be desperately needed by the armies in Europe. They had also captured a place called Kut-al-Almara, of which no one in England had ever heard, and then had pressed on towards Baghdad. But then everything went wrong. They were forced back to Kut and found themselves besieged, with only limited supplies of food and ammunition. In the early months of 1916 the papers had from time to time reported the failure of relief forces to break the siege, but no personal news could emerge from the beleaguered fortress. What was it that Libby had now learned?

> We've heard nothing from Bing himself, only a sort of official letter which I suppose is going to all the families. Kut was surrendered at the end of April. They had to do it because by then they'd eaten everything, even the horses, and they were all starving. Bing was still alive then. That's the latest, really, that anyone knows. All the survivors were made to march across the desert – in the heat – to prison camps in Turkey. It seems to have been quite terrible. Anyone who was wounded or just exhausted was simply left behind in the sun to die. I can't bear to think about it. Bing was always so fit and energetic and full of life. And that poor little boy, if he's never to see his father.
> We don't actually know what's happened to Bing. Grandfather's trying to find out, but it all sounds chaotic. Nobody on our side has had the chance to make any kind of record, and it doesn't sound as though the Turks are even trying. It makes me feel sick. Perhaps I ought not to have told you when you've got enough worries of your own. But it's difficult to think of anything to be jolly about at the moment.

Terts allowed the letter to fall from his hand. He and his brother were not close. Bing had never forgiven him for the Croxton incident and except for one or two essential politenesses had kept his vow never to speak to him again. This had attracted little notice from the rest of the family, because in practice Bing had never after that year spent very much time at Kinderley, living instead first with his crammer, then at Sandhurst and afterwards in India.

But they were brothers still. Terts found himself groaning in sympathy at this account of the ordeal. Simply to be a prisoner would be unbearable for someone like Bing and it seemed all too likely that the truth would turn out to be even worse.

For a long time he lay without moving. Then, changing his mind – because he was in need of solace – he set all but one of his other letters aside. He stared at the unopened envelope which was addressed in Venetia's handwriting, and allowed his imagination to picture the woman who had written it. Venetia as he had first seen her: the beautiful debutante. Venetia as he had last seen her, with tears running down her cheeks as she waved him goodbye. Venetia as she would look on their wedding day. Venetia as he would see her on the first night of their honeymoon: as no one else would ever see her. He spoke her name aloud, caressing her with his voice. Then, at last, he opened the envelope.

'Dear Terts,' it began. Not My Darling, or My dearest, or Sweetheart, but Dear Terts. 'I'm afraid this letter will come as a shock ...'

3

'You missed some decent grub tonight, for a change.'

Arthur's voice did not at first indicate surprise. It was not unusual for a stressful mission to put a pilot off his food. The cooks allowed for it, and were sympathetic to requests for late-night snacks to compensate for any missed meals. Then his tone changed as he realised that his friend, head buried in pillow, was not drowsing but weeping. 'What's up, old chap?'

With anyone else Terts would have tried to pretend that he was asleep. But Arthur was his closest friend. They had been through a lot together. They already knew most of each other's secrets. There was no reason why this one should not be confided as well. For a few seconds longer Terts's shoulders heaved and his body shuddered as he tried to bring his sick disappointment under control. Then he swung his legs off the bed and sat up, red-eyed.

'A letter from Venetia. She's breaking the engagement.'

'Someone else?'

'Yes. A patient at the convalescent hospital where she works. Just about to be discharged, medically unfit for further service. So she won't need to worry about him. It's the worrying about me that she's found so difficult to endure. What problems these civilians have to face, don't they? I'd never realised.'

His voice was bitter. All the fury which he had earlier felt for the gunners was now transferred to a faithless woman. 'What the bloody hell are we fighting for, Arthur? For king and country, all right, but for a country that's worth going home to? What's the point if there's no one there to welcome us? All those poor sods who are due to go over the top tomorrow. What are they doing it for? A few yards of mud! And how many thousands of them will die in the mud? Well, perhaps they're the lucky ones. They'll never find out that there was never any point to it. And that if they'd made it back to Blighty again, no one would have cared. Oh, Christ!'

He flung himself back on to the pillow again, turning his head away to indicate that even with his best friend he did not want to discuss the matter further.

Never before in his adult life had he succumbed to this degree of loneliness. Very often, flying solo during his training hours, he had exulted in the experience of being alone, king of the skies with the world literally at his feet. This was different. He needed comfort. He wanted to feel Venetia's arms around him. Or if not that, then the hug with which his mother had comforted him as a little boy. He had loved only two women in his life, and they had both deserted him.

A hand touched his shoulder. Arthur had not after all slipped quietly away. The touch was a brief one, as though his friend was shy about making physical contact, but was anxious that Terts should listen to what he had to say.

'It's because they're frightened, you know.'

Terts turned over on to his back. 'What do you mean, frightened?'

'I had a letter from Bridget about a month ago.' Arthur had never before mentioned anyone called Bridget. Had Terts been in a different mood he would have asked who she was and teased his friend for keeping her existence a secret. But as it was he merely listened to hear what relevance this statement had to his own misery.

'She'd been reading a page in some newspaper. I can't think how the censors let it through. Spreading alarm and despondency, to put it mildly. It set out what the life expectancy was considered to be for a young man arriving at the Western Front. A second lieutenant in the infantry was allowed six weeks, as far as I remember. The figure for an RFC pilot was three weeks. She was really upset. Of course, I wrote back straightaway to point out that the writer was talking about the new boys. Trained too fast and thrown into battle with no time to learn the tricks of survival. People like me – and you – have had months of experience in getting ourselves out of sticky situations. If we've survived that, there's no reason why we shouldn't survive months more. All the same, that article should never have been written. Think of all the women reading it, who were frightened enough already.'

'Are you trying to suggest that Venetia's telling the truth – that she's ditched me because she can't stand the strain of knowing I'm in danger? I don't believe it.'

'No. It's for herself she's frightened, not you. That would be my guess. Frightened of ending up alone. She looks round at all the young widows. All the women whose fiancés are dead. All the women who will never have either fiancés or husbands because the men who might have loved them have been killed. Girls find it very alarming, the prospect of being spinsters for the rest of their lives.'

'But she's so beautiful. She'd soon have found someone else, if ...'

'She's getting older with every year that passes. And she's probably beginning to wonder how much longer this show will go on. I'm not trying to justify that letter, Terts. Just trying to explain it, perhaps. Why she needs to grab at a husband. Any husband.'

'I ought to have married her on my last leave. I thought it wouldn't be fair. That it would be so much worse for her if she were left a widow, perhaps with a baby. I've been a bloody fool. Well, it's over. Sorry. And thanks.'

Once again Arthur's hand squeezed his shoulder. Friends, unlike women, could be trusted. A friend, thought Terts, would never let you down.

It was Arthur who came to wake him early next morning. Terts had lain awake for almost the whole of the night, tossing in bitter despair, and fell into a deep sleep only an hour before it was time to rise.

'We're three kites short this morning,' Arthur announced briskly as soon as he was sure that he had his friend's attention. 'Scott's and Douglas's, both write-offs. And your Parasol only has half an engine. God knows how you got it back yesterday. Young Spalding was due to come with me, but he's got a bad case of the jim-jams. So I've asked Cracker if I could have you as my observer instead. Today's the big day. I need someone I can trust to be quick and to get everything right first time. Okay?'

Rubbing his eyes, Terts needed a moment to work it out. It was unusual, to say the least, for an experienced pilot to act as observer on an important mission, or to fly with an officer of equal status. But it didn't take long to guess how the conversation had gone. A pilot who was tired and – for whatever reason – under stress and who could not be trusted to keep alert was a danger to his companion as well as to himself. What was it that Captain Sheffield had said a lifetime ago? 'Lack of concentration kills more pilots than the Huns do.' Major Cracknell had made a correct decision. Terts would not have trusted himself.

'Right,' he agreed, and hurried into his flying clothes. There was no further mention of Venetia.

Arthur had been allocated the BE 2c which Terts so much disliked; but on this occasion its disadvantages would not be so conspicuous, because there was to be no photography. In addition, for once there would be a fighter escort, making it less likely that the observer, sitting forward of the pilot, would need to use his own Lewis gun.

The flight was already in the air when the offensive began. The continuous barrage of the preceding week had seemed noisy enough to Terts, but the sudden thunderous explosion from all along the line pounded at his head. Even in the air, two thousand feet up, the sound was unbearable. How must it seem to the men on the ground, waiting for the order to leave the cover of their trenches and dash across the lethal area of no man's land: to be checked by barbed wire, mown down by machine gun fire, drowned in slime-filled shell craters? How many of those young lieutenants who had been promised six more weeks of life would be lying dead within the next six hours? And all of them, all the time, disorientated by this unceasing battering at their ears.

It seemed impossible that the barrage could continue for more than a few minutes. Surely there was not so much ammunition in the world. Women in munitions factories must have been labouring for months to produce what had been hurled across at the enemy in the past few minutes. But there was no more time to consider such matters, for now they were over the enemy lines.

Their duty today was artillery observation, but it was immediately clear to Terts that two of the three expected procedures could not possibly be followed. In normal circumstances an observer could be useful to an individual battery by letting out a wire aerial and using a Morse transmitter to tell the gunners exactly where their sighting shots had fallen, so that they could make any necessary corrections. Today, though, with every battery firing non-stop and so many shells falling at once, it was impossible to recognise who was firing what.

A second responsibility was to locate any enemy artillery which had moved during the night and indicate its new position. This also was almost impossible because of the cloud of smoke which by now was rising from the German lines.

Terts tried to concentrate on his third task. The infantrymen had begun their dash and it was necessary for the artillery to know exactly how far they had moved in order to keep out of range of them. To Terts, still smarting from the previous day's experience, this would have been a worthwhile job had he thought that the gunners would take any notice of his signals. But he could only do his best.

His heart beat faster in empathy with the hearts of the tiny running figures beneath him. From his bird's eye viewpoint, he could see, as they could not, that even if they were successful in breaching the wire and over-running the enemy lines, miles and miles more of this battered countryside still lay ahead to be captured. In one sense, he felt, this was like a medieval battle, fought to old-fashioned rules: the two sides taking up positions, the lack of any surprise. The difference was that in past centuries a battle might actually settle something. Crowns would be won or lost. Whole kingdoms would change hands. Today's battle, by contrast, was unlikely to decide anything at all.

Recognising that his mind was wandering, he forced himself to concentrate on the task in hand. He pushed up his oil-splattered goggles to give himself a clear view. Then, shouting back to Arthur to keep a straight course above no man's land, he prepared to fire the flares which would indicate the points at which the range needed to be lengthened if British guns were not to mow down their own men.

Intent on what was happening on the ground, he failed to see the Fokker that was diving towards them. Their escort, a Vickers FB5, intercepted the attack and at the same moment Arthur flung his own plane sideways and into a tight turn. But the Fokker was faster. Like an angry hornet it sped towards them, spitting bullets through its propellers. Above all the noise which still continued unabated on the ground, Terts was conscious of one bang that physically hurt him, as though a certain level of sound was capable of jerking his head violently backwards.

For a moment or two – he had no means of knowing how long – he was unconscious. When he opened his eyes again, the first thing he saw was a neat bullet hole through the Triplex windscreen, with a crazing of cracks around it. He began to raise his hands towards his head, to feel if there was any damage, but his muscles refused to obey the orders of his brain. He was no longer holding the Very pistol. And the gauntlet of his right glove was filled with blood. But his arm had been outside the cockpit at the moment of the attack. How could it have been wounded by a bullet which came through the windscreen? He felt stupid: unable to think of an answer.

The Vickers roared past for a second time and the Fokker spun to the earth with flames spurting from its engine, but Terts hardly noticed. Moving slowly, because his eyes were not focusing properly and his head was dizzy, he pulled off his right flying glove to discover the source of the blood. It came from his wrist. The bullet must have severed the artery.

Forcing himself to stay conscious, he fumbled to find some point in his arm which he could press to block the flow of blood, but without success. Every heartbeat was pumping his life away.

He felt no pain but only a sense of incredulity. He supposed that he was dying, but he didn't much care. Venetia would be sorry, perhaps, when she realised that she had only needed to wait another month to regain her freedom without any guilt. Or perhaps she would simply think that she had behaved sensibly, because this was what was bound to happen. But it didn't matter any longer.

A hand grabbed his shoulder. Not in comfort this time, but in anxiety. Arthur had unstrapped himself and was controlling the plane with one hand while reaching forward to turn his friend's body round and see what the damage was. That was when Terts passed out again.

When he came to, the aeroplane was stationary in a field. The sound of the barrage could still be heard, but less insistently than before. Arthur, biting his lip in concentration, was using part of a muffler to bandage a pressure pad over his wrist. Then, for good measure, he applied a tourniquet higher up the arm, checking the time by his watch.

'Where are we?' asked Terts faintly.

'Somewhere in Hunland.'

What could Arthur have been thinking of! To land behind enemy lines in the middle of a battle was definitely not to be recommended. Quite apart from the danger of being caught and possibly shot on the ground, the plane would be a sitting duck as it slowly lifted itself into the air again.

'We shan't be staying long. Now look. Press down here.' Terts felt his left glove being pulled off and his fingers pushed down on a point just above the impromptu bandage. 'Hard as you can till we get back. Keep yourself awake.'

It was a bumpy take-off over the rutted field and the spiky remnants of hedge brushed the undercarriage as they laboured to gain height. Arthur climbed steeply and then circled as he looked for landmarks to guide him home. It should have been Terts's job to navigate, but he needed all his strength to hold on to consciousness.

The noise of gunfire grew louder. 'Got it!' shouted Arthur, presumably referring to the right direction. He began to sing: 'There's a long, long trail a-winding'. The wind carried the words away and the noise of battle provided a heavy bass which overwhelmed the tune, but Terts could hear just enough to know that the purpose of the song was to keep him awake. He smiled in gratitude as he pressed, pressed, pressed. Not until he felt the bump of a less than perfect landing did he allow himself to slip away into darkness.

4

The events of July 1, 1916, brought Terts's career as an RFC pilot to an abrupt end, for he had sustained not one wound but two. Whilst the damage to his artery would have killed him quickly had it not been for Arthur's prompt action, the damage to his head represented a time bomb.

After an emergency operation to extract the bullet, the hole in his head was dressed and bandaged and he was sent back to England. So huge was the number of casualties in the battle of the Somme that the military hospitals were swamped. It was in a civilian hospital in Devon that a surgeon, well past retirement age, performed a further operation and spelled out the possible consequences of his injury.

'I'm going to cover the hole with a small steel plate,' he said. 'But ... these are bone splinters.' He jabbed his finger at an X-ray. 'We've taken out everything we dare touch. But there are two left that we can't get near without causing more harm than good. They're dangerously near the optic nerve. But as long as they stay where they are, they won't cause you any trouble.'

'And if they move?' asked Terts.

'Well, with any luck, new tissue will anchor them in place after a while. Means you need to be careful of yourself for a couple of years. No very sudden changes in pressure or direction. No diving or underwater swimming. No flying. And don't turn too many somersaults.'

'No flying!'

'You've done your bit,' the surgeon told him. 'I imagine you'll have to go before a board, but I can certify that you're medically unfit for further duties. Give you a chance to get back into civilian life. Got a job to go back to, have you? A girl?'

'No,' said Terts. Definitely no girl. And even before the war began he had been bored with his work at Bradley's. To return to his office desk now, knowing that all his friends were still risking their lives every day, would be intolerable. 'No, I want to go back. Even if I can't fly, there must be other things I can do.'

'Suit yourself. I'd have thought you'd jump at the chance. Mostly it's the other way round. A bunion on the big toe and they're pleading with me to get them out.' His tone of voice, however, was approving. 'Well, I'll give you a letter. Carry it with you all the time, and tell your pals and your commanding officer. You'll get headaches, bad headaches, for quite a time. Don't worry about that. It's quite normal. But if you feel anything going wrong with your eyes, get yourself to the nearest hospital at once. At once. And show them what I've written.'

There was more to be discussed. The satisfactory healing of his wrist. The need for convalescence before as well as after the fitting of the steel plate. It would be a good many weeks, Terts realised, before he saw Arthur again. He had had no chance, before being carried off unconscious to the field hospital, to express his gratitude. He owed his life to the decision to land behind the German lines, and Arthur had risked his own life or liberty to do it.

The letter he wrote brought an immediate reply. 'Don't be an idiot. I know you'd do the same for me.'

That would have been true enough once upon a time, but now Terts was never likely to have the opportunity to act the hero. As he lay in bed after the final operation, keeping very still, as he had been ordered, he applied his mind to the future.

What did he want to do with his life? To spend every day in an office merely in order to draw a salary which would enable him to support a wife and children had ceased to be an attractive ambition. He was not interested in trading, in making money. The events of the last few weeks had taught him a lesson about the insecurity of life, and when he died he wanted to leave something behind him to show that he had lived.

Once he set all the possibilities out in his mind it did not take long to see where his thoughts were leading him. Why should he not turn his hobby into a career? Before the war, the answer to that question had always been that photography was no way to earn steady money; it did not provide a secure career. But security, without Venetia, was no longer of any interest to him, except for as much as would serve to keep him alive and pay for film. Would his grandfather, he wondered ...

Lord Mortimer, travelling down to Devon to visit the convalescent, introduced the subject even before being asked, showing his approval of Terts's war career with a series of over-hearty pumps of the hand.

Bing's role in the war, although it had ended so tragically, had been that of a professional soldier, to whom battle represented the opportunity for accelerated promotion. His grandfather had naturally been proud of him as a defender of his country, but at the same time had taken it for granted that he would want to fight.

Richard, by contrast, under pressure from his Bradley uncles, had not volunteered to serve. Although conscription had been introduced six months earlier, he was over thirty by now, and married, which might help him to remain in London for a few months longer until all the younger unmarried men had been called up. Lord Mortimer made no secret of the scorn he felt for this attitude. For the young man who had volunteered and had been wounded in his country's service, though, there was nothing but praise.

'I've put a bit of money into the War Loan for you,' Lord Mortimer announced without preamble. 'It'll bring you in three hundred a year. To top up what they pay you at Bradley's. Having years cut out of your working life like this will set you back a bit otherwise.'

Terts's heart swelled with gratitude. For a man without property to maintain, servants to employ or a wife to keep in clothes, three hundred a year was enough to live on. His thanks were sincere. He felt it only right, though, to confess what he had recently decided.

Lord Mortimer received the news without raising any objection. He had allowed his younger daughter to marry into trade, because Bradley's in fact came very near to being a bank and its owners and employees were never expected to handle goods in the marketplace. But Terts was well aware that in his grandfather's opinion it was the mark of a gentleman to be able to live on his private income, preferably derived from the ownership of land. It would probably provide him with a secret pleasure that the Bradley side of the family expected Richard to work for his living, while the Mortimers could afford to support Terts in a less commercial way of life.

'But photography, you say? What do you do with photographs when you've taken them? Not much interest, are they, to anyone except the family?'

'There are magazines which print photographs. To show people what other parts of the world are like.'

'You wouldn't be doing this for money, though, would you?'

Terts realised that he must step cautiously. His grandfather had made him the offer of an income precisely in order that he need not ask for payment. He tried to explain that to earn an occasional fee would be the only way of discovering whether his work was considered to be up to professional standard. His earnings, if any, would be erratic and insufficient, never matching up to the salary from Bradley's that he would be relinquishing. So his appreciation of the War Loan gift was whole-hearted.

'And how would you get yourself attached to one of these magazines you were talking about?'

Terts confessed that he didn't know. 'I suppose I'd need to build up a kind of portfolio of interesting pictures, so that I could show them to an editor. I haven't had time to think about it yet. And I certainly shan't be able to do much until the war's over.'

'Going back, then, are you?'

'Yes. As soon as I can stand up without feeling dizzy.'

'Good man. I might be able to top up that War Loan a bit. The country needs the money. And if you're going to start roaming the world, you'll have expenses.'

'You're very good to me, Grandfather.'

Lord Mortimer brushed the thanks aside. 'It's not easy, you know, for us old men, watching the young men doing all the fighting and dying. Money's all I've got to offer.'

'It was good of you to come here, too. Tell me about the others. How's Aden getting on?'

'Always at his books. Doesn't seem to know what the countryside's for. A clever lad, his tutor tells me. Ought to go to university one day.'

'Are you going to send him to Croxton?'

'Not this year. He's still small for his age. Never quite caught up after being born too early. Don't want the bigger boys picking on him. Next year, perhaps.'

'And Libby?'

'Ah, Libby!' Lord Mortimer gave a deep sigh and was silent for so long that Terts, alarmed, thought he had forgotten about the question.

'Hugh's missing,' he said at last. 'Missing believed killed. Same day that you caught yours. That's why Libby didn't come with me to see you. She won't leave Kinderley in case a telegram comes. But it's too long now for any news to be good.'

'Oh, poor Libby.' And poor Hugh, who had perhaps been one of those tiny insect figures whom Terts had seen from the air scrambling out of the trenches.

'Yes. What seems to upset her specially is that she didn't manage to get herself in foal before he went back. Well, we can only wait and see. I'm staying here overnight. Not in the hospital, I don't mean, but with friends. So I'll call in again tomorrow. Look after yourself.'

'There are plenty of people to do that for me.' Terts was joking, but it was true. The twenty emergency cases who had arrived at this quiet country hospital in July were the first military patients the nurses had had in their care, and their attitude came close to hero-worship.

Two of them in particular were responsible for Terts's well-being. Nurse Bayley, whom by now he thought of as Helen, was on night duty. When the nightmares of which the surgeon had forgotten to warn him woke him in the middle of the night, it was she who sat beside his bed, gently calming him down; and who teased him next morning about the terrible language which apparently he used in his sleep. She was sweet and kind and extremely pretty. It would have been easy to fall in love with her.

Staff Nurse Trelawney, on the other hand – whom Terts never called anything but Staff – was a stand-no-nonsense woman who reminded him of the Matron at Croxton. All rules were to be kept and there must be no deviation from standards of tidiness. Beneath her brisk efficiency, however, Terts recognised a heart that dared not succumb to sympathy in case distress should make her unfit to help her patients. It would have been easy to fall in love with Staff as well, although probably a good deal more difficult to persuade her to fall in love with him.

Terts did not in fact allow himself to fall in love with either. He had learned his lesson as far as girls were concerned. To tie himself down emotionally to someone who might at any moment abandon him was to put the rest of his life at risk. It gave him a certain satisfaction to consider that Venetia was probably making a great mistake.

The relationship between nurse and patient, he realised now, was an unnatural one. It was easy to see how romantic feelings might grow, but the men and women involved were likely to discover each other to be very different people when it came to spending the rest of their lives together. Libby had taken a more courageous path, marrying the man whom she knew and loved, and accepting the risk of losing him.

Poor Libby. Terts promised himself that next time the surgeon came round, he must ask if he could spend a week of convalescent leave with his sister. And after that it would be time to return to the squadron.

5

There was something different about Arthur. In the space of a few weeks he had somehow ceased to be a young man, although he was only twenty. Terts, on his first day back at the aerodrome, watched from the doorway of the mess as his friend climbed wearily out of the cockpit and walked across the tarmac, pulling off his flying gloves. He looked tired and grim, very different from the fresh-faced and light-hearted schoolboy whom Terts had first encountered two years earlier.

Probably the change was not as dramatic as it seemed. It might already have begun, too imperceptibly to be noticed, while the two men were seeing each other every day. It must be the ten-week separation which suddenly allowed Terts to see Arthur as he was now and not as he had been at the beginning of the war.

He took a step forward. Arthur looked up and the two men ran towards each other – although when they met, a handshake was the best they could do to indicate pleasure in the reunion.

'Good to see you back,' exclaimed Arthur. 'Cracker warned us to expect you. Grounded, though, he said.'

'Fraid so. How are things here?'

'Not good.' The smile left Arthur's face. 'Richthofen and Boelcke are both operating in this sector now, and they seem to run rings round our escorts. We've lost five men in the past month. In fact, I'm the only one of our batch still flying. And the new boys are keen enough, but they simply haven't got the flying hours behind them. Still –' Once again his face was lit by a grin. 'I'm to get my leave at last. I was due for it in July, but of course it was cancelled. Another ten days to go and then ...!'

'I wish you could have had it earlier. You could have stayed with me at Kinderley.' Terts knew that Arthur's aunt, who had brought him up, had died soon after he was posted to the Front.

'Another time, perhaps. Let's go for a stroll.' He pulled off his helmet and the two men walked together towards the perimeter of the aerodrome. 'I've got all my pay saved up. I can afford a few days on the town. And I'm going to meet Bridget at last.'

'Bridget?' Terts remembered that the name had been mentioned once before, when Arthur was attempting to console him for his broken engagement. He had been too sorry for himself at the time to ask questions, but now it was clear that curiosity would be welcomed.

'My fiancée.'

'What! How can you be engaged if you haven't met her yet?'

'I proposed by post.'

'But how –?' They reached the edge of what had once been a wood, and sat down on the trunk of one of the many trees which had been felled by shellfire.

'Seven or eight months ago, do you remember, we got a parcel of comforts. Socks and scarves, mostly. I was allocated a pair of socks, and inside one of them was a letter and a photograph from the girl who'd knitted them.' Arthur felt in his breast pocket, drew out a wallet and extracted a snapshot which he handed across.

Terts studied it with interest. It had not been very sharply focused to start with, and by now was creased by much handling. Unusually, the girl had chosen to be photographed in profile, so that she looked handsome rather than pretty; but certainly she was attractive in a slightly old-fashioned way.

'I wrote to thank her, of course, and she wrote back and, well, we've been corresponding ever since. I feel I know all about her. We like the same things. She's a great reader. And you know yourself, when things get grim out here, you need to know that there's someone special. Someone to go home to when it's all over. So I asked her if she'd marry me one day and she said she would.'

Terts realised that it would be unkind to express too strongly his feeling that Arthur was taking a grave risk, but no doubt his silence spoke for him.

'If it turns out to be obviously wrong we shall both know it and there'll be no harm done. But this last couple of months, flying six hours every day and no one like you to talk to and so many deaths and ... and ...' Without warning Arthur broke down, burying his head in his hands for a few moments. At last he let out a deep breath and made an attempt at a smile. 'It's been hard,' he said. 'And I don't see how it's ever going to end. I needed something. Someone.'

'Yes, of course.' The two men sat in silence for a little while. But Terts had a different subject to raise.

'I wrote in my first letter, but I need to say it face to face as well. I know what a risk you were taking when you brought the kite down behind the Hun lines that day. And I know that if you hadn't, I'd have been dead from loss of blood before we got back here. Thanks.'

'As I said in my own letter, I know you'd have done the same for me. There has to be somebody one can count on.' Arthur was smiling again, as apparently light-hearted as though the battle were not still raging. They strolled, chatting, back towards the base.

Terts looked at his watch. 'I'm due to report to the Cracker in ten minutes. To sort out what he can do with a pilot who isn't allowed to fly.'

The answer, it transpired when his commanding officer had welcomed him back, was that he would work at Wing HQ on the interpretation of reconnaissance photographs: a task for which he was well qualified. It was not, however, work which gave him much satisfaction. He missed the camaraderie of the pilots' mess and, of course, the excitement of flying.

To add interest to his work he tried to introduce an idea with which he had been experimenting during his convalescence. It involved photographing hand-drawn maps of the enemy lines so that negatives taken from the air could be fixed above them, with a light behind, making it easier to note any changes. But the task of matching the scales of the two sets proved to be beyond the capabilities of men who had never been trained to do much more than pull the string of a fixed camera. He was back at the aerodrome, reporting failure in this self-imposed exercise and pressing the advantages of training observers to use hand-held cameras, on the day that Arthur returned from his leave.

Oh, yes, he had had a ripping time. Theatres, night clubs, dinners. The comfort of sleeping in hotel beds. The bliss of waking in the morning with the knowledge that the war was miles away and he could go back to sleep again. He had brought back some new gramophone records from the shows. Terts must stay to have dinner in the mess and hear some of them afterwards.

'And what about Bridget?' asked Terts when this flow of enthusiasm came to an end. 'Have you become a married man since I last saw you?'

'Married? Heavens, no. What made you think –? I only had ten days.'

'I thought there was some sort of special licence you could get.'

'Well, perhaps, yes. But it's not something to rush into, is it? She's a very nice woman. Very good company. And kind. She let me visit her one day at the school where she teaches, and she was marvellous with the children.'

'But?'

'There isn't a but. It's just a question of ... well, not rushing things. If she gets married, for example, she has to resign from her employment. I hadn't realised that. It's a big thing – and what would be the point when I'm still out here?'

It was clear to Terts that the meeting had in some way been a disappointment, but he accepted that this was too private a matter to be discussed even between close friends. Nevertheless, he could not refrain from sounding a note of warning.

'Do you remember,' he said cautiously, 'when I got that letter from Venetia? You told the Cracker that I wasn't fit to fly, didn't you? Unable to concentrate, I expect you said – and you were quite right. Don't you think perhaps you ought to have a couple of days to ... to get back into routine. That sort of thing.'

'The quickest way to get back into routine is to take a kite up! Now, how about these records? Will you stay?'

'Yes, of course.' Terts did his best to enjoy the evening, singing along with the others to the tunes of the newest shows, *Chu Chin Chow* and *The Bing Boys*. But his heart was heavy. There was an instinct which many fighting men shared, of guessing who was likely to be the next casualty within their group. It would be the man who, while not wishing to die, had briefly relaxed his determination to remain alive.

His instinct was right. Afterwards, Terts was to ask himself many times whether he could have done more to keep his friend on the ground for a day or two longer. On October 14, 1916, Baron von Richthofen notched up yet another kill. Arthur Lennox did not return from patrol.

6

Six weeks after Arthur's death Terts was summoned to the chateau near St Omer in which the GOC had his headquarters. Spread out on a table in front of the Major-General were half a dozen blown-up photographs.

'I'm told you sent me these?'

'Yes, sir.'

'Take them all yourself, did you?'

'No, sir.' Terts pointed at three clear aerial views of the battlefield. 'I took these three a few months ago, using a hand-held camera of my own. That meant I could focus properly. These other three, which are more difficult to interpret, were taken in the normal way by fixed cameras using plates. There's quite a contrast in sharpness of detail.'

'Indeed yes. There's a danger, of course, of a loose camera falling into the wrong hands.'

'All the enemy would discover would be pictures of its own lines.' Terts could tell that the objection was not a serious one.

'Yes, well. I'm sending you back to England, Captain Bradley. As Training Officer (Photography). This is a new post. We've got plenty of chaps capable of teaching men to fly, but it looks as though the new recruits need to know rather more about the use of cameras. My ADC will give you your

Orders. Sign off from your squadron before you go. You may take five days' leave before reporting in.'

'Yes, sir. Thank you, sir.'

Orders were to be obeyed, so it didn't make any difference whether Terts was pleased or disappointed to be sent home; but as he hitched a lift to the aerodrome he tried to decide what his feelings were. On the whole, he was pleased. He would miss the excitement of battle, the feeling that he was doing his bit – but he had in any case lost most of that sense of shared participation since being wounded. And all the men with whom he had trained were by now dead or invalided out. Yes, it was probably time to go, while he still had his life and all of his body except for a small piece of skull.

Back at the aerodrome, Major Cracknell made all the appropriate remarks before putting forward a request.

'You were a friend of Captain Lennox. There's a problem about his effects. I wrote, naturally, to his next-of-kin, an aunt. But the letter's been returned, Not Known.'

'She died, sir,' Terts told him. 'Quite soon after he enlisted. He didn't have any other relatives. But there was a fiancée.'

'Do you know her address?'

Terts shook his head. 'There might be letters, though.' There would certainly be letters. He could guess what he was expected to say next. 'Would you like me to call on her, sir?'

'Well, since you're going back to England in any case. You could hand his things over in person.'

It was not a duty which offered any pleasure. But Terts had often thought what an appalling shock it must be for the parents or wife of a dead man to receive through the post the bundle of miscellaneous objects which was all that remained to remind them of their loved one. It had even been known for the parcel to contain the bloodstained, bullet-ripped uniform in which he had been killed. Reluctantly he nodded his head and made it his first task when he arrived in England. A schoolteacher would not be working on a Saturday afternoon.

The address was that of a semi-detached house in a south London suburb. England by the end of 1916 was a shabby country as well as a hungry one, but there was a neatness about the front garden of 3, Jubilee Street that spoke of standards being upheld. Terts rang the bell. It was only at that moment that an appalling thought presented itself to him. Perhaps she didn't even know that her fiancée had been killed? But he was allowed no time to consider how to deal with that possibility, for the door was already being opened.

'Is Miss Bridget Adams at home?' he enquired.

'I'm Miss Adams.'

'Oh!' Arthur's photograph had shown a girl who appeared to be aged about twenty, but this woman was surely several years older. Perhaps it was just that she was strained and unhappy, and there was reason enough for that. She was not looking straight at Terts. Instead she had turned her face in profile – just as in the photograph – so that she appeared to be looking over his shoulder at a house further up the road. 'My name's Bradley,' he said. 'A friend of Arthur's. Had you heard ...?'

There was a long pause before she said, 'Won't you please come in, Captain Bradley?' She led him into the sitting room and indicated a chair. 'Yes, I know that he's dead. I read the lists in the papers every day. I haven't told my parents yet, though. They're out at the moment. If they come back ...'

'I understand,' said Terts politely. He understood that he was not to reveal the purpose of his visit to them, but not why she should wish to keep the matter a secret in the first place. There was a second long pause.

'Arthur used to write about his friends and the other men in the squadron using initials,' she said at last. 'S and D were both friends of his, but they were killed. I think you must be T.'

'Yes, that's right. T.' For some reason he was reluctant to tell her what the T stood for. There was something about the situation which made him uneasy, and he was anxious to keep at a formal distance from her.

'Arthur told me a lot about you.' She was still refusing to look directly at him. Was there something wrong with the other side of her face? He determined that he would see it before he left, but for the moment was content to express his condolences and to say how much he missed his friend.

'I was asked to bring you his personal effects,' he said when that part of the stilted conversation was over. He had left most of his kit in the left luggage office at Victoria, bringing with him only a small suitcase. Now, rising to his feet, he moved quickly to one side before setting this down on a table. She had no time to turn away. On the left side of her face was a large purplish-red lupus. He looked directly at her and saw that her eyes were beginning to flood with tears. She put a handkerchief up to dab at them, allowing it to cover her cheek.

'It's always a bad moment, seeing these personal things,' said Terts, pretending that he had noticed nothing unusual as he laid out the Bible, the cigarette case, the bundle of letters, the shaving kit, and one of Arthur's tunics on to which was sewn the Wings badge of which he was so proud.

'You didn't say anything. About my face.' She was not looking down at the table. 'That's nice of you. It was a shock to Arthur.'

'Hadn't you told him? Before you met, I mean.'

Sadly she shook her head. 'I didn't really expect that we *would* ever meet. I read that article about how dangerous it was being a pilot. It seemed to me he was certain to be killed. And if he had pleasure writing to me and getting my letters before that, well, I'd be glad. And of course, from my point of view ... I'd never had a young man. I didn't think I ever would. It was hard for me, when everyone else had someone at the front. Because I was writing to Arthur, I could talk about him as if ... as if ...'

She broke down in tears, but Terts felt little sympathy. It was not just the disfigurement that she had concealed, but her age. The photograph she had sent to his friend was a lie. And it must have been the discovery of her deception which had so greatly unsettled Arthur as he wondered how far he was committed to marrying her. It would not be too strong a statement to say that by distracting his concentration she was responsible for his death. But of course Terts could not possibly go as far as to suggest that.

'When did he find out?' he asked.

'On the first evening of his leave, I met him in the West End. For the theatre. If I put powder on, it covers the mark up for a little while. I wore a hat with a veil. And he was very shy. He didn't even kiss me at first. But after the theatre, he ... well, he was excited and I was as well. I went back to his hotel. I've never done anything like it before. I told him I didn't want the light on. But of course, next morning, when he woke up ... Oh, I know it was stupid. But I felt sure he liked me from reading my letters, and I hoped that if we could just have one night together he'd realise that I was no different from other women really and then it would be all right. My mother always says that she doesn't notice it any more. Oh, I've been a fool! But you feel so lonely, knowing that people won't even look at you and that you're a sort of freak. And now I'm pregnant and I don't know what to do.'

'What!' Terts, with no more words of comfort to offer, had been closing his suitcase, on the point of leaving.

'I thought nothing could happen the first time. And anyway, I hoped that Arthur was going to marry me, so it wouldn't matter whatever happened. He could have got a special licence, but he didn't. I shall lose my position at the school, and my father will turn me out of the house. His views are very strict. I've got nowhere to go and no money and ... and ... What can I do, Captain Bradley?'

She abandoned any attempt to check her tears and began to sob uncontrollably. Terts, unable to offer any comfort, watched her uneasily.

'You can't be sure yet, can you? It's only six weeks ...'

'Eight. I've missed twice.'

Terts calculated the time in his head. Yes, she must be right. It was almost seven weeks since Arthur's death, and there was the period of his leave before that.

'Aren't there ways of getting rid of –'

'Oh, I couldn't do that!' she exclaimed. 'It would be a sin. And I wanted a baby. I still want a baby. To have something of Arthur. And to be like other women. But of course I wanted it to be born in marriage. He would have married me in the end, I'm sure of it. He did say in his letters ... I would have made him a good wife. I could have loved him and cared for him. If only –' She shook her head sadly. There was no comfort to be found in 'if only'.

Yes, he thought, probably Arthur would have married her when he found out, because he was a decent chap and that was what decent chaps did. That wouldn't necessarily have meant that he would have wanted to, or that he would have had any expectation of the marriage being a happy one. No wonder he had looked so disturbed on his return from that leave. She had set out to catch herself a husband, and it was only Baron von Richthofen who had cheated her out of her prize.

'I gather you haven't told your parents yet?' he said.

'I haven't told anyone except Father Kelly, in confession. I can't ever tell them. They won't want anything more to do with me.'

'I'm sure they'd come round in the end. It would be their grandchild, after all.'

She shook her head. 'They'd feel disgraced in front of all their friends. My father will turn me out before anyone can guess.'

'Couldn't you pretend, then, Miss Adams? I take it that somewhere you've got a letter proposing marriage? Couldn't you pretend that it did actually take place during that leave?'

Once again she shook her head. 'My father would want to see the certificate. He'd be on to the War Office straightaway, you see, demanding to know why I wasn't getting a pension. They'd ask for documents and I wouldn't have them, but he'd never give up until they told him the truth. He's very determined, my father.'

'It's difficult for you, I can see that.' Terts stood up. It was her problem, not his, and she was going to cry again.

In that last respect he was wrong. As she shook hands and said goodbye, she managed to control her unhappiness. What was more, she looked him full in the face instead of persisting in her earlier attempts to conceal the lupus.

This small act of courage was not, however, enough to make him warm to her. She was a disfigured thirty-year-old spinster who had tried to trap his friend into marriage. It served her right if the attempt had backfired on her. All the same, Terts found it more difficult than he expected to put her problem out of his mind. For more than six months her letters had made Arthur happy. And the child she was carrying was Arthur's child. It was not as easy as he had hoped simply to walk away.

He had intended to travel on to Kinderley that night, but no one there would be expecting him, for in normal circumstances he would have had to wait much longer than this for leave. He booked himself into a hotel and began to look for company.

From his season as Libby's escort he was acquainted with all the debutantes of her season. The first one he tried, Muriel, was delighted to have dinner with him. He chose a restaurant where they could dance, and marvelled at the new freedom which girls were enjoying these days.

'When I remember how rigorously I was vetted and how strictly you were all chaperoned!' he exclaimed as they returned to their table after a vigorous valeta.

'Things have certainly changed,' she agreed. 'Anything goes nowadays. Well, almost anything.'

'Are there ever any, shall we say, unfortunate accidents in your set?' he asked, trying to keep his voice casual.

'Well, most of us are married.' More than three years had passed since the Season in which he had participated. All the young women would be twenty-one by now. 'As for the others, if anything were to go wrong there'd be jolly swift action taken. A baby without a father is social death. You can imagine.'

'What sort of swift action?'

'Oh, Tertsy darling, have you been getting a girl into trouble? No reason why you shouldn't make an honest woman of her, is there? Now that Venetia has traded her hopes of Kinderley for the reality of a draughty castle in Scotland.'

'She's married already, is she?'

'She certainly is. That's one kind of swift action.'

'Are you saying –?'

'My lips are sealed. But it wouldn't come as *too* much of a surprise to any of us if the first fruit of the marriage should prove to be a seven-month baby.'

Terts felt his breath snatched away by anger. How dare she! In spite of his disappointment at the time, he had respected Venetia for her refusal to sleep with him before they were married; and during all their months of separation it had helped him to believe, as a result of that refusal, that she would certainly not lower her standards with anyone else. Yet all the time, if Muriel's hints were to be believed ... Well, he was well rid of her. He didn't care where she was now, or with whom.

'My question had nothing to do with me personally,' he said. 'I've got a friend who needs to know. And marriage isn't a possibility in this case. What about the other kinds of swift action?'

She didn't believe his mention of a friend. People who enquired about problems like this always pretended that they were asking on behalf of a friend. He wouldn't have believed it himself from anyone else. But it was probably just because she didn't believe him that she did her best to be helpful.

'I can send you an address if you like,' she promised. 'I'd have to get it from someone else. I've never needed that sort of thing, thank God. You'd need to bustle your lady friend in as soon as possible, otherwise I believe it can get rather grim. And you must promise not to sneak. It's all thoroughly illegal, of course.'

'I don't think that's the sort of solution they're looking for either, my friends.'

'They may be less choosy when panic sets in. Come on, let's dance again.'

Even the style of dancing had changed with the coming of war. Muriel's body was pressed up close to his, making it easy for them to move fluidly to the music, as though they were one person. When he looked down, he could see her breasts swelling into her low-cut dress. Her head rested against his shoulder as she hummed the music to which they were dancing. She was telling him that she was available. Her fiancé, he knew, had been killed in the first month of the war and perhaps she had regretted ever since then the code of behaviour which at that time had insisted that a woman must be a virgin on her wedding day: the code that Venetia had apparently already discarded.

The war had changed more than merely a few rules of etiquette. Men whose future lives might be measured only in weeks were impatient for love; and the women they loved were anxious to give them whatever they wanted. It was not surprising that moral standards had slipped. *Carpe diem* was the order of the day. Terts was a young man made handsome by his uniform, and Muriel, infected by the mood of the times, would give him a good leave if that was what he wanted.

With their bodies so close together it was impossible for him to pretend that he was not aroused. He had not realised until now how much he needed a woman. But not this woman: not one of Libby's friends. At the end of the evening he kept the taxi waiting as he saw her up the steps to her mother's front door. She raised her eyebrows slightly when he turned down the invitation to come in, but did not try to persuade him. Anything goes.

Where Terts went was back to the West End, to Soho. He followed the first girl who smiled at him back to her room and flung himself on her almost before she had concluded her perfunctory routine of undressing. Afterwards, he lay for a few minutes without moving, almost light-headed with physical relief. In the old days, the days of peace, the tart would have hustled him straight out, but it was not only society debutantes who felt a softness towards young officers in uniform. The girl pulled on a robe, lit a cigarette and sat down beside the bed as though aware that he wanted something else for his money.

'Do you – any of you – ever get caught with a baby?' he asked at last as he began to dress himself.

'All of us, darling, in the end.'

'Has it happened to you?'

'Once.'

'So what did you do? I really want to know.'

'There was a mother and baby home. Run by nuns. I thought nuns would be kind. But it wasn't like that. More like prison, wasn't it? They didn't ask for money, though, so ...'

'So what happened to the baby?'

'Never saw it, darling. Heard it cry once, that's all. Never even knew whether it was a boy or girl. That was the condition of being in the home, to let the baby go for adoption. They said it would make it worse if I saw it.'

'Do you ever think about it?'

'I have nightmares, don't I? Wondering if people are being kind to him. It felt like a little boy, somehow. He'd be four by now, wouldn't he?' She slipped her robe off and began to dress again. 'But it wouldn't be any good bringing him up in a place like this, and I don't know anything else. I'd like to have met the other people though, to be sure they were kind. I have to say to myself, don't I, they must have wanted a baby very much. I expect he has a better life. Well, of course he does. But it would have been nice to know.'

That was the answer, then, thought Terts as he paid the girl and walked back to the hotel. Bridget would have to disappear from her home and her work for a few months. Perhaps her parents would be supportive after all if local opinion was the only thing that worried them. As soon as the baby had been born and adopted she would be able to return home as though nothing had happened. Terts himself would offer to put up the money for her period of seclusion if she failed to find the kind of free berth that the prostitute had spoken of. He would be able to afford it when his new income from the War Loan stock started to come through; and making sure that Arthur's child was born safely and given a happy home would be a fitting memorial to his friend. It was the least he could do.

That thought sent him contentedly to sleep at the end of a long and tiring day. It was only towards the end of a luxurious lie-in next morning that a sense of unease began to trouble him. He ought not to be thinking in terms of the least he could do for the man who had saved his life, but rather the most.

7

It was three o'clock on Sunday afternoon when Terts returned to 3, Jubilee Street and rang the bell. Once again it was Bridget who opened the door; but on this occasion she looked alarmed when she saw who her visitor was. Perhaps, if her parents were at home, she could not trust him to back up whatever story she had pitched to them.

'Would you care to take a walk, Miss Adams?'

'That would be very nice, yes. I'll just put my hat and coat on.'

She was more smartly dressed today; presumably wearing her Sunday best. Not knowing the neighbourhood, Terts left her to suggest the direction of the walk. She led him to what had once been a spacious recreation park. There was still a small play area for children, but most of the land had been turned into vegetable allotments. They walked in silence round the edge of the ground, coming to a halt beside a pond in which a few small children were sailing boats.

'Shall we sit down?' Terts waited until she had made herself comfortable on a long wooden seat. She chose the very end of it, so that he had no choice but to settle himself on her good side.

'I'd like to ask you two questions,' he said. 'Have you considered the possibility of giving the baby up for adoption as soon as it's born? And going away somewhere before that, so that no one would know?'

'Yes, of course I've considered it. It's the usual thing, isn't it? But even though I didn't intend it, I want the baby. I want someone of my own to love and to love me, and there's never likely to be anyone else. Besides, if I gave it away, I should never know whether he, she was having a happy life. It's not just my child, it's Arthur's as well. I have the responsibility to look after it myself.'

'Yes. Well. I understand –' he could not remember whether it was Arthur who had told him or Bridget himself '– I understand that you are expected to resign your post as a teacher on marriage.'

'Yes.'

'So your position is that if you marry you lose your job, and if you don't marry you lose your father's love and support.'

'And my reputation. That's right, yes.'

'Which of the two is the more important to you, Miss Adams? If you had to choose between your job and a marriage certificate, which would you choose?'

'The certificate.' The answer came without hesitation. 'Because I could always get some kind of war work, and then after the war I could move away and pretend ... But I haven't got that choice, have I?'

'I'm about to give it to you. If it would be useful to you, I would be prepared to go through a ceremony of marriage with you.'

How pompous he sounded! How different this was from the passionate eagerness with which he had begged Venetia to be his wife! But Bridget had turned to look at him with an expression which revealed not just astonishment but an excitement which alarmed him.

'Before you say anything, Miss Adams, there are several things that I'd like to make clear.' He had spent a confused hour already that day making them clear to himself; wondering whether he was being a complete idiot.

'Arthur was my closest friend. He saved my life once. When I tried to thank him, he said that he knew I'd do the same for him if he ever needed me. Well, there's nothing I can do for him now. But I could prevent his child from having to live with the label of illegitimacy round his neck.'

He did not intend to pretend even for a moment that he was making the offer for Bridget's own sake. He still considered her deceptions to have been the indirect cause of Arthur's death, and beneath the formality of his words there was a bitter anger.

'I'm not offering to be your husband in any way except that of words on paper. I should not consummate the marriage. I should not see you again after the ceremony. Until the end of the war you would have an automatic entitlement to part of my pay, and if I were to be killed you would get a pension – but that's not very likely, since I'm no longer at the front line. But you wouldn't get *me*. I'm suggesting this only in the hope that it will reconcile your mother and father to the prospect of becoming grandparents.'

'Yes. Yes, it would do that. You're very kind, Captain Bradley. Unbelievably kind. But have you thought about yourself? You might want to marry someone else one day.'

'That's my business. But it won't happen. You're the one who's more likely –'

She gave a short, bitter laugh. 'When this is over, how many men will be left to look for wives? Not enough for all the women who'll be waiting. So they'll be able to choose the prettiest ones, the ones unencumbered with children. No one's likely to come courting me.'

'So?'

'So I accept your very generous offer, Captain Bradley. On your terms. I won't bother you afterwards in any way. Although if you should ever feel –'

'No!' He spoke more vehemently than was perhaps polite. 'I've no wish to tie myself down ... to live with a woman.'

That way of phrasing it made it sound almost as though he might wish to live with a man, which was not at all the impression he had intended to give. But probably she did not even know that there were men of that sort. Or, if she did, it might make the strangeness of the arrangement more understandable.

'I'll get a special licence,' he told her. 'Are you on the telephone?'

'No.'

'Then I'll send a telegram with the time and the place.'

'Shouldn't it be in my own church? I'm sure Father Kelly would say –'

'No.' Although Terts did not share his grandfather's intolerant views about Jews and Roman Catholics, he was not prepared to put himself out for any Father Kelly. 'I've no time for that sort of thing. It'll be a register office. And I'll book a hotel room for you for the night. So that your parents won't be too surprised when you announce your news.'

There was no more argument, but she had a shy question to ask.

'Will you tell me your Christian name, Captain Bradley?'

Some of his anger and tension fell away now that the die was cast, and he was able to laugh in a friendly way.

'Yes, you certainly ought to know that. Mortimer.' It was the name on his papers. Although his friends called him Terts, Bridget Adams was not a friend. 'But if you've spoken to your parents about Arthur, you can use that name if you like. It would be easy enough to pretend that you don't like the name Mortimer. I can't stand it myself. I expect you could make up some romantic tomfool story. King Arthur and his knights. Something to do with that.'

'I suppose –' The question came hesitantly. 'I suppose you couldn't pretend to be Arthur altogether? Arthur Lennox. So that the baby could have his real name.'

'And how would you explain the fact that his marriage certificate was dated eight weeks later than his death certificate?' He was angry again. She was dishonest. Hoping for Arthur's pension, perhaps, and too stupid to realise that checks would be made. He stood up, ready to leave her.

'After the ceremony you can say whatever you like. Nothing to do with me. Look after the baby, that's all I ask of you. He's Arthur's immortality.'

She faced him with as much courage as on the previous afternoon, no longer trying to conceal her cheek.

'Did you love him – Arthur, I mean? Like Oscar Wilde? That sort of thing?'

So she was more sophisticated than he had expected. Well, she was an educated woman. And Arthur had said that her letters were full of the books she had read.

'Not like Oscar Wilde: not at all. But I loved him, yes.' Although that statement was misleading, it might provide her with a reason to accept without humiliation the fact that he would be marrying her and rejecting her in the same instant. 'I'll see you to your door,' he said.

'There's no need.' She held out her hand. 'Thank you very much, Captain Bradley. I can tell that you think I tried to trap Arthur, but it wasn't like that. I loved him, I really loved him because of his letters. But I do realise ...' She gave a sad shrug of her shoulders. 'It isn't easy for a woman, being ugly.'

'How long ago was the photograph taken, that you sent him?' Terts asked.

Her face flushed, but she answered honestly. 'Nine years. When I was twenty-one.'

'I'll take a new one. Your parents will want one. And your child, when he grows up.'

Her expression was doubtful, but already he was pulling from his pocket the small folding Kodak camera that he carried with him everywhere.

'Stand over here.' He decided to take four shots from different positions. 'No, don't move.' Automatically she was trying to keep her good side towards him but he was determined that the record would be a true one. Perhaps she would be surprised when she found that in black and white the almost full-face picture would show the lupus as little more than a shadow which might have been thrown by her hat. For the last one he tempted a smile out of her. 'Pretend that this is your wedding day,' he said.

Her lips parted and her eyes brightened in excitement, as though this was the first moment in which she could believe that the wedding would really happen. As he took the photograph he realised that he had captured not perhaps happiness itself but the expectation of happiness. She would be pleased with this picture, he thought to himself as he folded up the camera. When she was an old lady she would look at it and remember a moment in her youth when she had managed to escape from self-disgust.

The picture would be his wedding present to her; and he would also post to her, next time he was at Kinderley, a snapshot of Arthur standing beside an Avro after his first solo flight and another more formal photograph which showed the whole group of young men just after they had been awarded their Wings. Arthur's child must be allowed to see his father; and Terts had other prints that he could keep for himself.

It looked as though he would not be able to get to Kinderley during this short leave, though. There was the special licence to be obtained, and a ring must be bought, and then the ceremony itself.

That night he once again lay awake for several hours. Had he made a ghastly mistake? Well, if he had, it was too late to change his mind now. And in any case his self-questioning brought him back to the same conclusion. He was never likely to be short of female company if he wished for it.

It had been one of the surprises of Libby's season as a debutante and the year that followed it: the only half-secret lives of society women. Lord Mortimer, living quietly on his own estate and content with country pursuits, had never been part of society in the fashionable sense, so that Terts had found himself with almost as much to learn as Libby.

One of his earliest discoveries was that it was taken for granted that a husband would not be faithful to his wife for more than the first year or two of marriage. But there were strict rules about where he might look for his extra-marital excitements. Unmarried girls were out of bounds and so were young married women until they had provided their husbands with at least two heirs. What nobody had ever explicitly acknowledged was the logical consequence of this: that for every unfaithful husband there must be an unfaithful wife. If she were to be found out, the consequences would be disastrous for her. But she was expected to be discreet, and as long as there was no public knowledge of what was going on there was likely to be a high degree of husbandly complaisance. Terts himself had agreed with Venetia in the first rapture of their engagement that they would never behave in such a way; but he felt sure by now that her promise would not have been kept.

Bridget had been right to point out that after the carnage of the past two and a half years there would be a great many women who could never hope for a man of their own; and amongst those who had found one, there would be widows and bereaved fiancées. Although Terts was not handsome as Arthur had been handsome, he knew that women found him attractive.

At the moment, no doubt, it was the uniform which drew them. But he had discovered much earlier, when he was photographing the members of Venetia's set, that there was a sense in which girls were seduced by a camera. As they put themselves on display, their smiles proclaiming the sense that they were looking their best, some of their excitement attached itself to the man behind the camera. They wanted to be approved of; they wanted to please him. He could earn a living, if he chose, by photographing beautiful women; and perhaps he would indeed choose to do that.

But beautiful women could not be trusted. Beautiful women, knowing their power, would always be liable to discard one catch in favour of a better one. Never again, he had already promised himself, would he allow himself to be tied down to one particular woman. Never again would he allow himself to be hurt as Venetia had hurt him. A form of marriage with Bridget Adams would make it impossible for him even to consider marrying anyone else. And so by tying himself down legally, he would in practice ensure his own freedom. Yes, although his motives for the offer had been unselfish, even from his own point of view he had taken the right decision.

Part Four

Eye-Openers

1

As a man who had been one of the earliest to volunteer and an instructor whose instructions were no longer needed, Terts was demobilised with exceptional promptness at the end of the war and so was able to spend the Christmas of 1918 at Kinderley. It proved to be a sombre celebration.

Lord Mortimer, now eighty-three years old, had been sustained during the war years by his determination to support the families of all the men who had left his estates to fight, and at the same time to grow more food on his land in spite of the shortage of labour. Now, although the support and the food were needed more than ever, he seemed abruptly to have lost all his energy. In his sixties and seventies his body had been on the plump side, whilst the healthy colour of a man who spent much of his life out of doors had been deepened by a taste for good wines and spirits. But by 1918 his skin had paled into greyness and the clothes that he did not bother to send to his tailor for alteration hung loosely from his stooping shoulders.

It was not only his body that was wasting away. Depression had eaten into his normal good spirits. He devoted most of Terts's first evening at home to a gloomy recital of the bereavements suffered by all his friends.

And not only his friends. By this time it was known for certain that one of his own family would never return to Kinderley. Two years after the defenders of Kut were marched away by the Turks on the long journey to Antalya, the War Office had written to confirm that Bing was amongst the many who never arrived at the prison camp. Weakened by starvation and further exhausted by the heat and inhumane conditions of the exodus, during which no clean water was supplied for drinking, he had collapsed on the way and was left behind to die beneath the burning sun.

Aden, whose fifteenth birthday was celebrated on Boxing Day, should have provided livelier company. But he was a quiet boy, still small for his age and tending to plumpness, with no interest in parties or country sports. He borrowed book after book from his grandfather's library and was always to be found reading.

Terts had little in common with him. The thirteen-year gap in their ages would have been enough in itself to prevent the two brothers from being close, and the war years had aged Terts while hardly affecting Aden at all. Besides this, Terts would never be able to forget what had happened on the traumatic day of Aden's birth. His own unthinking action had killed his father, brought his younger brother too soon into the world and indirectly caused his mother's early death. He would have preferred not to be reminded of it by the existence of this bespectacled and precociously clever boy.

Like his brothers Aden had been sent to Croxton, but was outshining all three of them by the speed of his removes up the school. 'Don't know where the boy gets his brains from,' commented Lord Mortimer with a mixture of admiration and disapproval in his voice as he passed on the end-of-term report for Terts to read. For him it was more important to be a gentleman than a scholar.

To Libby the coming of peace was not exactly an anti-climax, but neither did it bring the relief and joy which might have been expected. For three of the wartime years she had undertaken the task of assisting the village schoolmistress – and had very much enjoyed the work. But the schoolmaster she replaced had already returned, one-armed, to take up his duties again, leaving her only with domestic responsibilities.

These were demanding enough. In 1914 she had been forced within a very short time to change from a happy and carefree young bride to the mistress of a large house which no longer had all the staff needed to run it. As her grandfather's representative she had for four years been visiting the sick and hungry on his estate, carrying food and other small comforts. It was a part she played well, but its effect was to make her somehow middle-aged. Terts could tell that she was finding it hard to make plans for the rest of her life, but it seemed to him that the first step must be for her to realise that she was still a young woman.

Kinderley had always been a cold house. Its occupants were accustomed to hurry from one pool of warmth to another along chilly corridors or across the icy hall, and Libby was rarely to be seen without a warm shawl round her shoulders. In the small morning room which she had adapted to become her private sitting room, however, a log fire burned all day, and Terts was glad of the invitation to share it. It was here, on the day after Aden's birthday, that he enquired about her plans.

'I shall stay here as long as Grandfather needs me,' she told him. 'The house that Hugh and I had hoped to live in was never built, so I didn't have time to think of Trelowen as home. And although Hugh's family are all very kind whenever I visit them, I don't really belong. If I'd had a child it would have been different. But as it is, it's almost as though I'd never been married at all.'

'Why don't you live in London for a bit? Get back into society. You could stay with Richard. You're only twenty-three, Libby. Far too young to rust away here. You should marry again and have babies.'

'There are lots of different answers to that. I don't know anyone in London any more. All my friends are bringing up their children in the country. When I go to stay with them it just makes me even more unhappy about not having a child of my own. As for Richard, I hardly know him. I was only seven when he left home, and even before that he was away at school. Living in his family I'd just be a kind of dependent old maid.'

'Don't be ridiculous!'

'But the real thing is that I don't want to marry again. I've thought about it, of course I have. In a general kind of way, I mean. And it isn't that I think Hugh would have minded, or anything like that. It's just that although our time together was so short, it was absolutely perfect. There wasn't time for anything to happen to spoil it. And I want to keep it like that: a kind of diamond in my memory. Living with anyone else would chip away at it, somehow – and it would be hard on the chap as well, because how could any ordinary living man, growing older every year, compare with someone who will always be young and marvellous?'

Terts made no further comment. Libby was making a mistake. She needed to plan ahead and consider how she would live when her elderly grandfather no longer needed her care. But perhaps it was too soon to expect her to think of herself as young again. Terts himself, although he was not yet thirty, felt old and tired. Like Libby he had been robbed of what should have been care-free youthful years – and also like Libby, he could not yet see clearly into the future.

Had they but known it, a letter which was to affect both their futures was being delivered to Kinderley even as they spoke – although it was not until later in the day, when as usual they joined Lord Mortimer in the library for afternoon tea, that they were told about it.

'Letter came today from Bingham's wife. Widow, rather. Violet. It's taken some time on the journey. She must have written as soon as she got the confirmation of Bingham's death. And before she had my letter inviting her to come here. But that's what she wants to do.'

'To live here permanently, do you mean?'

'She didn't put it like that, because she hadn't had my invitation. All she's suggesting is a visit so that the family can get to know her – and the boy, Victor. All the same, she spelled out her situation clearly enough. Her father was a Resident in Rajputana. Died just before war broke out. Her mother was dead already. Until she married Bingham, she'd spent a good deal of her life living in what she calls a pavilion attached to a maharaja's palace. It sounds as though she almost became one of the family. Anyway, after she had to leave her married quarters the maharaja offered her a bungalow near her old home and she's been there ever since. I suppose she's beginning to feel that she can't stay there for ever.'

'She may want to look for a second husband,' suggested Terts.

'Wouldn't blame her if she did. But what she's saying is that the climate isn't good for small children, and I expect she's right about that.'

'Well, of course she must come!' exclaimed Libby. 'When you write to her, Grandfather, I'll add a note to say how welcome she'll be.'

'Something else I was going to suggest,' said Lord Mortimer. 'Why don't you go out and collect her, Mortimer? Escort her home. Not too good for a woman with a small boy, travelling across India on their own.'

'But won't Bradley's –?' It was Libby, not Terts himself, who could see an objection from the firm which was presumably expecting him to return to work as soon as he had settled back into civilian life.

'He's not going back there. Am I right, Mortimer?'

It was a moment of decision in Terts's life. In one sense the decision had already been taken over two years earlier, as he lay in a hospital bed and listened to his grandfather offering him financial independence. But since then every tedious wartime moment had made it more and more difficult to believe that there would ever again be such a thing as a peace in which he might make his own choices on how to live his life. This, presumably, was exactly the lack of imagination from which Libby also was suffering.

But it had all been promised and arranged. The decision had been taken already. He had lacked the courage to hope that it would actually come into effect; that was all. The whole of Terts's body swelled into a smile of happiness.

'Yes, that's right, Grandfather,' he agreed. 'Thanks to you.'

A week later, after New Year, he walked into the marble-panelled hall of Bradley's. The clerks at their desks were so young – hardly more than boys – that Terts was a stranger to them. They looked up in surprise as he confidently announced that he had an appointment with Mr Richard Bradley. By now Richard held the title of general manager, although the three partners who were his uncles were still in charge.

'So you're back. Well done. It's good to see you.' Richard held out a welcoming hand. But the smile faded from his face when he learned that his brother did not intend to return to the post which had been kept for him.

'It's Grandfather, isn't it? At heart he always thinks of us as being in trade. Not quite gentlemen.'

'No, it's not that.' Even as he made the denial Terts wondered whether he was speaking the truth. 'It's myself. For four-and-a-half years I've been obeying orders. And giving them as well, granted, but always within a framework I couldn't change. I want to be independent. To see a bit of the world. How other people live. There's a specific reason why I'm going off almost at once.' He explained about the journey to escort Bing's widow home. 'But I wouldn't want to leave you thinking that I'd be coming back here after that, because I don't think it will happen.'

'For all those four-and-a-half years we've been paying your salary into a special fund, on the assumption that you'd be returning here. Not just yours, I don't mean: all our staff. Although for most of them the important thing has been to feel that their jobs were secure. In your case, as family, I didn't think it necessary to tell you about the payments because we all took it for granted...'

He sounded so aggrieved about the money which clearly he saw as wasted that Terts was tempted to smile. Instead, he repeated a polite apology. 'Is there anything I can do for you while I'm in India?' he asked, as a peace gesture.

Richard gave an immediate demonstration of the fact that he had become an efficient man of business.

'Well, as a matter of fact ... India, yes.' He rang a bell and asked the secretary who answered it to bring him a folder.

'This is a new proposition,' he explained. 'There's a firm in Agra which we already support. They make carpets. They were probably one of your accounts when you were on the India desk. Now they've applied for a new loan, a large one, to build another factory nearby. For high quality silk weaving. They'd need new machinery. Expensive. The idea is that the carpet factory would act as security for the new venture.'

'So you'd like me to make sure that it exists?' Terts's pre-war apprenticeship at Bradley's had been long enough to teach him that it was never wise to take anything for granted. 'Yes, I could do that.'

'More than simply its existence, of course. The general reputation of the firm. Financial stability. I'll give you all the documents. Very often just the fact of someone turning up is enough to bring any skeletons there may be tumbling out of cupboards. Not that I really think... The carpet business appears to be doing very well. Exceptionally well. Thanks, Terts. If you can call in tomorrow to pick up all the figures? And I'll have your nest egg ready for you as well.'

He was not really too upset, Terts realised. Perhaps, indeed, he was glad that he would be the only member of the younger Bradley generation in contention for the privilege of running the firm one day – for by now the whole family took it for granted that young Aden would choose to devote his life to academia rather than account books. The two brothers were able to smile and shake hands in as friendly a manner at the end of their meeting as at the beginning.

And now, thought Terts, once again passing the rows of clerks who had started work at eight o'clock that morning, as they would continue to do until the day of their retirement – and now he was free!

2

Like most men of his generation Terts took pride in the British Empire. He saw it as a modern version of the Roman empire, bringing law and order to the barbarians. When early in the war, he had come across Indian troops in Flanders, he felt critical of the maladministration which had condemned them to a winter of cold and wet in the muddy trenches while still wearing their tropical uniform, but it had not occurred to him to wonder why they should have been willing to endure so much in order to fight a war which did not concern them in an unknown part of the world. It must be because they recognised their good fortune in enjoying British rule.

Nothing in the first hours of his arrival in India challenged this assumption. As the ship slowly approached the Ballard Pier in Bombay he was impressed by the monumental buildings which greeted his eyes. Although the Customs House was crowded and noisy as all the passengers competed to clear their luggage, the system worked more efficiently than he might have expected, and had he planned to embark on the journey upcountry at once he could have embarked immediately on one of the first-class trains already waiting at the pier.

Instead of that, he had arranged to spend a few days sightseeing. It was likely that the letter of welcome from Lord Mortimer and Libby would have travelled out on the same mail ship as himself, and the delay would give his sister-in-law warning of his arrival. Besides, this was an opportunity to explore. Although his wartime leaves had afforded necessary respites from the stresses of battle, it was more than five years since he had last enjoyed anything which could be described as a holiday. To travel straight to Gwalior and then return almost immediately to England would be to waste the opportunity of observing an unfamiliar way of life.

While his luggage was being loaded on to a waiting *ghari* for the short journey to the hotel, Terts made his farewells to his fellow passengers. Many of them were young; boys and girls sent back to England for their education before the war and trapped there by the lack of passenger shipping. In some cases their mothers were with them; women who had not seen their husbands for five years and whose excitement at the coming reunion betrayed an element of nervousness. Like every other unattached young man on the boat, Terts had enjoyed romantic evenings in the moonlight. But he had been careful never to suggest any lasting interest, and now the girls who had danced so dreamily on the deck with him had already put the voyage behind them as they prepared for the next stages of their journeys.

The hotel was a substantial building which could have been anywhere in Europe had it not been for the profusion of brightly uniformed servants wearing feathered turbans such as he had last seen in King George's retinue when Libby was presented at court. The air was cooled by the movement of sea breezes from one side of the peninsula to the other through the louvres of the open but shuttered windows. In the larger rooms, such as the restaurant, the same effect was produced by sheets of cloth suspended from the ceiling, which swung silently to and fro as the unseen punkah-wallahs outside each room lay back and steadily pedalled their feet to pull the controlling ropes.

Only when he went outside, intending to take a little brisk exercise after the comparative inactivity of the voyage, did Terts become aware of the heat and humidity. His pace slowed, allowing him more time to appreciate the buildings and monuments which made it clear who was in charge of the country: banks and clubs, the fort and the mint, the cathedral and the old customs house, schools and colleges, a hospital and a palatial railway station. It came as something of a shock when, pressing on beyond this very British area, he suddenly found himself stepping into an Indian area of India.

Here, everything was different. The streets were narrow, lined with small shops and stalls, and so crowded that it was difficult to make his way along them – crowded not only with humans but with cows; ghostly white cows, with skin stretched tightly over their ribs to reveal that even the vegetable refuse tossed carelessly on to the ground was not enough to sustain them. When they obstructed the road, no one tried to move them. When they sniffed at the food on display, no one tried to distract them. When they defecated in the middle of the street, no one showed disgust – and perhaps that was not surprising, since the men who stepped round the mess were not above following their example. Foul water ran down gulleys in the middle of the streets and the stench was too great to be overpowered by the pleasanter smells of the spices which were stacked in colourful displays.

Terts was taken by surprise. He had been brought up to believe and feel proud that the British had brought peace and order and incorruptible justice to India – and perhaps they had, but no one had warned him that they had not succeeded in imposing cleanliness and sanitation. No doubt, though, it was only the unaccustomed heat which was making him feel queasy. He turned back towards the hotel, understanding for the first time why the taking of an afternoon siesta was a wise custom in such a climate.

A day of tourist exploration followed. His camera worked overtime as he took a small boat to the island of Gharapuri and photographed the huge sculptures in the Elephanta caves. The technical problems of adjusting to an unaccustomed brightness in the open air and then to the dimness of the caves kept him happily occupied, but on the boat returning to the hotel he was depressed by his ignorance of what he had seen. Who were Siva and Brahma and Vishnu and Parvati, and what was the significance of the stylised attitudes in which they were depicted? It was not surprising that he should know so little about Hindu gods and legends, for he had embarked on the visit to India with hardly any notice; but it meant that the images trapped within his camera would always be cold. He had seen them, but had been unable to feel them.

Did that matter? Yes, in a way which he found hard to explain to himself, it did. He cast his mind back to those days before the war when he had been young and carefree: the days when his only anxiety was whether or not Venetia would marry him one day. The photographs he had taken in that period – the London Landmarks, for example – were frivolous and unimportant. But, all the same, he had put his heart into them, understanding the young men and women who were his subjects and feeling with them. He promised himself that before any future journeys of this kind he would prepare himself more thoroughly for what he was about to see.

He had planned, after consulting a guide book, to start on his journey to Gwalior next day but to leave the train at Manmar junction for a diversion to Aurangabad. From here it would be possible to visit the Ellora and Ajanta caves, with their ancient sculptures and paintings. It seemed an expedition not to be missed; but how could he appreciate it without understanding the ancient stories that were illustrated there? Perhaps Violet would be willing to break the journey on the way back, by which time he might have acquired a better background to the sights on offer. Perhaps, indeed – since she had spent so much of her life in India – she would be able to help him understand the meaning of what he saw.

So instead of making that excursion he returned to the Indian part of Bombay, this time taking his camera with him. He photographed beggars sitting on the ground and displaying their amputated limbs. He photographed half-naked small boys stealing fruit. He photographed the cows, taking care to do so unobtrusively since by now he had learned that they were sacred. He photographed what at first he thought to be dead bodies, but eventually realised were just men wrapped in blankets sleeping on the street. And as he pressed on further he photographed hovels constructed from boxes and parts of old bicycles and corrugated iron, surrounded by fetid puddles of standing water. He was building a picture of poverty, more real and more important than the sculptures of Elephanta.

One thought came to cheer him as, sweating inside his unsuitable clothing, he returned at last to the cool of the hotel. Bradley's must be performing a social service. Thanks to its loans, factories had been built and men were able to support their families in a style which would be far removed from anything he had seen today. Because they had wages, they could have dignity. Their children would not need to beg or steal in the streets, but could go to school. He was glad that Richard had asked him to visit one of the factories, so that he would be able to see for himself the good that was being done.

Next day he left for Gwalior on the Punjab Mail. The train was comfortable, stopping at intervals so that the passengers could enjoy a leisurely lunch or dinner at a station. From time to time they passed other trains with a very different standard of comfort, their passengers sleeping on the roof or clinging to the outsides of the carriages. It was a contrast just as striking as the difference between the parts of Bombay which belonged to the rulers or the ruled.

Just as the first-class train was strictly for the privileged, so were his sister-in-law's living quarters. The maharaja's home, set within a huge park in the New City of Gwalior, was a nineteenth-century building bizarrely intended to resemble an Italian palace rather than a Hindu one; but it lacked nothing in ostentation. Every pillar and portico, every fountain and lawn, was designed to display the wealth of its owner; and it was surrounded by a complex of lesser but still palatial residences. Violet had described her home as a bungalow; and so it was, in the sense of being a single-storey building. But its three wings, built round a courtyard paved in marble, would have housed a dozen or more of the families that Terts had seen in the slums of Bombay.

Violet herself was out playing bridge when he arrived, but the servants had been warned that a sahib was expected at some time and he was immediately swept up in their welcome. His luggage was carried in and unpacked, a bath was prepared for him while he was being shown to his room, a cool drink was brought on a silver tray and the clothes he had been wearing on the journey were whisked away to be washed. Terts had been brought up in a house run by servants, but he had never before been left with this feeling that he need do nothing at all for himself except breathe.

This impression was strengthened when, cleansed and refreshed, he was drawn by the sound of a child's voice towards the nursery quarters. He had come to India prepared to be loving towards his fatherless nephew, but it took only a few moments to realise that such feelings might not grow easily.

At the age of four, Victor was already a tyrant. He was attended by two servants, both of whom he was bullying as Terts stood unobtrusively in a doorway. He threw his toys out of reach and then demanded that they should be brought back to him. When his ayah was slow to pick up his wheeled horse, he screamed in fury and flung a wooden building brick in her face. Automatically she put a hand to her cheek where he had bruised it, but made no attempt to remonstrate with him, merely putting the horse within his reach. Although Terts made no comment aloud, he shook his head disapprovingly. All the Bradley children in turn had had a nurse when they were small; but she was a nurse who imposed discipline, and they would have been whipped by their father had they ever assaulted her. Victor, without any doubt, was spoilt.

Violet, Terts realised when she returned an hour later, was spoilt as well.

No doubt it was not her fault. As the daughter of a Resident she, like her son, had been brought up in a palatial home with servants to pander to her every whim. For a few years she had been sent back to boarding school in England, but then had returned at the age of seventeen to find herself courted by young Indian Army officers who were in competition for the limited number of suitable English girls.

No doubt life had been harder for her since her marriage, as she waited with less and less hope for news of the husband with whom she had shared only three weeks of married life; but as Terts embarked on the process of getting to know her, he found something oddly passive in her personality. She was content to be waited on, and she had taken it for granted that someone would come to escort her to the new home in which she apparently intended to settle down. Terts couldn't help wondering how Libby would get on with someone who appeared to have no domestic skills at all and whose son threw tantrums every time he failed to get his own way. She would not want to be regarded purely as a kind of housekeeper. Perhaps she would decide to move to Cornwall after all and leave the new arrival to keep Lord Mortimer company.

No, that wouldn't do. Terts was surprised at the strength of his feelings. Ten years earlier, he would have felt no surprise or resentment had Bing been designated his grandfather's heir. But that was no longer possible, and he was upset by the possibility that Violet might become the chatelaine of Kinderley, with Victor growing up to take over.

Well, it was none of his business. His grandfather had the right to do whatever he liked with his own property. All the same, he told himself, once he was back in England he would not behave in quite such a disinterested manner as before. There could be no harm in making it clear how much he loved Kinderley and how willing he would be, if the occasion arose, to manage its estates and care for its workers. Anything would be better than to see it pass into the hands of someone who was hardly a member of the family at all.

3

'We shall dine tonight with the maharaja,' Violet told her guest. 'I've sent a message to say that you've arrived. Nothing formal. Just the family and us. I go regularly once a week. There'll be bridge afterwards. Do you play?'

'I'm afraid not.'

'Never mind. Nor does Daulat. He'll be glad of your company.'

'Who's Daulat?'

'His Highness's younger brother. He and I were playmates when we were small. He's about your age. Educated at Harrow and fought in Flanders. I'm sure you'll find something in common.'

'Just the family' proved to mean, when the time came, that there were only twenty-two diners at the banquet, and the number of servants on this 'informal' occasion was only twice that number. Terts couldn't help wondering how much the boys who were sent away for their education had enjoyed the hard beds and basic food of an English public school. The maharaja himself talked mainly of cricket, a game which Terts had been in no position to follow for the past five years; but with Prince Daulat he struck up an easy rapport.

Confessing his ignorance of Indian culture, Terts was given an immediate invitation.

'You must let me show you round the fort tomorrow. I can tell you of six hundred years of its history and three hundred years of legend before that. This may be more than you wish to know. Our great rock sculptures also, you must inspect. They are Jain. You shall have a lecture. I hope you are planning to see more of our country before you bear our dear Violet away. It is only a day's drive to Khajuraho, which has the finest erotic sculptures in the world. They will open your eyes, I think. You should go there with me, but certainly not with your sister-in-law. And there are many other treasures close at hand.'

'I have to go to Agra, to do an errand there. So I look forward to seeing the Taj Mahal.'

'Many times you should go to it. At sunset, by moonlight, in the early morning. In every light it is different. Also, there are other most beautiful buildings nearby. I shall give you a book. And send a servant with you to act as your guide and make sure that you are not cheated by hotels and drivers.'

So cheerfully did Daulat smile with the delight of being able to provide whatever the visitor needed that Terts grinned back.

'No – no servant, thank you very much. I like to be alone. I think I'd better not stay in India too long, or I shall forget how to look after myself altogether.'

'It is necessary for a man to be relieved of mundane duties so that he can devote himself to matters of the soul. I myself write poetry. And you, I'm sure ...?'

'I take photographs. Does that count as a matter of the soul?'

'Indeed, yes. So tomorrow you will bring your camera and we will walk through palaces until you beg for rest. Tell me, will Violet be happy in England?'

'I don't know her well enough yet to answer that question. She will certainly be welcomed by my family. And I expect she has friends ...'

'No. No friends. All her friends are here, in India. This makes me anxious for her. My brother has tried to persuade her to stay here, but it is true that our climate is not healthy for English children. It is to be hoped that she will marry again. Luckily there is no custom of suttee in your country.'

'Suttee?' Terts had never heard the word before.

'In the past here it very often happened that when a man of high caste died, his wife was expected to follow him. To die by fire.'

'Good God! Voluntarily?'

'In many cases, yes. To achieve honour and even worship after death. Where there were several wives, they would even dispute which of them should be allowed the privilege of burning. Nowadays, suttee is forbidden by the British. But that doesn't mean that it never happens. It must be more secret, that's all. But Violet is in no danger of that kind.'

'Indeed not.' But the earlier part of this conversation did reinforce Terts's anxieties about the kind of life which Violet might expect to lead after her return. As Libby had discovered when she was younger, it was no simple matter to find new friends while living at Kinderley. Perhaps it would be easier now that the war was over, but in the past few years there had been few opportunities for casual social life. If the young widow was to be found a new husband, that would involve deliberate matchmaking on somebody's part.

How easy would that be? Although Violet was still in her twenties, there was something washed out about her – the result, perhaps, of too much reliance on servants. No doubt it was difficult in a hot climate to be energetic and full of initiative. She might well become more vivacious when she was back in England. In any case, the fact that Terts himself did not find her attractive didn't mean that nobody else would.

Three days later he set out for Agra. Violet had promised that by the time he returned she would have packed up all her possessions and said all her farewells.

On the day after his arrival Terts decided to deal with his business duties first. In a gesture of politeness he sent a messenger at dawn to inform the manager of the carpet factory that he was about to pay a visit, and arrived there himself at nine o'clock. He first of all walked round the factory, taking the photographs which would prove to Bradley's that the building actually existed. By England standards it was a shack, with walls on only two sides; but no doubt in a hot climate it made sense to let any breeze move through the building unchecked.

A small boy, about seven years old, ran out in front of him, his broad grin revealing a double gap in his front teeth. He must have seen a camera before, because he was posing to be photographed. Smilingly Terts obliged and gave the boy an anna so that he ran off crowing with pleasure.

Then the factory manager appeared to welcome him and – this time in words rather than gestures – requested politely that his own photograph might be taken in front of the factory. Terts was glad to oblige, for he had no wish to appear in any threatening light. For the same reason, as he was led into the office to be offered tea, he at first shook his head when he was offered for inspection two ledgers containing accounts. All Bradley's had asked him to discover was whether this factory, as a property, would provide adequate security for the loan of capital required to build another one. But the books were pressed on him. It became clear that his approbation was desired. So he glanced through the pages politely before returning the ledgers with a smile.

'May I see the machines?' he asked.

'Of course, of course, sahib. This way, please.'

The word 'machines' proved to be inappropriate, with its connotations of metallic noise and movement. Instead, the open space was furnished with large upright looms and the only movement immediately apparent was that of a supervisor pacing round the area. But, although unobtrusive, there was in fact a great deal of movement going on. When Terts paused in front of one of the looms he could see the fingers of the two workers, who sat by the side there, going non-stop like those of a pianist practising exercises at top speed.

What brought him to a halt there, and widened his eyes with incredulity, was the size of those adeptly moving fingers. He had always known that the carpets were hand-made, but nobody had ever told him that the hands would be those of children.

'How old are these boys?' he asked the manager abruptly.

'These two, very fast, eight years old. Other boys and girls, nine, ten, eleven, twelve years old.'

'Eight!' Appalled, Terts looked round the factory floor at the rows of children hunched over their work, their eyes fixed on their fingers. Not one of them had raised his head to look at the visitor. His mental picture of skilled men working to support their families and maintain their dignity as providers had been shattered. 'Do you not employ any adults?' he asked, doing his best to keep any note of criticism out of his voice lest it should prevent him from being given honest answers to later questions.

'For cheaper carpets, in our other factory, there are women. But here are the highest quality, the most expensive. For the British market. After twelve years old, fingers become too large. You and I, sahib –' he held out his hands, palms upward, to show his fingers '– could never make such fine work. You will know that it is not the design which speaks of quality, but the tightness of the knots only. In each square inch, so many knots.' He picked up the corner of a finished carpet and bent it so that Terts could see the closeness of the work.

'I'd like to speak to some of the children.'

'Alas, sahib, they are not speaking English. Also, they must be completing their task every day. They will not be wishing to make an interruption.'

'How many hours do they work?'

'For thirteen hours only, unless there is some fault or too much slowness. They are here from six in the morning and go home at eight o'clock in the evening. We have built homes for them and their families, very near. For one hour in the day they may rest and we are giving them food at no cost.'

'Don't they go to school?'

'They are not wishing to go to school. In the villages they would be looking after goats. Here they are earning money. It pleases them to help their families in this way. Their fathers have great debts. They bring their sons to us so that the debts may be repaid. Although,' the manager added honestly, 'very often the fathers are foolish and borrow still more money, so that a child must stay here, or a younger one must be sent.'

It sounded to Terts as though the fathers were selling their sons into a kind of slavery. A considerable effort was needed for him to conceal his shock.

'Well,' he said with a pretence of cheerfulness, 'I'll take some more photographs inside the factory now. Which is the best of your carpets? Perhaps you would like to stand in front of it for another picture?'

The manager was delighted. Six boys were sitting side by side on a bench in front of the largest of the carpets. There was not a great deal of their work to be seen, because each finished strip of work was gradually rolled down in order that the boys should always be working at the same level. They must be ruining their eyesight, thought Terts, seeing how they leaned forward to peer at it; and the hunching of their backs would surely bring health problems in later life. But he made no comment on that as he took a series of photographs, some of them showing the whole area but most of them as close to the boys as he could get. He talked as he worked, promising the manager that he would be sent a picture of himself to keep, and asking him to choose one of the finest completed carpets and have it held up in order that the design might be photographed. The bustle caused by this request gave him the opportunity to distract one of the boys from his work to look up at him. The sad and tired young face made a depressing contrast with the gap-toothed grin of the lively youngster cavorting outside the factory – a boy who would perhaps himself be entering this prison within a year or two.

The need to keep a pleasant expression on his face increased the indignation which was building up inside him. Surely it must be illegal to employ such young children to do this kind of work? If it was not, then it ought to be. Did the people who bought these carpets in England realise that in order that their houses should be adorned, boys and girls who ought to be laughing and playing were being robbed of their childhood?

Probably not; because Terts could remember from the trading accounts which he had at one time had to scrutinise that by the time they reached London the finished products were as expensive as they looked, bringing profits to shippers and importers and indirectly to Bradley's, which had provided the original capital for the business. Did the uncles know, he wondered, that part of the income on which they led such comfortable lives was drawn from a kind of child slavery? Well, if they did not, he intended to tell them.

4

Rising from an afternoon siesta, Terts prepared for the first of his visits to the Taj Mahal: he intended to take Prince Daulat's advice and see it in several different lights. His plan was first to enjoy the overall view in the late afternoon, which he had been told was the best time; then to explore the building and its decoration and gardens in detail, and then to wait for the change of colour which sunset would bring.

But although the first glimpse of the calm white marble dome was as thrilling and satisfying as he had expected, when he sat down just inside the gateway to enjoy the vista he found that the expected peacefulness eluded him. He was still disturbed by his morning visit to the carpet factory. Unable to keep still in contemplation, he began almost at once to take photographs, moving nearer and nearer to the tomb until after an hour he was focusing on tiny details of the leaves and petals of semi-precious stones with which the marble was decorated.

Even this occupation, which normally absorbed all his concentration, could not calm him today. The thought that the children he had seen were still working away at their repetitive task was unbearable. He wished he had after all paid more attention to the ledgers which were placed in front of him; but one of his skills was to recreate from memory any page which he had once seen, as though the words and figures on it were part of a picture. He set his mind to that now, isolating the figures which represented the wages of the young workers before counting in his mind approximately how many of them would have shared that total.

Naturally the result of his arithmetic needed to be interpreted and related to the extremely low costs of living. Even so, his disquiet grew until with a grumble of impatience he realised that he was not doing justice to the beautiful building he had come to see. Promising himself that he would return the next day, he set off to walk back to his hotel.

He had made the earlier journey by taxi; but the air was cooler now and he was in need of exercise. It should be possible, he reckoned, to take a short cut along the bank of the Jumna, because the grounds of the hotel extended to the river. He hoped that this would not involve him in trespassing, and was relieved to see that a good many people were walking in the same direction. He was still thinking about the children in the factory as he walked, until he was distracted by the sight of a procession. In the centre of it was an open palanquin, decorated with flowers, in which was carried a woman richly dressed and laden down with gold necklets, bracelets and anklets. Naturally Terts pulled out his camera, wishing that he could capture the colour of the scene, for the servants who carried the palanquin and the women who thronged around it were all brightly dressed.

Terts guessed the woman to be on her way to a betrothal ceremony and could not resist following, although he was careful to keep a little behind and almost out of sight rather than to intrude on a family occasion.

The procession came to a halt beside the river. The woman was helped out of the palanquin and stood in calm dignity while her companions rearranged themselves in a circle, joined by many of the citizens who had been walking with Terts along the river bank. Half a dozen men – Brahmins by their dress – appeared from the opposite direction. Two of them came forward to escort the woman into the middle of the circle. She took one or two steps forward and then came to a halt, her mouth opening in fear. The two men no longer politely supported her arms, but instead began to drag her forward. Although she did not resist, it was clear even from a distance that she was on the point of fainting. No one was looking in Terts's direction. He moved nearer, his camera still in his hand.

What he had seen that morning had disquieted him. What he saw now filled him with unbelieving horror. As the crowd parted to admit the woman into the circle he saw that in the centre of it was a funeral pyre, on the top of which lay the corpse of a man. Incredulously he remembered what Prince Daulat had told him about the custom of suttee. But it was forbidden: that had been made quite clear. If the British authorities knew what was happening they would undoubtedly halt it; but how could any official be found in time?

Whether or not the woman had originally been willing to be sacrificed, she was not willing now. Terts could hear her moans as the two Brahmins who were apparently in charge of the ceremony lifted her high before placing her on top of her husband's body.

'No!' shouted Terts, unable to keep quiet any longer. He began to run towards the pyre, but from nowhere four men appeared with drawn swords. They were ceremonial swords, and held horizontally only as a barrier, without any attempt to strike the foreigner down, but it was clear that he would not be allowed to go any nearer.

By now the two Brahmins were emptying jugs of some kind of oil on to the dry timber of the pyre and at the same time they thrust flaming torches into it. The swordbearers turned their heads to watch as smoke and flames rose and Terts took the opportunity to use the rest of his film. Ghoulish though it might seem to record a death in cold blood like this, his pictures would be evidence that something was happening which ought not to happen.

As the flames and smoke rose, he heard the beginning of a high-pitched scream which was cut off by a choking sound. He could no longer see the woman's face, for it was engulfed in smoke, but from the manner in which her outstretched arm suddenly fell limply into the flames he guessed that she was probably dead even before the pyre collapsed and swallowed up her body. Sick to his stomach, he shook his head in disbelief.

The film was finished, and now Terts turned to run. What he had witnessed was barbaric, and it was not to be taken for granted that an unwanted spectator would necessarily be treated in a civilised manner. He retraced his tracks to the Taj Mahal where, as he had hoped, he found a taxi to take him back to his hotel.

That night he lay awake for a long time, wondering what to do. There must be a local British Resident; there might be a Christian missionary society operating in the area. But they surely must have known already what was going on and for some reason had decided to turn a blind eye. In the end, although it seemed a cowardly decision, he decided to say nothing until he was back in England.

It was the film which decided him. He had evidence of what he had seen, but could produce it only after it had been developed and printed. He had not come equipped to do that himself in India and it was all too easy to imagine some small inefficiency, whether deliberate or not, which could result in the loss of all the images. He would wait until he was back in England and then confront someone in authority at the India Office – just as he had already decided to confront Bradley's on the subject of child labour – and force him to take action.

Well, that was settled then. He tried to put it out of his mind during the next few days as he went through the motions of sightseeing and then embarked on the business of escorting Violet back to England.

Without Victor, this would no doubt have been a simple process, but the four year old proved to be an intolerable companion. He cried incessantly for his ayah, from whom he had never before been separated, and flew into tantrums whenever his wishes were not immediately obeyed. To make things worse, it became clear even before they embarked on the ship at Bombay that Violet had never looked after him herself and had no idea how to set about it.

'He needs a father,' she exclaimed from time to time when her son yet again showed who was master by refusing to do what he was told. Terts agreed, but resented the fact that he was expected to fill that role. It quickly became obvious that Violet was on the lookout for a new husband and was well aware of the romantic possibilities of a long sea voyage. There could be no objection to that, for it was almost five years since she had last seen her husband; but Victor was an impediment. It was one thing to mention, as Terts once overheard her doing, that her son was the great-grandson of Lord Mortimer of Kinderley Court, but quite another to inflict the boy on any possible suitor. So as she danced and flirted in the moonlight, Terts found himself in an unaccustomed and unwanted role of responsibility.

He gritted his teeth and put up with it, for by this time he had decided that he did not like his sister-in-law at all. It would suit him well if she could trap someone in the Red Sea and transfer herself to another family. So the only word of criticism he ventured to make was the unwisdom of continuing to wear the flimsy evening dresses which had been suitable for India on the deck of a ship which was fast approaching England's colder shores.

His warning was well justified. In the Bay of Biscay she retired to her cabin with a chill on the chest as well as an attack of sea-sickness, and she had not completely recovered by the time the ship docked. Terts hurried her off to Kinderley with her son but, although her welcome was warm, the house had always been a cold one. Within three days she had once again taken to her bed.

It was influenza, the doctor said. There was an epidemic sweeping the world, threatening to kill even more people than had died on the battlefields of the war. Perhaps, already chilled and weakened, she had been exposed to infection on the train from Tilbury. Perhaps it was simply caused by the change of climate. In either case, he would send along nurses, but there was nothing for the family to do except wait for the hour of crisis to come and go. It would happen at night, he told them. With any luck, they would all wake up one morning to find her sitting up in bed, asking for breakfast.

Violet did not enjoy that sort of luck. They woke up one morning to find that she was dead. It was a pitiful end to a sad and unfulfilling life.

She had no relatives to be consulted. Terts and Libby and Lord Mortimer met in the library to discuss the funeral.

'I'll write to the maharaja,' said Terts. 'All her friends in India can learn the news through him.'

'There's the boy.' Lord Mortimer was no more enamoured of Victor than was Terts, although during his mother's illness he had grown more subdued, frightened of the large and unfamiliar house and its unknown inhabitants.

'He must stay,' said Libby. 'We're all he's got. And he's Bing's son. There's no question about it.'

Lord Mortimer nodded his approval, but Terts could not restrain a word of warning.

'You'll find him a handful.'

'He's only four years old. I can see he's been spoilt, but his mother's death will have given him a shock. I think we'll find him ready to start again, so to speak; to fit in with a different way of life. Anyway, you have to remember that I'm an experienced schoolteacher now, capable of controlling twenty five- to seven-year-olds at a time. I know how to teach. I can get him ready for school. And I –'

She stopped abruptly and felt for a handkerchief. In the three years since Hugh's death Terts had never seen Libby cry, but she was crying now.

'I wanted to have children of my own,' she said, bringing herself under control. 'There wasn't time. But now ... I can give him the love that he needs and he can be the son I wanted. There are so many widows who are going to be alone for the rest of their lives. This is my chance to be luckier than the rest. I can take him to Trelowen if –'

'No, no.' Lord Mortimer interrupted the suggestion. 'He stays here. Bingham's son. And I don't want you going, Libby. I'm too old to have changes.'

'Thank you, Grandfather.' She leaned over his chair to kiss him. 'Then could I ask one more favour? It would do Victor a lot of good to have company of his own age. Not to live here, I don't mean that, but to share lessons and playtime. There's a five year old, Walter Purvis, in the village. His father was killed in the war as well, and he was very disruptive in class, but it was because he was cleverer than the other children and he got impatient waiting for them to catch up.'

'You don't need to ask my permission, my dear. Do what you like. You can use your old schoolroom. Set up a school for young delinquents if you like. Just don't let them make too much noise between two and four in the afternoon, that's all.'

'Thank you,' Libby said again. Her eyes were shining. It seemed to Terts an odd way for a young woman who had no need to work to find happiness but, like his grandfather, he was glad that she knew what she wanted.

Now it was time for him to decide what to do with his own life, and the first decision had already been taken. The people of England needed to know what was going on in India. They could not see for themselves, but he had seen for them. He had made himself their eyes. All that was needed now was to find a way in which they would be forced to look at what he had seen.

5

No one wanted Terts's pictures.

Richard had brushed aside the shots of the carpet factory with the comment that India was not to be judged by British standards. A very little money would go a long way there and the children must certainly feel proud to be the breadwinners for their families. No one forced them to take the work on offer. To use emotive words like 'slavery' was unhelpful in the circumstances, and since Terts was no longer working for Bradley's there was no need for him to feel that it was any of his business.

He was no more successful when it came to the Civil Service, to which he reported the second horrifying incident of his visit to Agra. Mr Bradley was thanked for his letter and the enclosures it contained, but informed that there was no need for him to waste his time by pressing for a personal interview with the Secretary of State. It was government policy to accept with tolerance the particular religious and social customs which were practised in the diverse areas of the British Empire. In the case of the ancient ritual of suttee, where lives were at stake, an exception had been made many years ago and the practice had been banned. This meant that any woman who was at risk could appeal to the authorities for protection. In cases where she chose not to do so, volunteering for death as a matter of honour, it was simply not possible for the police always to learn in advance about what was by definition a highly secret affair. The writer hoped that this information would be helpful and remained Mr Bradley's most obedient servant.

Terts turned to the press, with no better result. No longer willing to send his photographs through the post to offices in which they might be lost or pushed aside without proper consideration, he made the rounds of Fleet Street's newspapers in person, but to no effect. His pictures, he was told, were simply not suitable for a family breakfast table. In vain he pointed out that it would be enough to print only the first shot in the series, of the young wife sitting rigidly in her ceremonial clothes as she was carried towards the fire. It could be left to the text to describe the custom that had brought her to this situation and the agony she was about to endure.

Every conversation ended in the same way, with a shake of the head. In some cases there was even the suggestion that Terts was a traitor to his country; as though he was saying that the British were in some way responsible for the fact that these heathens were refusing to obey the laws laid down for their own protection.

By now he was running out of addresses to visit. As he emerged, rejected again, from the offices of *Our World* – a small magazine, but one which he had hoped might prove interested – he sat down in its tiny reception area to consider where to go next.

A tall, curly-haired man of almost his own age came in from the street and greeted the secretary with an ease of manner which made it clear that he worked in the building. He could hardly fail to notice Terts, and reacted in a curious way – as though he had recognised the visitor but was perhaps unsure whether the recognition would be welcome.

After a moment's hesitation he crossed the hall.

'Hello.'

Terts stood up politely but did not speak. They had never, so far as he was aware, met before.

'You won't remember me, but we were at school together. Very briefly. I mean, I'm right, aren't I? Bradley minor? Rose. Nat Rose.'

It took Terts a moment, but then of course he remembered. The blubbing boy with the bleeding back. 'Yes, of course.' They shook hands vigorously.

'I was so grateful to you, all those years ago, for helping me to get out of Croxton. I wanted to write and say so. But after my mother ... I mean, that was such a stupid thing to say. Your brother guessed, I expect?'

'Yes.'

'I was afraid so. It wasn't much of a return for your kindness. I thought probably you'd rather never be reminded of me. But – look, come up to my office, if you can spare a few minutes for a chat. And then we might have lunch. How about it?'

'You work here?' Without bothering to accept the invitation in words, Terts followed him into the tiny lift which juddered its way slowly up two floors.

'I'm the manager,' said Nat.

'That's very impressive.'

'I'd better not pretend to have been given the job on merit. My father owns a handful of magazines as well as the *Daily Bulletin*, but he's only interested in the newspaper side of the business himself. In here.'

He opened the door of a large, light room, very different from the cluttered editorial office which Terts had recently left, and gestured towards a comfortable armchair.

'So what are you doing here today? You obviously didn't come to see me. Have you been commissioned to do some work for us?'

'Unfortunately not. I brought some stuff in on spec, hoping Mr Nicholls might be interested in it for *Our World*.'

'And was he?'

'No. He and I live in different worlds, it seems. His world is cosier than mine.'

'Are you talking about words or pictures?'

'Pictures. I've moved on a bit from the old Brownie.'

Nat hesitated only for a few seconds before asking, 'May I have a look?'

'Of course.' Terts opened his attaché case on his lap and took out the folder containing the suttee series. He spread half a dozen of the photographs out on the low table between the two men. Then he watched Nat's expression of horror as the younger man studied each picture in turn before picking up the last and scrutinising it more closely.

'Is she –?'

'Yes, I think she was probably dead before then. From the smoke.'

'Tell me about it. Was this some sort of punishment?'

'Only if it's a crime not to keep your husband alive.' Terts gave a short explanation of what he had been told about suttee. 'Mr Nicholls seemed to think that this sort of thing wouldn't go with the breakfast marmalade too well. It would frighten the children.'

'People don't read magazines at breakfast time. Only newspapers. It's much easier to keep magazines away from children if you want to. Although you could argue ...' He checked the thought. 'Did you take anything else while you were there?'

'Masses of stuff.' Interleaving them with soft paper, Terts stacked the photographs back into a pile before leaning down to extract another folder. This contained the record of his visit to the carpet factory.

'These children are about eight years old,' he told Nat. 'They work a thirteen-hour day, or longer if they don't produce enough. It needs small fingers, apparently, to make the hundreds of tiny knots which create each square inch of carpet. It was difficult to get the situation absolutely straight, but I had a distinct impression that in most cases the children had been sold to the factory owners to pay off their father's debts. It came pretty near to slavery in my view.'

Nat burst out laughing, although there was an uneasiness behind the laughter.

'You haven't changed, Bradley. That was the first thing I thought when I caught sight of you downstairs. "That's Bradley and he hasn't changed a bit." I was thinking only of appearance then, but I see now that it goes deeper than that. This is another version of the boy with the bleeding back, isn't it? Wasn't there anything beautiful in India?'

'Yes, of course.' For a third time Terts opened a folder – and now Nat's laughter was whole-hearted.

'Magnificent buildings and sad people. Is that your message? Not a very cheerful one.'

'It doesn't have to be that contrast. I could have brought along a clutch of fat rajahs studded with diamonds and beautiful princesses bangled with gold. *They* were happy enough.'

'So you're making a political statement?'

'No, not really. At least, I didn't realise at the time that I might be doing that. I was just trying to capture what I saw, as I saw it.'

'Let's have lunch,' said Nat abruptly. 'Get up to date with each other. If you have time?'

'Yes, plenty of time.' Terts had almost run out of possible markets for his work. He packed the photographs away and closed his case.

'We can walk. Little place I go to quite often, just round the corner.'

The 'little place' smelled of money. Although Terts, as a guest, was offered a menu which showed no prices, he could tell that it was expensive. Nat was welcomed as a regular patron and shown to his regular table.

'Champagne!' he said. 'To celebrate a kind of reunion. And I recommend the caviar. Best in London. It's one of the advantages of not being recognised as an English gentleman: that I'm not expected to eat terrible club food in oppressive dining rooms.'

For a moment Terts was puzzled, until he remembered that of course Nathan Rose was a Jew. Lord Mortimer, whose views on the subject were extreme but not unusual, would certainly have blackballed him had he applied to join Brookes. Yet there was nothing about his appearance – except his comparative youth – which would have marked him out from other members of any club. The weedy boy had grown into a tall, well-built man, strong-featured and confident. The puckered white line of a scar over which his curly hair had not regrown suggested he had done his bit, and been wounded, in the war; but it did not detract from his good looks.

'You seem to be doing very well for yourself,' Terts commented.

'You're remembering how you last saw me, no doubt. There are some men, I suspect, who remain schoolboys all their lives, and other men who are never really schoolboys at all. I started living at the age of eighteen. Your health, Bradley!'

Terts raised his glass in reply.

'How many magazines do you manage?' he asked.

'Not enough to keep me in champagne. I have a generous father. He just has this foible, that I should pretend to earn the allowance which he would have given me anyway. To answer your question: three magazines. One for women, very cosy and full of knitting patterns. One for children, immensely educational. And *Our World*.'

There was a pause while they ordered. Then Nat continued as though there had been no interruption. 'I'd like to buy your suttee pictures, Bradley.'

'Your editor wouldn't.'

'I'm the one who holds the purse strings.'

'But he, presumably, is the one who decides what's actually printed. What I'm trying to say is that it isn't enough for me simply to receive money for them. That would just be a kind gesture on your part. What I need is to be sure that they'd be published. That people would *see*. What I'm trying to do with these pictures is to communicate something.'

'And you're afraid that I'm simply trying to repay a boyhood debt with cash? Well, let me ask you a couple of questions. Since I'm remembering the trouble you got your brother into all those years ago. I take it that the suttee business is frowned upon by the British authorities?'

'Forbidden.'

'So is there somebody who would be hauled over the coals if those photographs were printed? For example, is your brother now a District Officer in India, or anything like that?'

'He's dead; died as a prisoner of war in Turkey.'

'I'm sorry. I didn't particularly mean ...'

'I've no doubt that in each case there would be someone with a duty to stop the ceremony if he could. But the pictures could have been taken at any time, in any one of a great many places. So long as the text didn't identify ...'

'That's the second question. Would you be able to write an article to go with the pictures?'

'They're intended to speak for themselves.'

'And so they do, from their starting point. But they'd still need a little background.'

'I could provide that, yes.' Terts watched appreciatively as a waiter put down a mountain of caviar, set into an ice-chilled silver bowl and surrounded by foothills of chopped egg and onion and lemon.

'Then let me explain the way my mind's working. *Our World* is a cosy little world, as you've already discovered for yourself. I'm not sure that it ought to be like that. We're supposed to be not just entertaining but educating our readers about places they'll probably never be able to visit for themselves. But I do often ask myself whether it's right that they should think that it's only England that is grey and petty and class-bound and philistine and sometimes heartless. There are slugs under the stones of other countries as well. And it's particularly important to be honest when we, the British, are the ones who are responsible for allowing the slugs to thrive.'

'So?'

'If I try to change the whole attitude of the magazine we shall lose our existing readers without gaining new ones. But to have just one feature in every issue which doesn't necessarily print a rosy picture shouldn't do any harm. A regular feature. Readers who wanted to remain comfortable could ignore it. But others might buy the magazine because of it. The daily papers – well, the *Bulletin*, anyway – might take the subject up, give the magazine publicity. I'd like to see the circulation increasing. To show my father that I'm doing a proper job.'

'And what will Mr Nicholls have to say about all this?'

'The editor is responsible for making sure that the right number of words and pictures are commissioned and printed every month. I am responsible for hiring and firing the editor.'

Terts's mouth twitched with amusement, and Nat had no difficulty in guessing what he was thinking.

'You're quite right. We don't need to talk about Croxton after all. I'm not the same person. Not a victim any longer. And that's thanks to Bradley minor, aged fifteen. If I hadn't managed to escape ...' He thrust that subject aside and continued to talk about *Our World*.

'If you'll sell me the suttee pictures, I probably shan't use them straight-away. It'll take a little time to get three or four subjects in hand, so that once we start there won't be any gaps. I wouldn't want to have two India-based stories too close together, but all the same I'd like to buy the carpet factory shots as well, if you don't mind them being kept on ice for a time?'

'I'd need to check, before they were printed, that nothing had changed.'

'Of course. And in the meantime, how would you fancy a trip to East Africa and Zanzibar? I've heard nasty stories about Arab slave traders there. Although, of course, it could be dangerous. Have you any dependants?'

It was a long time since Terts had last thought about Venetia. Now a picture of her flashed into his mind once more. Somebody else's wife, looking after somebody else's children and spending the money that somebody else had to provide. What a marvellous thing it was to be free!

'No,' he said happily. 'No dependants.'

Part Five

Inheritance

1

'Have you got any idea of the trouble you've caused?' exploded Richard. 'How could you do this to us? Your own family!'

Terts, waiting for a chance to put in a word, hardly recognised his eldest brother in this red-faced, middle-aged man who was not only angry but, beneath the anger, frightened.

'You might at least have given us warning,' Richard exclaimed, still furious.

'I didn't know –'

'Of course you knew! *You* took the photographs. *You* sent them to this magazine which is determined to stir up trouble.'

'If you remember, I did give you warning. Years ago, when I came back from India that first time.' Terts was standing up for himself at last. He was no longer a baby brother or a school servitor to be ordered about, but a thirty-five-year-old man of the world in every sense: a photographer who in the past six years had acquired an increasing reputation for recording scandal and distress – and for attracting beautiful women – in every country he visited. 'I showed you the photographs. I told you at the time that it was scandalous for Bradley's to be responsible for a trade which relied on such working conditions.'

'That was in 1919. The whole situation might have changed since then. To publish out-of-date material –'

'It might have changed, but in fact it hasn't. You don't really believe that a magazine would publish without checking, do you? The journalist who wrote the text went back to inspect the factory first. It makes it worse, that nothing had been done about it.'

Richard ought really to consider himself lucky that the question of

Bradley's involvement in child labour had not been raised years earlier. Nathan Rose had waited to see what the effect would be of the first series of exposés, starting with the suttee pictures. Pleased by the publicity and consequent rise in circulation – and also distressed by some of the conditions depicted – he had planned well ahead, commissioning material from all over the world. It was in 1924 that each monthly edition for a year had included an article to show how children in many different countries were being exploited and robbed of their childhoods. Terts himself had contributed the photographs for half of these. The Indian carpet factory had been the first, while the last in the series had featured a workshop in China. In yet another industry funded by Bradley's, the work force once again consisted of children, this time using dangerously sharp tools to carve wafer-thin sheets of ivory to make fans.

'I warned you when I first told you about the Indian children that customers would be upset if they knew,' he added now. 'You ought to have taken notice. Then when the pictures appeared you could have claimed to have taken steps already to stop the exploitation. I couldn't have given you any further warning. I didn't know when the photographs were going to be used. I've been in Africa for the past two years.'

'I can't think why any country lets you cross its frontiers when you only arrive to go muck-raking,' grumbled his brother.

There was an answer to that which Terts did not intend to give. All his photographs were signed with the single word 'Terts' but his passport, naturally, was in the name of Mortimer Bradley. Only his family and a few old friends – including Nathan Rose – knew that the two names were used by the same person. Ever since he embarked on the role of a travelling photographer he had been careful not to reveal the connection to anyone else.

'Anyway,' he said instead, 'the circulation of *Our World* is a tiny one. The effect –'

'If it were only *Our World* I wouldn't care. But the *Bulletin* took it up as a campaign. In my opinion it's a personal vendetta. Bing told me exactly why he'd had to leave Croxton early. Obviously that man Rose is still trying to get his revenge on the family because somebody made his spoiled brat blub.'

'What's the *Bulletin* doing, then?' During his journey from the south to the north of Africa Terts had been completely out of touch with events in England.

'First of all, alerting the International Labour Organisation, which seems to think it has the right to stick its nose in anywhere it chooses. And then stirring up its readers to boycott any shop which sells goods made by cheap labour. The editor doesn't bother to explain that that includes almost everything, from all over the world. He's been concentrating instead on the companies we support, about which he seems to know a great deal more than he should. So the first thing that happens is that the factory in Agra goes bankrupt. Do you think those children you were so worried about are grateful that you've lost them their jobs and that their families are probably starving?' Richard's indignation would not allow him to wait for an answer. 'And as a result of the campaign, Bradley's is likely to go bankrupt as well.'

'Oh, surely ...'

'Don't play the innocent, Terts. You've worked here. You know how we operate. In order to make the loans which create employment and generate profits, we borrow money ourselves. When the lenders see that the profits are under attack, they call in the loans. We're not liquid enough to repay everything at once. A bankrupt factory in Agra isn't exactly an immediately realisable asset. I have a wife and three children to support and in less than three months I expect to have no income at all. Don't say you're sorry, because clearly you know exactly what you're doing.'

The conversation ended in anger, leaving Terts confused. He thought of the gap-toothed seven year old he had photographed in 1919. By now, in 1926, that lad would be fourteen, already too old for that particular form of employment. Would he have been glad to have kept his freedom, or was Richard right to suggest that for a few years his earnings would have been essential to the family? But all that Terts himself had done was to show the truth. There was surely nothing to be ashamed of in that.

He was still mulling the matter over as he travelled to Kinderley, but he put it out of his mind as the elderly butler admitted him to the house with a smile of welcome. Grainger was no longer the aloof figure whom Terts as a boy had often found alarming. He was well past retiring age and it was possible to recognise in his expression an element of fear that the family might decide to dispense with his services.

'Miss Elizabeth's in the schoolroom,' he said. By now the fact that Libby was really Mrs Kenward appeared to have been forgotten by everyone – perhaps even by herself.

'No need to announce me. I'll surprise her.' He made his way to what had been the schoolroom ever since the day of his father's death, and stood in the doorway without drawing attention to himself.

The room bustled with activity. Libby herself was sitting on a low chair. On her lap was a four-year-old boy who was proudly identifying letters from a book and being rewarded by a clap of the hands for each success. Another young woman – presumably an assistant who had been appointed since Terts's last visit – was playing a spelling game with a group of older children, while two others, seated at desks with their heads bowed in concentration, were working out sums. Silently Terts counted the number of pupils: nine altogether now.

It had not been long after Victor's arrival at Kinderley that a friend of Violet's, unaware of her death, had written to ask whether she would meet her small son off the ship from India and deliver him to the prep school at which he had been enrolled. Libby had undertaken the chore herself, but had returned distressed by the obvious unhappiness of a little boy who was too young to be separated from his family, much less to fend for himself in the rough and tumble of a school.

After two pathetic letters which begged her to help him escape, she had taken it on herself to supervise his education until he was a little older. A friend of his mother, arriving to check that all was well, was so impressed by the way he had settled down that she left her own son at Kinderley and spread the word after returning to India. Although Libby would not normally have expected ever to work for money, she accepted fees from the expatriate parents. From these she was building up a fund in order to offer a good education to those of the village children who were fitted to become more than farm labourers.

What she offered, as she had explained earnestly to Terts when he first enquired laughingly about what she was taking on, was a home as well as a school: and she herself represented the home element of it. No doubt that was why she had introduced a helper to play the part of teacher. Libby was a good teacher, as she had proved during the war, but her main role now was that of temporary mother. These children were substitutes for the babies she had never had herself, and she was able to let them go only because she could hope for others to arrive.

Looking up as the little boy slid off her lap, Libby caught sight of her brother and ran to hug him. Then, after a word to her assistant, she led him into the room which had once been used by her governess and was now her own small sitting room.

'You're too thin, Terts! Have you been starving yourself? We shall have to feed you up.'

'Every part of Africa has its own very special and very unpleasant disease to offer the traveller. I reckon myself lucky to have dodged half the opportunities on offer. I'll soon be back to normal on Kinderley cooking.'

'I hope you'll stay for a bit longer than usual this time. Grandfather –'

'How is he?'

'Not too good.' Some of the exuberance with which Libby had greeted her brother faded from her face. 'I'm glad you're back in time. He keeps asking when you'll be coming – afraid, I think, that he might never see you again. You've always been his favourite, haven't you? Actually, he's determined to reach his ninetieth birthday, but he spends most of the day sleeping. He gets very breathless if he tries to move around much.' She looked at her watch. 'Four o'clock. I'm longing to hear all about your travels, but this is his best time, while he's having tea, and I know he'll want you to himself. Perhaps –'

'I'll go now, yes. Library?'

'Yes.'

'It's good to see you again, Libby. To be home.' He gave her another kiss before making his way across the great hall and following the uniformed maid who was carrying a tea tray into the library.

He found his grandfather, tucked up in rugs in front of a blazing fire, much weaker in body than at their last meeting, but still as vigorous in conversation as ever.

After the first greetings were over, the expected questioning began. Terts had to be careful how he answered. His brief from the magazine which financed his expeditions was to discover and record shameful secrets, but because so much of Africa was painted red on the map, it was difficult to reveal the truth without denigrating British rule.

There was, for example, one subject on which he had prepared a portfolio which drew from every country through which he had passed; it recorded the rites and traditions with which different tribes marked the onset of puberty and the end of childhood in their young men and women. The cries of girls being circumcised against their will and without anaesthetic still haunted him, and he had every intention of encouraging his friend Nat to mount a campaign against it. But Lord Mortimer was a patriot of the old sort and would not be prepared to accept any implied criticism of British colonial officers who, he would insist, were doing their best to bring civilisation to barbarians.

'Which reminds me,' said the old man, apparently inconsequentially, after he had been given a brief and expurgated account of Terts's recent travels, 'what's going on at Bradley's? Nobody tells me anything, but Richard seems to be planning to take his family off to Australia. I don't hold with all this gadding about. Anyone lucky enough to be born an Englishman ought to stay in England.'

'I gather there's some financial trouble,' said Terts carefully – but it soon appeared that Lord Mortimer was more conversant with the situation than he had suggested.

'Declaring yourself bankrupt doesn't solve anything. They ought to press on with their business until they can pay their debts. Lot of bad feeling in the City, I'm told. And I'm not too pleased myself. Aden's twenty-one now. Should have had his share of his mother's marriage settlement. Money that came from me. Held by Bradley's so that they could invest it, but should have been in a trust. They had no right to use it for themselves. All gone, it seems. If it were anyone but family, I'd sue him for misappropriation. Don't mention it to Aden, though. I suppose I'll have to find something for him myself. Don't want to stir up bad blood between brothers. Though you seem to have done that successfully enough on your own account.'

'What do you mean?'

'You'll know better than I do. I had a letter from Richard nine months ago. Said he couldn't trust himself to write to you personally without calling you a sneak and a traitor. But wanted you to know that he never wishes to see you again and that if you ever expect any of the Bradley fortune to come your way, you'd better think again because for one thing it doesn't exist any more and for another thing he'd rather give it to a beggar than let you profit from it.' Nearly ninety though he might be, Lord Mortimer delivered his message with gusto.

In view of his recent face-to-face quarrel with Richard, the message came as no surprise to Terts. But it reminded him uncomfortably of Bing's similar ultimatum at the time of his expulsion from Croxton.

'All the fault of that Jew-boy friend of yours, in my opinion,' added Lord Mortimer, pulling his rug more tightly around him.

'I won't have that, Grandfather. I know your views on the subject, but Nathan Rose is one of my closest friends and I don't like to hear him described as a Jew-boy.'

Lord Mortimer's approval of loyalty was just about strong enough to override his distaste for the whole Jewish race. 'Well, all right,' he conceded. 'But in return, tell him to keep his hands off Libby.'

'What are you talking about now?'

'He had the cheek to come down here. Said you'd sent him some photographs but wanted them to be kept here when he'd finished with them.'

'And so I did. It was kind of him to bring them in person.'

'Yes. Well. Libby gave him luncheon. And tea. Chattering away all the time in between. Next thing I know, he's here again. More photographs. More meals and walks. And then he has the nerve to ask her to spend a weekend with his parents. House party.'

'And did she go?'

'Certainly not. Had the good manners to ask me for permission. I made it clear there could be no question. No question at all.'

Poor Libby, thought Terts to himself. She had been imprisoned at Kinderley for far longer than she could originally have expected and now was refused the treat of even a temporary escape. In only two meetings, the relationship could not have developed very far, but Terts himself would have been happy to encourage it. Nat was a decent man with strong feelings of compassion and a good sense of humour. Even his father, who was almost universally hated by politicians and other newspapers for his delight in investigating wrongdoing and exposing hypocrisy, was in private life charming and cultured. Terts liked Mrs Rose less, but not for any reason to do with race or religion.

For a second time Lord Mortimer, speaking in an apparently casual manner, fitted his thoughts into Terts's.

'They'd never have accepted her, those people,' he said. 'Looked down on her for not being one of them. Her children the same, if she had any. Probably even have booted their own son out for not providing grandchildren of the right line. It's the mother's blood that counts, you see. She'd have been unhappy. She recognised that. A good girl, Libby.'

They were interrupted at that moment by the maid returning with a second tea tray, this one laden with a substantial cake in the interest of a younger appetite. Neither of the two men spoke until they were alone again. Then Lord Mortimer, although looking tired, was the first to resume the conversation.

'Something we have to talk about,' he said. 'I can't last for ever. If you go away again on one of these long trips of yours, I may not be here when you come back. India, Zanzibar, China, Africa. Time you had a rest. And there's the matter of the Kinderley estate.'

He paused, putting his thoughts in order.

'I made a new will after Bingham died,' he said. 'Thought Richard would always do all right from the Bradley side. May not be true now, of course, but I expect he's tucked enough away. Anyway, the estate will be yours. Money for Aden and Libby, of course, and something for young Victor when he comes of age. The title will go to that cousin of mine in Canada. Can't do anything about that. But the house and land to you. Listen, though. Land has to be managed, even when it's let. You can't just go away and hope it'll look after itself. It's not only a matter of your own income. Other people, workers, tenants, dependent on you. I need to know that you'll stay at home. There'll be enough for you to live on. You won't need to do this photography business, not for money.'

Had Terts never given the matter any thought, he might not have known what to say now. There had even been a brief period – when Victor was at his most obnoxious and Aden was still a schoolboy – when he might have accepted that he was the most suitable heir. But his travels had changed his mind, and he was able to answer without any doubts or reservations.

'Now that I'm back in England, I'll stay as long as you need me, Grandfather,' he said. They both knew that what he meant was 'until you die'. 'But after that, I can't promise to settle down here. I can't live a comfortable life while I know that all over the world people are suffering in ways which could be prevented if only the rest of the world knew what was happening. And I'm someone who can tell them. I can be their eyes. It doesn't go with sitting at home and collecting rents. I'm sorry. It was kind of you.'

There was the silence of disappointment before Lord Mortimer, suddenly sounding weaker, said in a hurt voice, 'You mean, you're turning it down? So what am I supposed to do? Aden doesn't know anything about land.'

'He'll be finishing at Oxford this summer, won't he? And he cares very much for the house,' Terts assured him. 'Although he'd need to hire an agent to deal with everything, he's going to need an income for the sort of life he wants to lead.'

In the excitement of winning a scholarship to New College three years earlier, Aden had confided his ambitions to his elder brother. One day he intended to write a history, coming as nearly as possible to the present day, which would rival the works of Macaulay and Green. First of all he must get a good degree, and then work for a doctorate and in time become a university professor. It would be a good many years, on this plan, before he could expect to earn anything at all, and even at the top of the academic ladder the financial rewards would not be great. A scholarly reputation, he had said then, would be sufficient recompense. But in the meantime, he could hardly live on air.

'Look at it this way, Grandfather,' Terts said earnestly. 'Aden could spend all his life in university libraries, doing his best to climb up the ladder of academic life and teaching undergraduates who'd rather be rowing or playing rugger. Or he could work in the Kinderley library, your library, as a gentleman and a scholar, studying and writing whatever he chooses. A gentleman,' Terts repeated, knowing that this more than anything else would appeal to his grandfather, who had never shared the Bradley attitude to working for money.

There was another long silence. Lord Mortimer sighed. 'Well, think about it for a little longer. Aden will be back here on vacation at the end of March. If you still feel the same then, get Notcutt to come over.' Notcutt was the family's solicitor.

Terts nodded and left his grandfather to enjoy another nap. Although he felt guilty about disappointing someone whose only wish was to behave generously to him, he had no intention of changing his mind. To become a landowner would be to become a prisoner, and he had chosen freedom as his way of life.

2

Was this really Aden? Thirty months earlier Terts had said goodbye to a brother who, although about to start his first term at university, was still little more than a schoolboy swot, quiet and shy. The thick-rimmed spectacles that he wore at that time had given him an owlish look, but since leaving Croxton he had adopted a new style that made him almost handsome. He would never be as tall as Terts, but he had learned to carry himself well instead of sidling around in a furtive way as though he were afraid of being noticed. But the biggest change was in his eyes. They had always been intelligent but now were bright and confident, interested in life as well as in books. The little brother had grown up.

'We were all sorry you couldn't be here for my twenty-first,' he said to Terts when the first flurry of his arrival for the Easter vacation was over. 'Libby put on a marvellous party for me here. She said it was like the old days, with dancing in the ballroom and a scrumptious feast.'

'Dancing, you!'

'Why not?' Aden gave a twirl or two to show off the neatness of his footwork.

'Did Grandfather –?'

'He only came down for long enough to propose a toast. I think he felt the noise and so many strangers milling around would be too much for him. He's very frail these days. Well, you'll have seen for yourself.'

Terts hesitated for a moment, wondering whether to put into words what was on the tip of his tongue and tell Aden what the future held for him. Yes, he would. With a little advance warning, the twenty-one year old would be able to express a proper gratitude to his grandfather instead of perhaps being rendered speechless by surprise. Besides, Terts himself could not help feeling guilty about the manner in which he had betrayed each of his two elder brothers in turn, even though he could not believe that he had done anything wrong in exposing the truth. Perhaps it was selfish to want this third brother to know, by contrast, who was the cause of his prospective good fortune. In that case, he was about to be selfish.

As he expected. Aden was momentarily silenced by astonishment before stammering out his gratitude for such a self-sacrificing gesture.

'So you can see yourself as a country gentleman, can you?' Terts asked, smiling.

'Oh, yes, I could work here.' Aden's eyes were even brighter than before, with a new excitement at the prospects opening before him. 'I'd still need to stay attached to Oxford. I have to have a supervisor for my doctoral thesis, to start with. But to have an income and a home – and not just any home, but Kinderley! Yes, that would be marvellous. And it might help to bring Jessie's parents round.'

'Who's Jessie?' asked Terts, already guessing the answer.

'She's the most beautiful girl in the world and I adore her and she adores me back.'

Terts gave a sympathetic smile. Once upon a time he too had been in love with the most beautiful girl in the world and he could still remember how it felt.

'Are you engaged?' he asked.

'Not officially, no. I mean, we know how we feel. But I've got another term to go at Oxford, and anyway she's only just eighteen. She'll need her parents' consent to get married before she's twenty-one, and she's not sure that they'll give it.'

This also was a situation familiar to Terts. He nodded understandingly.

'So we thought we'd have to wait for a bit, because my allowance isn't enough for two people to live on and I shan't be earning anything while I work for the doctorate. But this ought to make a difference to her parents. If she could look forward to being mistress of Kinderley ... This is frightfully decent of you, Terts. Absolutely stunning. I know Grandfather was definitely going to leave the house and land to you, because he told me and Libby on my twenty-first birthday what his plans were. So for you to let me have it instead ... gosh, I can't get over it. Grandfather will see you right money-wise, I take it?'

'He said so, yes. It doesn't really matter.' Lord Mortimer had already given Terts a degree of financial independence, and his income was augmented by a publisher who had invited him to collect together photographs linked by subject or geography for publication in book form. *Our World* covered his expenses while he was travelling in search of features for the magazine and recently the *Daily Bulletin* had also begun to pay him a retainer, with generous fees for pictures which were currently newsworthy. On top of that, although he had little interest in taking portrait photographs, he knew that he could earn a living in that field alone any time he chose.

As it happened, that was a thought already in Aden's mind.

'Could you do something else for me?' he begged. 'You know those marvellous photographs you took of Libby in her debutante year?'

'Don't tell me. You want me to take your beautiful Jessie?'

'Would you? I say, thanks terribly, Terts. What I'd like is one to go in the *Tatler* when the engagement's announced. You know the sort of thing: all hazy. And then some others with a bit more life to them. She's a dancer – moves like an angel. You could catch that. It would make a nice change for you, a beautiful girl, after all these wizened old women and starving children you usually take.'

'Right you are.' But Terts was curious. 'How did you come to meet a dancer?'

'Well, not really a dancer. Not professionally. She'd like to be, but her parents are so stuffy, they won't hear of her going on the stage, not even in ballet. But she's gone to classes ever since she was three. Passed exams or grades or whatever they call them every year.'

'But how –'

'– did I meet her? Well, the college had a Commem Ball last summer. There are never enough girls at these things to go round, so one of the chaps got his sister to bring some of her friends from her ballet class with her. I didn't have a partner of my own, and Jessie and I hit it off straightaway.'

'Have you seen her since? To get to know her?'

'She stayed on in Oxford – they all did – for a couple of days. And she came to my twenty-first, of course. But anyway, there are some things you know are right from the very first minute.'

'A dangerous principle, when it's the whole of your life that's at stake.' Terts himself had fallen in love with Venetia at first sight, so he understood his brother's feelings. But there had been no happy-ever-after ending to the romance, and perhaps – now that he could look back on it calmly – it had been just as well that there was time for his fiancée's fickleness to reveal itself. And there was another reason for expressing doubt in Aden's case. 'I'd have thought you'd want a wife on your own intellectual level. Don't you meet girls at Oxford? Undergraduates, I mean.'

'Who'd want to marry a blue-stocking? Yes, of course I meet some, and they all look already like the headmistresses they're bound to become. If I want to have a scholarly conversation, I'll have it with scholars. Chaps. What I want in a wife is someone who delights my eyes. And is lively and fun to be with when I'm not working. Besides, I feel obliged ...'

He came to a halt in sudden embarrassment.

'Go on,' said Terts.

'Well, at the ball, dancing with her ... I'd never been with anyone who moved so beautifully. So close to me, and looking into my eyes, and – oh, I don't know. I suppose you could say I was swept off my feet. And by the end of it I was a bit drunk. We both were. And tired, by the time it got to five o'clock in the morning. I took her up to my rooms to rest before the breakfast. And ...'

'And you made love to her?'

'Yes.'

'Aden, you don't have to marry every girl you sleep with! If you did, there wouldn't be a bachelor left in England.'

'But it was her first time. Well, and mine, as a matter of fact. But it mattered more for her. She was still only seventeen then. I ought not to have ... And she's been very strictly brought up. Respectable parents who'd have a fit if they found out. I've spoiled her, in a way, for the sort of marriage they might want for her. But that's not the point, really. It's not just that I *ought* to marry her. I *want* to. I want to frightfully. It was so – well, I just can't tell you how marvellous it was.'

Terts made no attempt to conceal his doubts. If only his younger brother had had a father to introduce him to the ways of the world instead of leaving him to stumble alone. And whose fault was it that Aden had never known his father? Terts would have continued to play the part of the concerned elder brother had Aden not brought the conversation to a close.

'Well, you'll meet her for yourself, and then you'll see.'

'Yes, all right. She'd better come here.' With so many rooms in Kinderley Court that were never used now that Lord Mortimer had ceased to entertain, Terts had furnished one of the bedrooms as a studio. Its original dressing room, equipped with everything he needed for developing and printing and with all light excluded, provided a more spacious darkroom than the tiny box room he had appropriated as a schoolboy. 'Have you got her telephone number?' In spite of Lord Mortimer's objections to everything new-fangled, Libby had insisted on having a telephone line installed so that the parents of her pupils could get in touch easily.

Aden knew the number off by heart, but gave it only after a slight hesitation.

'It might be better if the invitation came from Libby. Jessie's parents –'

'Aden,' said Terts, 'have you met her parents? Do they know yet that you exist?' He hardly troubled to wait for an answer before slipping back into the role of the father-substitute elder brother. 'It's important, getting to know a girl's family, because you'd be marrying into it, after all. If you don't get on together for some reason you could be storing up all sorts of trouble for the future.'

'It doesn't really have anything to do with them,' Aden said stubbornly. 'A marriage is between a man and a woman. That's all that matters.'

'Not in practice, it isn't. A girl never completely cuts herself off from her parents. If for some reason they don't accept you ...'

But why should they not accept a young man who was clever and good-looking and now was assured of a great inheritance?

Or at least, he would be assured of it any day now. There was a necessary word of warning to be spoken.

'You'd better not mention your expectations of Kinderley until Grandfather's told you himself,' Terts suggested. 'He hasn't altered his will yet. He wanted me to think about it for a few weeks. In case I changed my mind and decided I'd like to take over after all. But I shan't. After he sends for Notcutt, that's when you could tell her.'

'Yes. Right. Thanks again, Terts. And the photographs?'

Terts still felt a slight uneasiness about whether Aden had chosen the right girl for the right reasons; and taking a formal photograph would make any engagement one degree more difficult to break. On the other hand, it would give him the opportunity to meet her and form his own opinion.

'Certainly I'll do that. I'll get Libby to invite your Jessie here,' he promised.

3

Yes, she was indeed beautiful. As he held out his hand to Jessica Stone at the moment of their introduction Terts could understand how it was that Aden had been bowled over by her looks.

Although he did his best to resist it, that thought brought back into his mind the memory of his first glimpse of Venetia at Lady Glencross's ball, and the surge of desire which had overwhelmed him as he waited to be received.

The two women were very different in appearance. Venetia was blonde-haired and blue-eyed and fair-skinned; Jessica's hair was dark, her eyes were brown and her skin was a smooth, sun-kissed olive colour – a Mediterranean complexion. Her face was oval while Venetia's had been heart-shaped, narrowing to a small mouth and chin. Both women, compared at the same age, were slim but Venetia's body had rarely been still. Her natural exuberance had shown itself in a kind of restlessness, as though she were perpetually dancing to unheard music; and the changing expressions of her face were the outward manifestations of her vivacity of spirit.

Jessica, by contrast – even now, when she was smiling in greeting – exuded a peacefulness which almost presented itself as placidity. Yet in spite of all these differences there was one feature which the young woman standing in front of Terts had in common with the remembered woman whom he had taken into his arms beside the lake on the night of Libby's ball. It was a straightness of back, and the way she held her head high on a long, slender neck, which gave Jessica's whole body a stretched appearance – and Venetia too had had this quality. It tempted him to touch, to stroke, to feel beneath that smooth skin the outline of a perfect shape. But Venetia had never allowed him to succumb to that temptation, and of course in the case of his brother's fiancée the thought must not be entertained even for a second.

With the handshake over, Jessica retreated once again into stillness. But this appearance of placidity could surely not be permanent. Aden had talked of her as being 'lively and fun'. No doubt she was simply showing a polite restraint in meeting a stranger. Well, that wouldn't prove to be a barrier for very long. Although it was several years since Terts had last agreed to let an eighteen-year-old English girl sit for him, it had always been one of his talents to make even the stiffest of his subjects respond to the mood in which he wished to capture her likeness. He would soon put a sparkle into Jessica's eyes.

There was one respect, though, in which today's sitter could not rival those of an earlier decade. The current fashion for short skirts did Jessica no favours. How much more delightful Venetia and her contemporaries had always looked in their long, flowing dresses! Or was it just that the fashions with which a young man first fell in love remained for ever his touchstone of elegance? Jessica had good legs, straight and slim. But the knee-length line of her skirt destroyed the natural proportions of her body. Even though he tutted at himself for having become an old fogey at the age of thirty-five, he found the style ugly. Already, as he showed her the way up to his studio, he was deciding that her picture for the *Tatler* should be a half-length, taken sitting down.

He opened the door for her to go in first and then found himself walking into her as she stopped dead in amazement.

'Did you do these? Are they photographs? No, they can't be.'

She was staring at a white wall to which had been fixed rows of horizontal battens. On these were displayed forty or fifty images in various stages of treatment. Some were proofs and some were finished but unmounted prints.

Some were straightforward representations, even though it was not always clear what they represented, while others depicted impossibilities. It was towards a girl with five legs, each kicking higher than the one before, that she now began to move.

'Why can't they be photographs?'

'I thought – I suppose I'm being silly – I thought you could only photograph what was there. What you see.'

'And you've never seen a girl with five legs? But I'm sure you could kick one of your legs up like that and pass through each position.'

'Well, of course.' With a startling lack of modesty she hitched up her skirt until Terts caught a glimpse of suspender. She raised her right leg until it almost touched her nose before gracefully lowering it again. 'But –'

'They're only a bit of fun.' After his long absence abroad he had returned to England to find European art in a state of revolution. It was no longer enough to hide the subject of a painting beneath shapes designed to distort it, as Braque and Picasso had done. Now a new generation was producing absurdities, paintings made all the more surreal by the meticulous skill with which each incongruous element was depicted. Why should photography not take the same path? Since he had promised to remain at home for as long as his grandfather was still alive, Terts had looked around for some way of amusing himself and these technical experiments, imposing images on top of each other, were the result.

The effect on Jessica was extraordinary. A moment earlier she had been calm and characterless. But now, as she moved along the display, her body reacted to everything she saw. Sometimes she tried to mimic a pose. Sometimes she moved her hands and arms to copy a shape which was not the shape of anything which had ever existed. Sometimes she laughed aloud as she succeeded in identifying some common object which had been photographed from an unfamiliar angle.

She was still laughing as she turned to face him, and Terts had a struggle to conceal his astonishment at the change in her. Aden had told him that she moved marvellously and it was true: movement transformed her. To make her interesting as well as beautiful was not going to be the struggle he had feared.

He still owned the heavy Gandolfi camera that he had used for Libby's debutante portraits in the far-off life that had ended with the war. But since his return he had bought a Leica and here was the perfect opportunity to take the same poses twice and compare the results. He had already arranged the lighting and reflectors and needed only to pull up a chair for her now that he had decided on the half-length.

This part of the session did not take too long. When he expressed himself satisfied Jessica stood up, expecting that he had finished; but Terts shook his head.

'That was for the magazine,' he told her. 'But Aden wants me to take some more, for himself. To show you moving, he said.'

'Can you do that? Doesn't it just blur?' She began to move around the room as though she were in her dancing class, her arms moving expressively as she extended one slim leg behind her.

'I certainly can't do it while you're wearing those clothes. They're very smart, but there's no fluidity. Hang on a minute. I have an idea. Come with me.'

He led her down to the schoolroom in which Libby was, as usual at this hour of the day, teaching the youngest children to read.

'Sorry to interrupt,' he said. 'But I wondered whether you still have any of your fancy dress costumes. Not the dressing-up clothes that we played with as children, but from your Season.' There had been a plethora of fancy dress balls in 1913, he remembered; and although many of the costumes were hired, several of them had been run up by the family dressmaker.

Libby smiled at the memory. 'Yes, of course.' In a house as large as Kinderley there was never any need to throw anything away. 'Help yourself. Although the moths may have beaten you to it, of course.'

She told him where to look, in an attic storeroom in the other wing of the house. Jessica gasped in disbelief as they made their way along dark corridors and up several flights of stairs. 'What an enormous house! When I came for Aden's party, all those grand entertaining rooms were breathtaking enough, but I didn't realise how much further the building spread out. You must feel it quite a responsibility that it will all be yours one day.'

So Aden had accepted the warning that it would be wise to keep quiet about his expectations until Lord Mortimer's new will had been drawn up and signed. It was tempting to see how Jessica would react if she was told that she might before long be mistress of Kinderley; but Terts resisted the impulse. That would be for Aden to reveal. Assuming, of course, that the attachment persisted.

The room which Libby had described was furnished with nothing but three huge wardrobes. As Terts opened one of them, Jessica burst out laughing.

'The moths never had a chance!'

It was true: the smell of mothballs was overpowering. He could hardly expect Jessica to try on any of the dresses until they had been well shaken out and hung outside to air. All the same, he pulled out the particular garment that he had had in mind.

None of the costumes had ever been expected to bear much relationship to reality. This one – a simple sleeveless white robe, full length, with a golden cord at the waist – had been assumed to turn Libby into a Grecian priestess.

'If Aden had told me what he wanted, I could have brought some of my dancing costumes,' said Jessica.

'Then you must come here again and do just that. There's no need to rush everything into one day.'

'Aden's going off tomorrow on a reading party, whatever that is, with his tutor.'

'He doesn't need to be here. Even today you're officially Libby's guest, aren't you?' The casual question resurrected his curiosity on the subject. 'Aden told me that you didn't want your parents to know about him. Are you expecting them to disapprove?'

'They'll say I'm too young. But I'm afraid, yes, they don't really believe that young people should marry for love. I hope that in a year or two ... But I don't know.'

'If not for love, how do they expect anyone to marry?'

'By matchmaker,' said Jessica simply. 'There's probably some old woman who's got the perfect husband lined up for me already and is just waiting for the right moment to introduce us.'

'Matchmaking!' Terts could hardly believe his ears. Surely nobody in England went in for arranged marriages any longer. Unless ... He looked at her more closely. 'Are you Jewish, Jessica?'

'Yes. Why do you ask?'

'Does Aden know?'

'I'm not sure. I've never particularly either said or not said anything about it. I'm sure he wouldn't feel –'

'No. No, I'm sure he wouldn't. But I ought perhaps to warn you that our grandfather's views are, well, intemperate. He's a very old man and I'm afraid his prejudices are too strongly engrained by now ever to change.'

'So you think I ought to pretend –'

'No need to pretend anything, no. But it might be as well not to bring the subject up.'

'It sounds as though that's another good reason for keeping our engagement quiet for a little while, then.'

She meant, of course, until after the death of Lord Mortimer. Terts found the thought distasteful – and yet wasn't he behaving in slightly the same way himself when he assured Nathan Rose that he would be ready to set out on another expedition as soon as he was free?

'I'll tell Aden,' Jessica said. 'In so many words, I mean, just to be sure that he knows. And to be sure that there's no problem.'

'I think that would be wise. Because you don't want to have secrets. So you'll come here again, will you? For a weekend, not just a day. With clothes that you can dance in.'

She nodded her head enthusiastically, and then her smile became shyer.

'It's terribly nice of you to be so friendly,' she said. 'I mean, I met Aden at Oxford first of all, and his rooms were just like anyone else's. I didn't know that his family was anything special. So when I came here for his twenty-first, and saw Kinderley Court, well! But Libby was so welcoming, and now you have been as well. I really do appreciate it.'

Leaning forward, she kissed him lightly on the cheek. He was still holding the Grecian dress, and as it was pressed between them the smell of the mothballs rose almost to choke them. Coughing and laughing, they made their way down three flights of stairs so that Terts could hand Jessica back to his brother.

4

Jessica arrived at Kinderley for the second of her photographic sessions on a bright March day, a week after Aden had left for his reading party. Libby watched in some surprise as all her guest's luggage was unloaded from the car which had brought her from the station.

'Don't worry, it *is* only a weekend visit,' said Jessica reassuringly. 'But I was asked to bring lots of different clothes for the photographs. And the tutu needs a suitcase to itself.'

The tutu was not what Terts had had in mind as a dancing costume. He was not a ballet enthusiast and found the bulky layers of tulle ungainly. Luckily Jessica had also packed another ballet skirt, this one of mid-calf length. It was full enough to allow her complete freedom of movement and was far more becoming. This was the first garment he picked up when she laid out all her clothes for his inspection.

This time he intended to use only his new Leica, so that there would be no need for her to pose in any fixed position. He had already carried a gramophone into the ballroom and now, taking her there, he wound it up and asked her to dance to the music. Jessica followed his instructions with a complete lack of self-consciousness. Although he was no expert, it did seem to him that she danced remarkably well and he could sympathise with her regret that her parents would not allow her to go on the stage.

After prowling around for a few minutes he lifted the needle off the record.

'I'm going to start the music again,' he told her. 'This time, if I say "Freeze!" I'd like you to hold the pose if you can. I'll be very quick. Then I'll tell you to go on again. They won't all work, but if I take a dozen shots we should get a few good ones. I'll develop them while you're here, so that we can try again tomorrow if we need to.' He rewound the gramophone. 'Right. Off you go.'

Anyone watching might have laughed to see the speed at which he now scurried round, making sure he was always ready at the point where Jessica was about to arrive, and poised for exactly the right angle. She herself was quick to understand what he wanted and to position herself as he wanted her. Her balance was good, and she had a dancer's ability to hold her head dramatically high. 'Good,' said Terts, over and over again. 'Yes, very good.'

'Are you going to give me five legs?' she asked teasingly when he indicated that he had taken enough.

'I doubt whether that's exactly what Aden has in mind. But I'd like to try some more with the dress I showed you on your last visit. I can promise you that it smells of nothing but sunshine now.'

He held out Libby's Grecian gown and watched in surprise as Jessica unfastened her skirt at the waistband and let it drop to the floor. Underneath it she was wearing only a tight-fitting garment which resembled a swimming costume, except that it revealed very much more of her thighs than would have been regarded as decent on a beach. They were beautiful thighs, long and slim, with just the faintest bulge of muscle, but Terts had not expected her to display them with such insouciance.

'Oh, I'm sorry,' she said, flushing slightly and picking the skirt from the floor so that she could hold it in front of her. 'We often have to make quick changes in class and on performance nights, and as long as we're wearing our leotards we never think anything of it.'

Terts ought not to have thought anything of it either. Often enough in his recent journey across Africa he had come across women who wore much less than this, revealing their breasts and buttocks with no sense of embarrassment. But he had somehow not expected Aden's girl to behave in such a way.

The Grecian dress suggested a more dignified style of photograph. Terts led the way outside and posed his subject in turn on the terrace, at the top of a flight of stone steps, beside a pillar with one hand raised to touch it, looking at a statue and, at the end, with both arms raised as if in praise of the beauty of the day. Then he paused for a long time, staring at her, while she waited patiently for her next instructions.

'I have an idea,' he said. 'You said you'd brought your tutu. I could take a picture of you to resemble one of Degas' ballet dancers. It was seeing you beside the pillar which made me think of it. Wearing one of Libby's other old costumes, you could be a Gainsborough lady. Wouldn't it be fun to surprise Aden with a whole set of Jessica as different painters might have painted her?'

She clapped her hands in pleasure at the idea, and showed her familiarity with at least one of the Degas paintings by moving straight into the pose of a dancer tying her shoe. When she went off to change, Terts rang for a maid to carry down the other fancy-dress costumes, all of which within the past week had been well shaken free of mothballs and aired in the sunshine. For his own part, he went to fetch a book which illustrated many of the world's greatest paintings. Jessica would have no trouble in suggesting the stillness of a Vermeer woman; and there was a Raphael, he felt sure, whose subject had exactly her type of dark-eyed beauty. Yes, there it was: *La Velata*. By the time Jessica returned, she found him scribbling notes in excitement.

By the time the Degas and the Gainsborough imitations had been successfully recorded, it was time for Jessica to change yet again, this time for dinner. This was nowadays the only meal for which Lord Mortimer joined the rest of the family. He had not met Jessica before, because at Aden's twenty-first birthday party he had appeared only for a moment or two. Out of politeness he asked her questions, trying to discover what her interests were; but she was perhaps inhibited by Terts's earlier warning that she would be well advised not to reveal her Jewishness. Her answers were brief and nervous. After a while her host gave up the attempt and instead chatted to Libby, who was always delighted to describe the latest doings of the children in her school and to pass on news of his great-grandson, Victor, who in a tribute to her teaching was now doing well at an ordinary prep school before going to Croxton like his father and uncles.

Next morning, while Jessica was arranging one of Libby's shawls to transform herself into Raphael's model, Terts was summoned to see his grandfather. He found Lord Mortimer propped up on pillows in his four-poster bed. His body was frail but his eyes were aggressively bright and there was nothing feeble about his tone of voice.

'Just wanted to ask whether you'd changed your mind? About not settling down at Kinderley.'

'No, I still feel the same. Still tremendously grateful that you were prepared to give me the opportunity. But Aden will do well here, I'm sure.'

'Hm. Well, if I can't persuade you ... Have a word with Notcutt on that telephone instrument, will you? Ask him to come up here and I'll tell him what to do.'

'Certainly I'll do that.' Terts assumed that this had been the reason for his summons and turned to go; but there was another matter to be discussed.

'That girl at dinner last night,' said Lord Mortimer. 'Your friend or Libby's?'

It was easy to tell there was trouble on the horizon. It seemed wise to give a cautious answer.

'I've been taking photographs of her,' Terts said truthfully. 'In different costumes, so I needed longer than a day.'

'That's all right, then, if she's just one of your models. I was afraid it might be Libby, forgetting what we'd agreed.'

'What had you agreed, Grandfather?' But even as he asked the question, Terts guessed what the answer might be.

'She's Jewish, isn't she, this Jessica girl? I can sniff a Jew a mile off. I told Libby years ago, when that friend of yours started hanging around her, that I never wanted to see an Israelite at my table again. Not your fault. I never said it in so many words to you. But don't do it again. I'm right, aren't I? A Jewess.'

Terts picked his words carefully. 'If I want a particular person as the subject of a photograph, I don't ask them that sort of question. I don't even ask myself. What they look like, or what I can make them look like, is all that matters.'

He was making things worse; fuelling his grandfather's suspicions instead of extinguishing them.

'Thing I've always like about you, Mortimer, is that you're straight with me. Never known you tell me a fib. Straight out now, then. Are you in love with this girl?'

'No, certainly not.'

'But she is Jewish?'

The sincerity of his first answer made all the more conspicuous his hesitation before the second.

'Come on, Mortimer. Out with it.'

'I think so, yes. But I do feel –'

'Doesn't matter what you feel. Still my house. I decide who I want and don't want sleeping under my roof. Too old to change now. No need for you to be discourteous and pack her straight off. I shan't come down to dinner tonight. But don't ask her again.'

'I'm sorry to have upset you, Grandfather.' As Terts left to rejoin Jessica, he had an uneasy feeling that he had been deceitful: telling the truth, certainly, but not the whole truth. Ever since the one shameful act which he had never dared confess to anyone – the causing of his father's death – he had indeed tried always to be straight with his grandfather: but today's conversation fell short of that standard.

But there was something different that worried him even more. Should he have lied for Aden's sake? Had he by his admission wrecked Jessica's chances of ever becoming mistress of Kinderley? He paused for a moment, looking down at the Great Hall from the gallery which encircled it, while he tried to sort out his thoughts.

It would be all right. No damage had been done. In fact, it was as well that Aden should know for certain that he would be wise not to introduce Jessica as his fiancée. If he wanted to remain the heir to Kinderley, he would have to keep his secret until his grandfather was dead. But since he was already expecting to conceal the attachment until Jessica was twenty-one, that would be no great hardship. Terts dismissed his anxieties and returned to the studio, where a Raphael beauty awaited him.

5

It was the Bonnard which was the cause of all the subsequent trouble. While Terts was being quizzed by his grandfather, Jessica had amused herself by turning the pages of his book of paintings and finding several examples of costumes which would be easy to copy. The Bonnard, which she showed him laughingly once they had finished with Raphael, would be easiest of all, since the woman rising from her bath was completely naked.

'Oh, I hardly think ...' But Terts checked his own protest. He had noticed a dancer's flesh-coloured body-stocking amongst the clothes which Jessica had laid out for his inspection. Presumably she intended to wear this. 'Well, why not?' he agreed.

While Jessica divested herself of her Italian costume he went to choose a bathroom. He half filled the bath and stirred the surface with his hand, observing the way in which the light reflected off the water. Then he retreated for a few minutes, waiting for her to take up the pose.

She called him in when she was ready and he stepped forward with the camera to his eye. He had already taken the first exposure before he realised what he was seeing. He had found Jessica at their first meeting beautiful in her ordinary clothes, and even more beautiful in the leotard which fitted over her slender body so closely; now she was more beautiful still, wearing nothing but her own smooth, tautly stretched skin.

'I thought ...' His mouth was suddenly almost too dry for speech. 'The body-stocking ...'

'Wouldn't give at all the same glint to the water, would it? But you're wasting the wetness.' She lowered herself into the water before rising to take the pose again. She was facing away from him. Beads of water glistened on her long, straight back and on buttocks as firm and pointed as those of a young child. Since the situation had arisen, he might as well take advantage of it. Sunlight and skin and water would combine in his camera to produce a perfect picture of a perfect body.

What they produced in himself was lust. He told himself that this was Aden's girl and that he must not touch. He told himself that she was behaving badly and that he ought to despise her for it. He knew that he needed only to continue holding the Leica in front of him for it to act as a barrier, a defence of decency. But now she was turning towards him, holding out a hand so that he could support her as she stepped out of the bath. As he set the camera down on the bathroom stool he cursed himself for weakness and disloyalty. But once it had left his hands and she was standing in front of him, he paused only for long enough to lock the door before tearing off his clothes.

It was because she had so surprisingly offered herself to him that what happened next was passionate and physically fulfilling. But in a curious way it was that same invitation which made the whole episode sordid: a writhing of two animal bodies on a cold linoleum floor. He had not courted her. He had not really wanted her. His body had moved, in a sense, against his own wishes. As his heartbeat steadied and he began to breathe normally again, he had to swallow a lump of self-disgust in a dry throat. In silence he helped

Jessica to her feet and in silence turned to pick up his scattered clothes. And yet he knew that he would go to her bedroom that night.

Had she enticed Aden in the same way? Ought he to warn his inexperienced younger brother and save him from any more formal entanglement with a girl who clearly held fidelity to be of little importance? But how could he say anything without revealing his own part in yet another fraternal betrayal?

By now Jessica had towelled herself dry and covered herself in her robe. Turning toward him, she kissed him on the lips.

'We could do some more paintings,' she suggested. 'Goya's Maja Unclothed. Dürer's Adam and Eve. They won't take so long to set up if there are no clothes to fiddle with.'

'You obviously studied that book with care.' Terts managed to return her smile and deliberately set himself the task of feeling light-hearted again. What was done was done. In twenty-four hours she would leave Kinderley and he would make it clear that the episode must be forgotten and certainly never repeated. She would be glad to know that she could trust his discretion. In the meantime – yes, some more nudes could be copied. Why not?

The next day, after a night in which neither of the two slept very much, Terts delivered the lecture he had prepared: reminding her of her duty to Aden and promising not to reveal what had happened. To his surprise, she appeared not to find this a relief.

'Aden's only a boy, really. Not a man like you.'

'I'm almost twice your age,' he pointed out, alarmed by the thought that she might be proposing to transfer her affections.

'That's what I like. What a fine couple we'd make, you and I, here at Kinderley.'

Terts stared at her in astonishment. Was that what had been behind her provocative behaviour? Had it all the time been the house she wanted, rather than the man? Aden would have told her when she first came to Kinderley that his elder brother was expected to inherit it, and had accepted the advice not to talk about his own improved expectations until Lord Mortimer confirmed them. Well, that time would come very soon. Terts had already telephoned the solicitor, who would be arriving to take his instructions in three days' time. There would be no harm in letting her know.

'This won't be my home after my grandfather dies,' he told her. 'Although no doubt Aden will invite me to stay whenever I'm in England. I shall be away on my travels again before too long. I'm not interested in settling down anywhere. Or marrying,' he added, to make the situation clear.

'Aden?' she queried, picking on the only point that puzzled her.

'Yes, he will inherit Kinderley Court one day. I don't want it. So, as I said a moment ago, you'd better put the past twenty-four hours out of your mind. We've behaved badly. The least we can do is never to let him know. Will you promise that – for my sake as well as yours?'

It was almost amusing to see her struggling to come to terms with the changed situation. She was subdued as she made her promise and said goodbye. After she had left, Terts scribbled a note to his brother.

Jessica has just been here for me to take the dancing photographs. I'm afraid I let slip the fact that you are about to become Grandfather's heir: Notcutt is due to call later this week. Sorry to deprive you of the drama of making the announcement – but I can guarantee that the news took her by surprise. She obviously believed that it was a homeless undergraduate that she'd agreed to marry.

Would it be kind to add a warning that Aden had better continue to keep the engagement secret during his grandfather's lifetime, since Lord Mortimer was not likely to accept Jessica as future mistress of Kinderley? Terts decided not to put that in writing but to mention it next time he saw his brother. For the next eight weeks all Aden's concentration would be on the need to do well in his Finals. There was no danger that he would unexpectedly turn up at Kinderley with Jessica in tow. Nothing was likely to happen.

In this belief he was wrong. A few weeks after the bathroom episode, Jessica arrived unannounced at Kinderley.

'You shouldn't really have come,' Terts told her. 'I did warn you, didn't I, that my grandfather is, well, unreasonable on the subject of welcoming Jewish people into his house. I can see that you must find this very offensive, but –'

'I had to speak to you.' Jessica interrupted him with a note of desperation in her voice. 'Is there somewhere we can talk? With no servants listening.'

'We'll walk in the rose garden.' He led the way there and they sat down side by side on a circular bench in the centre. He waited for her to explain her arrival, but at first she seemed unable to speak. 'So what –?'

'I've fallen,' she said.

Not understanding the phrase, Terts looked her up and down, expecting to see signs of bruising or fracture; but she shook her head impatiently.

'I'm expecting a baby. Your baby.'

Terts's first impulse was to protest that it was impossible. But of course it was not impossible at all. He felt his throat grow dry as he struggled for words.

'It's too soon, surely, for you to be certain?'

'I'm three weeks late,' she told him. 'And I keep being sick. Certain enough.'

'But what makes you so sure that it's mine.'

'Because there's been no one else.'

'Aden said –'

'At the Commem Ball, yes. But that was a year ago. And it wasn't something I'd meant to happen. I never drink at home, and all the champagne ... I was a bit drunk. So was he. Afterwards, we agreed we'd forget about it, sort of, and wait until we were married, like we should have done anyway.'

She began to cry. 'My parents will kill me. Well, not kill me, but turn me out. They're so strict. I need to get married straightaway.'

'I thought they wouldn't give you permission? Wasn't that why you and Aden were going to wait until you were twenty-one?'

'They'll give me permission for the baby's sake. They'll have to. But they won't ever speak to me again. It's bad enough on its own, and you not being Jewish makes it worse. I have to get married. I know Aden will be hurt. I know it means I shan't ever live in Kinderley. But it's your baby and you have to look after me.'

Although he had had a moment or two in which to see this coming, Terts was thrown into confusion by the demand. It was true that he had lusted after Jessica. She had a beautiful face and a beautiful, marvellous, perfect body, and she had deliberately put temptation in his way. He had proved unable to resist the temptation; but that didn't mean that he liked her.

It seemed to him that she was an unprincipled young woman. Almost certainly she had presented herself at her most seductive in the belief that he was his grandfather's heir and had happily transferred her affections back again to Aden once she was told the true situation. No doubt, too, she would equally happily stay with Aden if he could be persuaded that he was the father of the child she expected. Remembering her behaviour in the bathroom, Terts had no doubt at all that if she were to hurry down to Oxford the next day she would be capable of setting up a situation which would allow Terts's full-term baby to appear as Aden's premature one.

Perhaps that would be the best solution. But it would not be an honest one. Was it right that Aden should be deceived in such a way? Ought he to be told the truth?

He might in fact be happier in a false situation. He wanted to marry Jessica as soon as possible, he wanted to live with her at Kinderley, he presumably wanted to have children and, since the baby would be his own brother's, he would no doubt be able to recognise genuine family likenesses when it was born. All those things could happen if the shameful secret were never revealed.

The alternative would be for him to see the woman he loved marrying someone else, and what happiness could that possibly bring him? Or else Jessica might in desperation try to abort the baby. Given the strictness of her upbringing, such an act would be likely to prey on her conscience for the rest of her life. Terts realised that all he was doing was trying to argue away his own pangs of conscience, allowing expediency to overrule truth.

What did it matter, when the expediency fell in Aden's favour? To his surprise, he discovered that it mattered very much. He had no reason to disbelieve what Jessica had told him. The child was his. His responsibility; his own flesh and blood. Because he had never wanted to be tied down by a woman, he had always managed to thrust out of his mind the other possible tie, of fatherhood. It was astonishing to discover that he wanted this child, so unintentionally conceived. He wanted to love it and to be loved. He wanted to watch it grow up. He wanted to make sure that it had a happy life and a useful life. He had given a great estate away to Aden with hardly a second thought, but how could he bear to give away also this tiny scrap of life?

He shook his head almost in disbelief at the unexpected strength of his own emotions. It was necessary to spell the situation out to himself, because it was still not clear-cut. To accept his role as a father would condemn him to the unforgiving anger of his brother and to life with a woman for whom he felt no respect. Would the company of his son or daughter be enough to compensate for this?

He was just about to tell himself that yes, it would, when he remembered something that had happened a very long time ago: something that he had completely forgotten, because it had meant nothing to him at the time except a chivalrous gesture on behalf of a dead friend.

He remembered a woman standing in a suburban recreation ground, twisting her face away to conceal the lupus which disfigured it. He remembered her tears of desperation, as bitter – and for the same reason – as those which Jessica was shedding now. And he remembered the stiff formality of the offer he had made to her.

'*If it would be useful to you, Miss Adams, I would be prepared to go through a ceremony of marriage with you.*'

He had never seen her since the day after the wedding and had no idea where she was now. If she had tried during the intervening years to divorce him on grounds of desertion, presumably someone would have told him.

So that was that. The choice he had been agonising over did not exist. Aden would get the land, the girl and the baby, and Terts himself must be generous not only in giving but in taking care that the last gift at least was never revealed.

He gave a single sigh before turning to face Jessica.

'I'm very sorry,' he said as gently as he could. 'But I'm afraid you'll have to stay with Aden. I can't marry you. I'm married already.'

6

Five weeks after Jessica, confused and tearful, had left Kinderley, Terts came down to breakfast to find a letter awaiting him in a handwriting he knew well.

'This is from Nat Rose,' he told Libby. 'You've met him, haven't you?'

A faint flush came to his sister's cheeks. 'Yes, I remember him. Nice man. Very intelligent. What does he want?'

'It's about the miners.' So self-sufficient was the Kinderley Estate that the General Strike of 1926 had begun and ended without any more serious effect than the non-appearance of *The Times*. But the miners' strike, with which the dispute had begun, was still dragging on.

'*Our World* doesn't usually concern itself with British stories, but he's decided that that's perhaps a mistake. Since I'm not prepared to travel abroad at the moment, he's asked me to do a feature on the miners. Some of them are in a bad way, apparently. And there are a lot of casualties from the past, with injuries or industrial diseases. I'd like to have a go. What do you think?'

Libby would know what he meant. Their grandfather was not suffering from any particular illness, but now that he had achieved the target of his ninetieth birthday he seemed to be allowing himself to fade away.

'Yes, you should go,' she said without hesitation. 'You could telephone here every evening to make sure there's no change, and it wouldn't take you more than a few hours if you had to come back, would it?'

'No. Right, then. I won't be away for long. It'll be a bit different from trekking through a jungle and then trying not to let anyone become aware of what I'm doing. Presumably the miners and their families will be glad of the publicity.'

He left the next morning and returned five days later, shocked by what he had seen but pleased by the knowledge that he would have a dramatic portfolio of pictures from which to choose. There were hungry children, dirty and poorly dressed; worried women in curlers and pinafores; the miners themselves, making each cigarette last as long as possible as they gathered on street corners, weary from days of doing nothing; and the stark silhouettes of the deserted collieries. Terts hurried up to his dark room to process the films. Only when the prints were hanging up to dry did he report his return to Libby.

'There was a frightful row last night, after you'd telephoned,' she told him. 'Aden came home yesterday.'

'Of course, his term must have ended. How did he get on in his exams?'

'He won't know for a bit. But that's not what the row was about. He announced at dinner that he was engaged.'

'Oh.' Terts's heart gave an anxious thump. He had never got round to warning his brother that Jessica had better be kept in the background for as long as their grandfather was still alive. 'He didn't bring her with him, did he?'

'No. She'd been to visit him at Oxford, apparently, a few weeks earlier. For an Eights Week Ball. That was when they got engaged. She stayed a couple of days and then she went back home, to let him get on with his work. The problem last night was that Aden mentioned her name. At least, he said

Jessie, and then Grandfather went very quiet and said he supposed that was short for Jessica and Aden said yes, and then –'

'Grandfather remembered that he'd met her?'

'He asked whether she was the same Jessica who'd come to pose for you, and of course she was, and then he just flew off the handle. Said that she was a Jew, and Aden needn't try to pretend because you'd told him, and he wasn't going to have her living in his house and Aden had better go straight off and disentangle himself and needn't come back until he'd done it.'

'Oh, my God! Libby, it's so unreasonable!'

'Yes,' she agreed. 'Although – I must say, I didn't take to her much. She's good-looking but – well, common. Not really the right sort of wife for Aden.'

'That's for Aden himself to decide.'

'Agreed. Just as it's for Grandfather himself to decide who he wants to have living in his house. Anyway, if Aden's got any sense he'll keep quiet about her from now on. It may not be much longer. After Aden had stalked out, Grandfather looked absolutely terrible. I got the doctor to come this morning. He took his blood pressure and didn't seem to like what he found.'

'Is this what happened with you and Nat, Libby?'

This time her flush was deeper.

'We hardly knew each other. There was no question of an engagement. I don't suppose there ever would have been. It was just that we felt, well, friendly, right from the start.'

'But Grandfather said stop and you stopped.'

'Yes. I thought ... He's been so good to me. Well, to all of us. I was sorry it was necessary to make a choice, but I decided my loyalty ought to be to him. So. I haven't seen Nat since. I don't suppose he even remembers who I am by now.'

There was a moment's silence between them. Terts felt sure that his sister's next question would be to ask whether Nat was married; but instead she pushed away her half-drunk cup of tea and left the breakfast table, leaving Terts to consider his brother's position.

Aden would want to postpone any thought of actually marrying while Lord Mortimer was still alive. But if Jessica's visit to Oxford had gone as Terts suspected she intended it to, it would not be very long before she would be urgently pressing her fiancé for a ceremony to make sure their child was born legitimately. Well, that would be all right so long as it was kept secret. Aden had better find himself somewhere else to live. His allowance would not be enough to pay rent and support two people – and a baby – so Terts determined to make him a gift of money. It would be some recompense for the fact that, although he had dropped a hint to Jessica – who, if she had had any sense, ought to have passed it on – he had failed to send Aden a specific reminder about their grandfather's prejudices.

Before he could be generous, however, he needed to discover his brother's whereabouts. From New College he learned that the only forwarding address they had was still Kinderley Court. This oversight on Aden's part was to have unfortunate repercussions.

It was in July, about three weeks after the end of the Oxford term, that Terts was summoned to the library. Grainger was standing beside Lord Mortimer's chair, still holding the silver tray on which he had carried in the afternoon's post.

'What do you know about this?' Red in the face and panting with fury, Lord Mortimer held out three envelopes and a small package. Each of them was addressed to Mr and Mrs Aden Bradley.

It was all too easy to guess what had happened. Aden must have told some of his college friends that he was married and then had perhaps disappeared on a honeymoon without leaving behind an address to which any congratulations could be sent. The little idiot. He had done for himself now.

'Nothing,' he answered truthfully.

'He's married that girl, hasn't he? That Jessica. After what I said. Deliberately defying me. Well, I won't have it. Get Notcutt back here. Telephone him now.'

'Wouldn't it be better to wait until you're less upset?'

'Now!' repeated the old man.

To argue would merely be to increase the anger of someone who needed to feel that he was still – if not for long – in control of his own household. Terts made the call and reported that the solicitor would call at ten o'clock the next morning.

There was not, on reflection, any point in trying to effect a change of mind. Undoubtedly the will which had so recently been made in Aden's favour was about to be torn up. But if Terts himself were to be reinstated as his grandfather's heir, he would not need to be imprisoned by his inheritance. Once the house was his, he could make it over to Aden if he chose. That was exactly what he would do, for he was guiltily aware that it was his baby which was responsible for the badly timed marriage – and by making the gift, he could ensure that the child would be brought up in the gracious surroundings of the family home. Everything would be all right in the end.

Three days after Mr Notcutt's visit – the first of two – Lord Mortimer had a stroke, from which he never regained consciousness. He died forty-eight hours later.

Aden must have seen one of the obituaries; he telephoned to find out when the funeral would be held and took his place in the village church just as the service was about to start. He came alone, and shared a car back to Kinderley Court with his brother and sister after the interment. It had not been thought necessary to bring Victor, the only other member of the family still in England, over from his prep school.

'I'd better warn you, Aden,' said Terts. 'Grandfather found out that you were married. He had Notcutt up again. I imagine he's ditched the will he made in your favour. But don't worry about it. I'll see you all right.'

Aden did not seem to be particularly grateful.

'If it weren't for you, none of this would ever have blown up,' he said sulkily – and for one anxious moment Terts thought that Jessica must have confessed about the baby's parentage. 'Why did you have to announce to Grandfather that Jessie was Jewish?'

'I didn't announce it. He guessed. I couldn't deny it, that's all.'

'Please don't quarrel,' said Libby in a low voice. She had been crying during the service and was still upset. Unlike the boys, who had been sent away to school, she had spent her whole life since the age of nine in her grandfather's house.

The servants were waiting with sandwiches and sherry to welcome the mourners. It was a sunny summer day, and the atmosphere soon became that of a party – or rather, two parties, as Lord Mortimer's tenants congregated on one side of the terrace and his few surviving friends from the House of Lords on the other, with the three grandchildren moving from one group to another. The old gentlemen, reminiscing about past shooting parties, asked bluntly who would inherit the estate. The tenants, knowing their place, did not put the question directly, but they were the ones who would be most affected by the settlement, and the desire to be informed shone from every pair of eyes. Only the solicitor had no need to be curious.

'We all assume that Grandfather changed his will just before he died,' said Terts, coming straight to the point as the party began to break up. 'Is this the occasion on which you tell us what he decided?'

'The lawyer in the library? I can if you like.'

'Well, all three of us are here. It would be convenient.'

They assembled half an hour later and found Mr Notcutt in a happily unlawyer-like mood. No doubt he had been generously served with the sherry.

'I could read it straight out to you with all the notwithstandings and hereafters,' he said. 'But you'll understand better if I just give you the gist of it and then leave you a copy so that you can mull over it afterwards. This is Lord Mortimer's last will and testament, which supersedes all others. His signature was witnessed –' he turned to the last of the foolscap sheets to show them – 'by John Rendall, a clerk in my office whom I brought to Kinderley Court for the purpose, and by Robert Sidwell, Bachelor of Medicine, who will declare if necessary that his patient was of sound mind. Not that I expect that any of you will doubt that.'

There was a murmur of agreement and the lawyer continued.

'There are gifts to a number of the servants, which are listed in a codicil, and pensions for Mary Meadows and Frederick Grainger to be paid until their deaths. There are cash gifts of two hundred pounds each to Richard

John Bradley, his three children, and Aden Henry Bradley. A trust has been set up from which an income will be paid annually to Mortimer Bradley and to Victor Bradley. Once the second of those two persons has died, the capital from the trust will revert to the estate. The residuary beneficiary, who will inherit Kinderley Court, the Kinderley Estate, and any money remaining after all other obligations have been met, is Lord Mortimer's beloved granddaughter, Elizabeth Anne Kenward.'

There was a moment of astonished silence, broken by two exclamations.

'Libby?' Terts could hardly believe it. A woman!

'Me?' Libby could not believe it either.

Mr Notcutt set the will down on the library desk, smoothing its long pages flat and adjusting the pink ribbon with which the pages were tied.

'Lord Mortimer made his wishes very clear,' he said. 'He wished to express his appreciation for the loving and dutiful care afforded him by his granddaughter over many years. However, although I tried to dissuade him, he did insist on adding what he referred to as a penalty clause. Under this –' Mr Notcutt picked up the will again – 'Mrs Kenward's inheritance is conditional on her promise that all persons residing permanently at Kinderley Court during her lifetime shall be of the Christian faith.'

Terts was aware of Aden, beside him, emerging from the shock of the paltry bequest and giving a hiss of anger. But the solicitor had not finished speaking.

'I have to tell you, as I tried to persuade his lordship, that such a condition might not stand up to challenge in court. If you wished to dispute it, Mrs Kenward, I would be pleased to seek a counsel's opinion on your behalf.'

He was not taking long, Terts realised, to transfer his loyalties from the past owner of Kinderley to the present one. But it seemed that Libby was equally quick to make up her mind.

'I know why my grandfather inserted that provision,' she said. 'Some years ago I began to develop an affection for a Jewish gentleman. My grandfather asked me to promise that I would not allow the friendship to develop further. I made that promise and I intend to keep it. I will accept the condition.'

Did Libby realise what she was saying? It was impossible now for Terts to perform the act of generosity which he had planned, but Libby could still offer Aden and Jessica a home. Only, though, by challenging the will.

He took his sister by the arm and steered her into a quiet part of the garden.

'I'm glad for you, Libby,' he said. 'You deserve it.'

'I'm glad too. I can take more children now. I've been nervous about building up the school too much in case I found myself without a home suddenly. I knew Grandfather wouldn't let me starve, but I never thought he'd leave me the house.'

'The only thing is, Libby ... I mean, if it had been me, I'd intended ...

Well, what about Aden and Jessica?'

'What about them?' she asked. 'I think Aden's behaved very badly. He had the right to disobey Grandfather if he chose to do that and take the consequences. But instead he tried to deceive him. I think that was sneaky. And I don't want to share a house. There'll always be a home here for you, of course, Terts, between your journeys, because I know it suits you to be only a visitor. But if Aden had inherited, I should have left here and found somewhere else to live myself.'

'It's such a huge house!'

'Yes, but any house has to have just one mistress, and with Kinderley it's going to be me. I shall be able to use much more of it for the school. How do you think Aden and Jessica would like it, being sort of lodgers, poor relations, tucked away in a corner?'

'Since they *are* likely to be poor relations, they'd have to put up with it.'

'Well, it would make me uncomfortable. Besides, I told you, I don't really like Jessica. I don't want to be permanently exposed to woman-to-woman chats with her. Aden's twenty-one and a married man. It's time he started to stand on his own feet. I'll give him money to get him going if necessary. But I love Kinderley, Terts. Really love it. I'm happier than I can tell you that it's going to be mine. And I want it to be *all* mine. Something that I can enclose in my arms and – oh, I'm being sentimental. Sorry.'

'I do understand how you feel.' He could tell that no persuasions were likely to make her change her mind. 'I hope you'll be very very happy here. And thank you for saying that I can drop in.'

He had not expected Libby to be so hard-hearted. But no, that was unfair. All her generosity of time and money and space was devoted to the small children whose mothers she temporarily replaced. She was making a choice, and Aden was the loser.

Someone else would be a loser as well. It had been one of the motives behind the gift which Terts would have made had the legacies fallen differently: that his own son or daughter, although calling Aden 'Father', would have been brought up here, living a privileged life in spacious rooms with the freedom to explore the grounds; enjoying the fresh air and developing a feeling for the land and the plants and animals which lived on it. What sort of upbringing, he wondered, would the child have now? But it was too soon to make any enquiries of such a sort. He was not supposed to know yet that any child was on the way.

Libby was moving away towards her younger brother. 'Do stay the night if you want to, won't you, Aden?' she said. 'I told the maids to air your old room for you.'

Whether or not she was speaking out of kindness, the words emerged as the ultimate put-down. Only a few weeks had passed since he had left Kinderley for his last term at Oxford, assuming that this would be just another temporary absence from the house in which he was born: the only home he had ever known. Now, without warning, he had become merely a guest. As he stared at his elder brother and sister there was a bitter hatred in his eyes.

7

In the autumn of 1927 Terts emerged from the Amazonian jungle shivering with fever, covered with sores and with one arm agonisingly inflamed from a scratch with a poisoned arrow. Twelve months earlier, in an arrangement of mutual benefit, he had attached himself to an expedition of plant-hunters so that he could share theit transport and camping arrangements while in return making on their behalf a professional record of each botanical discovery in its natural habitat.

When the members of the expedition turned back towards civilisation he had entrusted them with all his exposed films and then pressed further into the jungle with a single guide, drawn by stories of Amazonian Indians who were being robbed of their land by groups of miners.

The stories were true, as he quickly discovered, but unfortunately he was assumed by the tribesmen to be carrying out a reconnaissance on behalf of the miners and was lucky to escape with his life. Only after a spell in an airless and insect-ridden hospital in Belem was he fit to travel on to Rio de Janeiro, the town in which any correspondence might be waiting for him *post restante*.

The post office, when he called there in early afternoon, was closed for the siesta period. Rather than go back to his hotel on the beach, he took a taxi towards the shanty towns which even from a distance could be seen clinging to the mountain side. On the edge of the city the taxi driver refused to go any further – and indeed, could not have done so. The huts, sometimes little more than pieces of corrugated iron perched precariously on poles, were packed close together, leaving only narrow paths which were obstructed by fires, children and running sewage. Terts removed from his hip pocket the passport which he would have needed for collecting his letters and concealed it inside his shirt. Then he began to walk.

In the eight years that had passed since he first encountered extreme poverty, in the slums of Bombay, he had photographed many shanty towns in many countries, but rarely had he seen this degree of squalor at such close quarters to a rich modern city. In Africa and China he had stayed in villages which were poor in the sense of being completely dependent on the weather for survival, having no cash income of any kind. But even there, even when drought or flooding had brought disaster, he had always been aware of a kind of self respect, a dignity, which prevented their society from collapsing.

There was no such dignity here. The adults, apathetic, had given up hope. Unmoving, unspeaking, they seemed oblivious of the stench. Only the children were active. Those of them who were not begging or stealing or offering themselves for prostitution in the streets near the hotels were busily scavenging in the huge refuse heaps, keeping their families alive with the discards of a richer class. As the only white man in the area Terts could not hope to pass unnoticed, and was soon being pestered by the young scavengers. But he had taken as many shots as he needed, and was happy to leave the boys scrambling for the small coins which no doubt to them represented wealth. It was time to return – although this time wearily on foot – to the post office.

Amongst the letters he collected was a very long one from Libby, which she had posted many months earlier, in January. Her news came from a different world. As he lay naked under a mosquito net to read it, it was hard to remember that he had once been part of that world, and no doubt one day would be so again.

The first excited pages were devoted to the expansion of her school. She described the changes she had made within one wing of the house in order to accommodate more children and the extra teachers and 'motherers' who were consequently necessary. She had begun to publicise the care she offered, instead of leaving the news to spread merely by word of mouth, and as a result was already – in January – showing round members of the diplomatic and colonial services who were about to be posted to the unhealthier parts of the world. Even before her inheritance had left her without money worries, she had each year offered free day places to some of the more intelligent children from the village and now was trying to expand the system to provide boarding care for others who were in no position to pay fees, as she explained in her letter.

'But it's difficult because if I take some bright child out of an orphanage for five or six years and give him a really good educational start, with a loving atmosphere thrown in, what's going to happen when it's time for him to leave? Does he go back to the orphanage and find he's got nothing in common any more with boys who've been going to the local elementary school every day? Or do I have to keep him until he's old enough to work – which would turn my school into something quite different. Not what I want. It's not as simple, that part of it, as I thought it would be.

Well, that's my problem, and no doubt it seems a very small one compared with those you see on your travels. Other news, then.

Aden sent me his new address soon after you left. He had to, I suppose, so that I could forward any letters. I went to see it and oh, Terts, it's the most horrid place! A nasty little semi-detached house in a London suburb, with a tiny front garden behind a privet hedge, and not very much more behind it, I shouldn't think. I'd meant to call, but I couldn't bring myself to ring the bell, because it must be so humiliating for him to land up in a place like that. When you think of Kinderley and everything he's been used to!

So I felt ashamed of myself for not being more generous, remembering what you'd wanted me to do. And although I still wouldn't want to have them living in Kinderley Court, there are houses on the estate which I could offer. When you and I were talking about it after Grandfather's funeral, I hadn't had time to think and realise that of course I could nominate a tenant next time a cottage fell empty. And when I did think about it later, I assumed that Aden would hate to live in something so small after being in the big house. But at least there he'd have space to breathe, instead of being imprisoned in a row of houses that all look exactly the same.

I waited till Christmas and then sent them money presents and details of a house they could have. Old Webster has just died. Aden turned it down. Because it's in the middle of nowhere and he needs to work and he's got a job as a schoolmaster near where he lives. And he wants me to know that he and Jessica are very happy and quite capable of looking after themselves without being offered charity, thank you very much. Big snub.

At the end of the letter he said that a baby daughter had arrived just before Christmas. Premature, but very healthy. Jolene, they're going to call her. Ugh! I expect it was Jessica who chose that. A common sort of name. I counted on my fingers and if it was a seven-month baby I suppose the Eights Week Ball is to blame. I suppose also that that must be why they got married so quickly. I still think it was all very sneaky, trying to keep quiet about it. So my spell of feeling ashamed and prepared to be helpful didn't last very long. If they're determined to cut themselves off, well, that's up to them. I shall send presents to the baby, though. Children need to know that they have relations, even if they never meet them.

The letter continued for two more pages, but Terts's eyes were swimming. He lowered the pages until they rested on his chest and then quickly moved them to one side as he saw the thin air mail paper darkening with his sweat.

A daughter. He had a daughter. For a second time he was overwhelmed with emotion at the knowledge that he was a father. It was necessary to remind himself that this particular child could never be his responsibility, since to lay any claim to her would be to betray Jessica. All the same, she was his. His blood flowed in her veins. She owed her life to him. What sort of life would it be?

He had condemned her, Jolene, to be brought up within the confines of a semi-detached suburban house by parents who no doubt loved each other at the moment but who might one day come to think of their first baby merely as the bait which had rushed them into the trap of marriage. Was there any way in which he could rescue her?

A perfect solution would be for her to become one of the children brought up by Libby until they were of an age to go to boarding school, so that the little girl would after all enjoy the ambience of Kinderley Court. But no doubt Aden would have other children, who must all be treated alike, and no doubt also he would maintain his refusal to accept 'charity'.

What was the point of all this day-dreaming? In the lottery of life baby Jolene had failed to draw the card which would promise her wealth and luxury, but compared to the children he had been watching on the refuse heaps only that afternoon she was a millionairess. She was the daughter of Aden and Jessica Bradley. They would bring her up in reasonably comfortable and healthy surroundings and give her a good education. There was nothing he either could or should do to interfere. After all, he had been given one opportunity to accept his parental role. Miss Adams – at this distance in time he could not even remember the Christian name of the woman who was legally his wife – would never have found out or cared if he had made a second, bigamous, marriage. In rejecting that possibility he had also rejected any possible right to be recognised as the father of Jessica's child. He must keep away and not allow himself even to think of the baby as she grew up.

When she was an adult, though, that would be different. Solemnly he made a vow to himself. On Jolene's twenty-first birthday he would demand the right to be recognised at least as her uncle. Although anger and disappointment might have made Aden determined to cut his own ties with his childhood, he could not deprive his children of their family for ever. But until December 1947 Terts promised himself that he would try to put Jolene's existence out of his mind and certainly would make no attempt to interfere in her upbringing. Except that, if Libby planned to send regular presents to her niece, he would ask her to make the tenth birthday present a camera.

Part Six

The Dying of the Light

1

Forty-nine. At the start of the second great war of his lifetime, Terts knew that he would be reckoned too old to take any active part in the fighting, but he did not anticipate the kind of war service that eventually came his way.

After eighteen months during which he photographed the sometimes comic activities of the Home Front, the heart-rending scenes of the Dunkirk evacuation and the stark effects of the Blitz, he was summoned to the Ministry of Information.

'I remember you from Croxton,' said a middle-aged man, rising from his chair to shake hands. 'Jenks.'

Jenks. The slavemaster who had not after all been responsible for the beating of young Rose.

'You never come to any of the Old Boys' things, do you? I never had a chance to say how sorry I was about your brother. Kut and all that ... long time ago. He and I were good friends. I thought I had a bad enough time in Flanders, but all that Turkish business seems to have been particularly nasty. Hoped we'd finished with that sort of thing in 1918.'

'Yes,' agreed Terts. 'I see all these young men rushing off to fight, just as we did. They don't know what they're in for, and nobody's going to tell them. You call yourselves the Ministry of Information, but I imagine the information you dish out is pretty tightly controlled?'

'Too true. And I'm one of the controllers, so I'll come straight to the point. I saw those pictures you took of Coventry after the raid. I got someone to look out some of your past stuff. He went back further than I'd expected. That was how I first realised that you were you. Bradley Terts. You've had a busy life! Getting around.'

Terts nodded, waiting to hear the reason for his summons.

'One of my chief responsibilities here is trying to keep the United States sweet,' said Jenks. 'The President is on our side, but he can't move faster than the country will let him. We send lecturers over there with the job of explaining to people who aren't quite sure where Europe is –' He checked himself. 'No, that's not fair. Half of them are Europeans themselves. But they need to be told just what Nazi Germany is doing. It may not be possible to get them to come in actively on our side, though we're trying, but we need their neutrality to be benevolent. Are you with me?'

'Certainly. But where do I come in?'

'The chap who brought in the copies of your photographs, that I'd asked him to collect, is an artist in civilian life.' Jenks laughed. 'It was funny really. You took his breath away. He'd never thought of photographs as having any relation to art, he said, but some of your shots ... Well, to cut a long story short, we came up between us with the idea that you might take a travelling exhibition over to America. With your own choice of early pictures, but an emphasis on what you've been doing over the past eighteen months. You could give short talks in each place. To describe the beating that Britain's been taking. Nothing too blatant. Just enough to create an atmosphere of sympathy. Mixed with a dash of fighting spirit to make it clear that with a bit of help we'll be certain to win. We've got people over there who could make the local arrangements.'

'I'm not a professional lecturer.'

'Doesn't matter. We'd provide you with what you might call the propaganda bit, to come at the end. You could start by chatting about one or two of the early photographs and how you came to take them. And to get from one to the other ...' Jenks opened a folder which lay on the desk in front of him. 'When Avery – that's the artist – produced these pictures for me, he'd also found a newspaper cutting. You won a prize back in the twenties for one of your photographs. The paper sent someone to interview you.'

'I remember that, yes.'

'"Terts, the eyes of the world". That was the headline. The interviewer got you talking about how ordinary people couldn't expect to see for themselves everything that went on all over the world, especially in the case of cruel customs which were naturally kept secret. It was the job of the photographer, you said, to be the eyes of the world and let people know what was happening.'

Terts laughed, remembering. 'Somebody said that to me when I was just a boy; when I was given my first camera. There was a period when I used to quote it too often. Became quite a bore on the subject.'

'Well, the judges who awarded you the prize seemed to think you succeeded rather well. "Proving that reportage can also be art," they said. There's no doubt that you could do a good job for us if you chose. What do you say?'

What Terts said had the extraordinary consequence of turning him within twelve months into a cult figure in the United States. The Ministry acted in a more subtle manner than he would have expected, playing down its own involvement so that the exhibition was allowed to draw audiences in its own right. Sophisticated Americans, he soon discovered, had already taken on board the concept of photography as a form of art. In both New York and Los Angeles he could have sold every item in the exhibition within a week had he not needed them for the rest of the tour. As a result of this enthusiasm he arranged to exhibit the photographs again when he returned to New York before leaving for London – and sold out within five days. It was good to feel that although he himself might go down in a torpedoed ship, his work would hang safely on the walls of expensive apartments.

He acquired an American agent. There was no torpedo and he was able to ship over more photographs. Never since his head wound in 1916 had brought Lord Mortimer to his bedside had he been penniless, and since his grandfather's death his income had been enough to keep him in comfort, had comfort ever been what he sought. But this was the first occasion on which his work had brought him in a large sum all at one time. It was odd to feel rich when there was almost nothing on which he could spend the money. Food and clothes were rationed and even restaurants were restricted in what they could charge. It seemed only fair to refund to the Ministry of Information the money it had invested in his travel arrangements, although to judge by Jenks's expression no one had ever done such a thing before.

The United States entered the war, due rather more to the Japanese than to Terts's exhibition. His photograph of a very tall black GI offering an orange to a very small white English girl who had clearly never seen either the fruit or a black man before made the cover of *Time* magazine. On this side of the Atlantic *Picture Post*, although unable to persuade him to join its staff, offered more commissions than he had time to accept. Probably to the disgust of those who had been the first to recognise the quality of his work, he had become fashionable.

When the Allied armies invaded Europe in 1944, Terts was at first refused War Office accreditation on grounds of age. It was Jenks who came to his rescue, pointing out in a supportive memo that this was a man who had spent his whole adult life surviving in hostile surroundings. Only a few weeks late, Terts was able to attach himself to a Highland regiment. It was in their company that, six months later, he entered the camp of Bergen-Belsen.

Terts had seen horrors before, but that day in April 1945 was the first occasion on which he was literally frozen into immobility with shock and incredulity, unable even to perform the automatic action of raising his camera to his eye. The delay didn't make any difference. None of the emaciated bodies at which he was staring was likely to run away. Most of them were dead, and the rest lacked the strength to move anything but their eyes.

Such hopeless, pleading eyes: a few of them silently expressing the thought, 'At last!' but more of them sending the message, 'Too late!' The group of officers who had led the way into the camp were all by now hardened observers of many forms of death, but they too were silenced for a moment by disbelief.

This inactivity did not endure for long. Whilst all around him orders were given and obeyed, Terts set to work in his own way. He photographed the almost fleshless corpses as they were shovelled into ditches or on to lorries. He photographed small children playing listlessly beside the bodies of their mothers. He photographed the medical officer as he moved at speed amongst the prisoners who were only just alive, pointing out any who could be carried to a makeshift hospital with some hope of survival. He photographed – and this was a shot which later went round the world – one of the Highlanders as he held out a biscuit from his rations to a starving man who lay on the ground, too weak to reach out for the food. The private was looking round with an angry and unbelieving expression on his face at a medical orderly who had just appeared to prevent the gift.

'No food! Captain Craig's orders. Ye can kill a starving man with food. Liquid only for the day.'

Like an automaton Terts moved round the camp. At one point his presence averted a probable lynching when the British troops came across half a dozen of the camp guards cowering in a bunker.

'They'll go on trial!' He shouted at the Highlanders to stand back as he recorded the faces of the terrified women. 'Put them to work for now. Make them useful.' He had no authority to give orders, of course, and did not wait to see whether or not they were obeyed.

He found himself, at the end of the day, in a hut filled with men and women suffering from typhus. Many were still alive and he sent a message to tell the medical officer where to find them. They were all lying, crowded together, on the ground and for the most part were naked; little more than skeletons tautly covered with skin. As he stood in the doorway, he saw one clawlike hand slowly stretch out to tug away a rag which was covering part of an adjacent body. This second person, as he quickly realised, had just died. Perhaps she was a recent arrival at the camp, killed by disease before starvation could claim her, for in her case it was possible to tell that she had been a young woman. The stolen rag had been covering flesh still recognisable as female breasts.

Terts stared down at the dead girl. He was at the end of his tether, both physically and emotionally. None of the many horrors he had seen in his life had prepared him for a day like this. Some of the cruelties he had witnessed during the past twenty-five years were the result of indifference rather than malice. Some, like the examples of female circumcision, were believed by the perpetrators to be justified and again were not exactly malicious. Some practices were indeed atrocious, but were performed one at a time against one person at a time. This was the first time that he had witnessed what could happen when murder was committed in the mass, its victims chosen merely for the crime of being Jews or Poles or gypsies.

In a mental daze from which he was unable to escape, Terts remembered his grandfather's antipathy to Jews. Lord Mortimer would never have killed with his own hands as a consequence of his prejudice, but it was a dangerous prejudice all the same: a prejudice which allowed things like this to happen. The woman lying at his feet might have been Jessica if history had taken a different turn. Beautiful Jessica with her smooth skin and graceful body, hated for the single reason that she was Jewish.

Or his own daughter, Jolene. The daughter of a Jewess was Jewish. The child he had never seen might, if England had been invaded, have lain in some charnel house like this, with no one to know where she was. And all because there was so much evil in the world. He felt himself surrounded by the evil: smothered by it. It rose, like the actual scent of death which surrounded him, to fill his nostrils until he could no longer breathe. Giving a single groan, he turned to one side and began to bang his forehead against a wall. Over and over again, and harder and harder, until suddenly he was checked by a pain which was greater than all the headaches he had ever experienced in his life put together. He opened his mouth to shout out in agony; but before any sound could emerge he lost his balance and fell spinning to the ground.

His first thought, as consciousness returned, was that he must be dead. The scenes of horror and despair that had filled his eyes, the smells of murder and disease that had stifled his breathing, all were still clearly in his memory but they had vanished from his present experience. He could see only blackness and could smell only flowers. But he could hear the sound of human voices somewhere in the distance. No, he was not dead after all.

With the realisation that he was still alive came a moment of panic when he found himself unable to move – not from any weakness of muscle, as far as he could tell, but because he was restrained by straps. Was he in a coffin, its lid already hammered down to exclude all light? Was it a wreath rather than a posy of flowers that was scenting the air? Was he about to be buried alive?

His shout of protest, his appeal for help, was only a noise, with no distinguishable words, but it was enough to produce an immediate response. A soft hand gripped his own. A soft voice spoke. It was Libby.

'Keep very still, dearest. You're all right, but you mustn't move.'

'Where am I?' The question emerged thickly from a throat that was very sore.

'In Oxford, in hospital. You've had an operation to your head and you mustn't move it for a bit. That's why you're fastened down, to prevent you from suddenly thrashing around. You've been drifting in and out of consciousness for a couple of days. I'll tell the nurse that you're with us again. And then the surgeon can explain what's been going on.'

'You tell me first.' He needed time to take the situation in, so that he would know what questions to ask.

'You hit your head. No one knows exactly how it happened. You were found lying on the ground.'

He remembered. It would not have been the fall which caused any damage, but the moment of sick disbelief in which he had banged his forehead against a wall. But that, surely, would not have been enough to cause more than a slight concussion?

'You were flown here, to St Hugh's, because they specialise in head injuries,' Libby continued. 'And when they saw the steel plate in your head they contacted me to find out how long you'd had it and who put it there and what was the reason for it. Whatever's happened now seems to be directly related to what happened in 1916.'

1916. He had been a young man then. Twenty-six years old. A German fighter pilot had put one bullet into his wrist and another into his head. Terts lay now, as instructed, without moving as he remembered what a kindly surgeon in Devon had told him.

'You'll have to be careful for a while. No sudden changes of pressure. No diving or flying. I've had to leave two splinters of bone dangerously near to the optic nerve. You'll have to be careful ...'

In Bergen-Belsen Terts had ceased to be careful. But he was only to be careful 'for a while'. Almost thirty years had passed since then. Surely, after so long ... He experienced a second moment of panic.

'Take the bandages off my eyes, Libby. I want to see you.'

'I can't do that. I'll call the nurse now. You're going to be all right. Now that they've done the operation, you'll just need a little while to recover and then you can come back to Kinderley with me.'

What did she mean by 'all right'? He was alive, certainly, but there were some circumstances in which life would not be worth living. As Libby slid her hand out of his and went to report his return to consciousness, his mind raced with speculations which gradually hardened into certainties. Even before the surgeon arrived to describe the problems he had faced, Terts knew what he was about to be told.

He would never be able to see again.

2

'There's a letter for you. Would you like me to read it out?'

Even as she asked the question Libby was slitting the envelope open with the silver paper knife. Terts could identify the sound and could see in his memory's eye the knife which was engraved with his great-great-grandfather's initials.

'Thank you,' he said. During the past two years he had learned to control the rage and despair he felt at the darkness which cut him off from everything that made life worth living. Over and over again he told himself he was lucky to be able to live in a house whose geography was well known to him. He was lucky that he could afford to employ a personal servant who made sure that he always appeared correctly dressed and well shaven. And, luckiest of all, he had a kind and loving sister who noticed whenever he needed help and provided it as unobtrusively as she could. It was not her fault that sometimes he felt as though he were one of her four-year-old pupils, as yet unable to read.

His outgoing letters were still under his own control. No doubt his typing was full of mistakes, but he assumed that the general purport must be understandable. To know what answers came back, however, he needed Libby.

'It's just a card. From Jessica. Very abrupt.' Libby's habit of looking through the whole of each of his letters before allowing him to learn what it said was something which always annoyed him, but he could not afford to show his impatience. In her own good time she read it aloud.

> There will be no twenty-first birthday party. Last December Jolene abandoned her Cambridge degree course and disappeared. We are both very hurt and disappointed and angry. She went originally to Switzerland, but we have no idea where she is now. It doesn't seem that she ever intends to return.

Hardly able to believe what he heard, Terts stretched out his hand, as though only the feel of the paper would convince him that its contents were true. Libby, for her part, expressed puzzlement.

'Did you write to Jessica, then?'

'Yes. It's been ridiculous, all these years, Aden refusing to accept anything from us. I thought, when Jolene was twenty-one, an adult and independent, I could give her something then.'

'Money, you mean?'

'Yes. To cushion her against poverty. To give her the freedom to lead whatever kind of life she chooses, without always having to wonder whether she can pay her way.'

Terts did not have any great capital sum at his disposal. The War Loan which was his grandfather's first gift to him had lost much of its value over the years, and the later inheritance was of an income just for his lifetime. But his wartime lecture tour of the United States had greatly increased his savings, and during the past two years he had spent practically nothing. The belief that on his daughter's twenty-first birthday he could make a generous gift without arousing any suspicion of the reason for it was the only thing that had helped him to be patient.

'I didn't say anything about money in my letter, though,' he added. 'Just hoped that if she were going to have a twenty-first birthday party, I might be invited to it. She ought to be allowed to know who her relations are. But if it's true that...'

No. What Jessica wrote could not possibly be true. Twenty-year-old girls did not simply disappear. Even supposing that there had been some terrible quarrel within the immediate family, Jolene would surely have kept in touch with somebody. If indeed there had been such a quarrel, that was when she would need support.

'Did she, Jolene, correspond with you at all, Libby?' he asked. 'You sent her birthday presents, didn't you?'

'I did for ten years. And to Timmy for six. I never got started with the third one, Yvonne. For Jolene's tenth birthday I sent her a camera. You 'specially asked me to, do you remember? Her own thank-you letter was full of enthusiasm. But Aden wrote at the same time. A really horrid letter. As though I were a stranger, not a sister. Jolene was very happy in her home and family, he said, and he didn't wish her, or the other two, to be disturbed by any further contact with the very different kind of life which was represented by Kinderley Court. I've still got the letter somewhere. It upset me. But I thought, if I pressed on, it would only cause trouble for the children. So I stopped.'

'I really don't understand why he –'

'Oh, I do.' Libby's interruption was a confident one. 'He's a disappointed and petty-minded man. He's never forgiven me for inheriting Kinderley, even thought I hadn't expected it or asked for it. I imagine he thought I ought to have disclaimed the inheritance and passed it straight on to him. But I believe that people should be able to leave their property as they choose and that they need to feel confident while they're still alive that their wishes will be carried out. So because I wouldn't give Aden everything, he wasn't prepared to accept anything at all. A kind of emotional blackmail.'

'That ought not to have affected his attitude to me. After all, I *did* give him everything, in a sense. I persuaded Grandfather to make Aden his heir when he really wanted to choose me. It wasn't my fault Aden was such an idiot as to spoil everything,' Terts protested.

'He thinks it was. Because you told Grandfather that Jessica was Jewish.'

'I didn't have any choice. A direct question.'

'I know that. But Aden's never going to believe it. He's cut off his nose to spite his face and I stopped feeling sorry for him a long time ago. It's a pity about the children, I agree, but perhaps he's right to say that if they're happy as they are, it may be best not to dangle in front of them a picture of how they might have been.'

'When a girl of twenty leaves home, unmarried, in the middle of a university course, with nowhere particular to go, that doesn't suggest any great happiness with things as they are.' Terts stood up, pushing his chair backwards so jerkily that it toppled and fell.

'You haven't finished your breakfast. There's a rasher of bacon –'

'I'm not hungry. You eat it for me.' Although more than a year had passed since the ending of the war, bacon was still on the points ration and not lightly to be thrown away. 'Bit of a headache. In fact, one of the bad ones.'

'Take one of your pills.'

'Yes, I will.'

He made his way up to his suite of rooms. Although far fewer servants were employed at Kinderley than in its great days before the first world war, he knew that there would be someone silently preceding him to make sure that no unexpected obstacles had been left in his way, so that he was able to cross the great hall and climb the stairs with as much confidence as any sighted man.

Nothing in his day was left to chance. Everything was organised for him. After breakfast *The Times* would be read aloud to him by Warner, his valet, although he had little interest in the world's daily affairs. He would write letters. He would go out riding, allowing the horse to make its own way round the same route each day, and knowing that the groom was following a short distance behind. After lunch he would listen to the wireless. He had never had much love of music, so the gramophone that Libby had given him was little used. Very often the dragging of the afternoon hours would lull him into sleep, even though he knew he would pay for the nap with a restless night.

After dinner Libby might read out clues so that he could complete the daily crossword. Or perhaps she would suggest a game. But although blind men were supposed to develop special skills of memory, Terts suspected that blindness had come to him too late for that. However often the state of the chess board was described, he was unable to see more than a single move ahead. And the spoken word games that she might suggest instead soon became too reminiscent of children's parties. More and more frequently he retired early to bed, allowing his sister to read quietly on her own, as he knew she wished.

Every day was a wasted day. His career was over. He could think of nothing that he wanted to achieve and would still be capable of achieving. Every moment that passed saw him settling a little further into depression.

Although he tried to cheer himself up with the constant reminder of how fortunate he was to have lived for thirty fulfilling years since the Battle of the Somme came within a millimetre of killing him, a second thought always intruded to kill the cheer: that the fortunate years had come to an end.

Only one hope had kept him going during the black months since he was exposed to the horrors of Bergen-Belsen: the hope that before too long he would meet his daughter for the first time. His need to know what sort of a woman she was and what she hoped to do with her life was a physical ache. And now that his hopes had been dashed, the ache spread from his heart to his head. He had told the truth to Libby: this was going to be one of his bad days.

Upstairs in the sitting room which had once been his studio, he sat down at the desk and began to type.

The words clattered fluently on to the paper; he had rehearsed them often enough in his head. When the letter was finished and signed, he folded it and sealed the envelope, not caring that the hot wax burned his skin. Stretching two fingers of his left hand widely apart to act as a guide, he wrote the name of Jolene Bradley on the front. Then he penned an undated note of instructions, to be fastened to the envelope.

> Libby. I would like Jolene to read this letter, but only after Aden dies. Will you arrange this for me?

The request might lead Libby to suspect the truth, but she would keep any guesses to herself. It was not his intention to cause his brother any hurt. Twenty-one years earlier, without intending to, he had indeed deceived Aden, but had imposed his own punishment by being strict with himself to ensure that the truth should never be known. Worse, far worse, than being the unknowing victim of deceit would be the discovery by Aden that his wife had been disloyal and that his eldest daughter was not his own. But once he was dead, everything would be different.

With the letter written and pushed into a drawer, it was only a question of passing the hours until nightfall. He pretended to listen to the day's news. He whipped his horse into an unaccustomed gallop, remembering how his father had died and wondering whether the mare might do him the same favour. But she was too sure-footed for him, returning him safely to the stable. In the afternoon he listened to talks on mental illness and the taking of geranium cuttings. After dinner he played Nebuchadnezzar with all the enthusiasm of a ten year old. He went early to bed.

As midnight struck he made his way up the dark and narrow stairs to what had once been a range of housemaids' rooms in the days when maids were easier to come by. In his hand was a decanter of whisky. In his dressing-gown pocket were all the tablets that the doctor had carefully counted out ten at a time over the past eighteen months and which he had collected in readiness for the time when he would really want to use them.

Sipping and swallowing took longer than he had expected – long enough for all the despair and depression to slip peacefully away. He was a photographer who could no longer take photographs. But it didn't matter. Every life was a story which had a beginning and an end. This kind of ending was all the more satisfactory for being his own choice; because the plot had run out and there was no further incentive to keep turning the pages.

And afterwards? He asked himself the question but could not answer it. Terts didn't believe in God. He had seen too many horrors for that. Nor, when he was being rational, did he believe in Heaven. All the same, it was difficult to resist the hope that in some future time he would be able to see again; to look down on the earth and discover what was going on there – although there was only one discovery which would interest him. It was his last thought as he slipped heavily into sleep.

What kind of life will my daughter enjoy?

BOOK TWO
Jolene

Part One

Sunset in Colorado

1

The sun is going down, about to take its bow and disappear behind the solid curtain of a mountain. There must still be two hours to go before the sunset proper, but it is not likely to be spectacular. I am a connoisseur of sunsets. My most popular book contains photographs of nothing else. Once, eavesdropping on a hotel terrace as the sky flamed into a kaleidoscope of orange and red, black and yellow and grey, I heard a woman exclaim to her husband that this was a Jolene Bradley sunset. My fifteen seconds of fame!

Tonight's display will not qualify for such an accolade. Resting on my ski sticks on the crest of a ridge, I watch only for a moment as the sun falls flatly through the sky like a huge crimson frisbee. Then, turning away to enjoy the sparkle of light upon snow, I see my shadow lengthening, stretching me into a stick woman. In my youth I was slender; in my thirties, slim; in middle age I was thin and now I am scraggy. Adjectives have an ageism of their own. This one doesn't bother me. I have passed my seventieth birthday and stopped counting. Scraggy is fair enough.

In front of me the undulating surface of the snowfield is unbroken. Pristine. No one has come this way since the last snowfall. No one has seen precisely this view. I revel in the feeling of being alone in the world as I shift my grip, preparing to push off for the last descent of the day.

The last descent of the season, in fact. Spring has come too early this year. It seems no time at all since the first silent snowfall of winter: that soft, smooth, glistening sheet of whiteness which acted as the invitation to a party. What a pity it was that such purity could not survive. All too soon, in the streets of each resort, the delicate skin was packed hard by the tramp of ski boots. Its sparkling surface became ridged like waves on a beach at low tide, although edged with black instead of frothing with white foam. But the partygoers have continued to trudge towards the ski slopes with energy and enthusiasm: until now.

It is still early in April, and some of the higher resorts must certainly remain in action. But in Winter Park, to which for reasons of economy I transferred myself when my work in Aspen and Vail was completed, the foot of the lowest ski tow is already surrounded by only a mess of brown slush. The nursery slopes have changed colour to become a muddy green, turning the last stage of any run into a country walk. Higher up, where the chair lifts endlessly circle above the piste, sharp spikes of black rock have begun to pierce the surface: a tank trap for the unwary. The party is over. All that dirty brown sludge is in its own depressing way the herald of spring.

To tell the truth, the party has been over for some days already, but the host has been too polite to show his guests the door. Now, down in the resort, hints are being dropped; one by one the lights are dimmed. Shops offer sale bargains and restaurants are closing their doors to allow for a month of rest and refurbishment before the summer season begins. There is an atmosphere of tiredness and anti-climax. Not up on the high slopes, in the snow; but down there, yes, every arrow is pointing in the same direction. It is time for beginners to go home.

I am not a beginner, but I came to Colorado to do a job of work, and the job is done. There is no excuse to stay any longer; I have a living to earn. With a single sigh which mingles pleasure and regret I steady my balance and prepare to go.

But I am not after all alone in the world. Someone is approaching from behind at a speed great enough to carry him up the rise to the top of the ridge with a whoosh and a sizzle of tightly controlled skis breaking through the powder snow.

'Hi there, Jo.' It is Warren, turning his skis to brake him to a halt behind me. 'The snow cat driver told me he'd brought you up here. I've been following your track.'

'Hi.' I am glad to see the young man even though he has shattered my solitude. It is with Warren that I have been working for these past few weeks. Together, at a leisurely pace, we are preparing a magazine feature on The Seasons of the Wealthy.

Warren is the heir to the Backer fortune. Recently graduated from Princeton, he will never need to work for money, but he is ambitious for journalistic fame – and since his mother owns two newspapers and a stable of magazines, he is likely to achieve his ambition. The feature is his idea. I don't think much of the theme myself, but over a twelve-month period it will offer me some pleasant social interludes to subsidise my serious work.

With the Colorado winter season particularly in mind, Warren originally asked the art editor to assign him the best photographer who could ski. It still amuses me to remember how his face fell when he was introduced to this elderly Englishwoman. But a little showing off on our first day together left him adequately impressed, I think, by my agility and skill on the piste; and by now he has had time to study the rough proofs of the portfolio I am assembling. For my part, I have been glad of his introductions to his mother's rich friends and neighbours. There's a sense in which I've felt for a long time that any kind of street – or snow – photography is an invasion of privacy; I wouldn't have wanted to act as a *paparazza*, skulking to snatch candid and unflattering shots of the wealthy and famous at play. My shots have been unposed but still, in a sense, by appointment.

In spite of the difference in age, we have become friends, Warren and I. It is friendship which he thinks now gives him the right to criticise. Pulling up his goggles, he shakes his head at me disapprovingly. 'Hasn't anyone ever told you how dangerous it is to go off-piste by yourself? Especially in April, with the sun so hot.'

'Lots of people, yes.'

'Then why do you do it, Jo? I mean, it's *truly* dangerous.'

'Because I decided a great many years ago that when the time comes I would like to meet my death alone on a mountain. Preferably at sunset. There's something very suburban, I always feel, about lying in bed and waiting for death to happen.' 'Suburban' is just about the most pejorative word in my vocabulary.

'So I guess I have to apologise for disturbing your solitude. You're standing here ready to commit suicide, are you?'

'Of course not. Come on. If we don't get cracking soon it will be dark before we're down.'

'You first,' Warren insists. 'I take it you'd be happy to die in my avalanche, but I'm too young to die in yours. See you at Pat's.'

Nodding in agreement, I pull my goggles over my eyes and push off. I have a feeling for snow; an instinct for what lies over the next ridge, and the next. Warren is a competent enough skier, but he has not yet had time or experience enough to develop my eye for the right line. He will follow in my track. There is very little danger of avalanches, in my opinion, but his decision to go second is a wise one all the same.

It allows me the pleasure, the thrill, of being the one to mark the pristine surface of the snow. The short, broad skis which I am using today feel like a part of my body. They seem to float above the powdery surface. Because it is necessary to keep going at high speed, I am not so much skiing as flying. I am tempted to sing aloud as I swoop down the steep incline, but exhilaration chokes my throat and robs me of breath.

Just the fact of still being on skis at all at my age is a miracle. I tell myself that to enjoy an activity indefinitely it is only necessary never to stop. But I do have to give credit to the Fat Boys and Snow Rangers which need so much less effort to control than the unwieldy long skis on which I had my first lessons fifty years ago. Modern inventions not only keep people alive, but also keep alive the joy of living.

Just such a joy chokes my throat as a cliff of snow falls away beneath me and I lean forward into a jump, confident of my landing. I hope that Warren, behind me, has noticed what he is approaching.

Warren, when he joins me at our rendezvous, Pat's Parlour, is limping. I would have pretended not to notice, but he admits at once to an awkward fall.

'Don't you ever damage yourself, Jo? I thought older women were supposed to have brittle bones, and you must fall sometimes.'

'I like that phrase "older women". In the mouth of a young man, it suggests a woman who's reached the advanced age of forty. You're allowed to call me old.'

'Okay then. Haven't you ever broken anything, old lady?'

I answer the particular point he has in mind rather than the more general question he has actually asked. So many of my bones have been broken and pinned back together over the years that I carry a doctor's letter in my passport to explain why I'm liable to set alarm bells ringing at airport checkpoints. There's a working explanation for each fracture: a bullet, a car crash, a distinctly inexpert parachute landing. But that's not what he means.

'I've had plenty of falls on skis. Who hasn't? But I've always managed to roll out of them undamaged.'

A waitress arrives and by the time we have ordered the subject of falls has been abandoned.

'I guess you'll be glad to get home after living out of your baggage for so long?' Warren suggests. 'Where is your home, Jo?' He sounds surprised at himself for not knowing, but it is the first time he has asked that question directly.

'Home? I haven't had a home for years. Just a series of addresses.' In New York City once upon a time, the cost and effort of domesticating the empty hugeness of a loft seemed to impose a longer stay than usual to make it worth while, but even that was more than ten years ago.

'Oh. Well, where's the present address?'

'A rented house in Santa Fe. I have it for a year. In September the owner will take possession again and I shall move on.'

'You enjoy the gypsy life, do you?'

'I don't like the feeling of being tied down by property.' What I don't add is that in one of my several careers, as a photo-journalist, I have spent so many weeks on so many roads crowded with refugees that I have become almost ashamed of having a settled roof over my head.

'But there must be some place you think of as home. If not a house, then at least a country.'

I find myself sighing with the difficulty of producing an honest answer. But yes, there is no doubt that I think of the country of my birth in that way.

For most of my adult life, although my work takes me all over the world, I have been based in the United States. But I was born in England. I still think and mostly speak in English, adding American words to my vocabulary only as I need them, in the same way that I produce from my memory the necessary smatterings of French, Spanish, Arabic or whatever is appropriate on particular missions. I still carry a British passport, although doubtless on its next renewal I shall become a citizen of Europe.

'Yes,' I have to agree. 'I think of England as home. But that doesn't mean I ever want to live there again.'

'England's a wide term. There must be one special house there. The house where you were born. That sort of stuff.'

'The house in which I was born, in which I spent my childhood, is simply one of those addresses; nothing more. From a very long time ago. It was two days after my twentieth birthday that I closed the door of it behind me for ever.'

'Heavy!' Warren's eyes shine with curiosity, but I have no intention of mulling over old history for him. Instead I check the details of the meeting, some way in the future, in which we shall fit together the words and pictures for this section of the feature. Then I stand up, ready to get back to my room and pack. Warren is right. It is time to return to my temporary home.

2

On the day after my conversation with Warren I drive southwards at the steady pace which will avoid the attention of police helicopters and radar guns, thinking about the declaration which he would so much have liked me to explain.

Two days after my twentieth birthday I closed the door of 43 Woodside Road behind me for ever.

Well, yes. Sort of. Like most would-be-dramatic statements, this one is not strictly accurate. There was one icy return when I picked up my clothes and tried to explain what had happened. And I did go back again when my father was dying, and stayed for his funeral. It's sad, I suppose, that death should draw people back in a way that the living can't; sad but not unusual. I would have attended my mother's funeral as well, in spite of our unhappy relationship; but at the time I was half way up Everest and Yunga's message didn't reach me until six weeks too late.

The dramatic effect is even further weakened by the fact that when I left home I didn't know I was going for good. All that I had planned was a holiday. 'See you in a fortnight,' I said as I waved goodbye. It simply happened that I never returned.

Nevertheless, that departure proved to be a decisive moment in my life. If the peoples of the world, as anthropologists claim, are divided into cultivators and hunter-gatherers, then it was at the age of twenty that I chose my side of the great divide: I pulled up my roots and set out to hunt.

Over the course of a long life, it's proved to be a very successful hunt. As far as most people are concerned, photographers are men – usually – who freeze weddings into albums or immortalise young graduates in their hired gowns: men who become famous only when they sleep with glamorous models or marry princesses. So the name of Jolene Bradley doesn't mean much to the man in the street. But it rates high with the people who really matter to me: art editors and publishers and gallery owners and collectors – and, of course, other artists.

I'm not saying this to boast, but just to get things straight. Usually it's the failures in life who daren't go back to the homes which they left in a spirit of high ambition. It hurts too much to be reminded of those youthful hopes if you've never managed to live up to them. People who do well are normally quite happy to let themselves be shown off to the neighbours by a proud mummy and daddy. Not me, though. Yunga, I know, has always thought it was because I was afraid of somehow being sucked back in: into the family, the house, the suburb, the stifling church society. It's nothing as positive as that. I'm just not interested.

Had it been the only way of keeping in touch with Yunga, I suppose I would have had to go back more often to Woodside Road. But almost from the start I was earning good money. Pretty well every year from the time she left school I've been able to offer her a holiday in whatever bit of the world I happened to be in at the time. She spent a month with me last year in Santa Fe. I'd only just moved in myself, so we explored New Mexico and Colorado together; it was a happy time. And then in the new year I agreed to do a fashion shoot and arranged a surprise holiday for her in the West Indies. It was to celebrate her retirement. I still think of her as my little sister, but she's passed her sixtieth birthday.

Between four and fourteen, eight and eighteen, there's a generation gap. It ought to have disappeared by now, though. Sixty and seventy: not much difference, you might think. Odd that the gap should still be important. Perhaps it's not so much a matter of age as of status. For Yunga, I have always been there. The first-born is the first-born for ever. While for me, Yunga has always been someone to be looked after. Time hasn't changed that. Whenever I invite her for a holiday I am in a sense offering a treat to a child: my little sister.

I am still thinking about those two happy periods in Santa Fe and then in Barbados as I pull up outside the adobe house in Canyon Road. Already I'm looking forward to reading a three-month batch of letters from Yunga. Although I've been writing regularly to her, I didn't give her an address for the skiing trip, because I knew that I'd be moving from one house or hotel to another, and even from one resort to another. She knew she could always reach me via my New York agent in an emergency; but what kind of emergency was there likely to be? Any one week in 43 Woodside Road is very much like another.

Within ten minutes of my return my next-door neighbour is on the doorstep, bearing milk and cookies as well as the mail which she has been collecting for me during my absence. Although I'm only a temporary tenant here, I was welcomed at once as the right sort of resident for a street which is strict about preserving its character.

The history of Canyon Road goes back to medieval times – to a period of history which a surprising number of Americans believe to have existed only in Europe. The street was first laid out by the Pueblos but took on a more formal line when the Spaniards arrived in the eighteenth century. Later on, each original clay-surfaced house was extended around a courtyard – which here is called a *placita*. The extensions proved later still to provide the ideal space and light for studios, so for much of this century the street was famous for being an artists' colony.

Its reputation persists, thanks to the enthusiasm of the local tourist office. There are indeed still some working artists in residence, but an increasing number of the sprawling compounds have become galleries or antique shops. They do good business. Holiday-makers wander along Canyon Road as sightseers but frequently become customers. It's part of my current tenancy agreement that I should open the gallery behind the house for five summer months, showing my landlord's sculptures as well as any of my own photographs that I may wish to put on display. Not yet, though. Winter may be over, but summer has not yet arrived.

Martha, my friendly neighbour, brings me up to date with local gossip and then leaves me to unpack. But first of all I sit down to read my mail. Mail, not post: there do seem to be some words which have driven their English equivalents out of my vocabulary.

There isn't a great deal and most of it is junk. Anything concerned with business goes directly to my agent, whom I phone (not call) regularly once a week. Out of the pile I first of all take a picture postcard. It is not, as for a moment I assume, a wish-you-were-here holiday card; its view of London's Houses of Parliament was painted by Monet.

The message on the reverse is brief: 'It didn't work. Y.'

I stare at the words without understanding them; but even without understanding I can sense the menace in the message. Glancing at the postmark, which is recent, I quickly extract every envelope which bears the queen's head on the stamp, and arrange them in order.

The first two contain nothing sinister. A thank you for the West Indies holiday. A cheerful essay about adjusting to life in retirement. But the third of Yunga's letters, after some general chat about books and piano pupils, ends with a paragraph, apparently casual, which my anxiety immediately pinpoints as being important.

> I don't think I bothered to mention it at the time, but I arrived home from Barbados with a slightly painful foot. "The economy class syndrome", I was told by friends who lectured me on how I should have interrupted the flight with a series of exercises. It conjured up an absurd picture of four hundred passengers all touching their toes in the aisles, but I shouldn't have laughed. The foot started to swell, and became very painful to walk on, and then after a bit it hurt even when I was resting it. I thought it was gout at first, but it wasn't.
>
> When I went to the doctor at last, he told me I'd had a thrombosis. I had a long lecture about how I ought to have gone to see him at once. It's one of the odd things about having a National Health Service. It tempts some people to call at the surgery for every little thing, just because it's free; but other people, like me, would find it easier to ask about some probably trivial symptom, if they knew they were going to pay for it. I do rather tend to put things off in case I'm wasting the doctor's time. Stupid, I know.
>
> Anyway, I shall have to have a day or two in hospital: I'm still waiting to hear when they can give me an appointment.

The gap before the next letter was much longer than it ought to have been. Yunga's handwriting has changed, I notice, particularly where she spelled out unfamiliar words, one letter at a time, like a child who has not yet been taught joined-up writing.

> What they did in the hospital was something called a lumbar sympathectomy. This was supposed to get the circulation going again in my foot, because there was a danger of secondary gangrene. Hearing that word came as quite a surprise. I've always thought of gangrene as something that only happens to soldiers with terrible wounds that have become infected. Which just shows that I don't know anything about it. Anyway, I've been going back once a week to make sure that all is well, and it isn't. The gangrene is there, and I shall have to have the foot amputated. In fact, maybe more than just the foot, to be on the safe side.
>
> It's all come as a bit of a shock. Such a silly little thing to cause so much trouble. And naturally I was depressed when I first heard the verdict. It would be worse for someone like you, of course, if you couldn't go on shinning up mountains and sliding down again. But even for a lazy lady like me it's a bit of a blight. I shan't be able to play the organ any more, and not even the piano properly, although it needn't stop me teaching. I have to remind myself that I'm a pensioner now, not a schoolteacher; and

I can probably carry on with my private lessons even as a peg-leg.

Anyway, those are small matters. The big question is whether the operation will be successful or whether the poison or whatever it is has escaped and will continue to spread. It's an odd feeling. With a cancer, I'd be able to visualise the cells of my body multiplying and forming lumps, but this has a more insidious feel to it. Sneaky and invisible.

I shall try to phone you when I know how things have gone, but I expect you're still skiing, so if necessary I'll leave a message with Fay.

Fay is my agent. She holds my archive, arranges copyright payments and exhibitions and puts my name forward whenever any work in my line is available. Because I spend so much of my life on the move, I contact her every Monday. Today is Sunday, but I have her home number. As I wait for a reply the picture postcard lies in front of me. I know what I'm about to be told.

'Hi there, Jo. I'm glad you called. Your sister wants to get in touch.'

'Did she leave a message with you?'

'Just that she's discharged herself from the hospital and is home again. She's hoping you'll contact her. And Jo, there's an offer –'

'Nothing for the moment,' I tell her, feeling sick with anxiety. 'I shall be flying to England as soon as I can get on a plane.'

Going home.

Part Two

Going Home

1

Home equals birthplace. As the plane takes off I try to concentrate my mind on birthplaces because I don't want to think about amputations and poisoned blood. I set myself a little exercise: to remember the origins of as many famous people as I can.

The list is a long one because, although I am not a great reader, biography is my favourite reading. It is interesting to notice how clearly the names which roll through my memory divide themselves into two distinct groups.

There is – especially from past centuries – the silver spoon brigade. Men and women – though mostly men – from a background of wealth and comfort, brought up to accept responsibilities and provide leadership. Men and women who return often to their childhood homes, at least in spirit, in order that family tradition can reinforce their dedication to duty. Men and women who almost certainly surround the structure of these childhood homes with a golden haze of memory. They can remember ballrooms and gun-rooms and stables and libraries, and they sieve their memories so that only the best of them remain.

Then there are the escapers, whose fame is a by-product of their struggle to put childhood poverty behind them. There are no ballrooms in their memories, but only outside privies: guns, perhaps, but not gun-rooms. What they have escaped from may be a share-cropper's shack, a miner's shanty, a city slum. They too may sieve their memories, but what they retain is the cold and dirt and hunger; the overcrowding and the moonlight flits. Hardly ever, as far as I can recall, is it a dormitory suburb which has acted as a springboard towards fame or fortune.

I am an escaper, of a kind, but from security, not hardship. Perhaps that is why I shall never be famous enough to have biographers beating at my door. I have no wish either to preserve or to destroy the kind of life with which my parents presented me seventy-odd years ago; merely to ignore it.

Kenbury, the suburb from which I have escaped, and to which I am now on my way, is a few miles north-west of London. It is a nowhere place. A place which provides shelter for unimportant people with no very great ambitions.

This – like my equally over-dramatic claim to have left it for ever at the age of twenty – is probably nonsense. I haven't lived there for fifty years. Everything may be different now. Perhaps. I am simply trying to keep my thoughts away from what is happening at 43 Woodside Road. Even in a nowhere place, important events occur. People die.

There is a little turbulence over the coastline; nothing much, but the need to refasten my seat belt provides a second distraction from an unwelcome subject, and this time I discipline my mind not to return to it. I eat an airline meal. I drink a tiny bottle of airline wine. I fasten shades over my eyes, incline the back of my seat and will myself to sleep. This is something in which I have had years of practice, and only the arrival of breakfast arouses me. We are approaching Heathrow.

It is thirty years since I was last in England. This fact is a tribute to the country's freedom from revolutions, civil wars, droughts and famines, hurricanes, earthquakes and floods. For much of my life I have earned my living as a vulture feeding on disaster, and there have always been better pickings elsewhere. So I have retained in my memory – as in my archive – a picture of bright-eyed young people dressed sometimes outlandishly but with a sense of style. A smiling, confident country. A happy country. What has happened to that country since 1967?

First impressions are not too bad. The view from the window as the plane crosses the coastline suggests that England remains a green and pleasant land; and an airport is just an airport. Perhaps London, at its heart, is still a vibrant and majestic city; but I have no need to go into the centre and out again. The north-western suburbs of the capital lie almost due north of Heathrow. It is on this part of the journey that my heart begins to sink.

On the assumption that Yunga's car will be at my disposal after my arrival, I take a taxi from Heathrow. Sitting as a passenger enables me to give my full attention to the scenery, and what I see appals me. Not by anything dramatically awful, but by a dinginess which lowers the spirits.

All the people I see on the streets are shabby. Not in the sense of wearing the rags of poverty, but in apparently not caring about their appearance at all. It is presumably a transient fashion whcih persuades young women to present themselves to the world with uncombed hair, but even members of an older generation are creased and untidy as they hurry to catch their buses to work. Children, eating their breakfast on the hoof as they dawdle towards school, wear no uniform and can only be described as scruffy.

As for the streets themselves, they are dirty. Empty crisp packets and torn pieces of newspaper flutter briefly before descending to litter the pavements, and empty beer cans clog the gutters. The vehicles which drive along the streets are dirty as well. The houses which line the streets are unkempt. It is a good many years since most of them last had a new coat of paint and their front lawns have been concreted over so that a car may block the view from a ground-floor window. The shops in the little arcades which punctuate the journey look dilapidated, as though their owners have lost heart. There are no window displays. Mini-markets offer only posters announcing special offers. Greengrocers stack their goods outside in the fume-heavy air in a jumble of crates. What has happened to the polished pyramids of fruit that I remember from my childhood?

It is necessary to remind myself that my childhood is a very long way away. And I should know better than to be shocked by such a petty collapse of standards, when I remember other journeys from other airports, past the squalor and stench of shanty towns in Brazil or India. Yes, but this is England. These are the outskirts of London, not Bombay. What has happened to pride – in one's appearance, one's home, one's community? Although by choice an expatriate, I have always felt proud of being English but now, confronted with the real England, my spirits sink.

I am being a stuffy old woman. When I was a schoolgirl myself I loathed the rules which forced me to wear hat and gloves and navy blue blazer and forbade me ever to eat in the street. Had trainers been invented at that time I would have longed to discard my black lace-up shoes. It is years – decades, even – since I last dressed in the neat skirt and stockings which I am expecting these suburban housewives to don for my benefit. And the shopping malls of the United States are crowded with obese women who stretch pink Crimplene trousers over their huge bottoms: compared with them, a little dinginess should come as a relief.

I ought to be reminding myself that it was because I found suburban life oppressive that I made my escape from it – and the oppressiveness lay in the very tidiness and rigidity of social expectation from which these people on the streets have so clearly freed themselves. There's a lack of logic here. I shall have to think about that later.

But now the taxi is approaching Woodside Road, and the outlook is improving. Since we have turned off the main road there is less dirt and less noise. The streets are wider, and tree-lined. These houses are well cared for and because they have garages there is no litter of parked vehicles. The driver asks me what number I want.

'Just stop here.' I need a moment to steady my emotions before I ring the doorbell. After I have paid and the taxi has driven away, I stare diagonally across the road at the house which was my home for the first nineteen years of my life.

It was four months before my birth that my parents decided to take out a mortgage and buy a house in the suburbs, rather than in the city or country. I've never really forgiven them for it.

The decision was for my sake, they told me later. What a child needs is a safe garden and a safe recreation ground to play in; safe roads to cross on the way to a safe school; safe friends and safe neighbours. They were wrong, of course, although it took me a little while to work it out for myself. What a child really needs is the possibility of adventure, the threat of danger. If I'd had a little more of that when I was five or six, perhaps I wouldn't have spent almost the whole of my adult life daring the most unpleasant parts of the world to kill me.

Well, perhaps. It did seem to work out differently for Yunga. And if I've enjoyed those dangerous years – and I have – perhaps too I ought to be grateful rather than unforgiving for that parental decision. More bad logic. Moving into my seventies does rather seem to be muddying my trains of thought.

For example: although during the taxi ride I have been startled to see how greatly street life has changed since 1967, I am equally startled to see that 43 Woodside Road has hardly changed at all. What I see at this moment must be very much what my parents saw in 1926.

I find it easy to picture them: Mr and Mrs Aden Bradley, standing where I am standing now and staring proudly at their new home. Perhaps they were holding hands, for at that time their marriage would still have been a happy one. My mother, no doubt dressed to disguise her swollen belly, would have eyes shining with the excitement of nest-making. Later in her life she became apt to talk bitterly about how she had sacrificed what would have been a brilliant career as a dancer; but at the time I am sure that marriage must have been what she wanted and that she was happy in this particular marriage.

My father, too, can not at this early date have succumbed to the disappointment which soured his later years. Although the responsibility of supporting a wife had prompted him to take employment as a schoolteacher, he must still have been hoping that it need only be temporary. Once he managed to complete his dissertation and earn his doctorate, the opportunity of becoming, eventually, an eminent university professor would surely present itself. So as he looked at the house, he would have been protective; proud that he was able to shoulder the responsibility of a mortgage and all the inevitable bills which descend on a householder. It was a big step.

They were both stepping into a cage; but if they realised the fact, they must have seen it as a golden cage. They did it for my sake, and no doubt that explains the depth of their anger when I ran away.

Well, I have been happy, as for most of their lives they were not. I have lived the life I chose for myself and, although it was not the life they had chosen for me, they ought to have been happy on my behalf. Perhaps they might have been if I had ever given them the opportunity to show it. I don't think so, though. I think that they both became and remained bitter because I escaped from the cage which they had built for me; the cage which remained their own prison even after I was free.

My mother was beautiful when she was young. I have seen a photograph that was taken to celebrate her engagement and, although I know better than most people how easy it is for the camera to distort the truth, I am prepared to believe that on that day at least she was as radiantly lovely and in love as she looks in the frame. It's sad that even the camera is not powerful enough to stand up against the memory of direct vision. I shall always remember my mother as I last saw her, on the day of my father's funeral: a querulous invalid, not quite able to conceal her delight in having the house to herself at last. She had not yet, on that day, discovered that her home had in fact been bequeathed to Yunga.

To the house, time has been kinder. It was never beautiful, but is no uglier now than seventy or fifty years ago. My dislike of it as a child came not from any precocious criticism of its design but from the fact that each pair of semi-detached houses along one side of the road was identical to every other pair. Red brick to halfway up, pebble dash above and a triangle of mock-Tudor beams in the gable. I remember the pebble dash as being a muddy grey, but Yunga has made a change here. It must have been after our holiday together in Greece that she decided to have it painted in a pale shade of apple green. It looks good.

Like all its neighbours, number 43 stands back from the road behind a privet hedge and narrow front garden bisected by a straight path of red tiles. The garden is covered with crazy paving in which gaps have been left for plants to grow. The first visual reminder of Yunga's illness comes from the clumps of daffodils whose flowers are dead but not dead-headed. I do not at this time recognise the significance of the fact that the gate and the gateposts have been removed.

The path leads to a black front door with a semi-circle of coloured glass above it. There is more coloured glass – this time depicting St George and the dragon – in the hall window on the right. On the left, adjoining number 41, is the bay window of what was the dining room when I was young, but later became my father's study after he found himself in need of a refuge from noisy children. Above it, also with a bay window, is the best room in the house, light and large – well, large for a semi-detached suburban house. This was my parents' bedroom until my mother evicted her husband from both room and bed and settled down to spend the rest of her life in it. The other front room, above the hall, was originally mine until the traumatic moment of my first confrontation with Timmy.

Still reluctant to move, I recall the shock of that moment again now, and spend a little time trying to imagine what different trauma it could have been that brought my parents' marriage effectively to an end. Such an ordinary family we were, living in such an ordinary house. But for a second time within a few hours I remind myself that important things can happen in unimportant places to unimportant people: things that are important to them, at least. That was something I didn't realise at the age of twenty.

A woman – a stranger – is looking out from the bay window; looking at me. I pick up my bags, cross the road and walk up the red path.

'You must be Jolene,' says the unknown woman who opens the door. She is wearing a nurse's uniform. 'I'm so glad you've got here in time.'

It is the wrong thing to say: a terrifying thing to hear. During my journey I have tried to persuade myself that I have misinterpreted Yunga's message. But this nurse is not going to let me kid myself. Dumb with misery I step inside. Home.

2

The nurse asks me to wait in the hall. No doubt there is a good reason for this. It is not yet half-past eight in the morning, British time. Yunga may still be asleep, or having breakfast, or sitting on a commode. She may need to be protected from even a pleasant shock. She may want to comb her hair and put on make-up before I see her. Nevertheless, the request irks me. I am being made to feel like a mere visitor. Since a visitor is exactly what I am, it is unreasonable to be resentful; but it spoils my picture, my expectation, of two sisters rushing into each other's arms.

Impatiently waiting, I study the hall. Like the pebbledash, it has changed for the better. In my father's lifetime it was a brown space. Dark brown stained floorboards, chestnut brown banisters and skirting boards, muddy brown dado: depressing in the extreme. Yunga – perhaps inspired by my New York loft or the house in Santa Fe – has painted walls and woodwork white. The floor is covered with a fair imitation of parquet. I can see the lines which reveal that the effect is produced by thin tiles; but it provides a light golden background to the bright rugs that she bought while visiting me in Pakistan after my precipitate retreat from Afghanistan.

There is a radiator as well, announcing that central heating has arrived to cheer up a house that I remember as being always cold. That was nothing particular to the Bradley family. Most houses in the England of the thirties and forties were cold. It is good that Yunga has managed to warm as well as lighten her home, but although my eyes register all these improvements, they do nothing to lift my spirits because they are cancelled out by the sight of a new piece of furniture. A wheelchair is standing just inside the front door. Yes, of course, that is why the front gate has been removed.

The nurse reappears, smiling. 'Your sister's delighted that you're here.

Have you had breakfast? Can I get you anything?'

Too impatient to answer, I shake my head. I am the one who has to do all the rushing, because Yunga is unable to move. But her arms are wide open to greet me. As I go down on my knees so that we are on the same level to hug and kiss each other, she is laughing and I am crying.

Only after a long time has passed do I sigh and draw a little way away to look at her, trying not to show how much her appearance shocks me. It is because she is ill that I am here. There is no good reason why I should be surprised. But I am.

I am ten years older than Yunga and my face looks older than I feel. It has become weatherbeaten over the years under the attack of a sun which glares with equal ferocity on mountains and deserts. I travel too lightly to bother with make-up or moisturisers, and it shows. Nevertheless, lined and leathery though it may be, it is a healthy face, bronzed from my recent weeks on the ski slopes.

Yunga's skin, in contrast, is unnaturally pale and smooth, stretched so tightly over her cheekbones that I seem almost to be looking at a skull already. Across my own face there is a strip of paler skin to show where snow goggles have been protecting my eyes, but Yunga's eyes are sunk deep into hollows of blackness. The flame of hope which I have been striving to keep alive in my heart during the flight flickers and extinguishes itself. I am looking at a dying woman.

Naturally I refrain from putting this thought into words. Instead, I jabber away, too cheerfully, telling Yunga how stupid she has been not to go to the doctor more promptly but how everything is going to be all right now that I am here. She will have an artificial foot fitted, almost as good as the real one. I shall force her to exercise and walk. We will go on expeditions together. And as soon as she is well enough she must come back with me to the pure air and clear skies of New Mexico. I am Little Mother again, protecting my baby from harm. But Yunga, of course, is no longer a baby. As I rattle on and on, she puts up a hand to stop me.

'Dr Morris will be here quite soon,' she tells me with the sweet smile that has always tugged at my heart. 'He calls in every morning before surgery, to give me an injection and grumble that I ought to have stayed in hospital. Have a word with him after he's finished in here. You may not want to believe anything I tell you, but you'll have to believe him. And then we can be honest with each other. Better that way.'

Her calmness silences me, and the silence is deepened by the impossibility now of saying anything encouraging until the doctor arrives. As Yunga's embracing arms drop wearily away, I look round for a chair.

We are in the room that has always been called the lounge: a word which I have never heard used by any other family. Drawing room, sitting room, the front, best room, living room, parlour or even salon; but never lounge, except here. It is surprisingly large for an unpretentious suburban semi. Even now, converted into a sick room, there is plenty of space. The sofa has been removed, but the baby grand piano is still there and so are two comfortable arm chairs. Against one wall is an ugly iron-framed bed which has presumably been hired to provide a height convenient for the nurse. Near to the bed is the commode which our mother used during her long illness: a substantial piece of Victorian furniture which successfully disguises itself as an ordinary chair. A nurse's trolley, covered with a white cloth, stands against another wall, but there is still room for the two oak bookcases which have always been filled with books designed to be admired for their appearance rather than read for their contents.

In the middle of the room Yunga sits, propped up by pillows, on a chaise longue. She can reach over to a table, on her left, on which stand a pile of books, a jug and glass, a telephone, a compact disc player and controls for television and video. Her legs are covered by a blanket which is held up by an invisible frame. From this position she can look out at the garden through the wide French windows, which perhaps will be opened when the sun comes round a little further. She has a view of the pear tree, which soon, no doubt, will produce a fine display of blossom – although I remember that the pears themselves were always riddled with the brown tunnels of wriggling maggots.

'It's a nice room,' Yunga says calmly, watching my inspection. Like me, she is trying not to talk about anything important until I have had my conversation with the doctor. 'Doesn't compare with the huge spaces you like to live in, but nice in its own way. I always thought it was crazy, when we were children, that it was only used on Sundays and for visitors and piano practice.'

'It made it into a treat, I suppose.' In the icy years of wartime fuel rationing, the ceremonial lighting of the coal fire in the lounge at two o'clock on a Sunday afternoon heralded a few hours of comfort as we played a family game of Ludo or Monopoly before enjoying toast and honey for tea.

'Your sunset doesn't go, of course.' She indicates a very large photograph which is hanging above the fireplace, where it can be seen from the bed. 'But I brought it down from my bedroom all the same. I wanted to have it with me.'

She is talking about the present which I gave her on her fiftieth birthday. I'd just published *The going-down of the sun*, a coffee-table book containing nothing but sunsets from all over the world with the black silhouettes of people or monuments in the foreground. This was a blow-up of one of the most dramatic. My favourite. Mountains and snow and sunsets are my three non-human passions, and here they are all combined. Unlike some of the other scenes in the book, whose setting can be identified by a pyramid or a Chinese fisherman in a coolie hat balancing on his narrow raft with a cormorant tied to his wrist, this sunset could be anywhere. It was actually taken in Mexico.

'When did it start?' Yunga asks me unexpectedly. 'Sit down, while you're waiting, and tell me about your very first memorable sunset.'

That's an easy one, because by coincidence it was part of the most important week of my life. Or was it in fact one of the experiences which made the week important? I take a moment or two to ponder the question. Yunga is in no hurry to hear an answer. She is holding my hand and smiling, but her eyes are closed. In happiness, I think; not pain. She is glad of my presence but doesn't need to hear my voice.

At the end of my fourth term at Girton, in the Christmas vacation of 1946, I went on a skiing holiday with a group of college friends. None of us had ever skied before. None of us had even been abroad before, because we were children when the war started and in the months since it ended neither transport nor hotels had been ready to receive visitors.

We were an inelegant bunch. Clothing was still rationed, and trousers were not at that time ordinary wear for girls – and in fact were forbidden for undergraduates in gowns. The problem was solved by army surplus stores: my own first ski suit was an ATS uniform. We were also very poor – not just in absolute terms, but because everyone at that time was forbidden to take more than a tiny amount of money out of the country. But that didn't stop us having a marvellous time.

Out of the group of eleven who slid and tumbled on the nursery slopes on that first hilarious and bruising day in Pontresina, four of us got the hang of skiing quite quickly. As a reward, our guide passed us up into a higher group after a week so that we could go on an all-day expedition instead of repetitively queuing for the ski-lift and whizzing straight down again.

We took the train to the next station along the line: St Moritz. St Moritz! The very name was romantic. It stood not just for winter sports excellence but for glamorous women in furs and diamonds sweeping out of grand hotels. Not that we had time to see anything of that sort before we were transported upward by a ski-tow, a chair-lift and finally a cable car. I had never been so high before. Altitude and excitement almost prevented me from breathing.

This was not to be a straight up and down day. We were to cover a great deal of ground, our new guide told us, and that meant that each sweep downwards was followed by a stint of trekking, digging our skis sideways into a slope as we regained some of the height we had lost until our leg muscles ached and shuddered. We were slower, I expect, than the guide had anticipated, because the sun was already setting as we began a gentle downward glide across the last snowfield, towards the head of the piste.

I was at the back of the group, and paused for a moment on a ridge to enjoy the view. It was a scene that I have remembered all my life. As sunsets go, it was not particularly dramatic: a soft rosiness in the sky, tingeing the surface of the snowfield with a sparkling pink. Below me, and rapidly moving further away, were the small black figures of my fellow-skiers in a single narrow line behind the guide. Above me were the mountain peaks. There was nothing else to be seen and no sound to be heard. I was alone at the top of the world.

The sun fell a little lower in the sky and sent a wide crimson path straight to my feet, as though to tell me not to linger. I gave a quick jump to clear my skis, bent my knees to press both sticks into the snow and pushed off at the best speed I could manage to catch the others up. The moment was over, but it remains as clear to me as any photograph I have ever taken.

No doubt there were special reasons for the effect this sunset moment had on the rest of my life. For more than six years I had been imprisoned by the war not merely in a suburb but in a country, and to an impatient young woman it had often seemed that there would never be any chance to explore the rest of the world. And in all my twenty years I had never before experienced such a sense of space. The grandeur of the mountains, the silence of the snow, the flushed beauty of the sky, all combined to excite me with the realisation that outside the confines of 43 Woodside Road and the corridors of Girton a wider world was waiting. It was almost certainly this experience which made me receptive to the adventure which the next day was to bring.

Yunga doesn't want to know all this – or, even if she does, a time of reunion is not the appropriate occasion for detailed reminiscence. It is enough to mention Switzerland, the year and the delicate shades of the sky. And now the front door bell is ringing. The doctor has arrived.

Once more the nurse asks me to wait outside. I meet Dr Morris in the hall and introduce myself.

'And before you go, Doctor –'

He nods his head, not needing to be asked. I pick up my bags and carry them upstairs.

The whole of the first floor is presumably at my disposal, since I have already been able to see that the front room on the ground floor has become a bed-sitting room for one of the nurses. I open each door in turn.

The large front bedroom which was once shared by our parents and later monopolised by our mother has obviously been appropriated by Yunga. She is never likely to return to it, but nevertheless it is hers. The small front bedroom which was mine for the first four years of my life is too closely associated with Timmy for me to be comfortable there. I avoid the room immediately above Yunga's head in case my movements in it should disturb her when she is resting, and dump my things instead in the small room which was mine during my schooldays. It is a square space without character and it arouses no sentimental feelings, but it will be somewhere to sleep. I sit on the bed and wait for the sounds which will tell me that the doctor is ready to leave.

He comes up to see me in my room, in fact, taking the stairs two at a time. No doubt he wants to avoid letting Yunga hear whisperings in the hall. My questions are answered sympathetically but definitely. No. No hope. Nothing more to be done.

'I can arrange a bed in a hospice any time your sister wants it,' he tells me. 'The pain control regime would be more satisfactory there. But she's been making it clear since discharging herself from hospital that she wanted to be at home when you arrived, so probably you're the only person who can persuade her to move. I call at this time every day, so let me know if you think she may be changing her mind.'

I nod my head, and he prepares to leave. But he has one more thing to say.

'Ten years ago, even five years ago, there wasn't a lot we could do about secondary gangrene,' he tells me. 'But nowadays there's no need for anyone to die of it. Not in England, at least. Your sister should have come to me much earlier, as soon as she was aware that something was wrong. I could hardly be expected to know without seeing her. And even after she'd been investigated, she took too long to agree to the amputation. As though playing the organ could be more important than staying alive!'

His voice is angry. I can tell that most of his anger is with the situation that has developed; with the fact that he is about to lose one of his patients unnecessarily. At the same time he is obviously feeling a need to justify himself to me. I can assure him honestly enough that Yunga has already admitted her own foolishness in her letter to me. Nothing is his fault.

After he has left the house I take a little time to steady myself. I have seen too many deaths to be sentimental about the subject in a general way. We live, we die; peacefully or violently, too soon or too late. It doesn't frighten me to contemplate my own death, because I shall have no awareness of any gap it has left. Yunga's death is different. Only when I put it to myself in such a way do I realise that what I am feeling is self-pity. That helps.

As soon as I can be sure that I am not going to cry again I go downstairs and once more take my sister into my arms, hugging her fiercely and silently.

'You've talked to Dr Morris, then?' she checks when at last we release each other.

'Yes. Three months.' I am pushing his estimate to its extreme limit, but this small dishonesty must surely be acceptable. 'Three months to make the most of. You must tell me how you'd like to spend it.'

Yunga smiles: a smile in which there is no trace of sadness.

'I don't feel quite up to saying that I'd like to go round the world before I die. Now that you're here, all I want to do is talk. I'm happy just being at home.'

I nod. Whatever Yunga wants she must have. For three months. Or three weeks. At home.

Part Three

Memories

1

Yunga's day is carefully organised. Gwen, who sleeps in the house, gives her supper and helps her to bed. Kate, the nurse who first greeted me, arrives at seven in the morning to bring her breakfast, give her a bed bath, help her to dress, move her on and off the commode and across to the chaise longue. After the doctor's visit she puts on a new dressing and administers any drugs which he prescribes. She stays until two o'clock and is replaced for a couple of hours by Maggie, who used to come once a week to do some cleaning but is now arriving daily and doing the shopping on the way. By the time Maggie leaves at four o'clock a tea tray has been prepared, so that any visitor has only to boil a kettle and make the tea.

There are visitors every afternoon, Yunga tells me, although never more than two. Somebody – either a neighbour or a member of the church congregation – is clearly acting as an organiser to make sure that she is never left alone.

On the day of my arrival, however, someone must have been keeping watch from behind a net curtain. After Maggie's departure we have the house to ourselves.

By now the emotion of our reunion has left Yunga too tired to talk much. She makes a comment to start off a conversation, but then seems happy for me to keep it going, meandering on even if she's hearing again what she knows already.

Because I can't always tell whether or not she's still listening or has fallen asleep, I fall silent from time to time, continuing the conversation in my head. Sometimes she allows the silence to lengthen; sometimes her eyes open almost at once, willing me to go on.

We have talked about her illness and about my flight. Now she asks me to turn over the pages of one of my books, the airport book, and puts up a finger to pause at the picture for which I am most famous: the terrified child cowering away from the man who has bought her to be his bride. This photograph has won awards, although it is not for that reason that I am proud of it. Yunga gives a sigh.

'You can't imagine how much I wanted to be you, when I was young.'

'To be like me, you mean?'

'No. To *be* you. Even if I'd left home, even if I'd done everything that you did, I still wouldn't ever have been you. We're too different. I've never been ambitious. It was something I always envied you: your ambition.'

I consider this in silence for a moment before beginning to think aloud, keeping up the pretence that this is a dialogue. There's nothing very praiseworthy about ambition. Wanting to be the best. To get the furthest up whichever ladder you've chosen to climb. The richest businessman, the fastest runner, the biggest-selling author. Fulfilling an ambition tends to be a question of comparisons, of being able to tread on the fingers of other people on the same ladder. Not a lot to be proud of in that.

What *is* enviable is the ability to choose the right *ladder*, the one and only ladder which leads up to personal fulfilment. If you get that choice right, happiness is built in. No risk of the disappointment which comes from setting a goal too high and then falling short. The happiness comes simply from doing the work, not from doing it better than anyone else.

'Well then, that's what I envy you. Choosing the right ladder.'

I'm not sure that even that is quite how it works. Perhaps the ladder chooses the climber. This metaphor is getting out of hand, isn't it? I suppose what I'm talking about is vocation.

It's an odd thing, this business of vocation. I remember reading how Tortelier's mother gave him a miniature cello when he was only three years old and then watched him become one of the greatest cellists of his generation. I have a friend who was in such despair at the resentments and rebellions of her newly acquired stepson that she enrolled him in a fencing class. She didn't know the first thing about fencing and nor did he, but within three years he was world junior champion. Everyone knows a story of this kind and it's always put down to some subtle instinct on the part of the adult concerned. But the stories wouldn't have sounded so good if Tortelier had decided at the age of ten that he wanted to play the flute or train as a hairdresser, and my friend would have kept a little quieter if her stepson had used his skill with steel to become a juvenile drug-dealer.

In one sense it's the child who chooses. All that any adult can do is to let it be known what choices may exist. But in another sense the skill or the career or the hobby, whatever it is, chooses the child. It seems to say: this is what you've been waiting for. Surrender to me, and I will make you happy for the rest of your life.

Yunga had a skill. A talent more obvious than mine at the same age, and more likely to offer a career. I remind her of it now.

'You've had your own vocation. Your music.' As a little girl Yunga was the star of the music festival which was held in Kenbury, winning first prize in her age group every year for piano.

'I was hardly Mozart. The best in Kenbury but an also-ran anywhere else. I realised when I got to college. Not good enough.'

'It gave you a career.'

She shakes her head. 'A way of earning money isn't the same as a career.'

I can't argue with that. Yunga has earned her living not by playing the piano but by teaching it, both in a local school and privately, in individual lessons. She has played for her own pleasure, as a hobby, and acted as organist and choirmistress at the church of which she is a member. In the years since our mother's death she has played to old people in residential homes, and even sometimes their own homes, and out of this developed a secondary career. Although she had no nursing qualifications she was prepared to sit with some elderly or demented person to give the regular carer a break, or even to move into the house and take over for a week, if it was within the school holidays. She is kind and patient, with an uncanny ability to soothe or stimulate a patient with her music. Her life has been a useful one, and I tell her so.

'Perhaps. But not a vocation. Different. We were talking about you. When did you ...?'

I found my vocation on my tenth birthday.

I was given dolls on my early birthdays, but they didn't make me want to be a mother. I was given a nurse's outfit when I was six, but I never chose to spend my life healing people. For my eighth birthday, I remember, I had a giant paintbox with thirty-six tiny rectangles of water colour and three brushes, and I liked painting pictures; but there was never any idea in my head that I'd want to become that kind of an artist. But on my tenth birthday I put my eye to the viewfinder of a Brownie camera and I knew, I absolutely knew what was going to be the most important enthusiasm of my life.

That might not necessarily have meant that I was going to be good at photography. Vocation and skill, vocation and success, don't always go together. But I didn't think that way as I took my first snap, of my mother and father and brother and the new baby – Yunga – in the garden, under the pear tree. I knew for sure that I was going to take marvellous photographs one day. That's what faith is, I suppose, and if you have it, it feeds on itself and makes itself come true.

It was the framing effect that did it for me, that first day. I saw that something quite ordinary changed its character once it was contained in a rectangle: the viewfinder. The spaces round the subject have always been important for me, but the spaces themselves only exist as shapes if they have limits.

The limits of a photograph operate in both time and space. They pick one tiny detail out of the whole wide world at one second out of the whirling torrent of seconds and tame it by keeping it still. That detail, whatever it is in life, loses its context when it becomes a photograph. It's no longer part of the flow of events. Naturally, whatever scene has been photographed has causes and effects in real life and the effects sweep on after the shutter has opened and closed. But if the photograph itself proves to have an effect, it's a different effect. You can change the course of history with a photograph. Don't ever let anyone kid you that all you're doing is to record it. That picture of mine, of the unwilling child bride at the airport, is sufficient proof of that. Laws have been passed; people have been sent to prison. In at least one country – to my pride – I am persona non grata.

How much of this have I said aloud? How much has only passed through my mind? Yunga can only concentrate on one thing at a time. She is more interested in ambition and vocation than in technique. She has asked for a simple date, and the answer is straightforward.

'When I was given a camera for my tenth birthday.'

'That was your vocation, then? Your calling. Did you realise straightaway that it would be your career?'

How many ten year olds know that it's possible to earn a living by pointing a camera and pressing a knob or pulling a lever? Not I, certainly – and I could not possibly have known that I might prove to have a talent for it, as my sister at the same age would prove – much more obviously – to have a talent for playing the piano. It was a hobby. An absorbing hobby; and because it was an expensive one for a child, I spent the next few birthdays and Christmases pleading for my presents to take the form of films and the equipment for developing and printing them. But it was a long time before the possibility of making money from such a hobby entered my head. That, as I explain to Yunga now, was why I allowed myself to be sidetracked to Cambridge.

'Tell me about Cambridge, then. Why you went. Why you didn't stay.' She knows – although perhaps she has forgotten – how I was offered the chance to escape from both home and university, but perhaps she has never understood why I was so quick to grab at the opportunity.

Meanwhile, she has lost interest in the book of photographs. I think she finds it an effort to focus her eyes on it for long at a time. I take it away and lay it down, closed, on the bedside table.

Then I have to make an effort of my own; an effort of memory. I haven't thought about Cambridge, England, for years; but for a few months of my life it was the most important place in the world.

I was a bright girl at school. Good at passing exams. Good at writing lively essays. Good at learning things by heart, so that I could always produce a useful quote. Good at debating and standing up for myself. English was my best subject.

My school sent most of its cleverest girls to London University; all they had to do in order to qualify was to pass a few Higher Certificate exams with reasonable marks. And of course it wouldn't have cost my parents too much to send me there. No maintenance payments, because I could still live at home and travel in daily; and most of my fees would be covered by a county grant. The money details mattered, because Timmy was still alive then and any money that my father could save for higher education was destined for him, not me.

But my English teacher was a Cambridge graduate: a Girton blue-stocking. She persuaded my parents to put me in for the Cambridge scholarship exam. I suppose she saw in me her chance of glory. It was to be glory for me as well, of course – in fact it would have to be: glory or nothing, since glory had a cash value. For my own part, I didn't need any persuading to have a shot. For the first time in my life I could see a chance of escaping from the suburbs.

A month after the decision was made, another factor entered the equation. That was the summer when Timmy died. Something in my father died with Timmy, but he wasn't a man to show it, Instead, almost overnight I became the one of his children who was to fulfil his own lost ambition. I should have to be the future professor; so, yes, of course I must go to Cambridge. Almost in rivalry with my school teacher he coached me for the all-important General Essay: the opportunity to show my future tutors that I had a mind which was logical, intelligent, retentive and capable of flashes of genius. A tall order!

So for six months, between the two of them, I was loaded with good books and stuffed full of great thoughts and invited to develop rational opinions. I didn't go to the kind of school which kept its sixth-formers on for a seventh term especially to cram them for Oxford or Cambridge. All the extra work was on top of the normal school syllabus. It was a hard slog. No time for boy friends. Mighty little social life at all. And the odd thing was that I didn't really know much about Cambridge. It was a possible bolt-hole, and getting there would be an achievement, but that was all. That was probably why it went wrong later. No sense of vocation there.

At the time, though, it was presented as so much of a challenge that the fun of having a go carried me along. The odds against getting into Cambridge at all – for a girl, that is, in 1944 – were long. The odds against getting a place from an ordinary grammar school, in competition with Cheltenham Ladies and the like, were longer still. The odds against winning a scholarship, especially in the most popular of girls' subjects, were horrendous. It was the fact that I didn't really think I had a hope which made me determined to succeed.

I took the examination at school towards the end of 1944, a month before my eighteenth birthday. Three weeks later I was summoned for an interview at Girton. This was a time when we were still being asked whether our journeys were Really Necessary, so only borderline candidates were to be interviewed. Which borders, though? Between place and scholarship or place and nothing? I was nervous, but excited at the same time.

The excitement didn't survive for long. Cambridge itself was cold and flat and grey. Since then, of course, I've seen the town in all seasons. The sun shining on the Backs: golden stone and waving daffodils and the graceful young foliage of willow trees and punts lazily drifting. None of that, though, was on offer on a drizzly December afternoon. On top of that, I discovered for the first time that Girton wasn't really in Cambridge at all. It was out on the fringe. I'd spent the whole of my adolescent years hating suburbs, but it looked as though I might only be moving from one to another.

The first flicker of doubt didn't stop me doing my best in the interviews. The last one, of three, was after supper. Travelling at night was dangerous during the war, so I'd been offered a bed in college.

I was led down a long, long corridor, past a score of dark brown doors. The undergraduate who'd been put in charge of me for the day opened one of the brown doors, showed me inside, hoped I'd sleep well and closed the door.

It's difficult to describe the peculiar claustrophobia of that moment. The room was actually a little larger than my bedroom at home. The furnishings were basic and shabby, but 43 Woodside Road wasn't exactly luxurious. I'd read my Virginia Woolf, naturally. I knew how important it was for a woman to have a room of her own. If I was invited to Girton, something like this – exactly like this – would be mine. I'd be lucky to have it, wouldn't I?

I sat down at the table which would serve as my desk. If I won a scholarship I should have to become a scholar. I should spend three years reading in libraries and writing on this stained slab of wood. Not writing creatively, but pulling to pieces what creative people had written. I think I knew as early as that, in my heart, that Cambridge was not the right place for me.

But I was young: much younger than any seventeen year old today. My teacher wanted me to succeed. My parents wanted me to succeed. I'd worked so hard that I wanted to succeed as well. To turn down a solid offer because of some nebulous qualms would have been idiotic. It wasn't as though I could think of any alternative training that I'd prefer to take. Photography was still firmly boxed into the leisure compartment of my mind. When I tried to imagine my future life, taking pictures would be just a hobby to give me pleasure while I was earning a living in some regular manner. Besides, when the offer – of the longed-for scholarship – did finally arrive, all the congratulations went to my head. My parents hugged me; teachers shook me by the hand; I was the heroine of the day at school. I'd fulfilled an ambition. It was asking too much of a schoolgirl to recognise that it wasn't the right ambition.

'I remember that day,' Yunga tells me now. 'I was seven or eight, wasn't I? Daddy produced a bottle of champagne which he'd had standing outside in the snow for an hour. He'd been keeping it for years, to celebrate the end of the war. I remember him saying that it didn't look as though the war would ever end, so he might as well open it while we were still alive to enjoy it. We all had some, even me. But I said that the bubbles were attacking my nose, so I was given a glass of Tizer instead. They teased me for years afterwards, about the bubbles. I've got some champagne here, under the stairs. Go and put it in the fridge. We need to celebrate your arrival.'

'Does Dr Morris allow –?'

Yunga's laughter is almost a giggle.

'I can have anything I want,' she says. 'A little of what I fancy. Because it can't do any harm now, you see. Let's get sozzled, Elda. Only one glass for Gwen, because she might get de-frocked or something. But you and I, we can get sozzled together. Why not?'

Why not? It can't do any harm now. This small word, 'now', brings tears back to my eyes. But Yunga doesn't see them because already I am standing up, turning away, moving towards the wine rack beneath the stairs. I am exhausted by a long journey and an emotional day. Yes, let's get sozzled, stewed, zonked, pissed, lushed out, blitzed, blotto. Why not?

2

Yunga is asleep. The second glass of champagne has combined with all the drugs she is taking to knock her out cold. I carry the half-empty bottle into the breakfast room and wait until Gwen, the night nurse, is free to join me.

'You must be tired,' she comments, when eventually she has completed her sickroom duties.

That's true enough. But I have my own rules for coping with jet lag. For any visit of less than forty-eight hours I try, if possible, to continue the eating and sleeping times of the country I have just left. For anything longer, I move immediately to the timetable of the country in which I have arrived. I shall not allow myself to sleep until ten o'clock British time. So I am glad of Gwen's company now to keep me awake.

It soon becomes clear, as we chat, that she has to do less actual nursing than Kate. Yunga's drugs usually ensure her a full night's sleep, although an intercom system has been set in place to pick up every sound from the lounge and relay it to Gwen's room, my father's old study. Gwen's main role in the daily routine is to act as a talker and listener. Since Yunga is asleep, tonight she practises her skills of interest and sympathy on me. I am not as a rule a garrulous person but, physically tired and emotionally drained, I find myself revealing situations that I haven't thought about for years.

'One thing surprised me,' says Gwen, shaking her head at the offer of champagne. 'Yvonne has always talked about her sister Jolene, but today when I went in she said, "Isn't it marvellous that Elda has arrived!" Same person, I take it?'

'Right. It surprises me almost as much to hear you refer to her as Yvonne. She's always been "Yunga" to me.'

'Yunga and Elda.' Gwen is quick to work it out.

'There's a ten-year gap between our ages, and my mother became ill after she was born. She so often told me to look after my younger sister that it seemed a good joke to a ten year old to rechristen the baby Yunga. Then as soon as she herself could talk she entered into the spirit of the thing by calling me Elda. They've been our private names for each other ever since. Just for each other. Professionally I'm Jolene and my friends call me Jo.'

Gwen raises an eyebrow, not needing to put the question into words.

'Jo,' I tell her.

'It's quite unusual for sisters with such a long gap between them to be so close.'

'My true feelings at the time came near to being maternal. There'd been an earlier disaster, some years before Yunga – Yvonne – was born. A failure of communication. So when my mother became pregnant again I was given good warning of a new baby's arrival. She, my mother, was so anxious that I should love the new brother or sister right from the start that there was a great deal of gush. You can guess the sort of thing. "This will be your baby, your special baby."'

Gwen nods in understanding. What she probably doesn't realise – since nowadays children seem to be aware of the facts of life even before they start school – is that at the age of nine and a half, more than sixty years ago, I had no idea, not the foggiest notion, where babies came from. I was told that the baby was mine, and I believed it.

'What was the great disaster?' she asks. She is not being nosy. She genuinely wants to know so that even after so many years have passed she can express sympathy.

'Ah.' I have to consider whether I want to answer. In the course of my work I have seen hundreds of traumatised children. Children who have seen both their parents murdered, children who have become lost in some mass exodus of refugees and don't know how to find their families again, children who are starving, children who have been raped. My own moment of suburban shock is small beer compared to these. But it mattered at the time.

Gwen does not interrupt as the silence lengthens. I have to think that long-past experience right through before I can decide whether it is possible to explain it. And so, as I struggle against the temptation of sleep, I remember a different occasion of drowsiness in this same house. It is the first important memory of my life.

I was four years old, and all I wanted was to go to sleep. My head hurt and my eyes refused to stay open, so why were my parents, usually more anxious to tuck me up in bed at six o'clock, so determined to keep me awake? They were taking it in turns to bend over the bed. My father tried to be jolly. He had not at this time grown the neat goatee beard which later became his most distinguishing feature. Nor had he yet abandoned all hope of finishing his doctoral thesis and obtaining a university post of some kind. He was an optimistic, sunny man who still knew how to smile as he told me jokes or recited funny poems. I didn't smile back.

My mother was less successful in disguising her feelings. She was a beautiful woman who wore her black hair scraped tightly back from her face and twisted into a chignon as though she had never relinquished her ambition to become a ballerina. This severe style accentuated the huge eyes which were her best feature and which flooded with tears when it was her turn to bend over me. At the age of four I was already seeing the world, as I was to see it for the whole of my adult life, as a series of pictures. I can bring those two faces back to the front of my mind now just as I saw them then. Loving and frightened.

Although of course I had no idea of it at the time, I was very near to death at that moment. In the event, my life was saved by the arrival of an ambulance to take me to hospital and the skill of a surgeon who pressed a pencil-shaped torch painfully into one ear, watched as a chloroform pad was pressed over my face to suffocate me, and then cut a large hole in my head. I have the hole still, and from time to time in hospitals medical students are summoned to inspect the lasting effect of a mastoid operation performed in the antediluvian days before antibiotics.

The days after the operation were painful. Twice a day a dressing was stuffed into my head and twice a day tugged out again. I suffered from headaches and nightmares. For quite some time I remained very ill. But as the weeks passed I became restless. No one else was being kept for so long in the children's ward. Some children recovered and went home; some died. Only I remained as a seemingly permanent inmate.

It was because of the dressing, the nurses told me. The daily routine of pressing in and removing the long gauze strip needed to be carried out in hospital. As a consolation I was allowed out of bed. Dressed in hospital clothes I could sit on the floor and play with hospital toys. I became boisterous, dashing up and down the long ward in a manner which can have done little for the peace of other and sicker children.

Another source of unhappiness was less easily explained away by the nurses. Visiting time in the children's ward was at two o'clock. My father, who was not free to come at that hour, had persuaded Sister to let him call in every morning instead. His visits were brief but regular, helping me to start each day in a happy mood. But my mother did not come at all. At two o'clock every afternoon I was made to return to bed, so that my noisy energy should not annoy the visitors. I was given picture books to read and a soft toy to cuddle. But nothing could compensate for the fact that I was the only child in the ward who never had an afternoon visitor.

At first I was upset. Then I was angry. In the end I almost managed to persuade myself that I didn't care. I loved my father all the more passionately because he was the only parent I had.

Three months after my first operation the reason for my continued detention in hospital became clear. I needed more surgery, this time to remove tonsils and adenoids. The surgeon had simply been waiting until I was strong enough. Once again an anaesthetic mask was pressed over my face. Once again I awoke in pain. This time, though, recovery was faster. It was not too long before my father was able to take me home.

He told me on the way that I was to have a bigger bedroom. All my toys had already been moved there; all my stuffed animals were sitting on the bed, waiting to welcome me. And of course Mummy was longing to see me again.

This news I received coldly. If she wanted me to overlook her neglect, she would have to work at it. Even when the front door of 43 Woodside Road opened and she held out her arms to hug me, I hung back; not so much in shyness as in hurt.

If she was disappointed by my unresponsiveness she didn't show it, but instead took me by the hand to inspect the welcome-home tea which had been prepared. Even after so many years I can recall every detail of the feast. There were sandwiches made with hundreds-and-thousands. There were tiny round biscuits, each with a star of coloured icing sugar on the top. There were gingerbread men and chocolate finger biscuits. There was an iced cake with my name written across the top, as though it were my birthday. And there was a quivering red rabbit made of raspberry jelly. I could feel myself beginning to thaw.

'We'll have tea straightaway, shall we?' she said. 'But first of all, your doctor wants you to take a spoonful of medicine before every meal. Just for a little while, to make you strong again. Let me get it now, and you can be holding a chocolate biscuit ready, to take the taste away.'

I opened my mouth obediently, because I had become used to taking medicines: but not this one. A spoonful of iron tonic seared my still-sore throat like paint-stripper. No chocolate biscuit was going to take that taste away. I gave a single roar of pain and rage and betrayal and ran upstairs.

In my fury I quite forgot that I had been promoted in my absence to a larger room, so it was the door of my old bedroom which I flung open. The space had not been left empty. In the cot which once had been mine lay a sleeping baby.

Recognising rather late in the day that it might have been better to give me warning, my parents hurried anxiously up the stairs after me.

'This is your new baby brother,' said my father. He put out a finger to stroke the baby's forehead. 'His name's Timmy.'

My sense of betrayal increased. They had had this baby, without telling me, for long enough not only to give him a name but to abbreviate it. I took hold of the cot and began to shake it violently. My father hurried to lift out the baby. My mother grabbed me from behind and pulled me away. Breaking free, I ran off to discover my new room and slammed its door shut behind me. I was crying, the baby was crying, and very soon my mother was crying as well. I never did get to eat the welcome tea; and I never loved my mother again.

This is too long a story, and how can a stranger be expected to care? I provide only a brief precis to answer Gwen's question.

'I had to spend a long time in hospital when I was four,' I tell her at last. 'My mother didn't visit me there. Apparently her doctor was afraid that anxiety about my illness might cause her to lose the baby she was expecting. She had to stay in bed. But I didn't know any of that. I only knew that I'd been banished from home for months and came back to find my place – my room – taken by a new baby.'

'And that was Yvonne?' Gwen is understandably puzzled. The story would hardly make sense if it were about the sister I love.

'No. My brother Timmy. It made things worse that it was a boy. I thought that must be the reason why I'd been replaced, because my parents would rather have a boy. No, the only significance of that episode is that when my mother became pregnant once again, six years later, she was determined not to make the same mistake twice. That was why I was given plenty of warning and allowed to feel so possessive about my new sister.'

Gwen nods. I can tell that she likes to get things straight. For a little while Yunga and I are her family, in a sense, before she moves on to her next job.

'Where is Timmy now?' she asks me. 'I've never heard Yvonne mention him.'

'He died young. Still a schoolboy.' I try not to make my voice too dismissive. Just as I never forgave my mother, so too I found it impossible to be friends with Timmy, although nothing was his fault. I haul myself wearily to my feet, a very different person from the spry old lady who only two days earlier was slaloming stylishly over the Colorado snowfields. 'I think I'll take a bath now and then get some sleep.'

Gwen stands up at the same time. There is something she wants to say.

'I haven't known your sister for long, of course. But long enough to realise that she's a very honest person. Honest with herself, I mean. Able to face facts.'

'And so you don't want me to jolly her along by suggesting round-the-world cruises or making advance plans for her seventieth birthday. No, I'd realised.'

'It's not easy to recognise that some conditions can't be cured. Our expectations are so high these days. And a lot of people can only cope by pretending. But it's what the dying person wants that's the only important thing.'

'Yes.' Tiredness and unhappiness combine to make me abrupt. I don't need a stranger to tell me how to behave with my own sister. I give her a goodnight nod and go quickly and quietly upstairs.

3

I awaken next morning at half-past six to a sense that something is wrong. Well, of course Yunga's illness is wrong, but it's not that. It takes me a moment or two to work it out.

I have chosen to sleep in the room which was mine from the time of Timmy's birth until the day I left home. For the last five years of that period I was awakened every morning by the sound of Yunga doing her piano practice. No one ever forced her to do it. It was simply the highlight of her day. No one is playing the piano now. It is the silence which is wrong.

The silence, however, is soon broken by the sounds of a household stirring. A kettle whistles that it is boiling. Cups are set on saucers. The front door opens and closes again. It is safe for me to get out of bed without disturbing anyone, but I take my time about appearing downstairs, not wishing to be in the way. Kate has arrived but Gwen is still on duty. They are discussing the day's arrangements as they have breakfast together.

By the time I make my appearance Kate is preparing Yunga for the doctor's daily visit. I earn approval by making my own breakfast without expecting to be waited on and sitting quietly with the newspaper until I am given permission to enter the lounge.

The air is full of artificial scents which do not completely succeed in disguising the odour of Yunga's decaying body. But as I give her a good morning hug, Kate is throwing open the French windows. The sun is shining outside but at this hour of the morning the air is cool. It refreshes and purifies the atmosphere, and tempts me to stand for a moment at the top of the steps which lead down to the garden, taking deep breaths. This is heavier, lower air than that of New Mexico, and even in sunshine the light is less clear; I am as much a connoisseur of atmospheres as of sunsets. But it promises a pleasant spring day, and provides a healthy antidote to the canned breathing material of the plane and the controlled hygiene of the sickroom. I breathe deeply, throwing out my arms to expand my chest.

'Have you still got your crystal tree?' asks Yunga.

I turn to face her in the room again, pleased that she has remembered. It was while we were in Barbados together that I told her about the crystal tree.

It's not really made of crystal. Just a perfectly ordinary tree in the front yard of my rented house: ordinary except that it's more stunted and distorted than it ought to be. I don't even know what species it is; nature is not one of my specialities. It was in leaf when I first moved in, and I hardly noticed it. But once the leaves came down, the bare branches proved to have a certain elegance: the sort of pattern you see in old Japanese prints.

So as winter nights became colder I took to going outside at midnight and spraying the tree with water from a hosepipe. The water clung to the branches and remained frozen all night, so that early-morning passers-by could enjoy the sight of sunshine sparkling on ice in every colour of the rainbow and in a curiously satisfying form.

'Yes,' I tell Yunga now. 'The tree's still there. Just coming into leaf. But quite ordinary again. No one gives it a second glance.'

'I took it as my text for a sermon once.'

'A sermon? You?'

Yunga laughs lightly at my surprise. 'It's one of the minister's new ideas. He still preaches the Sunday morning sermon himself. But in the evening a different member of the congregation each week is asked to give a very short talk instead. Participation. It's called Thought for the Week. When it was my turn, I used the crystal tree as my text. To suggest that even the ugliest or horridest people can be made beautiful if they're cared for. And of course that God is the one who cares for them.'

I don't believe in God. God is one of the things I escaped from at the age of twenty, and I've spent a lot of my life photographing people for whom no one has ever cared. Yunga, no doubt, needs her belief in God more now than at any other time in her life, so it is not for me to disturb it in any way. All the same, I can't accept her argument quite in silence.

'Dangerous, drawing parallels,' I suggest. 'I am the god who made my tree beautiful, but now I've deserted it. At this moment someone may be cutting it down, and I can't protect it.'

'Because you aren't God. We won't argue.' Quite deliberately she changes the subject. 'We were diverted by the champagne last night. My fault for falling asleep so quickly. You told me about getting to Cambridge. But not really why you threw your degree course up. It must have been something more than just the enjoyment of a single sunset?'

'Yes, indeed.' I am happy to reminisce on this subject, and move a chair so that I can sit down in hand-holding distance. 'It was a stroke of luck. Completely unpredictable luck. But I was ready for it, and I suppose the sunset was one element in that.'

I've had years since then to learn the lesson that good luck brings good fortune only to someone who's mentally prepared. Fate may deal you a good hand, but you still have to play it well. I've always allowed myself credit for having the nerve to grasp my chance when it came. Anyone reading my biographical details in a directory might reckon that the way I got started was simple and straightforward; but it needed courage at the time.

On the day after the sunset I abandoned my group of friends and went back to St Moritz. Over the later years in which I worked as a photo-journalist I developed a strong instinct of the right place in which to be at any particular moment, and something of that talent must have been stirring in me even at the age of only twenty. Pontresina, where we were staying, was a pleasant resort for a holiday, but St Moritz was the place which was buzzing. With still only six days' skiing behind me, I hadn't quite got the nerve to return to the highest slopes without a guide. But I managed one of the less ambitious runs without too much trouble. I was standing in the queue for the ski tow, ready for another go, when the accident took place.

Naturally I'd noticed the photographer at work. Because it was my hobby too, I'd even exchanged a few words with him earlier in the day. He was a young Canadian who was paying for his European holiday by snapping skiers as they shot past him or rested in a decorative pose or – more frequently – fell. The prints would be displayed in the window of a nearby kiosk two hours later. Their subjects bought the flattering shots to keep as a record of achievement and were even quicker to purchase the sprawling disasters in order to remove them from public view. Murray was supplied with the camera and film by the owner of the photo-franchise and was paid a small commission on each sale.

At eleven o'clock in the morning he was standing still on the nursery slope, facing downhill as he prepared to catch the moment when a beginner fell off the T-bar ski tow. He didn't see a different beginner, out of control, rushing down towards him with no idea how to stop. The resulting crash proved later to have left him with a broken arm and some badly bruised ribs.

I was the first to reach him, and he recognised my face from our conversation a couple of hours earlier.

'Better not move me,' he said, grimacing with pain. 'But could you get the camera off, d'you think, and take it back to the kiosk?'

'Of course.' I had to unbuckle the strap which was round his neck so that I could pull it away without hurting him more.

'Tell them ...'

I had a better idea. Stepping back slightly, on the assumption that he had been using a fixed length focus, I took three shots of the two prone figures. To support any insurance claim I made sure that there was a clear view of the face of the girl responsible.

I didn't immediately return the camera after Murray had been taken off to hospital. My decision to use up what was left of the film was made from purely altruistic motives: to allow him the commission on a few more prints which could be sold. But the care with which I studied the unfamiliar camera and chose the shots probably implied that I had already decided what I was going to do.

'You asked if you could take over the job!' Yunga, it seems, has never before heard in detail this part of the story – probably because in the end the plan was aborted before I'd had time to earn even a single commission.

'Right. They printed out what I'd done on Murray's behalf and it was OK. And of course they couldn't afford to have a day with nobody on the job. I wasn't as good a skier as Murray, not then, but it didn't matter because the nursery slopes were where most of the customers came from. The money was never going to add up to much but it would have allowed me to stay on for another couple of weeks after my friends had gone home. The Cambridge vacations were long ones. To start with, that extra couple of weeks was all I wanted. More skiing. More high mountains. More sunsets.'

'But then?' Yunga smiles happily, gripping my hand. She is a child, begging for a bedtime story. It doesn't matter whether or not she has heard it before. The ending will still come as a delightful surprise. And as it happens, she has not in fact heard the next part of the tale before. For fifty years I have kept a promise; I have kept a secret, even from my own sister. But everyone concerned must be dead by now. It doesn't matter any more. I can tell the true story of how I became a professional photographer.

In Pontresina there hadn't been a lot of après-ski excitement. A cream cake and a mug of hot chocolate was all that any impoverished undergraduate could manage by way of evening luxury. St Moritz, however, was different. Glamorous women in glamorous clothes ordered glamorous drinks and waited to be noticed. My new employer explained the arrangements he had made with various hotels and restaurants and offered me the opportunity to do an evening shift if I chose. I chose.

There was, however, a problem. Unprepared on that first evening for exposure to society's night-life, I was still wearing my ATS surplus uniform and ski boots. No grand hotel was likely to let me past the door.

The solution was to be found in the streets. Rich women wearing fabulous fur coats were delighted to be snapped as they stepped from horse-drawn sledges. It was in the street that I caught my first glimpse of a full-length sable cloak, hooded to conceal the face of its wearer, who was hurrying almost furtively into a surprisingly modest bar.

Modest enough even to admit someone like myself, it proved when I followed my quarry inside. I was just in time to catch the moment when, after flinging back the fur hood, she was extending her hand to be kissed. It was an elegant gesture that was going to make a striking picture. She would surely be delighted to have it for her family album. The camera flashed. All hell was let loose.

It came very near to being a stand-up fight, because the owner of the bar was not at all averse to enjoying the publicity which he – although not I – immediately realised that the photograph could bring him. He was on my side, and quick to prevent the camera from being snatched away.

They couldn't simply disappear, these illicit lovers, because they had to square me first, and that task was made particularly difficult by the fact that I was in every sense an innocent abroad: a sheltered swot who didn't even know that gossip magazines existed. Once the name Dana Delamere – Didi to her fans – was brought to my attention I did recognise her as one of the starriest of Hollywood goddesses. But I didn't know that the hand-kisser was a prince, and what I most certainly didn't know was that his wife was currently spending a small fortune on detectives to provide evidence of a liaison which would enable her to start divorce proceedings of a profitable kind. Or that Miss Delamere had a morals clause in her contract which would allow the studio to ditch her at the first sniff of scandal. So I wasn't simply playing dumb as negotiations proceeded. My dumbness was completely genuine.

It was the prince who was the first to cotton on to this and to realise that I was not a professional blackmailer; just stupid. No, I wouldn't sell the film, because then I should lose my whole evening's work. No, I couldn't sell the camera either, because it didn't belong to me. What was the problem? If he wanted the photograph, he had only to turn up at the kiosk next morning. His frustration grew. If he increased his offer to unrealistic heights, even this unsophisticated child might begin to suspect that the secret to be concealed was a valuable one.

Miss Delamere cut through the cotton wool. Her beauty was of the wispy, fragile kind, but her voice was businesslike.

'What do you want, kid?' she asked.

'What do you mean, what do I want?'

'Everybody wants something. Do you want to be in films?'

'No.' I didn't know what I was going to say next until I heard myself say it. 'I want to be a photographer. That's why every photograph I take is important to me.'

'This particular photograph is more important to me.' She wrote down a Swiss telephone number and held it out. 'Give me two days to fix it, and then call this number. Gerhardt Neumann. He'll take you on for a year. You'll have to do all the fiddly work, the setting up; but you'll learn and he'll pay you. Now give me the film.'

Two days. Two days in which this publicity-shy couple could slip away and pretend they had never been anywhere near St Moritz. I hesitated.

'You play straight with me and I play straight with you,' she said. 'The film. And you've never seen me in your life. Not a word to anyone, ever; not even Gerhardt. I get your silence and you get a career. He owes me. And he's the best.'

She was right. At that time I'd never even heard of Gerhardt Neumann, but he was to give me a first-class training in portrait and fashion photography. More than that: he had been a Surrealist in his youth and there was nothing that he couldn't do with film. The tricks he taught me had originally been intended to shock; but in my hands they became simply useful tools; unusual techniques. My year in his studio was to prove the best possible start to my new career.

But that evening in Bim's Bar I couldn't foresee any of that; not for certain. All I could see was that I suddenly had a choice between a safe, familiar life and a future which might be exciting but would certainly be frighteningly insecure. I was being asked to act on impulse, and that was not the way I had been brought up.

Nowadays, whether they like it or not, young people recognise that no job is for ever and it's often as well to jump before they're pushed. But it wasn't like that in 1946: not for the sort of family which lived in 43 Woodside Road. Suburban schoolgirls turned down party invitations and slogged away at homework in order to win scholarships. Suburban undergraduates slogged away to get a decent degree and get a foot on the first rung of a career ladder, so that they could slog their way up through the civil service or the law or whatever. If all else failed, there was always the teaching profession. In short, suburban people decided on goals and worked steadily to achieve them, holding on to a safety rope all the time. Safety was the key word. After so many years of always being safe it needed courage to step off the Girton ladder and go into free fall.

Trusting a stranger is always a risk. I took the risk. Removing the film from the camera, I watched the disappearance of my evening's work. But at that stage all I was staking was a brief holiday job and if I lost the gamble I was no worse off than I had been twenty-four hours earlier. The true courage was called upon two days later, when I made the phone call to a man whose name meant nothing to me, and was invited to Zurich. And the St Moritz sunset had a good deal to do with that decision. I was abandoning the narrow path which led from Woodside Road to Kenbury Girls' Grammar School and on to Girton College, Cambridge, because I had been allowed a glimpse of a wider, more dangerous and far more beautiful world.

'You never told me!' Yunga is breathless with a mixture of amusement and indignation. 'I mean, I knew about you working for Gerhardt, naturally. But you never told me how you first met him. About Dana Delamere.'

'I promised her that I'd never mention that evening to a single person. She'd kept her promise, so I felt I had to keep mine. Until she died, and by that time it didn't seem important any more.'

'So that was why you didn't come back in time for the next term! Daddy was furious, you know. And I cried for days. First of all I thought you must have done something so terrible that nobody would tell me about it. Like killing someone. And then when they said you were never coming back, ever, I thought you didn't love me any more. I didn't realise that they were the ones who said you couldn't come back. They didn't let me see your first letter to me. But I worked myself into such a state that they had to give in.

And from then on Daddy used to read the letters you wrote me. Whenever I asked him if he wanted to, he said no, but then he came and found them while I was at school. I used to set traps, so that I could tell. You know, a hair sticking out of the drawer, that sort of thing.'

'But he never forgave me, did he?'

'Well, he may have done. But perhaps he didn't know how to say so.'

'It was a mess.' I am silent for a moment, thinking about the failure of my family relationships. My mother adored me, but I was never able to forgive her for abandoning me in hospital. How can one force oneself to love? I adored my father, but I didn't know how to earn his forgiveness. How can one force someone else to love?

Is this the true reason why I have never wanted to marry? I have always attributed my single state to the gypsy life I lead and the professional impossibility of settling down in one place with one man for ever. But perhaps the problem goes deeper than that.

Well, at least my relationship with Yunga is one which I have never fouled up. As for the rest, it's not important now. I have never missed marriage or wanted children. But Yunga; why has she remained unmarried? She is a home body, a nest-maker. She would have been a marvellous mother. I can remember several times asking her, when she was younger, whether there was anyone special. The answer was always the same: no one special. Was that true? Any young woman, unless she's a complete freak, can find herself a man if she sets her mind to it.

The answer I have always allowed myself to believe, was that she let herself be imprisoned by duty. Our mother lived for thirteen years after the stroke which partially disabled her. For all those years Yunga ran the household, working full time in order to pay the bills. She acted, no doubt, out of love; but by the time she found herself free at last she was in her forties. Perhaps it really was too late by then. It wouldn't necessarily have to be because there was no one to love her. She might have discovered, as I had discovered years earlier, that freedom is not something to surrender lightly.

The conversation has upset Yunga. Perhaps she is reliving the distress of the little girl who wondered whether her sister had abandoned her. It is time to change the subject.

'Well,' I ask brightly. 'What shall we do today?'

4

My question doesn't expect a very startling answer, but is given one. 'Let's go shopping.'

I look at Yunga in surprise. 'Can you?'

'Why not? If you're willing to push me. Kate will get me ready.'

There is a new brightness in my sister's eyes and smile. Yesterday, anxious after the period of wondering whether I would come, and drained by the emotion of seeing me again, she was a dying woman. Today, although still a convalescent, recovering from a serious operation, she is back in the world again. A stab of hope pierces into the unhappiness which I am being careful to keep out of sight. Twice in my own life, on a mountainside and in a minefield, I have forbidden myself to die and have obeyed my own orders even though to die seemed the easier choice. I know that it can be done. Perhaps the doctor was wrong; or else, out of kindness, was giving me the worst possible prognosis in order that any surprises in the future may be happy ones. And the sun is shining.

'Why not, then?' I go to find Kate, who approvingly wraps her patient up even more warmly and fastens a kind of cage across the bottom of the wheelchair so that there can be no accidental bumps on the bandaged stump.

It takes about a quarter of an hour to reach the main road, probably because I am over-careful not to jolt the wheelchair. Although it is so long since I have lived in Kenbury, I find my way without hesitation. It has always been one of my talents to carry street layouts in my head, visualising them as though they were drawn like a plan. Perhaps this is the consequence of so frequently needing to be sure how best to make my escape if a street demonstration turns nasty or an invasion picks up speed. I could walk round Damascus or Jerusalem with almost the same confidence which I now bring to my birthplace.

Today, though, that very confidence leads to uneasiness. It was along this route that I once walked every day to school; to a school that I don't wish to remember.

'That's a pity,' comments Yunga when I pass on my misgivings. 'Because Sandy Lane is where we're going.'

I am just about to express surprise that she should wish to revisit a place of bad memories when I remember that of course her memories are different from mine. In the course of my life I have done Yunga two favours. Two is not very many, but they were huge ones. The first was when, at the age of fourteen and a half, I confronted my parents and persuaded them that it would be criminal to condemn their younger daughter to the institution in which they had imprisoned me.

Sandy Lane Elementary School was built in the 1880s and maybe it provided a marvellous educational opportunity for the children of that period. When I went to it, fifty years later, very little about it had changed. The windows were high, so that children at their straight lines of desks could not see out. The school was still lit by gas and heated by mean coal fires which warmed only the teachers. In winter we sat in our overcoats and sucked fingers to warm them before dipping pens into inkpots and splattering blots over paper and clothes.

Twice a day, for the morning and afternoon breaks, we were turned out – whatever the weather – into the playground. The asphalt area – the cause of many a grazed knee – was bounded by a high brick wall with three or four feet of wire mesh rising even higher above that. No doubt this barrier was intended to keep balls from flying into the street, but it served the secondary purpose of confining the owners of the balls as well. Our ages ranged from five to fourteen and not unnaturally it was the fourteen-year-old footballing boys who commandeered the ground. It may well be that I owe some of my later resilience to the need, as a small girl, to overcome my terror of playtime. But at the age of five, still wobbly on my feet after my long spell in hospital, I couldn't understand why my parents should condemn me to this daily torture.

It wasn't as though there was no alternative. Along Woodside Road at half-past eight every morning walked girls in royal blue blazers and boys striped like wasps in yellow and black, with neatly segmented caps on their short-haired heads. I longed to go to the royal blue school, where there would be no boys. But that would cost too much money, my father told me, and my illness had been expensive. Timmy, as a matter of fact, was to become one of the wasp-striped boys: but that came later.

As I push the wheelchair in silence I am suddenly overwhelmed by a remembered hatred of the school which I have not thought about for years. I recall the ceremonial canings, the regular rapping of knuckles, the sarcasm of teachers who were probably no happier than their pupils were to spend their lives in Sandy Lane, and had less hope of ever escaping. I bring the wheelchair abruptly to a halt and step forward so that Yunga can see me.

'I'm sorry, darling, but I don't want to go there. There must be somewhere else we can shop. I don't ever want to see that school again, or think about the years I spent there. What's the point of dredging up old memories?'

'You were happy yesterday to talk about your sunset memory.'

'That's different. When I was twenty I took my life into my own hands. If I made mistakes they were my own mistakes. But at Sandy Lane I was a victim. I have the right to erase those years from my recollection if I want to.'

'Indulge me.' Yunga smiles pleadingly – and of course she holds the whip hand. If she wants to drink champagne, she must have it. If for some incomprehensible reason she wants to take me back to my childhood, I must allow her to lead the way. It is natural enough that a woman who has no future should wish to spend her limited present in contemplation of the past.

And so with a sigh I move forward again. We are nearly there. I turn one more corner and for a second time come to a halt. In front of me I can hear Yunga laughing quietly as she visualises the surprise of my face.

Sandy Lane has been pedestrianised, partly covered, and transformed into a shopping mall. A designer has been at work. He has not done very well, but he has tried. On either side of a red-tiled walkway are long wooden troughs filled with tulips, and benches for the footsore. Above them globe lamps rise on black stems which must have been the height of fashion twenty years ago. But I spare little time for such details. Automatically I look towards Sandy Lane Elementary School. It isn't there.

Where it once stood is a store called Marks and Spencer. Yunga waves a hand to indicate that this is our destination.

'We need more champagne,' she tells me. 'You might like to get it from the site of your old enemy. You see, you don't have to worry about your memories. I thought you'd be glad to know. The school doesn't exist any more, so you can cut those years out of your life if you like.'

As indeed I have done for the past sixty years. Oddly enough, as a wide door opens automatically to admit the wheelchair, I find myself exploring the interior with my eyes in order to identify where the various parts of the school once stood: the classrooms, the freezingly cold outside lavatories, the piles of coal which provided the only playtime refuge from the rough big boys. But Yunga is pointing out something rather different: the food department; the wine section; the shelf of champagnes. We buy as much as we can carry. I am tempted to add a bottle of Scotch, which is my own favourite tipple, but am restrained by yet another of those darts which continually stab into my heart. While Yunga is alive I shall share the drink of her choice. The whisky would only be for after her death. If I don't buy it, perhaps she won't die. Oh, come on, Jolene. Be your age!

In order that our destination should come as a surprise, Yunga chose to approach it by a slightly roundabout route. For the return journey I automatically pick a different, more direct way. These are the quiet suburban streets along which I trudged or skipped four times a day between home and school, pausing to pick discarded cigarette packets out of the gutter in case a cigarette card might be tucked inside the silver paper. Whatever happened to my cigarette card collection, I wonder?

'We can take a short cut here,' Yunga tells me.

'Yes, I know.' We have arrived at the end of a narrow alley, fenced high on either side, which links two parallel streets and will save us walking round three sides of a rectangle. The excuse which I make to myself for almost walking past the entrance without stopping is that there may not be room for the wheelchair, but this is nonsense. My reluctance to enter is caused by the memory of a man in a mackintosh.

It's ridiculous. He must have been dead for years. Turning the wheelchair into the alley, I describe my childhood anxieties to Yunga as cheerfully as I can.

'There used to be a man who lurked here. Not every day: a couple of times a week. He knew what time little girls would be coming home from school. He must have had some way of seeing, because he would always wait until I was about halfway along before he appeared at the far end.' We are halfway already. I pause for a moment. The alley now seems very short, very safe, within shouting distance of the houses on either side. It is hard to recall the menace with which it was once filled.

'Did he molest you?'

'He was extremely fat,' I remember. 'So that when he walked towards me he seemed to fill the whole space. And then, just before he reached me, he would turn sideways, with his back to the fence, as though politely making room for me to pass. But he still didn't leave quite enough room, so I had to squeeze past him. Usually I started to run after that. But once I stopped and looked back, and he was unbuttoning his flies. I assumed he was going to urinate in the alley. Very naughty. Very rude. But molest me, no; he didn't touch me with his hands or try to stop me. The only thing I found frightening was never knowing whether or not he was going to appear.'

I move on, and after only a few paces we are out of the alley and into the lightness of a street. Nearly home now.

'On the plane coming over,' I tell Yunga chattily, 'I was reading about some report which says that one child in four suffers sexual or physical abuse. And I thought what a ridiculous statistic that was; but then I looked at the small print in which it defined sexual abuse and realised that it covered me, because of the lurker. Everything that's wrong with me as an adult is probably the fault of the lurker. Were you an abused child as well, Yunga?' I am laughing as I ask the question.

'What's the small print definition of physical abuse?' she asks.

'Oh, just as crazy. I reckon every kid who's ever been given a smacking qualifies for that.'

'Then, yes, I was an abused child as well. Mummy used just to sort of slap at my hand or arm if I was naughty, but for serious crimes it was report to Daddy and that meant knickers down and a slippering on my bare bottom.'

'I should think that pulls you into both categories – and me as well, now I think of it.' Our parents never knocked us about in any brutal way, but they believed in discipline – as, indeed, did the parents of all our friends. Children in those days only had duties, not rights. 'Ruined for life, the two of us. Seems to me we've done very well to survive. Here we are, then.'

Using the short cut has brought us quickly home, and Kate is waiting to help lift the wheelchair into the house. It is only when Yunga decides that she would like to rest on her bed for a little rather than on the chaise longue that I realise how much the expedition has tired her. She is very pale and her breathing is shallow; her arms hang limply as she is lifted. If she has wanted to prove to me that she is not as ill as she looks, the attempt is a failure. I shall not suggest this kind of outing again; and nor will she.

5

Yunga's eyes are failing. Already before I arrived she had ceased to read books. Now even the daily paper is too blurred for her. She asks me to read aloud from it after she has had her lunch and slept for an hour after it.

It's not easy to decide what items will interest a dying woman. So many words are devoted not to the true news of what has happened but to guesses about what may happen in the future, in days which Yunga may not be alive to see. I turn the pages, picking out paragraphs which catch my eye.

One story today concerns the effects of a civil war in Africa: a conflict which made headlines some years earlier as one tribe massacred another and was then in its turn forced to escape to refugee camps when the survivors of the first tribe began to take revenge. That conflict was driven off the front pages by the later tribal war in Bosnia, as though the world could only devote its indignation and sympathy to one area at a time. Only now has someone counted the cost in deaths and displacements. The numbers, which I read out, are huge.

'You went out there, didn't you?' Yunga remembers. 'I was surprised at the time, because you'd told me before then that you weren't going to do any more war missions.'

'True.' Earlier in my career I had spent ten years of my life acting as a photo-journalist. They were exciting and often dangerous years, but it wasn't because I was afraid that I decided I'd had enough. There's a nasty feeling of complicity which can creep over a photographer. You're taken to see a mass grave, a ruined village, a hospital full of limbless children. You kid yourself that what you send home will be an argument for the futility of war, but in practice by your choice of shot you are supporting one side, and one effect may be that that side wins in the end and proves that war isn't futile at all, for the survivors.

'Then why did you change your mind?'

'A little bit of charitable work in my old age. I saw some frightful statistic about the number of children in Rwanda who were either orphaned or lost. The Red Cross had a scheme for photographing them all, thousands of them, and putting the shots up on wall sheets to see whether anyone recognised them. Taking photographs, I thought to myself, is something I can do. I took two thousand. They told me afterwards that seven hundred and seventy-two of my batch had been identified and claimed by some family member. One of the best statistics I've ever been given.'

'Do you remember much about our own war?'

It's an unexpected question. Yes, I remember a great deal. It was an exciting interlude, an adventure, in what had been until then a dull life. I was twelve when the war began, and a child of that age doesn't know what she ought to be afraid of. After Timmy died, I saw what his death did to my parents and it made me grow up a bit; but that happened quite late in the war. For five years I almost enjoyed it. Perhaps I should be ashamed of that.

'I can tell you one thing I remember.' It's something that I haven't thought of for years. The feeling I've had so often since then, of recognising where the action is and wanting to be part of it. The buzz. 'I remember my fury at not being a Londoner. There was all this propaganda at the time of the Blitz: London can take it! Kenbury was so near to London, and we were having air raids as well, but of course they weren't nearly as bad, and in an odd sort of way I wanted them to be; so that I could feel proud of "taking it" like the Londoners. I suppose our generation, yours and mine, is quite an oddity in England now, of civilians who know what it's like to be bombed.'

Even as I make the comment I wonder whether Yunga does in fact remember the experience. In this respect, as so many others, the ten-year age difference between us is a generation gap. Yunga was not quite three years old when the war began: I was twelve. It made a difference. Perhaps she was too young to know what was going on. For small children, even ordinary, peaceful life is a series of inexplicable events, to be accepted rather than understood. The beginning of a war or a first journey in a train are probably of equal significance.

There is no time to continue any discussion of the war, however, for we are interrupted by the ring of the front doorbell.

'I'll get it.' It is four o'clock and Maggie is probably just changing out of her cleaning clothes, ready to leave.

The routine which my arrival disrupted has been resumed, it seems. Yesterday I was allowed time for a private chat with my sister, but now there is to be an afternoon visit as usual. The two elderly women who stand on the front path – they are probably ten years younger than I am, but I have not yet learned to think of myself as old – are dressed in exactly the neat manner which I had expected of the shoppers in the streets as I was driven from Heathrow. They wear jackets and skirts and white blouses and tights and court shoes. One has a string of pearls round her neck; one carries a pair of gloves. Compared with them I am far too casually dressed in black sweater and slacks. Their eyes take note of my tall, rangy figure, but I can be sure that even in their minds they are not criticising me. In my own home I may dress as I please.

They know who I am, of course, and introduce themselves smilingly, but take it for granted that in spite of my presence they will still be welcome. What they are saying without words, these two good people, is that it was never because Yunga would otherwise be left alone for these afternoon hours that they chose to visit her, but because they are her friends and genuinely enjoy her company.

I approve, and prepare to withdraw as soon as I have carried in the tea tray. But Yunga holds me back. She wants me to be there. I am a new subject of conversation. She is proud of me; my work, my life. Or perhaps she needs to show off on her own behalf the fact that I have come at last. Taking pleasure in the holidays I have been able to offer her, it has never before occurred to me to wonder whether she may in a sense have felt humiliated by my refusal ever to visit her in her own home. I try to make up for it now by following her conversational leads.

Mrs Johnson and Mrs Meads are not, as it happens, particularly interested in the adventures of an international photographer. They want to remind me instead that when I was fifteen and they were three they were members of the Beginners' Sunday School class which I took every Sunday afternoon. This interests me just as much as they think it ought to do, because I have a memory of that class. My nervousness at being promoted from pupil to teacher was overcome by astonishment at the discovery – new at least to me – that three-year-old children, especially boys, look exactly like the ninety year olds which they may one day become.

I was so taken by this theory that on the Whitsun Sunday School outing I lined up my class for a group photograph. The children assumed it was just a record of a happy day, but my intention was to keep it for fifty or sixty years and then compare the faces.

I haven't remembered that photograph for years, but now I wonder aloud whether it still exists. Every snap I took in my childhood was abandoned, of course, when I failed to return to Girton, and perhaps my father threw them all away in his fury. I put the question to Yunga. There is no need to talk about the shape of skulls beneath the curls and fringes of three year olds. Mention of the photograph is a perfectly natural response to the reminiscences of the visitors.

'It's all up in the attic,' Yunga tells me, pleased that the conversation is going so well. 'But you're not to go and find it now, because I know you: you'll start looking at everything and we shall never see you again.'

Smiling, I agree that I will have it ready for some future visit, and the chat continues. It is all about the church which I attended regularly for the first eighteen years of my life. For my sake Mrs Johnson and Mrs Meads talk briefly about how things were fifty years ago; for Yunga's sake they talk at length about the present. About last week's sermon, about how the choir is getting on without her, about who is ill and who is on holiday. It is cosy. It is claustrophobic. This, I remember now, is one of the reasons why, as a schoolgirl, I longed to get away.

While they chat, I allow my thoughts to drift. Fifty, sixty years ago the whole of my parents' social life was provided by the church. They went to morning and evening services every Sunday. My mother belonged to the church dramatic society and sang in the church choir. My father was a star of the church debating society and ran a Bible study class. For the Christmas Fair my mother knitted baby garments and my father made objects out of turned wood. They both played tennis at the club which was owned by the church. They went for rambles with other members of the congregation; they attended social evenings. The would-be professor and the would-be ballerina had settled for a pleasant suburban life and in those early years I feel sure that they must have been happy with it. All their friends were church friends. There were occasional clashes of personality but never any conflicts of opinion.

Yunga has settled for the same kind of small-town life. When I was younger and on the road, driving myself across America, I used often to find myself spending a night in the motel of some one-horse town which was hardly more than a bleak stretch of road. As a bored young waitress slammed a cup of coffee down in front of me I would wonder incredulously how she could bear to stay in such a place, confined to the tiny community in which she had been born and educated, with nothing to look forward to but marriage and children and passing the rest of her life in the same ugly and unstimulating environment.

It was only as I began to travel more widely in the world that I realised how general a human experience this is, at least for women. The village, the shanty town, even the refugee camp can all be tolerated because the need for a base, a home, is stronger than the need for excitement. For centuries it has been the exceptional, not the normal woman who turns her back on child-rearing, and the exceptional and not the normal woman who has not simply dreamed of a different life but has had the courage to escape. The unexceptional woman has recognised that life outside her home community is dangerous and lonely; she has stayed where she was. All these attitudes are disappearing fast from our Western societies, but Yunga and I are both of a generation born before the change.

Yunga has chosen to stay, and it is not for me to feel sorry for her. It is only those who long to run away from a closed community and are unable to do so who are imprisoned by it; and the ability to escape is a matter of mental strength rather than of walls and locks. If Yunga hadn't been happy here, she would have left; ergo, she must have been happy.

Listening with half an ear to the easy chatter of Mrs Johnson and Mrs Meads I recognise that at this final stage of her life the support of local friends is important to her in a way that it would not be to me. Twice in my adult life I have come close to death. In each case it would have been a death either alone or amongst strangers, and that fact, far from causing me extra distress, in an odd way made the pain easier to bear. If I ever have the chance to choose the moment of my own death, it will take place alone; but I recognise that not everyone feels like that. In fact, in the half hour between the departure of the two visitors and the moment when Gwen reports for duty, Yunga confirms that in so many words.

I have commented on how nice her friends are. 'Nice' is not a word I ever use in the ordinary way, but it seems appropriate in this context.

'Mrs Johnson's mother was one of the people I sat with, when she was dying. She had Alzheimer's. Drove her family almost frantic, asking the same questions over and over again, but when I came she'd keep quiet and listen. I don't imagine she had the faintest idea who I was, but she liked the noise. I used to play to her for hours. Nothing classical. She liked musical comedy songs: Ivor Novello, Noel Coward, that sort of thing. It didn't matter how often I repeated them.' She pauses, turning her head to smile at me. 'I often used to wonder, sitting in some unfamiliar bedroom, who it would be, holding my hand, when it was my turn. I'm glad it's you, Elda.'

6

If I try to return Yunga's smile I shall cry. Recognising that, she continues to talk about her recent visitors. 'I expect you found it all rather parochial, that conversation.'

'Parochial gossip is always the most interesting, as long as it's one's own parish.'

'I remember – ' This time Yunga laughs aloud. 'I remember writing to tell you that I'd been appointed organist. I was terribly proud; but you were horrified. "It means you'll have to go to church twice every Sunday for ever!" you wrote, and I had to point out that I did that already. You don't like being tied down to anything, do you?'

'I've never had to live in a routine. I can see that you've always been used to it, though. School timetables, bells. In all my life I've never had a nine-to-five job.'

'There must be times when that's a strain. When you have to think out from scratch how you'll fill your day.'

'It's never bothered me.' There have always been more projects swimming in my head than there are days in the year. By now I've saved enough money. I could sit and do nothing if I wanted to. Taking two or three months off every year to ski is the nearest I've come to retirement. But every year, as soon as the season ends, I'm on the phone to Fay with an idea for a new book or a new exhibition or a project to be put to a magazine. Except this year, of course.

Yunga, the accepter of routines, glances at the clock. Although she can no longer read, she can see the television screen. Very few programmes interest her, but Gwen has told me that she regularly watches the six o'clock news. I find it a little surprising that she should want to keep in touch with the world that she will soon be leaving, but perhaps it is this regular infusion of new interest which helps to keep her alive.

Today – or rather, last night – there has been an earthquake. The screen is filled with scenes of devastation while the newsreader speaks of remote villages from which nothing has been heard, of more lives which will be lost if a damaged dam collapses. We watch in silence.

'Have you ever been in an earthquake?' she asks when at last I turn the set off.

'I was never on the spot for any of the big ones.'

It was always after the disaster occurred that the call would come. Get yourself out to Agadir or Managua or Sichuan or wherever. For pictures of houses in ruins, fathers scrabbling in rubble for their babies, old women sitting blank-eyed in the middle of devastation with nowhere to go, no one to look after them.

Sometimes – well, to be honest, almost all the time – I felt like a parasite, feeding on people's misery. But the pictures were necessary to unlock compassion. Charity. The money rolled in with a speed that wouldn't have happened without me, or someone like me. Not everyone is capable of imagining the misery of nothingness.

Mind you, I wasn't always confident that the money would end up in the right hands. But it wasn't my responsibility to put the whole world to rights.

The answer I have given Yunga, though, is incomplete, and I add to it now. 'There are always aftershocks, and some of them are pretty near as fierce as the original. I've been in plenty of those.'

'Describe them,' demands Yunga. 'How do they feel?'

I am not good at painting pictures in words. I can précis written information and regurgitate the facts in a reasonably clear and logical form: that was the talent which won me my Girton scholarship. I can look and register what I'm seeing, and I can feel and understand my feelings. But verbal description is not one of my talents. Still, as Yunga closes her eyes and listens, I will try.

The noise comes first. Not always with the smaller tremors, but certainly with a full-scale quake. Like a plane crashing nearby. Or a truck, a lorry, running into the building. That's what wakes you up, fast, all senses immediately alert to the fact that the earth is moving.

In the strongest shock I've ever experienced, the highest up the Richter scale, what came after the bang was a feeling that the room was being pulled apart, with the earth beneath opening in a great crack. A vertical divide. Then it shuddered together again. It didn't last more than a few seconds, I don't suppose, but they were long seconds.

Smaller tremors have a more horizontal feel to them. Like someone shaking a sieve until the ash has fallen through and only the cinders are rattling from side to side. There's often a rumble while that's going on, as though a train is passing along a subway below. But you don't notice it because you're too busy listening for the sound of walls and ceilings cracking and starting to fall. Then a sort of shivering. A pause, perhaps, and another trembling. And then, if you're lucky, it's over.

'Is it a panic situation? People screaming?'

'In the primary quake, maybe. But I guess those would be people actually falling or hurt. I've always been in bed, every time, and half expecting it. And by the time the moment for feeling frightened might have come, it was all over. I can remember reading about the San Francisco earthquake at the beginning of this century. It happened early in the morning. Everyone waited until the shaking stopped and then they got dressed and brushed their hair and went out into the streets, just in case there should be another one. But all quite calmly.'

'I've heard of that San Francisco earthquake. I thought it was a great disaster.'

'And so it was, in the end. In terms of property, mostly. But that was because people drifted back inside and lit the gas to cook breakfast and set all the fractured gas mains alight. So the city burned down, because the water mains were fractured as well.' Why are we talking about San Francisco? What possible interest can it hold for a dying woman?

Yunga recognises the irrelevance herself. Out of the whole world, it is only my life that she wishes to explore.

'But weren't you ever frightened, Elda? Lying in bed with the earth shuddering.'

'No.' There is a moment in which I am tempted to tell her why: to describe an incident from my childhood. I have already been reminded of it once this afternoon, in the conversation that was interrupted by the arrival of the visitors.

Everyone knew in 1939 that there would be bombing. Even on the fringe of London, as we were, every family tried to provide itself with some kind of air raid shelter. In the case of my own family it was a distinctly makeshift affair. As war approached my father had arranged for a trapdoor to be cut in the floor of the breakfast room. Through this we could jump down into the foundations of the house, which were about four feet deep. Another opening had been cut through the rockery at the back of the house, to act as an escape route if the building collapsed on top of the trap door.

The snag about this arrangement was that the space beneath the house was not a proper cellar but – well, merely a space. There was no kind of reinforcement to protect us against blast. The ground, being of earth, was dirty and damp, the lack of height was claustrophobic and there was no ventilation. An electric cable was fixed to the joists beneath the floor boards, with a single light bulb dangling from it, and camp beds and torches were taken down as soon as the need arose.

It was while lying on my camp bed that I experienced something worse than an earthquake. It was one of the worst raids to hit Kenbury. The earth trembled and the air shuddered with noise. Much of the noise was made by anti-aircraft guns, but that was not much comfort. In an earthquake the ground, as it slips and stretches itself, is behaving in a natural manner, without malice; but in an air raid the knowledge that someone is deliberately trying to kill you increases the tension. They may not stop until they've succeeded.

The bombers came in waves. There was a pause, and then another plane passed overhead; another stick of bombs began to fall, screaming, towards the ground. A good deal of unscientific myth was developed in playground gossip at school. It was the fifth in a row which was the dangerous bomb; after that you were all right. As usual I began to count. On this occasion it was number four which fell close at hand.

The foundations of the house were columns of brick. From my camp bed I could see two of them and, as I watched, they bent into a curve. It seemed to happen very slowly and perhaps I only imagined the feeling that the ceiling – the floor of the house – was pressing down towards my head. What was certainly not imagination, though, was that if those columns arched out for even another millionth of an inch the curve would explode and the whole weight of the house would collapse on top of us. My mother screamed. I was frightened as well, but in my case fear brought silence. I shut my eyes. It seemed certain that in a few seconds I would be dead.

When I opened my eyes, the columns were straight again. The house, as we discovered later, was damaged but still standing. The raid continued for an hour or two, but at last the guns fell silent and we went to sleep.

What I learned that night as the ground shuddered and steadied, as the brick foundation pillars bowed out and straightened again, was that only a tiny fraction of a second, a time too short to be of any significance, separates life from death. The anticipation of death and the process of dying may be longer, but that's a different matter. There is no point in wasting hours, months, years in fearing the coming of that split second. And so ever since that night in the cellar I have been unafraid of death.

Yunga on that night was only four years old, and never knew how close she came to dying. I try now to describe a little of that experience to her, but not all. Death in the abstract is a difficult subject to discuss with a woman who is facing death in reality. She must be the one, on any occasion, to speak of it first. In a way she does so when I have finished speaking.

'I remember, when I was about five or six and very bored, you taught me to play clock patience. I could never get it out, that first day, and I got cross with myself, thinking that I was being stupid. But you told me it was nothing to do with me.' Yunga pauses, trying to remember how I had phrased it.

'"There's no skill in it, this particular game," you said. "It's all in the cards. From the moment you deal them out, the course of the game is settled. If the bottom card in the middle is a king, then the moment you turn it up the game is over. Finished. And that king was there all the time, waiting.

Nothing to be done about it. The game was never anything more than a way of passing the time."'

I nod, understanding what she means. There is nothing to add. She has found her own form of comfort.

Part Four

Bombshells

1

The earthquake is yesterday's news. Today the focus of attention has moved to a tribal war in the middle of Africa. A different tribal war; not the one to which I contributed my photographs. Once again there has been a massacre. Once again refugees are streaming out of their country, abandoning homes and crops, preparing to appeal for the world's charity.

As I turn the television set off, Yunga sighs. 'Why is the news always so depressing?'

There are a good many answers to this question. With very few exceptions – weddings, perhaps, or the births of babies, or some sporting triumphs – happiness is a continuing emotion. To pick out and record a few moments of it in anyone's life is to shatter the very quality you are trying to capture. It is only when happiness is disrupted by disaster of one kind or another that it becomes news. The finances of television coverage ensure that once a team has arrived in an unhappy area it will remain there while the tragedy continues to develop but leave as soon as life returns to normal. But even in my own career as a still photographer it has always been the pictures of disruption rather than ordinary life that my editors wanted to see. Sometimes extreme joy was allowed as a contrast, but if I chose to photograph calm, ongoing happiness it could only be for a book or an exhibition.

'I remember once reading an article from some photographic magazine,' I tell Yunga now. 'It was when I first started training with Gerhardt. The author of the article, Terts, had been a friend of his in the twenties, when they were both young Surrealists.'

'Terts? Terts who?'

'I don't know. Just Terts. It was a professional name, I guess. I never knew him to be called anything else. You must have heard of him. He was just about the most famous British photographer in the thirties. I mean, Beaton posed pretty ladies in gauzy dresses, but Terts –'

I must check my enthusiasm, which Yunga cannot be expected to share. In the world of photography, Terts is my hero. If I have a social conscience it is because when I was twenty-one Gerhardt, my teacher, spread in front of me copies of Terts's greatest pictures. Tiny children knotting carpets in India. Young girls screaming with the pain of female circumcision. A slave market in Zanzibar. A lynching in Tennessee. An Indian widow burning to death. I have a vivid recollection of my first reaction to my own picture of the child bride, the marital slave, at the airport: Terts, I thought, would have approved of this.

But why should Yunga know his name? He died soon after the war – while I was in Switzerland, in fact. It was his death which had prompted my teacher's reminiscences. Yunga would hardly have been in her teens at the time.

She shrugs off her ignorance. 'What did the article say?'

'It was called "Here and there", as far as I remember. He was writing about still photography, of course: my sort. About the relationship of the magazine reader to the subject of the photograph. What you feel when you look at most photographs is, "I am here, they are there." There's a gap, a contrast, a difference.' Not for the first time, I am finding it difficult to explain myself in words. 'If the subject is a happy one, you look across the gap and feel envy and perhaps discontent.'

I don't personally, as a matter of fact, subscribe to the discontent part of this theory. There are enough good-hearted people in the world who take pleasure in knowing that other people are happy. But I am quoting; and so many important persons in the media agree with this opinion that their views dominate what is printed and shown. So I continue with Terts's argument.

'If it's a sad picture, though, what you feel is relief and contentment. "I am here. I'm glad I'm not there." Editors like to make their readers or viewers feel good. That's one way they can do it.'

'But surely –'

'Oh, yes, there are ways to bridge the gap. Compassion is one way. But in most cases the gap remains. "I am sorry for you and I will try to help you. But I can only do that because I am not you, but someone quite different. None of this is happening to me."'

'You say "in most cases" ...'

'What made Terts different, and what he went on to describe in his article, is that sometimes the photographer can bridge that gap by the intensity of his own feelings. When you look at a Terts photograph you feel the pain, because he was feeling it himself.' I could explain myself more clearly if I had an example to produce. 'And as a consequence, instead of a vague desire to help, you're likely to be stirred into a passionate belief that something must be done. The illustrations to a magazine article cease to be simply a form of entertainment and become political weapons, designed to make things happen.'

Steady on, Jo. I am overdoing the defence of my hero; partly through enthusiasm but mostly because I have tried throughout my life to copy him but only rarely have attained his standards. I produce the kind of smile which contains an element of apology and an invitation to change the subject. Yunga takes the hint.

'Let's look at your own photographs,' she suggests. 'The ones you took while you were here. Perhaps you'll be able to find the one you were talking about yesterday. The children in your Beginners' class.'

'Are they still around? All that old stuff.'

She nods. 'There's a tea chest up in one of the attic cupboards. Well, actually, there are two. One of them's full of business papers belonging to Mummy and Daddy. Bank statements and tax letters and all the stuff about proving wills. I thought I ought to keep it for a bit after they died, in case there were any queries, and I never got round to looking at it again. The other one has got old games on the top. I went through it a little while ago and sorted out anything that was good enough to be given away. I noticed then that there were a lot of your old snaps underneath. Bring the whole box down and sort things out where I can watch you.'

'Right.' The excuse to stand up comes as a relief. Although I want to spend as much time as possible with Yunga, the atmosphere in her sick room is oppressive. The artificial scents which keep at bay the natural odour of her illness leave me longing for a breath of fresh air.

'And on the way, would you tell Gwen that I'd like the bedpan?'

'I can deal with that myself.'

'I don't want you to. You're a sister, not a nurse.'

I'm a sister who feels no squeamishness about the workings of bodies, but I accept Yunga's decision, give the message and make my way upstairs.

The attic, on what in England is called the second floor, is simply the roof space. The ceiling rises high in the centre of the room and slopes down towards the floor on three sides. Only the party wall with number 41 is tall enough to allow an adult to stand against it. The wall facing this has been built up to the height of four feet in order to create two large cupboards which extend right to the end of the roof.

In the slope which faces the garden is a small dormer window. I fling it open for a moment to banish the musty, dusty smell. At the age of about eight – perhaps demonstrating for the first time on a small scale the love of mountains which was to become a passion – I once climbed out of this window and scrambled up the tiled roof until I was sitting with my legs astride the central ridge.

There I stayed, at first triumphantly and later uneasily, until a worried neighbour shouted from her garden to alert my mother, who in turn shouted up that I must stay quite still until the fire brigade arrived. I had no intention of being rescued like a kitten, so I conquered my fear and slithered down on to the jutting gable of the window before cautiously easing myself back into the room. By the time I had been hugged and slapped and shouted at, I had learned two useful lessons: that anxiety makes people angry, and that it is always easier to climb up than to come down. My mother had learned a lesson as well, and before long there were metal bars across the window. They are still there: a tribute to the fact that the motto of our household was Safety First.

In those days – because our bedrooms were small and the lounge was open to children only on Sunday afternoons and for piano practice – the attic was our playroom. The floorboards were bare and there was never any heating in the room, but we accepted coldness as the price of privacy. Here Timmy could lay out his model armies or the rails of his train set. Here, later, Yunga could play with her dolls' house. And here, in one of the low eaves cupboards, I made my first darkroom experiments.

They were not very successful. It was one of Timmy's pleasures to fling open the door at inconvenient moments; and even after I had bought a bolt and screwed it on, it was a struggle to follow instructions learned only from books, using makeshift equipment in a space which did not allow me to stand up. Although since that time I have had to become proficient in all the technical aspects of film processing in order to create by experiment the effects which I can see clearly in my mind, I have never taken great pleasure in this part of my work. It is the act of taking a photograph which produces in me, if I feel that I have got it right, an almost sexual excitement. What happens to it afterwards is just hard slog.

The two boxes to which Yunga has referred are in that old darkroom cupboard now. I pull them both out, but leave the box full of papers untouched. From the other I remove the battered boxes of board games which must have been set aside for a younger generation: a generation which was never born. Ludo, Snakes and Ladders, Halma, Draughts, Monopoly, Tri-Tactics. Now I have reached the photographs which Yunga noticed, and can start to riffle through the contents.

How tiny the snapshots are, and how incompetent! To give my younger self her due, these loose efforts are the rejects which were never good enough to be mounted in an album, but even so I shake my head over fuzzy focus or schoolfriends without feet. They would have been thrown away long ago had I continued to live at home. I am still turning them over when Gwen comes into the room.

'Your sister says, she doesn't need this long just to have a pee.'

'Sorry. I'll be right down.'

'Let me carry one for you.'

'No, they're dusty. And only one of them is going down anyway.'

But Gwen is not wearing a nurse's white-aproned uniform. Like me, she is casually dressed in sweater and trousers. Puffing off some of the dust, she picks up the box of photographs and, leaving me only with the task of opening and closing doors, carries it into the lounge.

'I shall need a large –' For a moment I pause, having to search for the English word. Trash is wrong, although trash is what I am holding. 'Waste paper basket,' I remember triumphantly.

'I'll find something for you.' Gwen sets her burden down on the carpet and disappears.

'But you're not to throw a single thing away until I've had a look at it,' Yunga commands. There have been more visitors this afternoon and after summoning the energy needed to entertain them, she is tired, but is making a visible effort to be bright again for me. I'm not sure that it's a good thing to encourage her. Why shouldn't she be allowed to flop? But perhaps to pass these childish efforts in front of her eyes will not drain her energy too much. Except that there are too many of them.

'If you're going to look at each one, we shall have to divide them into daily rations,' I tell her firmly. 'Not more than half an hour a day. Too boring, otherwise.' If this were something important, I should want to hurry, hurry, before it was too late. But it will be only a way of passing the time, as though she had all the time in the world. A waste, really, but it is not for me to say that. If I were measuring my own future in hours, how would I wish to spend them? Should I try to answer that question now, I might come up with some last ambition to be fulfilled, some project to be finalised; but perhaps when the choice is a real one and not a hypothesis it is more tempting to coast along; to begin the process of letting go.

Gwen returns with a large black plastic bag and rolls down the edges until it forms a neat circle on the ground.

'Call me if you need anything,' she says. 'I'll be getting supper.'

Already, as I thank her, I am lifting the first small snapshot from the top of the cardboard box; but without warning I find myself unable to look at it. Sadness and regret surge through my body and then seem to freeze. I can't move. I can't speak.

'What's the matter?' Yunga is quick to notice what is happening. 'Is it something in the photograph that's upset you?'

Forcing myself to look down at what proves to be an over-exposed photograph of Timmy, aged five, sitting cross-legged in front of his wigwam, I shake my head.

'They thought I was going to come back, didn't they?' There is no need to spell out the fact that I am talking about my parents. 'They must have hoped that I would, one day. Why should they keep all this trash otherwise? Christ, how selfish can one get! I should have guessed ... But they never said. Not a word.'

'I suppose, since you chose to leave, they had to hope that you'd choose to return. But you were waiting for an invitation, were you?'

'It's not quite as simple as that. I was told in so many words that I needn't think this was my home any longer. And the really sad thing is that after a bit I didn't care. Hardly thought about it. Life was so exciting.'

I toss the snapshot of Timmy into the plastic bag and think about other photographs. Gerhardt did more than simply train me. He set me off on my career. I'd been with him for almost a year when he was invited by a magazine, *Harper's*, to go to New York. He was well known over there from before the war, but in 1948 he claimed to be too old for all the travelling and living in hotels. He sent me in his place, equipped with cameras which I was to pay for out of my first earnings.

An unknown twenty-two year old wasn't at all what the art editor had in mind when she invited Gerhardt himself, of course, and I wasn't allowed to take over the project she'd had in mind for him. But she didn't want to offend him and he had written me an enthusiastic reference. Also, I was on the spot and I was cheap. I was offered a run-of-the-mill fashion shoot. By the time she agreed, half reluctantly, that I had made a good job of it, I had a new idea to put forward.

Old masters and young pretenders was how I thought of it to myself, but Americans probably wouldn't have known what a pretender was, so it had a different headline in the end. The idea was simple enough: contrasting portraits of the present top people in their fields and those who might one day challenge their eminence. I didn't ask for a commission; only for a letter of introduction. I spent nine months on it, doing other jobs at the same time to keep alive; it was one of the most fascinating periods of my life.

All my subjects loved me. I've never been a beauty and even so long ago I was spending all the daylight hours dressed in black sweaters and slacks: no glamour about that. But I was tall and slim, young and bright-eyed and full of energy. The old ones, the ones who had already made their reputations and fortunes, were flattered by the completeness of my concentration on them. As I worked, I encouraged them to talk about whatever subject it was which had made them famous. Although I was never going to be a Cambridge graduate, I was of university calibre, you might say, and knew how to ask questions and how to comment on the answers. And because I didn't want to talk too much myself, I came over as a good listener.

It was very educational. They invited me to stay for a night, a weekend, a week in their often palatial houses. That was educational as well. They looked at the proofs of their portraits and ordered copies for themselves. Some of the women wanted the right to approve anything that was to be published, but the old men seemed to glory in all the wrinkles and laughter lines. They enthused about me to their friends, so that a social weekend house party became a major sales opportunity. I soon paid off my debts to Gerhardt.

The young men liked me as well. Although the word was not then part of my vocabulary, I soon came to realise that many of them were gay. This may have been because while it was easy even for an outsider to recognise who was at the top of any particular tree, it was more difficult to be sure who would have replaced each of them there in forty years' time. I needed to collect opinions and perhaps I didn't always recognise that I was being passed along a concealed network. Be that as it may, I was popular with these sitters also because although I was emphatically female, I was also single-mindedly committed to my professional career. They enjoyed flirting with me, knowing that nothing would ever come of it. Taking a vivacious girl to a party helped them, I suppose, to keep the closet door shut. I made some close friendships during that nine-month period. Forty years later – because several of my guesses were good ones – I was able to offer ten 'then-and-now' pairs of portraits of famous men; all from my own archive.

To describe this period of my career to Yunga will only emphasise the dullness of her own suburban life. I concentrate on sifting through these early efforts at portraiture, forbidden to throw even the worst duds away until Yunga has had a chance to see them.

At the end of half an hour I have spared hardly more than a dozen to spread out on her lap tray. As I expected, these also are all really discards. Anything worth keeping will have been mounted into an album. But even these unsuccessful attempts are enough to prompt an odd discovery. Every member of the immediate family is represented there, but no other relations of any kind. I comment on this to Yunga.

'I never noticed it at the time, but it's unusual, isn't it? Most children have grandparents. Aunts and uncles and cousins. Didn't we have any at all?'

Even as I ask the question, I think of a partial answer. Every Christmas for the first ten years of my life I did receive one present by post. 'From Auntie Libby' was the only message inside. No letter; no address. In fact, now that I consider it, it was Auntie Libby who gave me the camera for my tenth birthday. I remember that my father tried to put it away, telling me that I was too young for such a present; but I was physically in possession of it and refused to surrender. I wrote my thank-you letter as usual and gave it to my mother to post; but after that year there were no more parcels from Auntie Libby.

Yunga, who presumably never received any gifts from that source at all, is thinking along different lines as she answers my question.

'On Daddy's side, his father died actually the day he was born, and his mother quite soon after that, I think. His grandfather lived on to be very old, but even he died just about the time you were born. I don't know so much about Mummy's family, except that she was an only child.'

'But isn't that extraordinary, when you come to think of it? I mean, that we should know so little. And even more extraordinary that we should never have been interested enough to ask. What self-centred creatures children are!

Well, I'd better speak only for myself. What a self-centred creature I must have been, to assume that my parents' lives only really began on the day I was born.'

'It's not quite as simple as that. I did try asking questions, when I'd stopped being a child. And they didn't want to answer. So even if they never made that clear in so many words when we were young, I expect we picked up the impression that they intended us to have.' Yunga pauses for a moment. Talking so much is tiring for her, and when she resumes her voice is weaker. 'After all, the most extraordinary thing is that neither of them ever spoke about their own childhoods. Most parents say, "When I was a little girl", or "little boy", from time to time. Ours never did.'

Odd though that certainly may have been, it is my own lack of curiosity which dumbfounds me. It must mean, I suppose, that I have no family feeling in the tribal sense. Perhaps that's a characteristic of the hunter-gatherer. Roots don't seem important. But it is not too late to start being curious. I could at least discover where each of my parents was born, and into what kind of family. Not immediately, though. For Yunga it *is* too late.

She is still continuing the conversation.

'I can think of one explanation for why they didn't want to talk about their childhoods. What I did discover from Mummy, after Daddy died, was that Daddy's family – well, his grandfather at least – were furious with him for marrying a Jewess, and Mummy's family were furious because she converted. So both lots must have cut right off from us all. And maybe Mummy and Daddy found that the easiest way to deal with an unhappy situation like that was to do a kind of cutting-off themselves. To pretend they didn't care.'

'*What* did you say?' I am taken aback by the way in which Yunga drops her bombshell. 'Are you telling me that our mother was Jewish? How long have you known that? Why didn't you tell me?'

'I didn't know until quite late in her life. When she was ill, she told me, and asked me to find out whether her parents were still alive. They weren't. She didn't want anyone else to know. Not her church friends.'

'But a daughter is different from a friend! You should have told me.' Although the disclosure is startling enough in itself, I am almost more upset by the discovery that Yunga has kept secrets from me. I have always assumed that we have written frankly to each other on every subject.

'What difference does it make?'

I am still gasping with the revelation. 'Well, it's an unexpected thing to discover about myself in my seventies: that I'm Jewish.'

'You're not really.'

'Yes, I am. Really. And so are you. It goes through the female. We have a Jewish mother and so we're Jewish.'

'And you're exactly the same today as you were yesterday.' Yunga, whose voice for most of the day has been faint and faltering, is speaking with a firmness which takes me by surprise. 'I don't accept that there's any difference, knowing or not knowing what Mummy once was. I was born into a Christian family. I was brought up as a Christian. I have always thought of myself as a Christian and that's what I am. I could add "And so are you", except that of course I know you're not.'

She is right about that. My father's unchristian lack of forgiveness led me to abandon the faith of my upbringing as decisively as in the end I abandoned my home country. But at this moment I feel uneasily that the legacy of blood may be harder to evade than that of upbringing.

The lounge contains no mirror in which I can search the reflection of my own face for Semitic features, so I look instead at Yunga. She guesses what I am doing and meets my gaze with a smile.

There has never been any physical resemblance between the two of us. Even as a child I was always tall and thin, like our mother, while she inherited my father's plumpness and smaller stature. Our ways of life since then – hers sedentary and mine energetic – accentuated the differences, but her present illness seems to be feeding on her flesh in more ways than one. Her body is no longer firmly rounded; the skin of her upper arms is beginning to droop loosely.

This is not the change in which I am interested. I take her into my arms and kiss her fiercely.

'As you say, no difference. The same person today as I was yesterday.' We are still hugging each other when Gwen comes into the room with a supper tray, and the photographs must be hastily removed. Probably we shall not discuss this subject again.

All the same, I wish there had been no secrets. Later in the evening, lying awake in bed, I repeat the words silently to myself. 'I am Jewish. I am a Jewess.'

No, it's not important. I have never held any anti-Semitic views, nor ever said anything which, if applied to myself now, would anger or disgust me. In fact, so many of the magazine editors who employ me are Jewish that it would probably have been to my advantage to be recognised as one of themselves. But that Yunga should have failed to confide in me is a different matter. I have always presumed that we are as close as any two sisters could be. But now a gap has opened between us, and it leaves me uneasy. Is there anything else that I should have been told?

2

I have tracked down my old photograph albums. Searching deep into the attic cupboard while Dr Morris is paying his regular morning visit, I find a parcel wrapped in brown paper and tied with string, as though about to be posted.

My name is written on the front, but without an address. Smiling with pleasure at the discovery, I come down one flight of stairs to the landing and meet Dr Morris coming up.

'I've increased the strength of the injection today,' he tells me without preamble. 'You'll probably find that your sister needs to have longer periods of rest as a result. I have to warn you that her condition is deteriorating. It did seem to me earlier that she was making a great effort to stay alive until you were able to get here. Now –'

'Now I'm here. So she's letting go?'

He nods. 'Something like that. In a terminal illness, the will to live is often just as significant as any drugs which we may administer. I'm not saying that your sister has lost the will to live, exactly. It's more that she's gone into neutral. She seems happy just to let things happen. I wanted to warn you.'

'Thank you.' The words do not actually emerge from my throat, which thickens them into a croak, but Dr Morris interprets the effort. He nods again and goes back downstairs.

Half an hour later I carry the albums into the lounge. The cheerfulness of my smile is as shameful as Yunga's concealment of earlier secrets. The gap between us is widening. I have promised to be honest, but am unable to keep the promise.

There are three albums, and the first one I open reveals immediately the group of Beginners of which I was reminded by yesterday's visitors. Laughingly and without success we attempt to identify Mrs Johnson and Mrs Meads. 'But we should start at the beginning,' Yunga says.

That means a different album. The snapshots it contains were fastened to the pages by triangular mounts which formed pockets into which the corners could slide. After sixty years the adhesive has dried and the mounts have slipped. I have to catch the photographs as they fall from the page. I set half a dozen of them down on Yunga's lap tray and then move five away to the side, giving centre place to a tiny rectangle of black and white: my very first photograph.

'The start of a great career!' I announce – and then, looking at it more closely, mutter under my breath: 'Christ Almighty!'

Because I have always remembered the occasion of taking this particular snapshot as a turning point in my life, it comes as a surprise and disappointment to see the unsatisfactory result.

Naturally the family group is posed – and no doubt I kept them all waiting for an unreasonably long time as I aimed for perfection with the unfamiliar camera, stepping backwards and forwards to find the perfect distance. But I must have forgotten to ask them to smile. My father looks positively irritated about something. Timmy is restless, tugging to get away; and because he is standing in front of our parents I have cut him off just above the ankles. Even my mother, who is supposed to be proudly showing off her new baby, has an unhappy look to her whilst Yunga herself, serenely unconscious of what is happening, is little more than a white blob of face in a long white shawl.

'What a miserable lot!'

'Well, Daddy never liked being photographed, did he?' Yunga picks up the snapshot and holds it close to her eyes so that she can see it.

'No. But a mother with a new baby is supposed to look proud and happy.'

'Only if she wanted the baby in the first place. I suppose it took her a little longer than this to come to terms with what had happened.'

'What do you mean?'

'I mean that I was an accident. Completely unintended and distinctly unwelcome.'

'How do you know?'

'Because she told me. When she was giving me the usual facts-of-life talk. I was about ten, I suppose, and hugely embarrassed. Quite determined that none of this bleeding business was ever going to happen to me, even if every other female suffered from it. Then she went on to the business of having babies and how it wasn't safe to take a risk even once, because look what had happened to her – me. I cried all night. It's not much fun, finding out that nobody wanted you, that you shouldn't ever have been born.'

'That was a terrible thing to do – to tell you!'

'Yes. There was something odd about the conversation. She seemed very bitter. Said something to the effect that she ought to have learned from experience. By the next morning she'd realised that she ought to have kept quiet. There was a great lovey-dovey session about how she'd loved me as soon as she'd actually seen me, and ever since. That was all an act. For the rest of her life, she never really forgave me for existing. Anyway, then she went on to say that it was never going to happen again, now that she and Daddy slept in separate beds. More embarrassment on my part. Children don't really want to know this sort of thing, do they?'

Tired by so much talking, Yunga closes her eyes, leaving me to stagger my way through this second shock.

One forgets. Goodness knows, I am old enough to remember that trace of anxiety which accompanied every extra-marital sexual experience in the days before the contraceptive pill had been invented or abortion made legal. Rubber was never wholly reliable. I have a druggist in China to thank for the fact that I am not today the single mother of a half-Italian thirty-five-year-old. But one forgets that for married couples, loving each other and sharing a bed, the temptations were far greater and the risks just as great.

Now that Yunga mentions it, I do recall that soon after her birth my parents' bedroom was refurnished. Out went the double bed and the shabby wardrobe, to be replaced by a black lacquer bedroom suite. A wardrobe, a chest of drawers, a dressing table and two single beds, all decorated with willow trees and herons and bunches of grapes and bearded Chinese mandarins. At the age of ten I loved the pictures and thought the handsomeness of the new furniture to be a sufficient explanation for the banishment of the old. The significance of the twin beds was quite lost on me. As Yunga says, children are not interested in what their parents do or don't do after lights-out.

Now, sixty years later, I wonder about it in silence. Perhaps the severing of marital relations didn't matter much to her, my mother. In our own sex-mad generation, to live a celibate life seems almost unnatural, a deprivation. I suspect, though, that in the pre-Pill days married women may for many centuries have reached a stage when they yearned not to be 'bothered' any longer. My father, though; it would have been different for him.

There is always something disquieting about trying to imagine the love-life of a parent. I can only visualise my father as I always saw him: fully dressed, or at the very least with a dressing gown tightly belted over his pyjamas. What did he look like with his trousers off? I don't really want to know. Once upon a time, in the early years of his marriage, he must have been passionately in love with his wife, fumbling at buttons in his haste to take her to bed. But a child could know nothing of that. Even as an adolescent, if I had tried to picture him going to bed, the picture would have been of a plump little man with a goatee beard and a habit of looking over his spectacles; a man who at the end of the day would sit on the edge of a chair and take off his shoes one by one, setting them carefully side by side, in no hurry and not envisaging anything but sleep.

That can't be a true picture. He was only thirty-two when Yunga was born. Did he really accept at that age that his sex life had come to an end? Perhaps acceptance was forced on him, because where else could he look? The whole of his social life revolved round the church. The women he met at weekends and in the evenings were all the wives of his friends: out of bounds. The school at which he taught was co-educational, so there were female teachers on the staff, but from the evidence of my own girls' school I can feel sure that these unhappy representatives of the generation whose possible husbands had died in the Great War had by that time given up any attempt to attract male admirers.

Much more dangerous would have been the sixth-form girls he taught. He had first fallen in love with my mother when she was only eighteen, and there must have been moments when a young, bright-eyed face stirred memories of those early days. But to stray in that direction would have meant professional death.

What else was there? Prostitutes? Surely not. Better to return to my starting point and consider that perhaps in those days, sixty years ago, sex was simply not important. A temptation for the young, a bribe to make marriage attractive and then a ritual designed for the procreation of children and nothing more. But I don't really believe that.

Yunga has been lying back on the chaise longue with her eyes closed. Even without the doctor's warning I would have recognised that she is far more tired than even one day earlier. There is a moment in which I am frightened, because she seems to have stopped breathing. But then her body shudders with effort as she takes in more air, opens her eyes again and smiles, ready to continue the conversation and guessing the direction in which I shall take it.

'How did he manage?' Although in a sense I don't want to talk about it, the question blurts itself out. 'I mean, I can see that our mother may have had a strong enough motive, but for him, at that age ...'

She gives a little shrug of her shoulders, and her answer follows my own earlier thoughts. 'Nowadays, if the papers are to believed, everyone expects to have sex every day or night. But that isn't true for everybody even now. And we ought to remember that it wasn't always like that.'

Something else that I ought to remember is that Yunga herself has never had a lover – at least, not to my knowledge. Yesterday's revelation about our mother's Jewish background has left me uncertain about how much I can take for granted. But Yunga is right. In the nineteen-thirties and forties and fifties, as for centuries before, fear must have acted as a support to abstinence. All the same, though ...

Yunga has returned the photograph to its place on her lap tray. It is my turn to stare closely at it. This was supposed to be a picture of a happy family group; but if, as she believes, my parents' marriage had already in one sense come to an end, the picture was a lie. I pride myself on using my camera only to tell the truth. It makes me angry to learn that at my very first opening of the shutter I was being deceived. But I suppose that what I should be feeling is pity and sympathy.

The sympathy ought to be for my mother, who suffered the pain of childbirth against her wish. It is quite ridiculous that even now, more than sixty years after my first confrontation with Timmy, I remain as cold towards her memory as I did towards her in person while she was still alive. I am an adult, for heaven's sake. I was perfectly well able to understand what happened while I was in hospital and dismiss it as the small mistake which was all it was. But I can't do it. It is for my dead father that my heart aches now as I picture his loneliness within what must still have seemed from outside to be a happy family.

I have never stopped loving him, or his memory. If he disowned me, it was because he in turn loved me so much that he was unable to forgive me for running away from the life he had chosen for me. Even when I felt most hurt by his coldness, I understood it. It was all my fault. And if he had already had to suffer not only the death of his son but the loss of his wife's love, it was no wonder that my betrayal hit him so hard.

'Daddy was away from home for most of the war, of course,' Yunga reminds me. 'There may have been someone else then. We wouldn't have known.'

A schoolteacher in his mid-thirties when the war started, our father was in a reserved occupation, but he must have volunteered to help the war effort. His brilliant degree, although it had failed to earn him the university post he craved, apparently qualified him for some kind of intelligence work. What he did was secret, he told us at the time, and he was still not prepared to talk about it when I left home. Throughout the war years he quite often returned home on Saturdays or Sundays to see us, but did not always stay the night.

Thinking back to that period, I dredge out another memory. It was at the end of the war, when my father was once again living at home, that my mother's unidentifiable illness began. A heart murmur, a fibrillation, a sudden intense spasm of chest pain: whatever it was, it was enough to win her a prescription of frequent rests and no sudden exertions. Sex, almost certainly, came into the category of sudden exertion. And so I ask myself – and Yunga – again: 'But after the war, for all those years. What did he do?'

Once more Yunga's eyes are closed. Her lips are closed as well. They hardly move as she speaks. The words of her answer are forced out of her throat rather than by her tongue. I have to strain to hear them, and they die in the silence of the room almost before I have time to take them in.

'He had me.'

3

The front room which was once my father's study is Gwen's territory now. As I open its door, half an hour after Yunga's confession, I feel a double sense of trespass. The study was always off-limits to children except on the formal occasions when we were invited in to choose something to read. As Gwen's room it should be equally private. But knowing that she is out, I need to stand inside it in an effort to come to terms with what I have just been told.

The room is untidy. In her work Gwen is meticulously neat, carrying out all the necessary procedures of sterilisation and general hygiene and returning everything to its proper place. Perhaps it is in revolt against these professional necessities that she has left her bed unmade and has strewn discarded clothes over the furniture. She wouldn't want me to see it like this, but I have to be here.

Throughout the years of my childhood this was my father's private room. If my cautious knock was greeted with 'Yes?' I could open the door and wait, standing in the doorway, until he had finished whatever he was writing. In the early days it would be notes for his never-completed thesis. Later, it was more likely to be some comment on one of thirty Latin translations. Only when he was ready would he turn in his swivel chair and lower his head to look over his glasses at me, ready to show irritation if the interruption was unjustified.

Neither then nor now have I ever held this against him. As a child I accepted what he frequently told us: that only his hard work lay between the family and starvation. As an adult I recognise that I have inherited the same need for uninterrupted time in which I can concentrate completely on what I am doing. Because my life has been wilder I have not, like him, come to rely on a private space; but even in the middle of a battle or a hurricane I am liable to display anger with anyone who tries to distract me from the work in hand.

There is little left today to remind me of the years when the room was a study. Once upon a time every wall was clad with bookshelves reaching to the ceiling, but none of these remain except the three low shelves which curve beneath the bay window. A mahogany dining table, pushed to one side to make room for the bed, reveals that Yunga has at some point returned the room to the use for which the builder originally intended it. Half a dozen chairs are pressed wherever there is space for them: under the table or against a wall. A sideboard is acting as Gwen's dressing table, littered with hairbrushes and cosmetics. The place is a mess, but my thoughts are messier.

Over and over again, in the conversation which followed Yunga's confession, I have demanded to know why she didn't tell me at the time what was happening, so that I could protect her. But the answer was painfully simple.

'You weren't there.'

No, I wasn't there. I had run away from what I saw as my own prison without a thought for a fellow prisoner left behind. I was busy being happy. Roaming the world as I built a career, and thinking that letters and postcards and holiday invitations were all that was needed to maintain the links between us. For the first ten years of her life I had allowed my little sister to think of me as her best friend, her protector, almost a second mother. But when she needed me I wasn't there.

It was because I wasn't there, almost certainly, that the abuse first began. He had lost Timmy, he had in a sense lost his wife, and without warning he had lost his elder daughter as well. Is it so surprising that he should have been desperate to keep his only remaining child close to him?

'You should have told Mummy?' I haven't used the word 'Mummy' for years, decades, not even in my thoughts; it has always been 'my mother'. But in making that comment to Yunga I was trying to put myself into the skin of a ten year old. The effort made it easier, although not easy, to understand the answer.

'Well, of course he told me not to. She'd be jealous, he said, if she found out that he loved me more than her. And I was pleased about that. It was only a little while earlier that I'd discovered she never really wanted me to be born at all, and I was still feeling upset about it. This was going one up on her, in a way. And to begin with, what happened was nothing very dramatic. He just wanted me to stroke him, as though I were stroking one of my pet mice. I didn't know there was anything wrong about it. I didn't like the stickiness of it all, but ...' Yunga paused at that point, either because she needed a rest or because she was trying to set herself back into her ten-year-old mind. But after a moment she went on.

'He was reassuring about that, in a sort of way. Telling me that men and women were so different that I needn't think the same thing would happen to me. And all this was just after Mummy had been warning me about menstruation, so I suppose I thought, you know, that what was happening was a sort of equivalent of that. I didn't know anything about sex or men's bodies or anything. Mummy had tried to tell me something about babies, but I didn't really understand the mechanics of the business. And for years nothing changed. Me stroking him; him stroking me: that was all it was. He waited until I was fourteen before ... before ...'

At that point there was another long pause. Was Yunga remembering the unexpected night of pain, the first sense of sin? If so, it seemed that she was prepared to leave that to my imagination while she worked up courage to make another confession. 'I did tell her in the end, though. After he died. We were having a row. It was when she discovered that he'd left the house to me and not to her. It seemed quite natural to me, since she wouldn't let him love her and I would.'

'How did she react?'

The answer came as yet another bombshell. 'That was the day she had her stroke.'

So that was it. I had never properly understood why Yunga had spent so much of her life caring for a demanding invalid, and the recent revelation that she had always been treated as an unwanted child served to deepen the mystery. Until that moment, the only possible explanation had seemed to be that Yunga had a saintly and dutiful nature, but it must have been simpler than that. A sense of guilt. A need to make amends.

It was Kate's arrival in the lounge with a hot drink for Yunga which brought that conversation to an end. My excuse for leaving the room was that I wanted a cup of coffee, so I had better make that for myself before returning. I have been pacing up and down in the limited space of an over-furnished room for more than half an hour as I go over and over what I have just been told. Now it is time to pull myself back to the present. This is Gwen's room. I have no right to be here. She too needs to have her private space.

Arriving in the breakfast room I am surprised to see Kate sitting there with a mug in her hand instead of keeping Yunga company.

'Your sister said she'd rather be on her own until you came back,' the nurse explains, justifying herself. 'I looked in a moment ago, and she's asleep.'

There is a change in the atmosphere here as well. Kate and Gwen hold identical qualifications, but are completely different in character.

Gwen, who is in her forties and the widow of a soldier, is casual in her appearance and always patient and unhurried: a sympathetic listener and willing to play any role which her patient may demand of her.

Kate is twenty-seven, brisk and well-organised. I have already learned that she has a five-year-old son who is taken to school each morning by his father and comes out again at three o'clock, which is why the hours here suit her so well. The uniform prescribed by the nursing agency which supplies her is not quite as hierarchically detailed as that of a hospital, but it is nevertheless a uniform. It announces her status in the household. She is strictly a nurse and not in any sense a domestic servant. Although as a gesture of welcome she offered me breakfast when I first arrived, it has been clear to me ever since then that, to take a small example, if I want coffee, I am the one to make it. She is kind to Yunga, and gentle with her body, but belongs to the school of thought which supposes that too great a show of sympathy for a patient encourages self-pity.

But today, as she looks at me, there is a different expression in her eyes. Unable to meet her gaze, I go past her into the scullery and fiddle with the filter.

'Dr Morris had a word with me this morning,' I tell her over my shoulder. 'I don't suppose you needed to be told.'

'No. I ought to be in there, really. But she seemed a little upset. She only wants you. You will call me quickly, won't you, if ...'

'Sure.' I have been away too long already and abandon the filter in favour of instant coffee. Kate has left the door of the lounge open, and my trainers make no noise as I approach the chaise longue from behind. There is something about the silence in the room which alarms me; not simply the lack of music but the lack of any sound at all. Was Yunga's confession prompted by an awareness that her death was imminent? As I listen for the sound of her breathing, I suspend my own.

For a moment, or at least several seconds, there is nothing. But then, as has happened before, a rough fluttering of air tells me that she is still alive. I step quietly to her side. Her eyes are closed and her face is smooth and peaceful.

Conscious of my presence, Yunga opens her eyes and gives me a loving smile. 'I'm glad you know at last.'

This, I realise, is the reason for her peacefulness. She was not disturbed by what had happened in the past, but only by her failure to tell me about it. This is the confession she needed to make: that she has kept a secret from me for so many years.

'Why didn't you tell me before?' I ask her.

'Because you loved him, didn't you? Not in the same way that I did, obviously, but I know how much it hurt you when he was so angry about Cambridge. And Elda darling, you mustn't blame yourself for anything. I shouldn't have said that, about you not being there. I could have stopped it by myself if I'd wanted to. Well, not at first, perhaps, but when I was old enough to leave home.'

Is she telling me that she enjoyed the relationship? Even after she was old enough to know that it was wrong? Even when she must have felt at least a little guilty, however much she might have argued to herself that her father was entirely to blame for abusing an innocent child? Only a moment ago I have been imagining that the cause of my distress is that the truth has been kept hidden from me; but now I have to control an illogical anger that I have been told at all. The discovery that I have loved only an image of a father and not a real man is a hard one to accept. I conceal my unhappiness in an attempt at laughter.

'What a family! A God-fearing, respectable suburban family! Who would ever have guessed at all these emotions simmering away beneath our Sunday best as we set out for church! Me refusing to love my mother, while she longed to adore me. Mother herself refusing to love the baby she never wanted, while you ached to be accepted by her. Me wanting to please the father I loved, but not quite managing it. You pleasing him in a way you never dared to confess to anyone else. Timmy dying in such an unlucky, unnecessary way. And the two of them, our parents, grieving for their son, slowly sliding out of love and into coldness and separation, but not able to escape. What complicated emotions for four ordinary people to cope with!'

'Nobody's ordinary.' Yunga, tired, closes her eyes again. 'Birth, marriage, childbirth, family relationships, death; everybody has to cope with the big things. I funked out of some. Makes it all the more important that I should deal with this one in the right way.'

Her voice fades away so that I have to strain to catch the last words and for a second time I am frightened. Gwen has warned me that death is unlikely to arrive in such a peaceful manner, unless the regime of drugs is increased; but because I am praying that my sister will slip away without pain when the time comes I am frequently overcome by terror that the moment has already arrived and passed without me noticing it. For a second time, though, it is a false alarm. Yunga is tired. She is asleep, leaving me to accept what she has just told me.

Yes, it's true. Nobody is ordinary. Nobody is unimportant, at least to herself. And even if it were not true, it would make no difference. Tremendous things happen to little people in unimpressive places. I have been present in palaces or on parade grounds during bloody revolutions. I have seen rulers and generals gunned down and chopped to pieces, their lives brought to an abrupt end while they were still surrounded by the trappings of power. The ending of Yunga's life will be slower and less unexpected, in the lounge of a suburban semi-detached house, but it will all be the same in the end. And a little of my own life has died already, with the discovery that not all of it was quite what it seemed.

4

The house is stifling me. I need fresh air. I need time to think. I need to be on my own. But I daren't leave.

Yunga guesses how I feel. After lunch, as Kate is settling her down for her rest, she issues a command.

'Go out for a walk, Elda. You've been inside too long for an outdoor lady like you. I shall be asleep until half past three. I shan't even know that you've gone.'

'Well, I might just do that.' I bend over to kiss her before following Kate into the breakfast room.

'What do you think?'

'Yes, you go. I can stay for an extra hour today.' She is telling me that she is not prepared to leave Yunga only with Maggie. 'You can take my mobile with you, if you like. I'll ring through if there's any change. But there won't be, not in the next few hours. Perhaps you ought to have a word with the agency, though, and get someone to cover afternoons from now on. Anyway, have a good breath of air.'

Walking round the nearest streets promises no joy; I coax Yunga's car into life after its months of idleness. There are no mountains nearby to restore my spirits, so I make for the only point nearby which could perhaps be described as a hill. More of a pimple, really; but there is just enough of a slope to make me feel, as I park the car at its foot and walk up, that I am stretching my muscles.

When I was about sixteen I had a friend who lived up here. No doubt there is a photograph of her in one of my albums, but we lost touch years ago. After I had finished my training with Gerhardt and moved to New York, in the excitement of learning to cope with a new job in a new country I allowed all my contacts in England, except Yunga, to lapse. Jenny, who had new excitements of her own, may not even have noticed. Instead of going to university she married young and was already pregnant when I left home. By the time we were twenty-two we no longer had anything in common except our shared years at a grammar school. All the same, for at least two years we were best friends.

Jenny's family was prosperous and her home, to my sixteen-year-old eyes, very grand. I make my way towards it and see that, to judge by the number of bell-pushes, it has been divided into eight flats. Nearby is the church in whose graveyard the two of us, Jenny and I, liked to sit in all the self-indulgent gloom of adolescence, reading Keats or planning how society ought to be rebuilt from the ashes of the war years.

Perhaps it is because I have so recently been discussing that far-off war with Yunga that I remember, as I return to the graveyard today, the worst moments of those years for the Bradley family. It was on a sunny afternoon in July, 1944: the last day of the summer term. School broke up at noon and Jenny had invited me back to lunch to celebrate the start of six weeks of freedom. After the meal we borrowed a poetry anthology from her father's bookshelves and strolled with it to the churchyard. We were sitting on the wall – and I sit myself down now in the same place, reliving the incident – when we heard the doodle-bug coming.

Nobody under sixty in England will still remember the sound of a flying bomb, but nobody who heard it will ever forget it. It came out of a clear summer sky, that steady rasping noise. We all knew – Jenny and I certainly knew – that we were safe so long as we would still hear the engine. Only when silence fell would it mean that the bomb was diving towards the ground. The approach of each bomb stopped every conversation, and beneath the silence was a single unexpressed thought. 'Go on a little further. Fall somewhere else.'

That certainly was what I was thinking as this particular flying bomb made its slow way towards us. Now it was above us, so that we could see the flaming tail which propelled it forward. 'Go on a little further.'

It went on a little further. Then the engine cut out.

'That's Kenbury way,' said Jenny a few seconds later as we heard the explosion and watched the cloud of dust rise and swirl and slowly settle again. 'There go your windows again.'

'Not this time.' After the earlier bomb which had shattered most of the glass, the replacement windows had been criss-crossed with strips of brown sticky tape, so that only diamonds of light, as in a medieval house, penetrated into our brown and dingy home. It would take a closer explosion than this one had been to fragment the glass. I could tell from a row of trees near to the dust cloud that the bomb had fallen close to the recreation ground, several streets away from my home. We returned our attention to the poem we were reading. 'The Garden of Proserpine', it was. I had discovered Swinburne for myself a year or two earlier and was now introducing Jenny to my favourite example of his work. Later on, the choice of this particular poem seemed hideously inappropriate.

The bomb had killed Timmy. On the last day of the summer term, as he made his way home with a group of his friends. They were carrying their satchels and shoe bags, stuffed with everything that had to be carried back from school. They had diverted from their usual path, it transpired, in order to kick a ball around on the rec, since school had broken up half an hour earlier than usual that afternoon. Two of the boys were killed instantly and one was so badly injured that he died three weeks later.

There was no reason why I should feel guilt of any kind. It was a German who had invented the bomb and a German who had sent it on its way to kill children in the streets. And yet I did feel guilty: for wishing the bomb to travel on that extra mile, but even more for being only an observer and not a sufferer – as on many occasions since that time I have felt guilty for recording suffering without having to endure it. I feel it again at this moment, still unreasonably. 'I was here. He was there.'

Why am I thinking about Timmy when it is the revelation about my father which has driven me out of the house and into the fresh air? I suppose it is because there is a connection. Timmy's death was my father's war wound. Even at the time I noticed a change in him, but interpreted it only as a shift in parental ambition. His elder daughter would now have to have the brilliant career for which his son had originally been destined. At least for as long as I was still at school I accepted the new pressure and understood it. I was not mature enough to realise what might happen if he lost me as well.

Does it matter – after all these years – what happened? I pose the question within my mind, but it is my body that answers and I am suddenly, violently, groaningly sick. Over my shoes, over the narrow path which encircles the graveyard and over the headstone of Edith Petts, who died in 1804 at the age of fifty-two.

For a few minutes longer, even after my stomach has emptied, I continue to retch. Then, with my breath still coming in deep moaning sighs, I pull handfuls of long grass from the edges of graves and do my best to clear up the mess. The effort is not very successful and in the end I walk away, anxious not to be associated with it. Not in any religious mood, but because I need to sit down, I make my way into the church. It has a minder, knitting quietly in a corner to deter vandals. She smiles at me in a welcoming fashion and is luckily too far away to be aware of the smell which enters the building with me.

My distress has very little to do with my father. It even appears that I need hardly feel sorry for Yunga, whose innocence protected her as a young child and who appears to have enjoyed the incestuous relationship as she grew older. I am upset because I have always thought of my sister's life as being attached to my own in the same way that number 43 Woodside Road is attached to number 41. They are two parts of a single building, just as Yunga and I are two parts of a single sisterhood. But the word to describe the two houses is 'semi-detached', and it seems that that has always been our sisterly relationship as well – with the emphasis on the 'detached'.

My need for air is greater than my need to sit. I wander restlessly outside again, still thinking about my father. I don't want to imagine him in Yunga's bedroom, and yet I am trying to do so. Without much success, fortunately. It's unbelievable. The man I remember couldn't possibly have behaved like that.

The man I remember was someone I knew for only twenty years, and always in the relationship of child to parent. As soon as I succeeded in establishing myself as an independent adult, the relationship did not adapt itself, but snapped. And so my memory of him has been frozen in time; in the same way that one may look at a photograph without reflecting that the subject of the photograph is changing every day and no longer bears any resemblance to his picture.

Only a few hours have passed since I expressed incredulity at my ignorance of my parents' lives before their marriage. Now I must reproach myself for giving too little thought to their lives after my departure. There is more to it than simply self-centredness. It is a lack of imagination – and a second lack of sufficient sensitivity to recognise the need for imagination. The whole of my career has been devoted to recording what I can see: something that exists. When I use my imagination, it is only to transform something which is actually in front of my eyes.

The effort to use it in a different way now has exhausted me. Walking slowly down the hill, for the first time in my life I feel old. My body is faint and weak from nausea and my mind is still in turmoil. What Yunga has told me is impossible to accept. And yet I can't believe that she would lie to me.

My route home takes me past the site of my old school. Not Sandy Lane Elementary, of hated memory, but the grammar school which provided my escape from it. It lies halfway between my home and Jenny's, between her posh suburb and my drab one. Winning a place to it was part of the process of leaving my past behind – a process which I seem to have continued throughout the rest of my life.

The girls who won places at the grammar school were those who were able to pass an examination at the age of eleven, and very few of the Sandy Lane pupils – only three in my year – achieved this. Presumably my father, a schoolteacher himself, gave me coaching for the tests. Certainly there were cleverer girls than myself at Sandy Lane who failed to win a place and were condemned to stay in their educational prison until the age of fourteen before being turned out into the world of work.

Where are they now, I wonder as I drive slowly on. What kind of lives have they led? Excited by my own success, I never gave them a second thought. I lost touch with Jenny and my other grammar school friends when I moved on to university. I lost touch with my university friends, perhaps inevitably, by stepping out of academic life. I walked out on my family, except for Yunga. I have had lovers, and some of the relationships have extended over many years, although with the many interruptions which are an integral part of a globe-trotting career. But I have never been prepared to tie myself down in marriage and in every case, now I come to think of it, I have been the first to recognise that it is time to bring the affair to an end and move on. I have tended to pride myself on my ability to remain on friendly terms with my old lovers, without reflecting that it might have been more admirable to work at sustaining the relationship rather than changing it. It is dismaying to be confronted with the thought that what I think of as level-headed self-sufficiency is really emotional shallowness.

Throughout all this period I have assumed that at least my relationship with Yunga has never weakened. It is because she is the only person whom I have unreservedly trusted all my life that the confessions of the past few days have come as such a shock. Should I accept them in silence, or is there time for that trust to be restored by talking the whole situation through? The answer to that question is still not clear to me as I turn the car into the garage of 43 Woodside Road.

5

As she has promised, Kate is still in the house when I return. But instead of keeping Yunga company she is sitting on the bottom stair. She waves away my instinctive alarm with a reassuring gesture.

'Your sister's making her telephone call.'

The phrasing suggests that this is some regular occurrence. Raising my eyebrows in interrogation, I await more details.

'It's an arrangement she has for this time every week. In fact, I ought to pass on to you ...' The nurse pulls a piece of paper from her pocket. 'If ever she's unable to make the call at this time herself, she'd like someone else to do it instead.'

Most international telephone codes are familiar to me. This number is in Canada. Who is James Wakeham?

Kate answers the question before it is put into words. 'An old friend, I understand.' At that moment there is a faint noise from the telephone in the hall to suggest that the extension receiver has been replaced.

'Right, then.' Kate stands up briskly. 'I'll just go and see if there's anything she wants and then I'll be off. Maggie's baking. And Gwen's here, resting.' She gestures towards the door of my father's old study. I am not to worry about being left alone.

In reality, to be alone with Yunga is what I most desire, but I am not allowed to get my wish. Even before Kate has finished whatever she is doing in the lounge, the front door bell rings. Today's visitors have arrived early – and are quick to explain that this is because others will be calling at four o'clock and they know that dear Yvonne prefers not to have more than two visitors at a time. They don't want to tire her.

They do tire her, of course. By the time the second pair – a married couple – depart at a quarter to six, the pools of blackness which encircle Yunga's eyes have deepened and her face is so pale that it seems no blood can be reaching it. I can tell that she is longing to slip away into sleep, but there is something she is determined to tell me. It has nothing to do, unfortunately, with the only subject that interests me at the moment.

'I know you won't like this, darling, but I want to talk about what happens afterwards. I've had plenty of time to think about it. The funeral service; that sort of thing. I've already given the choir warning. It gives me pleasure, thinking in advance about the music they'll sing. And there are gifts. Not worth listing in a will, but I've written then all down for you to deal with.'

She points at a sheet of paper lying on the table. I nod to show that I have seen it, but make no movement to pick it up.

'The two who have just left: I'd like them to have the piano. You won't want it, will you? Their daughter, Hilary.' She lacks the strength to formulate complete sentences. 'My best pupil ever. Eleven. Has to practise at school. With a piano of her own, she might ... Drink, please, Elda.'

This is the first occasion on which she has not been strong enough to reach out towards the table beside her. I pour a glass of orange juice and hold it to her lips, using my other arm to raise her into a more upright position. She weighs nothing. Nothing at all. And yet when I release her, her shoulders fall back into the pillows as though they are too heavy for her to control.

The drink appears to restore her energy. She takes and expels one deep breath. When she speaks again it is with her normal firmness of tone.

'I've left you the house.' There is a hint almost of amusement in her voice. 'I know you won't want it and I know you'll hate being lumbered with selling it. It's a sort of late revenge for your part in making it mine in the first place.'

'What do you mean, revenge?' I am startled and indignant. I have always reckoned that it was one of the two great favours I have done for Yunga in my life. My father was on his deathbed when I suggested that instead of leaving the house to his wife absolutely, he should bequeath her a life interest only, with Yunga to inherit on her death. I had arrived too late in his illness to realise that by that time he and my mother were still married only because neither of them would have contemplated divorce. There was no love between them. Rather, although he accepted my suggestion of sending for his lawyer, it must have been spite – possibly as much against me as against his wife – which prompted him to leave the property directly to his younger daughter.

'I thought it would make you feel secure, knowing you had a home.'

'As a prisoner feels secure! I could hardly turn Mummy out, either to sell the house or so that I could live in it alone. And I couldn't afford to buy or even rent anything else. Of course, I can see now that I ought to have packed my bags and run, just like you did. But I was living at home while I was at RAMDA. I did have plans for after that, as a matter of fact. But then she had her stroke, and I knew I was responsible for that, and ...'

She shrugs her shoulders in a gesture of helplessness. 'No, of course it wasn't really your fault. Just teasing. I was too bloody feeble. All my life, too bloody feeble.'

My eyes open in astonishment. In the whole of my life I have never heard Yunga swear. More disturbing than that, though, is the implication that she has not, as I have always assumed, been happy to spend the whole of her life in Kenbury. But even that must be pushed aside by the subject which has dominated my thoughts ever since her confession that morning.

'What you told me this morning, Yunga. I can't –'

'I don't want to talk about that.' She closes her eyes in what seems almost an act of defiance.

'But –'

'I'm sorry, but no. I ought not to have told you. I'm sorry about that, too. Let's forget it, shall we?'

She must realise that I can't possibly forget it, but at that moment the sound of a door opening and closing tells me that Gwen is coming on duty. In only a moment or two she will interrupt us while she takes Yunga's pulse, asks questions about her day, studies the programme of medication and administers whatever is scheduled for this hour of the evening.

All this duly happens while Yunga, after a single smile of greeting, continues to lie with her eyes closed. How can I be expected to know whether she is truly exhausted or just putting on an act?

'No telly news today, then?' Gwen's voice is bright, not acknowledging any change in her patient's condition. 'Very wise too. I've been listening on the radio. Nothing but gloom. A plane crash in Russia. Thousands starving in Afghanistan. Girl babies being allowed to die in Chinese orphanages. You know what I think will cause the next world war? A kind of global Rape of the Sabines. All those spoilt little Chinese boys with no one to marry when they grow up! Just one more tablet and that's the lot. Would you like some music instead?'

'No. A poem. Elda, will you read me a poem?'

'Sure.' It's impossible to reintroduce the subject of sexual abuse while Gwen is in the room. 'Any poem in particular?'

'Yes. It used to be a favourite of yours. You wrote and told me, when I was fifteen. So then I read it and it's been one of my favourites as well ever since. I was thinking about it while you were out for your walk. Trying to remember it right through. But I got stuck and then I was asleep. Swinburne. "The Garden of Proserpine".'

There is a moment of silence in which my astonishment communicates itself at least to Gwen.

'Yvonne, dear, I think you ought to open your eyes and study your sister's face. She appears to have been hit by a thunderbolt.'

Yunga's eyelids flicker, but she lacks the energy to open them. I make an attempt at an explanation.

'It's an odd coincidence, that's all. I was up on the hill this afternoon. Remembering the day Timmy was killed, because I was up there when it happened. That poem is the one I was reading aloud when the bomb came over, so I was thinking about the poem as well.'

'Telepathy!' suggests Gwen lightly. 'May I stay and listen?'

'I'm not sure that I can remember ...'

'Over there, on the top shelf,' Yunga tells me where the book is to be found without needing to look. 'Green.'

So there is no escape. It is a long poem, but even as I begin slowly to read I know that there is a tear-trap near the end. Perhaps Yunga will fall asleep before I reach it. Just as I have recently found it hard to tell whether she is listening to the answers of questions she has asked, so on this occasion I am unsure whether she is still awake. And even if she is, she may not be applying her mind to an understanding of the words. Yunga's first language is music, and Swinburne's poem is music, of a kind.

Now I have reached the dangerous verse.

> 'From too much love of living,
> From hope and fear set free,
> We thank with brief thanksgiving
> Whatever gods may be
> That no life lives for ever ...'

It's no good. My voice croaks to a halt. Tears are streaming down my eyes and I can't go on. Very faintly, from the chaise longue, Yunga completes the verse.

> 'That dead men rise up never,
> That even the longest river
> Winds somewhere safe to sea.'

Neither of us is prepared to finish the poem. Gwen waits for a moment and then, as though skimming a stone across water, shatters the surface tension with a reference to supper. But Yunga is not hungry, and it is clear that Gwen has not expected her to be. She folds back the sheets on the high hospital bed, carries Yunga across to it and makes her comfortable for the night, although it is only half-past six. Then she disappears to the kitchen. Unlike Kate, she is prepared to undertake a housekeeperly role during her hours of duty. Every evening so far she has provided a meal for me as well as for her patient and herself, and she is about to do the same today.

This is my chance, I hope, to talk privately with Yunga at last; but it takes me only a few seconds to realise that my hope will not be realised. Whether or not she was only pretending to sleep earlier, she is not pretending now.

Sitting beside the bed, I find the pattern of her breathing disturbing. Sometimes she breathes in so heavily that it is almost a snore, and sometimes this is followed by an unduly long period in which she seems not to breathe at all. I hold my own breath to match hers, and more than once am on the point of leaning forward to prod her into wakefulness. But always at the last minute she splutters back into a more regular rhythm for a little while.

After a longer absence than usual Gwen opens the door.

'I've had my supper,' she tells me. 'So now I can be here while you have yours. That last tablet will have knocked her out for eight hours, so there's not really much point in your sitting with her this evening. Unless you want to, of course. I shall stay in here all night.'

She hasn't felt it necessary to do that in the past. The change of routine does nothing to cheer me. I do in fact return to the lounge after eating, but quickly recognise that I shall have to wait for a new day before we can talk. Instead, I put one of Yunga's compact discs on to play, keeping the volume low but hoping that the sound will penetrate her sleep to soothe her spirit.

At ten o'clock Gwen looks up from her book.

'Get some sleep.' It is an order, not a suggestion. 'If you want to sit with her again, I'll call you to come down at three o'clock. If there's going to be any change, it will be then.'

I go upstairs without question and take a hot bath; but how can I possibly be expected to sleep through what may be the last moments of Yunga's life? And yet I cannot bring myself to return to her bedside, lest I should be unable to resist the urge to shake her out of her refuge of sleep and force her to answer my questions. This is how a potential murderer must feel, balanced on a knife-edge of control and knowing that the only hope for himself and his chosen victim is to put distance between them. Instead, I sit down on a middle stair, hugging my knees and listening for sounds.

To my shame, I must after all have fallen asleep, for at some early hour of the morning I am awakened: by what? By a cry? It is over and gone before my senses are sufficiently alert to identify the sound, but there must have been something. I keep very still in the darkness, my ears straining to hear.

From the lounge downstairs there is a movement, a creak of furniture. A voice – it is Yunga's voice – begins to speak. I cannot make out the words, but the tone in which she speaks is a penetrating one. It is so high-pitched as to be almost a wail, and there is an urgency about it which fills me with alarm. Gwen will be in the room already, but I almost fall down the stairs in my haste to find out what is happening.

Yunga is still speaking, shouting, as I open the door.

'Tell her!' she says. Always before her voice when speaking to Gwen has been gentle and grateful, but now she is giving an order.

By the pale light which is left on all through the night I can see Gwen bending over Yunga's high bed. She looks up as I appear, and Yunga, sensing that she has lost the nurse's attention repeats the urgent command. 'Tell her!'

'Tell what?' But even as I ask the question something horrific happens. Yunga's back arches convulsively and her whole body seems to explode. A foul stench fills the air and as I hurl myself towards her I can see blood trickling from the side of her mouth.

'Get away, please.' Gwen is having to fight her patient to keep her in bed. Suddenly, though, Yunga's writhings stop and she collapses back on to the bed. Gwen, leaning over her, is shuddering with effort; and although I have been only a spectator, I am shuddering as well. This is not the peaceful passing I had envisaged. I can hear myself groaning aloud.

'Just sit down over there for a moment, will you?' Gwen has things to do and I am not to be allowed to approach just yet. I sit in one of the visitors' chairs with my head buried in my hands, unaware of how much time is passing.

'If you want to come now ...' Gwen has turned on a brighter light. She stands beside me as I look down. Yunga's face is clean again: bloodless in every sense. Her eyes are closed and she looks as though she is sleeping peacefully. There is a smile on her face. I bend down to kiss her forehead, but it is a cold gesture. There is nobody there.

After a little while Gwen takes my hand and leads me back to the chair. She must realise that I have something to ask her.

'"Tell her!" she was saying. Did she mean me? What were you to tell me?'

'She wanted you to know –'

I interrupt her. 'In direct speech, if you can. Exactly what she said.'

Gwen sits down to face me and the carefulness of her speech makes it clear that she is quoting directly, word for word, as I have asked. 'She said, "Tell Jo that it didn't happen. I was fibbing. Because I was always jealous. Because he loved you so much even when you went away. I'm sorry. Tell her."'

'That was all?'

'She repeated "Tell her!" several times, but yes, that was all.'

'What am I supposed to think?' Almost without realising it, I find that I am speaking – although only to myself – out loud. 'How can I know what to believe?'

Assuming that I am looking for an answer, Gwen provides one.

'According to lawyers, deathbed confessions are assumed to be true. As long as the person involved knows that she's dying, and Yvonne did. A confession is what this was, I take it.'

There is no point in arguing with Gwen, who isn't aware of what is at stake. But it's not as simple as she makes it sound. Yunga could simply have been saying what she knew I wanted to hear.

Oh, Yunga, why couldn't you stay alive one more day? Just one.

6

Through the whole of the day which follows Yunga's early-morning death I walk like a zombie. Something so expected ought not to come as a shock, but it does. Why doesn't the whole world come to a standstill for a few hours, out of respect? Instead of that, I am pressed into a bustle of activity. It is a conspiracy to prevent me from having any time to mourn.

Dr Morris arrives early, expressing his sympathy as he signs the medical certificate. Because I am in a sense a foreigner, he presents me with a booklet which tells me what to do after a death. 'Best to get cracking straightaway,' he suggests. 'It can all drag on a bit.' He gives me the address of the local registrar as a hint about where the getting cracking process should start.

By six o'clock in the evening I am exhausted. I have visited the registrar, a funeral director, the probate office and an estate agent. I have put a notice in the local paper and called the number of the mysterious James Wakeham, leaving a message with his answering service. I have made cups of tea for people who came to condole and have taken advantage of their visits to begin the process of making the gifts which Yunga has listed. I have thanked Gwen and Kate for their care and given them presents. What I have not been able to do until now is to sit down alone and think.

I ought simply to be mourning: indulging my personal sense of loss. But instead, as I at last collapse with a glass of whisky, I have to fight what is almost anger that Yunga should leave such emotional chaos behind her, because I don't know what to believe. If her first confession was true, then I not only have to come to terms with a new view of my father as a child abuser but must accept that Yunga herself has been keeping an important secret from me for almost all her life.

In the moment before her death she claimed that the story was untrue – but does that make the situation any better? Her only reason for lying could be that she had for a long time harboured some kind of resentment or envy which right at the end had spilled out of control: if Gwen's report was accurate, then she admitted as much herself. I find that just as hard to accept as the suppression of the truth which is its alternative. In either case, our relationship has been wrecked in a way that death on its own could never have wrecked it, while death has made salvage impossible. And still I don't really know which story to believe.

'Deathbed confessions are true,' Gwen assured me; but I'm not sure. There was too much detail in the earlier version for it to be entirely invented. Unless of course this was the kind of sexual fantasising that keeps therapists in business. Christ, what a mess! Can I still love the memory of my father, or must I feel disgust for him? And beyond all this is my sense of personal guilt. 'You weren't there!'

Three whiskies later I pick up the telephone. Dr Morris, who could reasonably be indignant about this interruption of his home life, is sympathetic as he feels his way cautiously through what may be the incoherence of my questions. Yes, anyone enduring the regime of drugs prescribed for my sister during her last few weeks of life might very possibly suffer confusion and hallucinations. These most commonly take the form of imagining the presence in the room of people who have long been dead or of claiming with complete conviction that nurses have been seen stealing or otherwise behaving improperly, but there could certainly be other manifestations. Could the drugs inspire false memories, for example? That's quite possible, yes.

Is he, out of kindness, deducing what I want him to say and therefore saying it? No. I have asked him a direct question and must trust him to have answered it honestly. Yunga was a sick woman who was not responsible for her words or actions. I am entitled to remember my father as the anxious and loving man who visited me daily during my long sojourn in hospital; as the careful and loving man who organised family treats and holidays in the years before the war disrupted every aspect of normal life; and as the clever and loving man who analysed my essays and trained my mind as I prepared for the Cambridge scholarship examination. Stop worrying, Jo. Time for bed.

If I want to be quiet, if I want to be alone, next morning I have my wish. There are no birds singing when I awaken. There are none of the sounds which would mean that Kate has arrived to be briefed by Gwen. No kettle is boiling. No window is being thrown open. The house, all its furniture put back in place, is no longer a hospital annexe; but it is no longer a home either.

Another day of chores lies ahead, but from one duty I am excused. There is a funeral service to be arranged, but not by me.

Who will come to my own funeral? Fay, I suppose, but after that? Each of the three men who have loved me for more than a few nights is dead already. My friends – and I have many – are scattered throughout the world. Even if someone were to go through my address book there would be no time to summon them; nor, I think, are they the sort of people who would think the journey worthwhile. My neighbours are always new neighbours. I attend no church, so that any minister of religion who was asked to deliver a eulogy could do no more than recite my entry from the *International Who's Who of Women*. In any case, who would there be to ask him? I have always assumed that Yunga would survive me. Now the thought flutters across my mind that as well as making a new will, I need to find a new executor. It flutters, but does not rest. By the time my funeral arrangements come to be made, I shall have no interest in the details.

Yunga has not shared this attitude. She has fixed everything but the date. Mary from across the road comes to call, worried lest she is intruding too early upon my grief, but anxious to let me know the position before I embark on unnecessary alternatives.

'It was in case you couldn't get here in time,' she explains nervously, but we both know that this is not the whole truth. I may think of myself as having been close to my sister, but I know too little about the details of her day-to-day life in Kenbury to avoid mistakes. My only contribution to the service is indicated by a gap in the programme for 'Hymn of Jolene's choice'. I am not even expected to provide the refreshments which customarily follow a funeral. 'There'll be too many people to come back to the house,' Mary tells me. 'It will be easier to manage in the social hall at the church. The ladies of the choir will look after all that.'

And so it is almost as a visitor that I take my seat in the front row of the crematorium chapel a few days later. It is the largest of the three chapels, but extra chairs are still being carried in as the service starts. It seems that the whole congregation for which Yunga acted as organist has turned up, and also, as I discover later, old pupils whom she has taught at school or at home and members of the families for whose demented or dying relatives she has cared in her time.

A double slot has been booked to avoid any feeling of rush and, as is suitable, there is a great deal of music in the service.

Most of the hymns, lively in a modern way, are unknown to me. When it comes to the hymn that I have been allowed to choose, however, it is the congregation which is at a loss. But the choir, assembled in a gallery, has practised it. Just as well, since this is the moment when tears close my throat.

> Lord, it is good for us to share
> The higher, purer mountain air.

It is a selfish choice. The mountain air is mine, not Yunga's; she has lived her life in the lowlands. But I was remembering, when I chose it, an expedition which she and I made together during her visit to Santa Fe less than a year before. The air was indeed high and pure as we explored the canyons of the Mesa Verde. Yunga was happy with me that day. There was no shadow on her future. I have a photograph of her, laughing, with her hair blowing in the wind. I want to remember her like that.

At the end of the service, the church choir which Yunga has trained for so many years stands to sing the last of her choices: the last part of Verdi's *Requiem*. They are joined by another thirty or forty singers, members of the choral society which she also trained and conducted for concerts. They are all amateurs, naturally, and here must make do with an organ rather than full orchestra, but the drama of the music carries them through. '*Libera me!*' they sing. 'Set me free!' Their voices soar, in triumph rather than sadness. This is happy music, but its effect is to increase my unhappiness. Have I been wrong to assume that for all these years Yunga has been content with her quiet, unadventurous life? Has she in fact always secretly longed to escape? *'Libera me!'* No. that's a ridiculous idea. She was a musician. She has chosen this because it is marvellous music. But I am unable to concentrate on the music any longer because a curtain has opened and rollers are turning. The coffin moves away and out of sight. This is an ending.

Not for me, though. Back in the church hall a feast has been laid out: sandwiches, biscuits, and enough home-made cake to feed the whole of Kenbury. The members of the choir, having made a quick exit from their gallery, are already pouring milk into teacups by the time the rest of us arrive.

I have no duties in the tea party. I have not laid out cups and I shall not be expected to wash them up. I am, nevertheless, in one sense a hostess. I make a little speech to thank everyone for coming, and also for the love and support they have given my sister during her illness. In these surroundings, it is easy to fall into church-speak.

People queue up to talk to me about my sister and then queue up again to say goodbye, squeezing rather than merely shaking my hand. As china begins to rattle in the kitchenette, only one of the tea-party guests remains, and it is clear from the way he approaches me that he has chosen deliberately to be the last to leave.

'Hello, Jo,' he says, holding out a hand and speaking in a Canadian voice. 'I'm James.'

7

'James Wakeham?' Even before he approaches me I have guessed, watching him work the room; the only stranger in a closely knit group. Socially confident in introducing himself, asking questions, nodding in recognition of some familiar fact or name. He is a tall, good-looking man with very thick and wavy white hair. His face is tanned to a degree that speaks of an outdoor life. He is smiling as though he has known me for years.

'Right. It was good of you to call me so quickly.'

'I hadn't expected you to come today, though. It's a long way.'

'Yes. Well. Yvonne was very special. I expect she's talked to you about me, has she?'

Another secret. Another part of her life from which I have been excluded. It seems best to be honest. 'No. Not a word.'

'Oh.' He is disconcerted. 'So I suppose –'

'I'd like to hear, though. If you're willing to talk about it? We might have dinner together, if you're free. Not in the house, I don't mean.' Quite apart from the fact that I don't know whether there is any food there, cooking has never been an activity on which I am prepared to waste time if someone else can be paid to do it for me. 'But there must be somewhere –'

We are both strangers to modern Kenbury, and the moment of silence suggests a shared doubt about its gourmet possibilities.

'My hotel has a restaurant,' volunteers James at last. 'I don't know anything about it, but ... Eight o'clock, say?'

'Fine. Except ... I don't know how long you're planning to stay in England. But Yunga – Yvonne, I mean – wanted you to take anything from the house that you'd like to have.'

'Why don't we go there now, then? I plan to fly home tomorrow.'

Glad at the thought of company in the empty house, I leave him alone for a moment while I thank the members of the choir both for their singing and for their hard work in providing the tea. A good deal of kissing and embracing goes on, to which I submit although I am not really a social kisser. Like James, they are anxious to tell me what a special person my sister was.

Half an hour later I unlock the door of 43 Woodside Road. James looks round curiously as he steps inside, and I am curious in a different way.

'You've been here before, I imagine? Before it was redecorated, perhaps.'

'No, never. Yvonne wouldn't invite me here. She said that after we were married she wanted to make a complete break from her past life. She didn't want to think of me as ever having been in this house. I thought it was a bit odd. But compared with the sort of girls who are always running home to their mothers, it seemed an oddness in the right direction.'

'You were actually going to be married?' After a moment's hesitation I lead the way into the lounge. It is a lounge again, with its full complement of sofas and arm chairs. The hospital bed has gone and the chaise longue is simply another article of furniture, unobtrusive against a wall. But the ghost of Yunga's last cry still hovers in the air. As I open the French windows to the garden, I am glad of a companion who doesn't know what has happened in this room.

'I thought she'd have told you.' He sits down and shakes his head at the offer of a drink. 'Not in the beginning, when it was all a secret, and not at the end, after she'd funked out; but there was a time in the middle when I thought she'd have told you.'

'Tell me now.'

'We were at college together.'

'RAMDA?'

'Right. I played the cello. You went to university, didn't you? Colleges of music are very different from universities. A collection of first-year students from all over the country, each of them used to being head and shoulders above anyone else on their own instrument in their own region. All ambitious to be soloists, virtuosi. All except one or two very gradually coming to terms with the discovery that they're good but not brilliant, that they're always going to be the supporters and not the stars. Teachers. Orchestral players. Ambition takes quite a knock. It's tough. Yunga and I went through that together.'

'And you fell in love?'

'Right. In a slow sort of way. I mean we didn't have any money between us, and we weren't likely to have any for some time. But there didn't seem any hurry. It was just fun, being together, doing things in London.'

'Did you –?'

'No. I'm talking about the fifties. Girls didn't much, then. Not till they were definitely engaged, anyway. The pill hadn't been invented, and nothing else was absolutely reliable. I tried to persuade her once or twice, because after all, if there had been an accident we could have got married quickly and hang the lack of money. But I knew she was a churchy sort of girl. It didn't really surprise me when she said no; wait. We had a sort of understanding. That we'd get officially engaged on the day we both graduated. And get married when the first one of us got a job.'

'But it didn't work out like that?'

'It was queer,' said James. ''I never really understood. When we were in our last year her father, your father, died. 1957, I think it was. You came home when he was ill; I remember Yvonne telling me. That was the time when I thought she might have said something.'

I shake my head, though I would have thought so too.

'After he died, she seemed to change. First of all she was upset, of course. Then she became excited in an odd sort of way. Started talking about how we might go off somewhere quite different. Make new lives for ourselves. That was when I started finding out what sort of jobs were going in Canada.'

James may not want a drink, but I do. I produce the bottle of whisky, which has been taking quite a beating over the past few days, and this time he nods his head.

'I got a summer job that year,' he tells me. 'In Brighton just for the holiday season. Yvonne came down for a visit. No last train home to be caught. No mother waiting up anxiously. I got excited, and this time she didn't say "Wait".'

He gives a sigh and a wave of nausea sweeps over me. I know what he is going to tell me.

'But?' I prompt him.

'I don't know. I really don't know. It wasn't ordinary shyness. I tried to be slow. I tried to be gentle. And she was trying too, in a sort of way. But she didn't seem able to come close, to go through with it. Obviously I wasn't going to force anything. I thought that maybe, church person like her, the inhibitions were too great. We'll leave it, I said. Get married first. Do things the right way round. The oddest thing was, she said no to that. It would be worse, she said, if we got married and then it didn't work. She promised to try harder next time.'

He laughs, a sad kind of laugh, as he raises his glass. 'Your health. Well, it doesn't do much for a chap's morale when his girl has to try harder. I was only twenty-one myself. Not exactly a man of the world. Not over-brimming with confidence. Next time we tried it wasn't quite so spontaneous. More like a scientific experiment. Which still didn't work. Yvonne was crying. Saying it was all her fault. Saying there was something she needed to do which would sort it all out. Next thing I knew, she'd run back to mother. And next thing after that, her mother had had a stroke and Yvonne was sorry, terribly, terribly sorry, but she'd have to stay at home to look after her. For as long as it might take, and I did understand, didn't I? Well, I bloody well *didn't* understand, excuse my language.'

I can understand all right. All the confusion of the past few days has fallen away. It is a relief, in a way, to know which of Yunga's two declarations is the truth. I can understand her feeling that she must confess something to somebody if she was to start a marriage with a clean slate. Admitting to James that she was not a virgin must have proved too much for her – and perhaps it was the first experience of a legitimate love which made her at last feel ashamed that she had not, when she became an adult, freed herself from her father's demands. In confessing instead to her mother she might have been hoping for sympathy or advice; but she certainly didn't get either.

Shall I give James the explanation which was denied him at the time? No, what good can it do? And in any case he is still talking. Probably he has never been able to discuss this with anyone else before. He is clearing his own mind as well as mine.

'I tried to get her to go to a doctor. On her own behalf, I mean, not her mother's. Or a psychiatrist. But she wouldn't even talk about it. I gave up in the end. Went off to Canada, as we'd planned. But on my own.'

'To play the cello?'

'No. To train as an accountant. I've had a good life. In Vancouver. Plenty of work, plenty of money, plenty of sailing.'

'A wife?'

'Yes, for a bit. Didn't work out. Two good kids, though.'

'But you kept in touch with Yvonne?'

'She wrote to me. After about a year. Repeated the stuff about being sorry. Said she'd had a bad experience as a child and now she couldn't bear to be touched. Nothing to do with me personally, she said. There'd never be anyone else. More apologies. She hoped perhaps we could be friends. That's what they always say, the girls who shove you in the shit; but there was something about this letter ... She meant it. I wrote back. It did happen – the friendship, I mean. A letter every month, each way, for forty years. The diary sort of letter, describing our lives, you know. Writing the sort of things that we wouldn't want to tell anyone close at hand. They meant a lot to me, those letters. I shall miss –'

He is upset. Putting down his glass, he stretches out a hand to take mine and for a moment we are as close as though we are the two who enjoyed the friendship.

'You never saw her again?' I check.

'No. It could have spoilt things. Even when I came to England I didn't look her up. That suited her as well. Did you know, Jo? This bad experience she mentioned: did you know about it?'

'Not at the time. I do now.' But I can tell that he doesn't want to know the details. I pour him another whisky and answer a few questions about Yunga's illness. Then I invite him to come upstairs, to the bedroom which used to be hers, in which I have spread out all those of her personal possessions which have not been specifically earmarked but are to be distributed amongst friends. There is a parcel already wrapped and addressed to James, but he can take anything else he likes.

'Photographs,' he says. 'I have one of her at the age of eighteen. I've only been able to age her in my mind since then. Are there any?'

That's an easy one. Every year I have snapped her on the holidays we have spent together, and she has devoted an album to those pictures alone. Setting it down in front of him I watch as he turns the pages, as Yunga moves through her twenties, thirties, forties, fifties. On the last page she stands on the edge of a Mesa Verde canyon with the wind blowing her hair, and then steps out of the sea on a Barbados beach, a plump but healthy little figure, her skin glistening with oil. 'All yours,' I tell him as we stare down at the page together.

'Thanks. Nothing else, then. And I think, if you don't mind ... I ate too much cake at that tea. Don't really have any appetite for anything else.'

'My own feeling exactly. Shall I call you a taxi?'

'No, thanks. The hotel's not far away.' He follows me downstairs, but ignores my outstretched hand. 'My nearly sister-in-law. Yvonne wrote so much about you. She was so proud. It's good to have met you at last.' He kisses me as an affectionate nearly brother-in-law and then takes a card from his wallet. 'If you're ever in Vancouver ...'

'Thanks.' Neither of us expects the offer to be taken up, but I might write. He might write. There is a link between us.

After he leaves I sit on the stairs, just as I sat on the night of Yunga's death. Peace descends on my spirit. There is no room for doubt and so the door is opened to acceptance. My father was a pervert, my mother was a tyrant, my sister was a victim and I have been grievously deceived. But they are all dead. There is no point in agonising any further. *Libera me!* Yunga is free, and so am I.

8

The estate agent has arrived with his camera and his tape measure. The house is about to be reduced to a set of particulars. Semi-detached, quiet street, favoured position, convenient to schools, shops, stations. Garage, front and back gardens (in untended condition, but this will not be mentioned). Attic room with good storage space. Bedrooms 1, 2, 3 and 4. None of them, unfortunately, with en suite bathroom. Two receps, bkfst rm. Kitchen in need of modernisation. That's for sure.

Particulars have no history. The dining room is just a dining room. No one, once I have left, will know that it was once the study of a schoolmaster who had longed to be a professor, or that more recently it served as the bedroom of an untidy but kindly nurse. Not important.

'How long do you think it will take to sell?' I ask the young estate agent, neatly dressed in white shirt and dark suit. I have read gloomy reports about the housing market in England and expect him to be cautious. But his eyes are bright with confidence.

'Not long at all, as long as the price is right. Inside the Golden Triangle, you see. There are always people waiting for something to come on the market.'

'Golden Triangle?' The words conjure up a picture of peasants driving in expensive cars to their opium fields. I have been to the Golden Triangle. But the young man is hurrying to explain.

'So much of Kenbury has gone downhill in the past twenty or thirty years. The larger houses converted into flats. And the smaller ones taken over by ...' He pauses, not knowing quite how to describe the influx of brown faces (which I have noticed for myself) without appearing to be racist. 'By families who don't always spend enough on upkeep of their homes. And of course the fact that the suburb was developed before car ownership became general means that so few properties have garages. But these three streets here –' He flips over the pages on his clip-board to reveal a map of the local area and points with a clean-nailed finger to Woodside Road, Grove Road and Brook Road. 'There's no through traffic. All the properties have garages. The gardens aren't large, but people don't want too much to manage these days. And the houses themselves are exactly the right size for family occupation. Most desirable. You must find it a wrench to leave?'

Only with an effort can I prevent myself from laughing. A wrench? When there are so many beautiful places in the world, so many exciting places, why should anyone want to live in 43 Woodside Road? But it's just as well that the agent at least can feel enthusiastic. I allot him the right to sell. I agree the asking price he suggests. I make it clear that he, and not I, must show round all prospective clients, and give him the name of Yunga's solicitor, now mine, who will handle the contract of sale as soon as he has obtained the grant of probate which makes the house legally mine to sell.

Once that has been done, a charity will find a use for any furniture which still remains after Yunga's friends have taken their pick. But a chore that I cannot avoid will be to go through the house and throw out all the junk. Starting now; at the top. I carry half a dozen black plastic bags up to the attic.

There are two large cupboards extending under the roof right to the eaves. My childhood darkroom I have already emptied in the search for old photographs. Now I pull packing cases out of the other space. Experience tells me that the fastest way to deal with them is to tip everything on to the floor, removing the temptation to linger in reminiscence or doubt when removing one item at a time. Confronted with such a mess, it doesn't take too long to toss away battered children's toys with which no grandchildren will ever play, theatre programmes which will stir no more memories, old newspapers which no one will ever consult. Parcels of moth-nibbled clothes serve as a reminder that my mother, living through years of rationing, saved everything which could be cut up and re-used to make clothes for Yunga, while a bulky bundle of black-out curtains perhaps reflects her fear that war might one day return. Ruefully I think of all the press stories which describe priceless antiques or long-lost Old Master paintings discovered in just such an attic turn-out. Not in this one.

Before too long, moving with ruthless speed, I have reduced the clutter to a pile of papers which require closer inspection; and now I do begin to linger. Over two scrapbooks, first of all: their large pages brown with age. The first records my mother's small triumphs as a child taking ballet examinations and appearing in a pantomime. Growing older, she added tap to her repertoire and won a competition. There are photographs of charity concerts, but the record comes to an end in 1925. The last pages of the scrapbook are empty.

The second book is very similar, although its pages are a lighter shade of brown. This records little Yunga's musical career as she progressed up the year-groups of the Kenbury music festival, always winning in the piano competitions and often also commended for voice. Her success in winning a place at the Royal Academy for Music and Dramatic Art is recorded, and so are two of her concert appearances there. This scrapbook also ends when its subject is twenty.

One cutting has been left loose between the pages. It announces that Jolene Bradley, of Kenbury Grammar School for Girls, has been successful in winning one of the coveted scholarships to Girton College, Cambridge. Nothing else in my own childhood, obviously, was worthy of press notice. Out go the scrapbooks.

Now for some more formal documents. Birth certificates, for example, which perhaps I had better keep because you never know. I note with interest that my father's place of birth is recorded as being Kinderley Court: where and what is that?

A large brown envelope, stiffened with cardboard, is filled with proof photographs – and now my eyes do open wide, because the beautiful woman they depict is unmistakably my mother. They must have been taken at much the same time as the familiar portrait which marked her engagement.

These are rather different from that silver-framed frozen moment of youth which stood on the grand piano while the lines deepened on its subject's face; although they show the same technical skill on the part of the photographer. Some of them depict her in period dress, and it is easy to tell that she is being posed in the style of different artists: Gainsborough, Degas, Manet. And Goya. This is the moment when I am knocked back by astonishment, for here is not only the Maja Clothed but the Maja Unclothed as well. The pose is copied faithfully, but the voluptuous body that Goya painted has been replaced by one that is small-breasted and slim-hipped: my mother in her youth. The sight is embarrassing, even shocking. Besides, parents ought always to be older than their children.

I am trespassing here, but the temptation cannot be resisted, for there is more nudity to come. A Botticelli. A Bonnard, with water glistening on a bather's skin. And then, right at the bottom, something different again. The photographer has fitted himself into the picture to be Adam to Dürer's Eve.

At first glance Adam looks a little like my father; but the resemblance ends with the face. This man is tall and thin. In his youth my father may have been slimmer than he was when I knew him, but he was always below average height.

How rash it is to assume that anything can remain hidden for ever! If my mother had died before her husband, what would he have felt as he discovered and studied these nude poses? It is hard to believe that he could have been aware at the time of what was taking place. It is equally hard to believe that this Adam and this Eve were nothing more than casual acquaintances.

Past history. The photographs join the black-out curtains in one of the plastic bags.

A single page from an old newspaper almost goes the same way without pause, on the assumption that it was merely wrapping something up, but the name 'Bradley' catches my eye just in time, and I smooth it out on the uncarpeted floor.

It is an obituary – and now the shocks are coming thick and fast, because its subject proves to be a man whom I have never met but have hero-worshipped throughout my adult life. Like almost everyone else, I have never known his real name, but the surname proves to be the same as my own. It is fifty years since he died, but as I read the narrow columns of type my heart thumps with as much distress as if it were today's unexpected news.

Mortimer 'Terts' Bradley

The death is announced of one of this century's outstanding photographers. Always professionally using his school nickname of 'Terts', he was able to travel unostentatiously under his real name so that the perpetrators of the many cruelties he recorded during his lifetime became aware of his visits only after he had returned to his own country and published his exposés.

Mortimer Bradley was born in 1890, the third son of Henry and Edith Bradley. After the early death of both parents he was brought up by his grandfather, Lord Mortimer of Kinderley, at Kinderley Court. He was educated at Croxton, and after leaving school went to work at Bradley's, at that time a prosperous investment and trading company of which his father had been the senior partner. It was during this period that his interest in photography, already sparked during his schooldays, took on a more professional aspect when his sister Elizabeth was presented at court and he was pressed to photograph many of her fellow debutantes. His first lighthearted collection, *The Season*, was published in 1915 but attracted little attention in the grimmer atmosphere of the time.

In 1914 he volunteered to join the Royal Flying Corps as a pilot. A serious head wound during the Battle of the Somme in 1916 left him unable to continue flying, but instead he used his technical expertise to improve the primitive system of aerial photography which had been in use until then.

A seminal experience in his life came when, during a visit to India after the war, he witnessed the suttee burning of a young widow: a custom forbidden but not eradicated by the British authorities. He began to roam the world, seeking out and recording cases of slavery, child labour abuse, torture, and extreme poverty. In this work, which was naturally unpopular with those responsible for permitting it, he was greatly helped by his friendship with Mr Nathan Rose, whose magazine, *Our World*, resolutely continued to publish his photographs in spite of pressure which on one occasion included the temporary withdrawal of an ambassador.

In 1939, at the age of forty-nine, Bradley offered his services as a war photographer; and for a time, as he recorded the often comic improvisations of civilians coping with the unexpected, he recovered the lightness of mood which he had not displayed since his experiments with Surrealist photography during the twenties.

At the end of the war, however, he accompanied the British forces who were the first to enter the Belsen concentration camp. The pictures he took on that occasion horrified the world, and the effect on Bradley himself was so traumatic that it reactivated the head wound he had suffered in 1916, causing him to lose his sight and so bringing his career to an end.

In a radio interview in 1933 Bradley claimed that his ambition was to act as the eyes of the world, enabling people everywhere to become aware of scenes that they could not hope to witness for themselves. Many of those who admired both his technical skill and his courage rated his work more highly even than that, describing him rather as 'the conscience of the world'.

During the years of his blindness, he returned to Kinderley Court, where he was cared for by his sister Elizabeth, who survives him. He never married.

When I come to the end of the obituary I read it through for a second time, this time hardly able to breathe. Mortimer Bradley, born in 1890, was brought up at Kinderley Court. Aden Bradley, my father, was born in 1904 at Kinderley Court. They have to be brothers. And Mortimer was cared for by his sister Elizabeth, who must be my Aunt Libby.

Terts was my uncle. Why didn't anyone tell me? Why didn't he tell me himself?

I am being stupid, although I am not aware of it yet. I still haven't cottoned on to the truth.

9

I continue to stare at the obituary as I put out a hand to grope for the next sheet of paper to be picked off the floor. It proves to be a letter, written by someone who is a careless typist – or, as I soon realise, a blind one. The errors in it are not spelling mistakes but mis-hit keys.

> Dear Jessica,
> I have kept my promise never to communicate with Jolene. But this year she will celebrate her twenty-first birthday. To such a celebration it would be reasonable, would it not, to invite all her relations as well as friends? If you allowed me to join you I would only be one amongst many, of no significance. It is too late for me to see her, but it would give me great happiness to meet her just once and to hear from her lips what she hopes to do with her life.
>
> T.

Along the bottom of the letter is written in my mother's round, still schoolgirlish handwriting: 'Told him, too late. Gone away'.

Yes, that's right. I celebrated my twenty-first birthday in Switzerland instead of in the church social hall. All I remember of the day is an intense relief that I was my own woman at last, because for the first year of my escapade I had never been quite sure whether my father might use some legal power to haul me home again.

Already the penny is beginning to drop; but it is another pair of letters, one of them written ten years later by my Aunt Libby, which sends it clanking down into certainty.

Dear Jessica,
After Terts's death I found the envelope which I now enclose. I don't know anything about its contents, but he left a note asking me to send it to Jolene after Aden's death. I have kept it with the intention of doing so – although I hope the occasion will not arise for many years yet. But I am about to go into hospital for an operation and, although naturally I hope that it will be successful and that I shall soon be back at Kinderley again, I have had to consider what might happen if things go wrong. I have set up a charitable trust in order that my work here may continue, so that should be all right. For the rest, I am just trying to tidy things up, and I think it would be better if you were to become the guardian of Terts's letter. I take it that he doesn't want Aden to know about it, whatever it is, so you may choose to keep it in a bank.

I have never understood Aden's refusal to let us help him, or even to recognise our existence. It's obviously too late now to patch up, whatever quarrel took place between the two brothers, but I hope that perhaps the letter I enclose may be intended to ensure that that dispute doesn't continue into a new generation.

With all best wishes,
Libby

The envelope which bears the single inscription *Jolene* has been torn open. By whom? I wonder. By my mother, anxious to know what I am about to be told? By my father, enraged at the discovery that something is being kept from him? I came home when my father was dying. I was here for his funeral. I could have been given the letter then. What is it that I have never been allowed to know? Even before I pull out the sheet of cream deckled paper, embossed with the address of Kinderley Court and dated in 1947, I have guessed the answer.

My dear Jolene,
When you read this, it will be because my brother, Aden, is dead. You are mourning him, I expect. I am sure that you have loved him, just as I am sure that he has been a kind and loving father to you throughout your childhood. Nothing that I tell you now should change that. But I have devoted my life to bringing the truth to light, and I would not want my own daughter to be the only person I have left for ever in the dark.

Yes, that's it. My daughter. Aden was not your father, Jolene. Your mother and I fell in love, although we ought not to have done, because she was already engaged to my brother. I have a great deal to be ashamed of. Perhaps by the time you read this you too will have learned how it feels to be swept out of the channel of decency by the swift current of passion. I would have married her as soon as I learned she was pregnant, but a previous marriage, almost forgotten but never dissolved, made this impossible.

She was young and frightened. I hope you will find it in your heart to forgive her for the deceit she practised in hurrying to marry her fiancé and ensure that you were born legitimately. She, I'm sure, is as much ashamed as I am.

You will probably find it more difficult to forgive me – for being your father in the first place, but in the second place for not being your father in any but the biological sense. I promised your mother that I would never do or say anything to jeopardise the happiness of her marriage, and I have kept that promise. It has cost me dearly. I have longed to know you and I have wished that you could know me. You can learn a little about the way I have spent my life if you are able to search out any of the books compiled by 'Terts', the name I have used as a photographer.

When your mother wrote to tell me, a little while ago, that you had abandoned your university course and left home to live abroad, I was dismayed in one sense but at the same time glad to recognise a spirit of adventure which I hope you have inherited from me. By the time you read this letter – no doubt many years after I am writing it – you will have had time to forge a career of your own. I hope you have had, and will continue to have, a happy life: and if you are ambitious for success in some field, I hope you will achieve that as well.

I recognise that it is selfish of me to 'claim' you in this way, when silence might have been kinder. But as I draw towards the end of my own life, I feel the need to say just once how much I have always loved you, the thought of you, growing up. My dear daughter.

With love, much love, from

Your father, Terts Bradley

There is silence in the attic. Not even a creaking or cracking of old bones disturbs it as I rise to my feet from the cross-legged position in which I have been sitting on the floor, but the need to make a noise is almost overwhelming. I am not sure exactly what is meant by a primal scream, but nothing less would encompass the mixture of anguish and rage which overcomes me now. I want the ends of the earth to hear me shout and scream; but my upbringing is too strong for me. The next-door neighbours must not be disturbed. Instead I pant and gulp in the effort to stifle my distress.

Terts, my father! Of all the people in the world, if I could have chosen my own father it would have been Terts; and to know that it would not have been simply a fantasy is too much to bear. How could they not tell me? Perhaps my father, I mean Aden, never knew. But my mother! After Terts's death perhaps, and after Aden's death certainly, she should have told me. I was a photographer myself by then. She must have realised how much the link would have meant to me. But because – I suppose – she was frightened that I would judge her harshly ... Oh, I hate her, I hate her, I hate her!

It is hatred as much as unhappiness and a need to be in the open air which sends me rushing down the stairs and out of the house. Rain is falling from a black cloud in the middle of an otherwise blue sky; it mingles with my tears and soaks my hair and clothes. I am not going anywhere, except round and round the Golden Triangle. Just keeping on the move, trying to bring myself under control.

At the end of the fourth circuit I come to a halt at the point where the taxi set me down on the day of my return. What a sentimental picture I had then of the moment when a young couple, proud and happy, prepared to enter their new home for the first time! It can't have been like that at all. My mother must have been anxious lest something about the baby she was carrying, or the date of its arrival, would alert her husband to the fact that he had been deceived. And Aden himself, a man born and brought up by Lord Mortimer of Kinderley in a house called Kinderley Court: how can he ever have felt anything but shame in being reduced to a semi-detached suburban house? Everything that I have ever believed about my father is turning out to be a lie.

Just as well, then – I am trying to reason myself back into calmness – that I am about to leave it all behind me. Rage and resentment and longing will not bring Terts back, but I can study his career with a new interest and feel a vicarious pride. I ceased to love my mother when I was four years old; what has changed there, except that I shall no longer feel guilty about it? Aden Bradley was a child abuser? Well, he was not my father. Little by little I bring myself under control. I may still feel guilt about my failure to protect Yunga, but it has been cancelled out, in a way, by her failure to confide in me. Anger directed against the dead is a negative emotion; a life-destroyer. It is the years of love and affection which must be remembered. The fact that they were based on lies does not make them any the less real. One last deep breath. Yes, I'm OK now, thank you.

This is supposed to be summer but I am very wet, and in slamming the front door behind me I have locked myself out. No doubt one of the neighbours holds a key, but before ringing any doorbell I make my way round the side of the house. In my childhood a spare key was always kept in the outside lavatory. Yes, it is there still, conspicuous on top of the cistern, an invitation to any passing burglar. How nice – that suburban word – to live in a community where there is no need to worry about such things! A safe community. A decent, dull community. Oh, yeah!

At some moment while I am stripping off my wet clothes and dressing again my feeling of betrayal is replaced by a new stirring of curiosity. I return to the attic and look more closely at some of the dates involved. The date on Terts's letter to me is that of my twenty-first birthday, although it was never intended to reach me then. Why does he talk of his life drawing to a close? According to his obituary he was born in 1890, so he would be under sixty: not an old man.

I study the obituary again. It is not specific about the date of his death, but the day on which it appeared in *The Times* was only three days after that birthday of mine. Did he know as he was writing the letter that he was ill? Or is there a nastier possibility? Did a man who had lived all his life through his eyes find the prospect of years of blindness too much to bear? Did a man who had hoped he might one day meet his daughter give up hope when he discovered that she had run away? Even had the obituarist suspected suicide, he would have made no mention of what was then a criminal act. But I wish I knew.

And Kinderley Court. What and where is that? Where did these two boys – and there were other children as well – grow up? That should be an easier question to answer, even though it may not explain why apparently Aden cut himself off from it. Yes, before I leave England, at least that one small mystery can be solved. And then I can turn my back on this whole mess of deceit and return to Santa Fe.

Part Five

Kinderley

1

43 Woodside Road has been bought by Mr Khan. The estate agent – good for him! – was right about the Golden Triangle. There was a rush to acquire this Desirable Residence in spite of its unmodernised kitchen and lack of en suite bathrooms. Not to mention its untidy garden. Although my upbringing was designed to instil in me the principle of delayed gratification, in which self-denial and hard work today will have its reward tomorrow, I have never lived long enough in one place to develop an aptitude for cultivation. When I arrived in Kenbury I was greeted by the sight of dead daffodils. I leave behind a garden edged with dead forget-me-nots. Few flowers look more reproachfully neglected than dead forget-me-nots.

'Annuals,' I confess with shame to Mr Khan, who has never before possessed a garden of his own at all. He has come for an extra visit to ask small questions about pilot lights and stop cocks and dustbin days: questions which I am not really competent to answer. 'But leave them there for a week or two longer and they'll seed themselves and give you new plants for next year.' This is what should be the pattern of nature: life and reproduction and then new life. Something the Bradleys don't seem to have been much good at in this generation.

Mr Khan's father came to England after his sister was a victim of the vicious days which preceded Independence on the Indian sub-continent. Mr Khan himself is leaving Tower Hamlets because his brother has been injured in a racial attack. Kenbury to him is a sanctuary in which there will be no murder, no fear, no looking over the shoulder at the sound of footsteps behind. So now his feet will tread on the carpets that Yunga chose. His hands will draw the curtains that Yunga sewed. I haven't charged him for any of the things left behind in the house.

On the day we exchanged contracts he wrote me a polite letter of thanks for not gazumping him and enclosed a photograph of two bright-eyed little girls, dressed neatly in grey skirts and red sweaters. He was happy, he said, that his children will be able to play safely in the garden. He has promised them a swing, and they can climb the pear tree. They will walk to school in no danger of attack. They will learn their lessons well and go to university one day. Their lives have been changed. In this new home they will not be expected to endure adventures. They are lucky little girls.

So now the moment has come and this time it is true that I am leaving 43 Woodside Road for ever. Without a backward glance. That part of my life is done. Finished. I pause at the pillar box only to post the last set of keys to the solicitor who has handled the sale. That's it, then. I suppose my repeated emphasis on this finality must mean that I am glad about it. If there is a doubt, it can only be because I am leaving Yunga behind as well.

With a list of road numbers written on a card attached to the dashboard, I make for the M40. I have already checked that Yunga's car, hardly used since the day of her amputation, is in good order and, although it is ridiculously small, it chugs along at a good rate. As a child – from a carless family – I used to be perpetually amazed by the ease and skill with which film criminals and private eyes could leap into unfamiliar vehicles without so much as a glance at the controls. Now, of course, I do it myself all over the world, but it still amazes me. I drive with confidence through the suburban streets.

I am booked on an evening flight from Heathrow, but am not going there directly. There is a call to be made first. So I ignore the M25 exit and proceed smoothly towards Oxford. Just as my spirits sank in the course of the journey from the airport to Kenbury, so they rise now. The motorway is lined not with advertisement hoardings, as it would be at home, but with trees wearing the fresh green fashions of early summer.

At home. What do I mean when I allow that phrase to pass through my mind? The rented house in Santa Fe – in which I ought by now to be putting my landlord's sculptures on display? The United States, region unspecified? I can't answer that question. But something quite significant has changed. For fifty years my life has been an escape from a fixed point. Now the fixed point has gone, leaving me in limbo. Something to think about as I head for the house which was once the home of my father: of both my fathers. Kinderley Court.

I leave the M40 for Oxford, skirt the city and continue to drive west. The colour of the countryside changes as the greenness of the past fifty miles is almost submerged by a froth of white. What is this tall, delicate flower which has invaded the wide grass verges? I have forgotten its correct botanical name, but the phrase 'Queen Anne's lace' comes into my mind. And behind these fluttering snowfields rise hedges of may in full flower, their ungainly arms sticking out at odd angles like the branches in a Rackham drawing. Above them again, tiaras of elderflower in a creamier white. The effect is cool, man, cool. I am getting into the mood to present myself as an American.

Checking the route I have written out, I turn right along a lane so narrow that if I meet another vehicle one of us will have to reverse. Presumably the locals are prepared for this.

The map is of no further use, so on reaching the village of Kinderley I draw to a halt and look around for help. There is no shop; no one on the streets. The only signs of life are the distant drone of a lawn mower and the handsome ginger cat who watches me with calm curiosity from its perch on a stone wall.

The whole village is built of stone: a dark grey stone which must look heavy and depressing in winter but which now, in sunshine, is brightened by the wide grass verges in front of every building. Off the main street there are several rows of small cottages, though a study of their curtains suggests that in some cases two or three have been put together to form a single home. The village school has been converted to become The Old Schoolhouse. Where children would once have skipped and kicked balls and played hopscotch, a Bentley is parked, and there is a satellite dish fixed above a doorway which still bears its stone inscription: Infants. This is of no ancestral interest to me. The Bradley children would not have attended a village school.

The school is not the only building which has departed from its original purpose. The Old Rectory, which stands next to the church, has surrendered what must once have been its walled garden to provide a site for the modest new rectory, but is still surrounded by an adequate acreage of neatly shaven lawns, neatly clipped hedges and neatly dead-headed herbaceous borders. Other equally substantial houses can be glimpsed at the ends of winding drives lined with shrub roses. Clearly, although lacking in amenities, this is a village that has come up in the world.

One amenity, of course, it still retains. The church, built of the same dark stone, stands on an island in the heart of the community, surrounded by a sea of gravestones. I wander amongst them but fail to find either Mortimers or Bradleys. Perhaps these have memorials inside the church instead; but the door is locked. Even this peaceful and secluded village, it seems, is afraid of thieves and vandals.

My approach to the nearest cottage is announced by a frenzy of barking from within and the door is opened before I ring the bell. There is time to observe a front parlour filled with computers, scanners, printers, copiers, its walls decorated with work-flow charts and clocks showing the time round the world, while a well-spoken young man in shirtsleeves apologises for the fact that he knows nothing about the arrangements for opening the church, but gives me directions to Kinderley Court. It is just up the hill, on the right. I can't miss it.

No, I can't miss it, for a wooden notice board beside the entrance to the drive proclaims its name and telephone number in neat gold letters. The notice serves to increase my curiosity about its present use. No private house would advertise itself in quite that way. What am I going to discover at the end of the drive?

Is this visit wise? Would I have done better to be content with a mental picture of some imagined dream-palace? Doubts assail me as I drive slowly up the long approach. But being so near, I couldn't not have come. I concentrate on becoming an American, ready to appear at once well-connected and brash. It will not be an act. I intend to tell nothing but the truth.

One last curve and the house appears in front of me. Not quite a palace, perhaps, but certainly the greatest possible contrast to the semi-detached nineteen-twenties suburban house in which Aden and Jessica Bradley found themselves. How could I ever have believed that they felt proud and happy as they took mortgaged possession of 43 Woodside Road?

Architecture is yet another subject in which I have little expertise, but the clusters of twisted chimneys which rise above battlemented parapets proclaim that the substantial central section of the house must be very old; whilst larger windows and a deliberate symmetry suggest that the two wings built out at right angles to it were probably added a century or so later. Within these three parts of the building is enclosed a large colonnaded courtyard which justifies the name of the house.

There are other groups of buildings as well: a stable block on one side and an orangery and conservatory on the other. I park the car near the stable block, conspicuously enough to show that I am not skulking, and then walk up a broad flight of steps and along the centre of the courtyard towards a pair of doors, standing wide open, which lead into the central block of the house.

Because I am subconsciously expecting to tug at a long chain which will jangle a high iron bell, my eyes pass over the neat modern bell-push and settle instead on the contents of the great hall, which is open to my inspection. The hall is huge, rising through two tall storeys. Slabs of pale grey marble comprise the floor; slabs of pale pink marble on the walls frame panels which are decorated with paintings of leaves or flowers. The only furniture in the whole of this vast space consists of one plain wooden chair and a variety of juvenile equipment: tricycles, cars, an indoor climbing frame, three swings, a large wooden engine with a selection of trucks and half a dozen easels to which large sheets of paper are fixed ready to be painted. What does all this mean? Is Kinderley Court being used as a playschool, or is it currently owned by a large family? Either way, there is a lack of dignity here.

All this modern equipment is brightly coloured, but my eye is caught by something hiding in the shadows at the back of the hall. It is a Victorian rocking horse. Unlike everything else, this is not scaled to the size of its probable user. A small child, lifted into its saddle, his legs stretched wide over its broad back, might feel dangerously high above the ground, dangerously likely to be tipped over its head.

The horse is shabby. There are few hairs left in its mane or tail and the saddle which once was brightly decorated has been rubbed into a shiny brown by a century or more of bare legs. Whether timorously or vigorously, Aden Bradley, I am sure, must have ridden this horse. I put out a finger to touch it and, beautifully balanced, it dips its head in confirmation.

'Can I help you?' A large man with a bushy red beard has come up behind me on silent sneakers. I am a trespasser. I am expecting the challenge. I have come prepared to answer it. Yet now that the moment has come I am unable to speak because I am struggling not to cry. Me, Jo, a woman who has seen terrible things without ever fogging my vision with tears, totally unmanned by the touch of a finger on a shabby old rocking horse. Talk about sentimentality!

What is unbearable is that I should know what that little boy could not have known as he happily rode his wooden horse: that he had been born to be a loser. He lost his father before he was born, and his mother soon after: that much I have learned only recently from Yunga. He lost his inheritance and his career, although I don't know why. He lost his only son. He lost the love of his wife. He lost his elder daughter to what must have seemed a whim; and then may well have discovered that she – I – had never been his daughter at all. It is all so unfair. What right have I to sit in judgement on a man struck down by so many bitter blows?

The bearded man, who cannot possibly understand why the gentle stroking of one finger along the edge of the saddle should produce such an effect, is sympathetically patient as I pull myself together and remember to produce my American accent.

'Hi! Sorry. Touching this ... I hadn't expected ... Guess I owe you an explanation. I'm over from the States. Santa Fe, in New Mexico. Flying back tonight. I only just discovered that my family used to live at Kinderley Court. My father was born here. I'm Jolene Bradley. How do you do?'

'Bradley?' Out of my incoherence one word has emerged to make sense to him. 'Then you must be related to our Miss Elizabeth.'

'My Aunt Libby. But I never met her. Why do you say "our"?'

'She was the founder of our institution.'

'What kind of institution would that be?'

I have asked, so I am going to be told. It takes some time.

2

I am offered a cup of good coffee and a seat on a comfortable sofa and sit patiently as Mr Yardley, my bearded host, delivers the well-rehearsed lecture that is presumably offered to social workers and probation officers and the parents of prospective pupils.

Miss Elizabeth, I learn, was really Mrs Kenward, but was so young and newly-wed when widowed in the Great War that she returned to her family home and continued to be called by her old name. She had no children of her own, but in 1919 accepted responsibility for the upbringing of an orphaned nephew. Her nephew: my cousin – yet another relative whose existence was unknown to me.

When, a little later, she was asked if she would provide a holiday home for some children who, for health reasons, were sent home to England while their parents remained in India, she was horrified by the young age at which they were expected to cope with boarding school life as well as separation from their parents.

'That was why she decided to turn Kinderley Court into a small school when she inherited it from her grandfather, Lord Mortimer. For children up to eleven whose parents were out of the country. So that she could mother the children and let them feel that this was their home as well as their school.'

'And that's still the case now, is it?'

'Not in quite the same way. Until 1939 all the children came from much the same social class. Their parents tended to be in the Army, the Foreign Office or the Indian Civil Service. But during the war she took in some evacuees as well, and discovered what a good environment could do for children who lived in poor homes and went to overcrowded schools where not much was expected of them. Before she died, she put the house and the income from the estate into a charitable trust.'

The lecture continues. Since I hope eventually to be shown over the house, I listen politely, even though my true interest is in the past and not the present.

At any one time there are twenty-five children at Kinderley Court. They are grouped into 'families' of five, each with its own house-mother and the range of ages which would be found in an ordinary family. Two out of the five will still be fee-paying, to help support the others. One will be nominated by a local school as being a bright child from an unsupportive home. One will come from council care, having no relatives and being unsuitable for adoption. 'This in practice,' says Mr Yardley, 'means handicapped in some way.'

And one – I wonder whether the fee-paying parents are warned of this – will be a tearaway: a persistent criminal who offends constantly because he knows he is too young for the police to touch him. 'None of the other children will know of his reputation; and once he's cut off from his gang and his probably criminal parents and any opportunity for offending, it's amazing how quickly he'll want to become one of the group. These boys – they're usually boys – are often very intelligent. Once they stop playing truant, they find they can cope with lessons.'

'Sounds like you're doing a great job. You don't, I suppose, have a photograph of Miss Elizabeth that I could see?'

There are two hanging in the great hall, it appears. I must have walked past without noticing them. Mr Yardley leads the way back.

The photographs have been mounted as a pair. They show an attractive young woman who looks to be about eighteen. In the left-hand picture she is casually dressed, with her long hair loosely fastened at the neck. She is nuzzling the head of a horse with her chin. 'Libby and Nutmeg. Christmas 1912', says the neat writing on the mount.

In the right-hand picture, full-length, she has been transformed into a debutante. She is standing very straight in a formal dress cut low over her shoulders and falling into a train at the back. Long white gloves cover her arms. Her hair is dressed into an elaborate crown from which rise stately plumes of ostrich feathers. It would be a run-of-the-mill formal photograph were it not for the fact that down on the floor a dressmaker is looking up, startled, from the hem she is adjusting with a mouthful of pins.

'Miss Elizabeth Bradley. May 1913'. That is on the mount, but there is more writing across one corner of the photograph itself: 'To my favourite sister, with love. Terts'.

'Perhaps you ought to keep this somewhere more secure,' I suggest to Mr Yardley. Other people, presumably could wander like myself into the great hall. 'It could be quite valuable.'

'A photograph!'

It is difficult not to smile at his astonishment. Very few people realise that some photographs can be as valuable as some paintings – and that photographers, like painters, have 'periods'.

'It's taken by a photographer called Terts, who was very famous in his time. People who collect his work try to get an example from each different stage in his life, and he only went in for this kind of portrait work for a couple of years before the Great War.' But I don't press the point. It's none of my business. 'You don't have any other photographs of the family, I suppose?'

As expected, Mr Yardley shakes his head. 'Miss Elizabeth's nephew was allowed under the terms of the trust to stay on in part of the house, and he would have inherited anything personal, I imagine. But he died in 1980. Before my time here. Would you like to look round part of the house?'

That was why I came, but my gratitude for the invitation quickly vanishes.

'The ballroom,' announces Mr Yardley, throwing open a pair of double doors. 'We use it as a kind of theatre now. Every summer each family either performs a little play or gives a musical concert, and at Christmas all the children come together for something more ambitious. Do come in.'

I surprise both myself and him by shaking my head. This is a room in which Terts, perhaps, swept his sister into a waltz in the summer of 1913. It should be lit by chandeliers. It should be lined with little gilt chairs on which chaperones could gossip. There should be an orchestra playing. Everyone in the ballroom should be handsome or beautiful as they dance their cotillions or quadrilles. In the past few days I have been trying to envisage the childhood and youth of my two fathers, and now I realise that it is better not to let modern developments – the amateur dramatics of orphans and tearaways – spoil my imaginings. The rocking horse, unchanged by time, has proved potent enough for one day.

And so I make my apologies, asking instead if I may wander into the grounds to take a photograph of the house. Mr Yardley, although puzzled, offers me Liberty Hall.

In the car I approached Kinderley Court from the north. Now I make my way round to the south side and stride downhill towards a crescent-shaped lake. Only when I have reached its further bank do I turn to contemplate my ancestral home.

From this viewpoint the two wings are invisible, so that although the house looks smaller, the proportions of the south façade make it seem grander. It is easy to identify the long windows of the ballroom and now, free from the distractions of the present, I can hear the orchestra playing and visualise the members of that golden but doomed generation as they dance and flirt.

Did Terts, I wonder, once stand where I am standing now and gaze at the ballroom as I am gazing? Did he take a beautiful girl into his arms and tell her he loved her? Although I tell myself not to be ridiculous, I can almost feel the two of them standing beside me now. But if there was such a romantic moment, it seems never to have developed into a happy-ever-after relationship. I wonder what happened.

The obituarist in *The Times* claimed that Terts never married. He himself, in his letter to me, told a different story. What was his phrase? 'A previous marriage, almost forgotten but never dissolved'. What kind of marriage could have been put out of mind in such a way, and kept secret from the world? There is a mystery here. How frustrating it is to know that I shall never be able to solve it.

The music of the orchestra fades into silence. Soon Terts and all his companions will be snatched from their privileged lives and sucked into war. Terts himself will be wounded, many of his friends will die and his sister will be widowed. The golden age is over and will never return, so I have no grounds for complaint that I never shared it. Aden's exile may have been involuntary, but Terts by choice spent the rest of his life in dangerous and uncomfortable places, almost as though he could not bear to live in paradise when so many others were condemned to hell on earth. Terts, the eyes of the world. The conscience of the world.

My need to learn more about him is physically painful: not Terts the photographer but Terts the man. I am a believer in causes and effects. I want to know not only what happened in the months before my birth but the reasons for what did and didn't happen. I don't suppose there is any way of finding out, though. It is all too long ago.

I must have been hoping that Kinderley Court, the building, would somehow present itself as an open book in which the lives of its occupants could be read. A crazy idea! All I have gained is a lecture on the care of deprived or delinquent children who – like Mr Khan's two daughters at 43 Woodside Road – have found sanctuary. Oh, and that brief contact with little-boy Aden which came from the stroking of a shabby rocking horse.

Time to go. I have been wearing one of my cameras round my neck, as would be expected of an American tourist, and now I lift it to my eye, zooming in until the south façade of Kinderley Court fits snugly into the frame of the viewfinder. I do not, however, release the shutter. When I take a photograph it is always for the benefit of other people. I don't need any print for myself. The act of composing the picture is enough to imprint my father's home on my memory for ever.

There are other ingredients of this moment that I shall remember as well. The lushness of the long grass in which I am standing. The calm surface of the lake. The cool green and white tapestry of the landscape, into which even the sheep grazing in the park are woven. The silence. The solitude. Even in a small country, it seems, it is possible to be alone.

Four hours later my plane takes off from Heathrow. Looking down as it circles, gaining height, I am as struck as on the day of my arrival by the pastoral richness of the countryside. A green and pleasant land. I can remember that exact phrase coming into my mind: the quotation which has become a cliché because it is so precisely true.

'Pleasant' is a suburban adjective, which is another way of saying that it doesn't rate high with someone who as a rule likes space and drama in her landscapes. Down there below me are millions of people who have never known what it is to be refugees. They have never needed to flee from massacres or droughts or earthquakes. Although some may complain of poverty or hunger, it can never be hopeless destitution or starvation. All those people who are going about their evening business beneath me are safe. I wonder if they realise how lucky they are.

Does that sound like a chink in my own search for adventure? Not really: there is a huge difference between walking open-eyed into danger and having danger forced upon one. A little while ago, needled by smug speeches as the fiftieth anniversary of the Second World War's end was celebrated, I published a book which I wanted to call *Fifty Years of Peace* – but that title proved unsuitable. Americans are not too hot on irony and in any case are too deeply wounded by Vietnam.

It became *On the Road*. There was very little text. Just a procession of refugees: Ibo, Tibetan, Tutsi, Hutu, Cambodian, Kurdish, Marsh Arab,

Afghan, Somali, Chechnyan, Bosnian, Serb and many more. All facing the same way, plodding on at each turn of the page with baskets on their heads and small children struggling uncomprehendingly to keep up. All with that expression of blank hopelessness which settles on those who know they must escape but have no idea where they may find sanctuary. The book was not exactly a best-seller. Surprise!

The roads which are now far beneath me have never been crowded with this kind of hopelessness. Instead they dance with elderflower and may and Queen Anne's lace. Goodbye, lucky little England.

Part Six

The Going Down of the Sun

A new day is dawning as I arrive at Albequerque airport, pick up my car and head north through the pure air and wide spaces of New Mexico. The light is brilliant and the world is empty. As I drive steadily along, my shoulders widen, my lungs fill more deeply; there is room to expand. I am no longer pressed down, oppressed, by clouds; the clear sky soars above me. I have escaped from the confines of a small house in a small town in a small island to a country in which spaces are huge and anything is possible. Well, perhaps I should be more careful with my tenses: in which anything has been possible. Choices narrow as time runs out. But one choice has already been made. I am still unhappy about Yunga's death, but I have accepted the unhappiness and in a geographical sense at least have left it behind me. I shall never go back to England. And this time never means never.

So when I pull up in front of the rented adobe house in Santa Fe, and inspect my crystal tree – which in this season, of course, presents itself as a very ordinary green shrub – it is not in the garden but in the yard. The luggage which I stowed away in the boot is unloaded from the trunk.

Neighbours begin to arrive even before I have had time to open all the shutters and windows. They bring offers of milk and invitations to supper. They enquire about my sister, and their condolences are sincere. None of them has known me for very long, but I have chosen to live amongst them and am entitled to the warmth of their concern.

I spend only one night in the house before driving off again. On the flight home I have come to a decision, and there is no point in hanging around.

The Mesa Verde, which is two hundred odd miles away, is a National Park. When I drive through its entrance gates I still have twenty miles to go before reaching the area which makes it memorable: twenty miles of hairpin bends and corniche roads, for I am driving up a mountain. At least, it would rank as a mountain in England, since it is almost nine thousand feet high. Out here, in Colorado, it is simply a high plateau, because the top is not a peak but a long, narrow, flat finger of rock.

The mesa is riven by deep, deep canyons. In the way of national parks, the area has been sanitised. There are Visitors' Centres and refreshment areas and camp sites; there are railed-off lookout points along the roads and, where steep staircases have been cut from the stone, thick ropes along each side give confidence to the nervous and strength to the breathless. No normally cautious person will come to any harm here. Nevertheless, the canyons are dangerous. Parents hold tightly to their children and the vertiginous stand well back from the edge.

I have no need to call at a Visitors' Centre, for I have been here many times before. Most of the photographs which entice the tourists in colourful brochures were taken by me – from places which no tourist is encouraged to reach. Strapped into a harness, lowered on a rope, swaying gently in the air several thousand feet above the ground until my heels touched a ledge and helped me to steady myself. The special glory within the Mesa Verde is not a fashion model who can be told to move this way or that, to pout or toss its hair. It is the photographer who must move, to portray something which has been frozen in time for more than seven hundred years.

Without the entourage of that earlier occasion, I drive along the rim of one of the canyons, park neatly in a designated lookout area, duck under the solid metal railings and scramble a little way down the side of the ravine. There is a faint track to show that others have dared this before me: amateur photographers, no doubt, whose husbands or wives held their breaths in anxiety until they regained the safety of the lookout. I am wearing two cameras myself; one slung round my neck and the other fitted into a leather holster which is buckled diagonally across my chest – and, in fact, before going any further, I sit down at the end of the track, with my feet dangling into space, and take half a dozen shots. Then, setting the camera down on the ground beside me, I stare at the wider view of what I have just trapped inside a rectangular frame.

The sides of the canyons are sheer, but they are broken by a series of huge caves. Level floors extend deep into the darkness of the rock and above them curve vaulted roofs, higher and wider than any cathedral. The caves, I suppose, are natural, but within them has been built one of the wonders of the world: a series of villages, densely packed into the space under each arched roof. Four-storey towers rise where there is room, surrounded by lower buildings which fit underneath the curve.

Seen from across the space of a canyon, as I am seeing three of them now, the cave villages present themselves sympathetically to the modern eye. They are built of sandstone blocks, sometimes covered with mud of the same colour. They have become a part of the cliff, and it would be easy, although wrong, to think of them as having been carved out of the rock instead of constructed within it. The combination of high square towers and the lower round walls of ceremonial rooms is also pleasing; and best of all are the sharp-edged dark shadows which move with the sun. In the moment when I zoomed in to fill the view-finder, I was composing a Cubist picture.

Today, though, I am not really looking at the scene with a photographer's eye. Instead, I am thinking about an abandoned culture, frozen in time.

For almost a thousand years this mesa was occupied, by people to whom the present-day Navajo have given the name Anasazi: the Ancient Ones. They cultivated the ground at the top of the mesa, descending to the bottoms of the canyons to find water, which they carried up thousands of feet by means of toe and fingerholds in the almost vertical rock face. As time passed and they became less primitive they constructed their amazing buildings in the caves of the canyons. They defended themselves against other, wandering, tribes and, living at such close quarters with each other, they must have evolved a structured social system. And then one day they left.

No one knows where they went and no one knows why. It may be that towards the end of the thirteenth century there were too many years of drought, which forced them to look for a safer source of water. Whatever the reason, the fact is certain enough. There was no battle and there was no plague. They were cultivators, like Yunga, not hunter-gatherers like me; they had chosen Home and not Away as a way of life. They worshipped the sun, and the sun still rose and set every day. But in spite of all that they recognised that the time had come for them to move on.

Their real name has been forgotten and their blood lines may well have died out; but for seven hundred years their memorial has survived. I find that satisfying. I am pleased for them, the Ancient Ones.

And so I take a moment or so to consider my own memorial. It must be hard to die and leave nothing at all behind. Did Yunga feel that? She had no children, and nor have I; but there are other things which may endure.

I think of my sunset series. My work is still hanging in small living rooms or, hugely blown up, in the reception areas of hotels and banks. Perhaps for a few years longer a few people may sigh with pleasure at some magnificent, real-life sunset and declare it to be 'as good as a Bradley'. There's that.

Sunset photographs are popular art. Vulgar in the Latin sense of the word. Too many people enjoy them for them to be taken seriously by critics. But in the course of my life I have devoted several periods to the creation of works of Art with a capital A. Perhaps this is a pretentious claim, but it has been my good fortune to live through a time when a photograph is no longer considered merely an instrument of record but has become valued as an object in itself. In books and exhibitions my name may survive for a little while.

What has earned me a steady living, though, is my career as a photo-journalist. Nowadays my breed is dying out. It is the television cameramen and women who are despatched to the world's disasters and disturbances. But there is still a need for people like me. A television camera attracts action as well as recording it. Placards are displayed, stones are thrown, fires are lit which would have not have been lit were no one looking.

It is easier for someone like me to be unobtrusive. There is little to distinguish my camera from those of many world-wandering tourists. I am a silent thief of other people's private moments. I can record scenes which the perpetrators would prefer to be unpublicised. And then, if I am lucky, I can slip quietly away so that no one knows about the hissing fuse until the explosion of publicity takes place.

That was how I obtained the picture in which I take the greatest pride. No doubt there are many places throughout the world in which young girls are still bought and sold in marriage against their will. But there is one country in which they became safe twenty-five years ago, and they owe their safety to a photograph of a child in an airport with terror in her eyes. A photograph taken by an unremarkable middle-aged woman who was behaving as though she had just bought a new camera at the duty-free shop. She was trying it out, wasn't she, as she pointed it at a check-in counter, a smart air hostess, a young couple who were perhaps on their honeymoon, a sleeping child and then, just as casually, a fat man in his fifties bending over a frightened girl of twelve. There had to be other shots to complete the photo-story and there had to be a text, but this was the picture which drew the world's attention. Most of a journalist's work is ephemeral, but here was a photograph that resulted in new legislation. No one in the future is likely to associate my name with it but it is, none the less, a kind of memorial.

And as I nod my head in satisfaction about that, something very important happens inside my mind, although I am not quite sure what it is. Does that make sense? There is a new thought somewhere within my consciousness, but it is not yet quite organised into words. All it tells me for the moment is to wait. I have come to the Mesa Verde with the intention of performing two separate actions, but the time is not quite ripe.

So I sit on the ledge without moving as the sun goes down. The camera remains untouched beside me. I have recorded enough sunsets in the course of my life and from my earlier visits to the Mesa Verde I calculate that this one is unlikely to be anything special. Okay, probably, but not marvellous.

It happens quickly, as is usual in mountain areas. Deep crimson bruises into yellow and black. The darkness of night begins to roll across the sky, but I continue to wait, knowing that I have experienced only the overture.

Above the mesa the dark clouds part. The curtains of a theatre are opening for the evening's performance. An arch of bright crimson rises through the gap. For a moment it reminds me inappropriately of the organist who fifty years ago used to rise in a blaze of light from the depths of the Dominion cinema in Kenbury. But perhaps this is not after all an inappropriate thought, because I can almost feel Yunga's little hand gripping mine in excitement as she stares through the cloud of cigarette smoke; as a small child she found the organ the best part of any performance. So real is the squeeze of her fingers that I find myself almost surprised by the lack of musical accompaniment to the exhibition which is now presenting itself.

Against the crimson background, golden haloes encircle the clouds while fingers of black and purple extend themselves, shooting upwards in a display of pyrotechnics. The Mesa Verde is doing Yunga proud. This sunset is after all more than okay, more than marvellous. It is magnificent.

So now, before the intensity of the colours begins to fade, it is time for me to perform the first of the two actions which have brought me to the Mesa Verde. Fumbling in my pocket, I pull out the little jar which holds Yunga's ashes and take off the cap. 'At the going down of the sun' – I speak the words aloud – 'I will remember you.' Slowly I scatter the ashes into the canyon.

I have chosen this place because we were happy here together, Yunga and I, less than a year ago; and I have already guessed what I shall feel as the grey particles fall and scatter and sink out of sight. There is no Yunga any more, and therefore there can be no Elda. It takes two to make a comparative adjective. Now I am simply Jolene. On my own.

Something else has to be considered as well. 43 Woodside Road has been sold. I can no longer claim any place at all, however far away in time or distance, as Home. And if there is no Home there can be no Away. It takes two to make a contrast. I no longer belong anywhere.

The pleasure of being a sister and the excitement of always being a foreigner are two of the elements which have given spice to my life for the past fifty years. Without either of them, living just for the sake of living holds little appeal. And so, as I drove to the Mesa Verde today, it was with the firm intention of allowing myself to fall from the edge of the canyon. To meet my death on a mountain, as I have always wished, and to merge the remains of Yunga's body with my own.

Why is it that within the last few seconds I have changed my mind? It is not through fear. To die now, quickly, would be far easier than the tedious business of living on as an increasingly old woman, alone in the world. It is thinking about memorials which has suddenly turned my thoughts in another direction. A quotation has presented itself to my memory – but presented itself as incomplete.

And some there be, which have no memorial. Those were the words which came into my mind as I scattered Yunga's ashes, watching them disperse and disappear in such contrast to the enduring monuments of the Anasazi – and even to the temporary survival of my own work. A trite thought, perhaps, but appropriate. Some there be which have no memorial.

Inside this elderly body, though, there still lurk traces of the clever ten year old who won prizes for Bible study by the simple expedient of learning whole books off by heart. Automatically now the first lines of that chapter of

Ecclesiasticus come to my mind: 'Let us now praise famous men, and our fathers that begat us.'

The father who begat me, my real father, was a famous man: Terts, who was acclaimed as the eyes of the world, but who was something more than that. The conscience of the world. Even, in a way, the suffering heart of the world, for in all his greatest pictures there is an overwhelming sense that the photographer is sharing the agony of the people whose lives he is recording. The bells which tolled for his subjects tolled also for him. No one who has seen them can ever forget his pictures of the suttee widow burning alive, the hunched children knotting carpets, the Belsen survivors for whom rescue came too late.

But by the time Terts died he was blind and reclusive, with no one whose business it was to preserve his reputation. There were glowing obituaries; and then silence.

I can give him a memorial. It is that realisation – forcing itself at last to the front of my consciousness – which has kept me safely on this dark ledge as Yunga's ashes fall out of sight. The world has forgotten Terts, but I can make it remember him. I can collect his work in a way which he never bothered to do himself. Whatever reputation I have acquired myself can be revealed as being an inheritance. I want to boast about my father; to tell everyone who will listen how proud I am to be the daughter of such a man. I wish – oh, how I wish – that he had lived to know me as an adult. That he loved me, sadly, from a distance, I feel sure, but I would have liked him to feel pride in me too.

Well, it's too late for that – and that thought overwhelms me here on the mesa just as it did a few weeks ago in the attic of 43 Woodside Road. In a suburb emotions had to be controlled, in order that the neighbours should not be disturbed. But there is nothing to restrain me now. Regret and anger and despair combine in a single shout, a moan, a scream which fills the canyon with my hurt and echoes back and forward again.

So violent is the effort with which I project my voice that for a few seconds my whole body trembles, and I almost achieve by accident what I have just decided not to do deliberately. A little stiffly, I stand up. Even in the Mesa Verde there are neighbours of a sort. Tourists will have heard my scream. The echoes may have made it difficult to determine its source, but already wardens will be on the move, patrolling the rims of the canyons. I make my way back to the official look-out platform before returning to the car and driving slowly away. I am doing my best to behave calmly and inconspicuously; but my hands are shaking and at the first opportunity I turn off the road towards a designated picnic spot where I can park again.

There is still the opportunity for second thoughts, but I have no regrets as I start to make plans in a businesslike way. It's time to get back to work. Proper work. Work fitting for Terts's daughter. Someone else can help

Warren to record the other Seasons of the Wealthy, pampered in a Newport 'cottage' or dressing up for an opening night at the Met. I shall go to China, to discover whether female babies are really being abandoned to die as a means of population control; or to Mauritania, whose society is rumoured to be based on a slave system; or to the parts of Asia to which paedophiles flock for their holidays and leave damaged goods behind when they leave. There are still dark corners into which the eyes of the world have not penetrated. Who is better able to take the risk of shining a light there than a woman who is in any case approaching the end of her life naturally and who has no domicile and no dependants?

All the same, I shall be cautious, for there is something even more important than that to be done. Fay will help me to organise an exhibition and assemble a book of Terts's photographs. And I shall write his biography.

The prospect is a daunting one. How can I hope to discover how a boy acquired his first camera almost a hundred years ago? Was there some seminal event which helped him to recognise his vocation? The published photographs themselves may steer me through the later years of his career, but how did it happen that he became estranged from his brothers? And – most important of all to me – what was it that prevented him from marrying the mother of his child?

I have had no training in this kind of research; but I am irrationally convinced that the intensity of my need to discover the truth will carry me through. I can feel the muscles of my body contracting and flexing with excitement. I have a new reason for living.

With everything settled in my mind, I start the car again. The day is over. But as I drive slowly along the twisting corniche, I feel hope rather than despair. The sun has gone down, but it will rise again tomorrow.